WESTERN

Rugged men looking for love...

Reclaiming The Rancher's Son
Trish Milburn

The Paramedic's Forever Family
Tanya Agler

MILLS & BOON

RECLAIMING THE RANCHER'S SON
© 2022 by Trish Milburn
Philippine Copyright 2022
Australian Copyright 2022
New Zealand Copyright 2022

First Published 2022
First Australian Paperback Edition 2022
ISBN 978 1 867 25159 0

THE PARAMEDIC'S FOREVER FAMILY
© 2022 by Tanya Agler
Philippine Copyright 2022
Australian Copyright 2022
New Zealand Copyright 2022

First Published 2022
First Australian Paperback Edition 2022
ISBN 978 1 867 25159 0

MIX
Paper from
responsible sources
FSC® C001695

Published by
Harlequin Mills & Boon
An imprint of Harlequin Enterprises (Australia) Pty
Limited (ABN 47 001 180 918), a subsidiary of
HarperCollins Publishers Australia Pty Limited
(ABN 36 009 913 517)
Level 13, 201 Elizabeth Street
SYDNEY NSW 2000 AUSTRALIA

Cover art used by arrangement with Harlequin Books S.A.. All rights reserved.

Printed and bound in Australia by McPherson's Printing Group

Reclaiming The Rancher's Son
Trish Milburn

MILLS & BOON

Trish Milburn is the author of more than fifty novels and novellas, romances set everywhere from quaint small towns in the American West to the bustling city of Seoul, South Korea. When she's not writing or brainstorming new stories, she enjoys reading, listening to K-pop, watching K-dramas, spending probably way too much time on Twitter and, since she lives in Florida, yes, walks on the beach.

Visit the Author Profile page at
millsandboon.com.au for more titles.

Dear Reader,

Welcome back to Jade Valley, Wyoming, where the crisp, sunny days of fall that we saw at the end of *The Rancher's Unexpected Twins* have given way to the cold, snowy depths of winter. But in the midst of the cold is the warmth of a mountain cabin, cups of hot cocoa and a totally unexpected blossoming romance between chipper newspaper editor Maya Pine and reclusive rancher Gavin Olsen.

While I personally don't like wintry weather (I moved to Florida to escape it), it's undeniable that it can be beautiful and romantic. That's what Maya and Gavin find out, despite obstacles that stand tall between the moment they meet and the moment they realise they've fallen in love with each other. I hope you enjoy the sometimes bumpy, snowy road they travel to happily-ever-after.

I love to hear from readers. You can contact me through my website at trishmilburn.com.

Trish Milburn

DEDICATION

To all my fellow journalists out there still fighting the good fight of fact-based truth telling, no matter the obstacles. You are doing important work. Thank you.

CHAPTER ONE

MAYA PINE ALREADY had a newspaper deadline, a demanding boss and an approaching snowstorm on her plate, so the last thing she needed to add was a matchmaking mama. But she was getting it anyway.

As she listened to her mom encourage her to go out with Rory Tillman, Maya grabbed her camera, purse and car keys. She should be on her way to conduct an interview before the predicted snowstorm moved into Jade Valley, but here she stood in the tiny office of the *Valley Post*, cell phone to ear, listening to the hopeful tone in her mom's voice.

"Nope, not happening," Maya said as soon as her mother took a breath.

"Why not?"

"One, I don't have time to date. And, two, do you not remember that Rory was the mastermind behind my car ending up parked in the middle of Mr. Eagle's front lawn? And with the radio blaring 'Loser' by 3 Doors Down as the cherry on top." Maya had thought the little dirt-brown compact with one yellow door had been stolen, but Rory and his buddies had temporarily relocated it to the principal's yard, much to Maya's and Mr. Eagle's mutual displeasure.

"Really?"

"Yes, Mom, really. So you can stop searching high and low for a man for me as if my expiration date is nigh."

Maya was pretty sure her mom had been looking under rocks on the Wind River Reservation for a potential son-in-law.

"I hate to see you alone."

"If it doesn't bother me, it shouldn't bother you. But if this is about your sisters outpacing you with grandchildren, you're just going to have to enjoy being a great-auntie."

"Well, I feel called out."

Maya laughed. "I know how you think, woman."

"They're just so annoying with their grandbaby stories."

"You love those kids every bit as much as they do. I've seen you slipping them sweet treats when their moms weren't looking."

This time it was her mom who sighed, causing Maya to laugh again.

"Listen, if a hot man crosses my path, I'm not going to look the other way. But I'd say the likelihood of that is on the slim side. I mean, Sunny snatched up one of the few decent-looking eligible bachelors in the valley."

Not that Maya had been interested in Dean Wheeler. They'd known each other too long. And despite him being attractive, Maya had never been attracted to him. Which was good since her best friend and he were currently sappy newlyweds.

Most of the rest of the unattached men in the area fell into one of three categories: too young, too old or not in a million years.

A gust of wind rattled the front door, reminding Maya that she'd best get on the road.

"Mom, I've got to go. The paper doesn't write itself."

Before her mom asked any further questions that might lead to Maya fibbing about what was next on her schedule, she hung up the phone. Her mom didn't need to know that Maya was heading up the mountain when a snowstorm was supposed to move into the area in a few hours. She locked the door behind her since Janie Oberlin, the only other employee of the *Post*, was at the high school interviewing the basketball coach about the boys' season so far and the plans for the upcoming tournament.

As Maya headed to her car, the cold, humid air already smelled like snow. She was going to have to conduct this interview with as much speed as possible to maximize her time with elusive mystery author Benjamin St. Michaels while allowing enough to get back to town before the mountain road became dangerous.

But she couldn't miss this opportunity. St. Michaels hadn't given an interview in years, and for her to score one with him was a big deal. His legions of fans would likely give the paper at least a one-week bump in sales. Every little bit helped when the Clarkes, the family who owned newspapers and radio stations all over Wyoming and Montana, were constantly on her case to increase the paper's revenue. That was difficult when the population of Jade Valley was five hundred and some of those were too young to read.

She'd even gotten the wild idea to possibly ask St. Michaels if he might become a regular contributor to the paper, maybe write some short fiction. It all depended on how this interview went.

As she rolled through the small downtown area, which was free of any traffic lights, she waved to half a dozen familiar faces. One of those belonged to Sherriff Angie Lee, so Maya made sure not to go over the speed limit until she was a mile outside of town. Even though she and Angie were friends and had gone to school together, Maya knew Angie wouldn't give her a free pass to break the law. Angie had a fairness streak a mile wide, so that was how she policed and what she also expected from the deputies who worked for her.

By the time Maya was ascending the mountain road and halfway to her destination, the sun had disappeared behind the gunmetal-gray clouds. Why couldn't this interview have taken place yesterday when the sky had been a beautiful blue and the temperature several degrees warmer?

Oh well, it wouldn't be the first time she'd done her job in unpleasant conditions. Also wouldn't be the last.

When she reached the turn onto the gravel road that led back to St. Michaels's vacation cabin, she mentally went through her list of questions for him again. She'd read all of his books about a Wyoming-based FBI agent, so she hadn't had any trouble coming up with questions many of his fans might have. Such as, was the protagonist's brother a good or bad guy? With each book, Maya's opinion on that changed.

She had to laugh when she saw the "cabin" because the house she rented could probably fit inside it twice. Some of those sweet, sweet bestseller dollars had obviously gone into the vacation home. She would bet it had expansive windows on the eastern side, affording stunning views of the valley and the stretch of mountains that lay on the other side.

Maya didn't see a vehicle, but it was probably tucked away in the garage. She glanced up at the tops of the surrounding lodgepole pines, noting the way they were swaying in the breeze. Nothing to be concerned about yet, but she didn't have time to dawdle either.

She grabbed what she needed and stepped out of the car. It was noticeably colder thanks to the gain in elevation. This spot would be beautiful with a white powdery coating of snow, but she didn't plan to be here when it started falling. Pulling her coat's collar up around her neck, she hurried toward the front door. Before knocking, she noted how the small pane of glass at the top of the wooden door was etched with a feather quill. How appropriate for the home of a writer. She wondered if some of the Hank Gulliver series had been written mere feet from where she stood.

She lifted her hand and knocked, then waited for St. Michaels to appear. But not only did he not open the door, she also didn't hear any approaching footsteps. Wondering if he was in a part of the house that made it difficult for him to hear her, she knocked louder the second time. Still no answer. Was it possible the man was asleep or listening to music through headphones? Occupied in the bathroom? Was he the absentminded sort who'd already forgotten their appointment?

After glancing to the side and seeing there wasn't a doorbell, she knocked even louder. Still facing a closed door, she retrieved her phone from her purse and called the number St. Michaels had given her. When the call also went unanswered, her frustration grew.

Okay, she'd tried the professional, front-door approach. Time to do some exploring. She left the porch and rounded the house to find an expansive deck and, yes, a wall of floor-to-ceiling windows that afforded an incredible view of the valley, the river winding through it, and the snow-capped mountain range in the distance.

Maya climbed the steps to the deck and repeated her knocking at a side door just around the corner from the picture windows. By this point she wasn't surprised when she received no response, especially because it looked as if the visible interior was unoccupied and perhaps had been for a while.

She paced the deck as she called again and left a message, hoping that perhaps the man was on his way. While she waited, she pulled out her camera and took some photos of the incredible view. It didn't matter that she called the valley below home and had probably covered every inch of it since starting first as a reporter for the *Valley Post* and then becoming the editor two months later when the previous one decided to retire early. Despite her familiarity with Jade Valley, it still managed to take her breath away when she looked at it from this type of vantage point.

After she'd taken several photos, she lowered the camera in time to see a few snowflakes fly past on a sudden gust of wind. She lifted her gaze to the sky, which had grown darker.

No, no, no. Why was this storm moving in faster than had been forecast? Even if St. Michaels had opened the door after her first knock, they would barely be getting started with the interview. Resisting the idea that this opportunity was a bust, she knocked one more time, placed another unanswered call and paced the deck for a couple of minutes.

But she wasn't a fool. You didn't live in Wyoming your entire life and not respect the weather's mercurial nature. If you didn't respect it, you could end up dead. So she hurried down the steps and back around the house to her little blue hatchback, which already had a few flakes sticking to the windshield. This storm was impatient.

By the time she'd traveled the short distance to the end of the gravel drive, the pace of the snowfall had picked up. Yeah, not good. She wanted to race down the mountain, but that also wasn't smart considering the temperature at this elevation already had some white flakes sticking to the road. And while her car did fine in the valley, snowy, mountainous roads were another story entirely.

Biting her lip, she tried to balance her driving between the urgency to get to a lower elevation, and thus hopefully out of the snow, and her desire to not slide off the road. After about five minutes, she eased around a curve, thankful her car seemed to be handling the conditions well so far.

"Way to go, Blueberry."

She'd give the dash an affectionate pat if she didn't need to keep both hands on the steering wheel. But the tension in her shoulders actually eased a bit, and she exhaled a deep breath.

In the next moment a flash of brown jumped in front of her car, and she instinctually hit the brakes. She knew immediately it was a mistake when she started to slide, but it was too late to correct it. She gasped when the front wheels left the roadway, pointing her downhill into a thick stand of trees.

THE FIRST THOUGHT to surface after Maya woke was that her head throbbed. She slowly blinked to focus her eyes, which led to her second realization—that she'd been knocked out long enough for the world around her to be coated in white. Considering the pace at which the snowflakes had been increasing when she'd swerved to avoid what she now realized had been a deer, she might have only been unconscious for a few minutes.

Moving slowly, she reached for her purse in the passenger seat, only to realize it was on the floor with the contents spilled everywhere. She pressed her hand to her forehead and unbuckled her seat belt. Again moving slowly, she leaned over and scooped up all her belongings. She needed to call for help and hope that the road conditions were such that someone could reach her.

But when she grabbed her phone, it wouldn't turn on. Either the battery had died or the phone had been damaged internally in the crash.

This was not good. Really, really not good.

Though her head continued to throb, she knew she couldn't stay where she was. To do so would almost certainly mean she'd freeze to death. She might be used to Wyoming winters, but that was not the way she wanted to go.

Even though she felt addled and must have hit her head on the window, she was careful to make sure she was fully covered in her coat, gloves and the hat her mom had knitted for her last Christmas. Then she crawled over to the passenger door since the driver's side was wedged against a tree. But she was thankful for that tree or she might have tumbled even farther down the mountain and not woken up at all.

By the time she was standing outside in the snow, she was already ridiculously tired.

"Come on, Pine. You're not going to end up a skeleton in the woods."

She shivered, though whether it was because of that mental image or the cold she wasn't sure. Her feet slipped some on the fresh snow, but she managed not to fall as she climbed up the incline toward the roadway. She was fairly certain she'd aged a year by the time she stepped onto the pavement, which was now totally white. Trying not to panic that it was unlikely a vehicle would come along, she set off down the road. She had to keep moving if she hoped to survive the day. Even if no cars passed, she'd eventually come to someone's house. Now, if she could just remember where the nearest house was to where she'd gone off the road.

As she hurried down the side of the road, she did her best to focus on anything other than how much her head hurt or how cold air seemed to be seeping straight through her coat. She thought about how Benjamin St. Michaels had stood her up, and how that had led to her being at exactly the wrong spot when that deer had decided he absolutely must be on the other side of the road despite the oncoming car.

Of course, with the weather turning bad quicker than expected, she probably would have left before being able to complete the interview. That or not have been able to leave. She laughed. Being trapped at the home of someone you didn't know didn't sound like the most awesome time ever. More like awkward at best.

When she thought she heard a vehicle, she turned quickly to look behind her. But not only was there no approaching help, she also managed to send a fresh wave of throbbing pain through her head.

She picked up her pace, hoping her blood would pump hard enough that her feet would warm up. If she thought she wouldn't fall or it wouldn't cause further pain in her head, she'd start running. Better to keep a decent walking pace than risk further injury.

She had no idea how much time had passed when she realized she was shivering and that taking a nap on the side of the road had started to sound appealing. She fought that thought, somehow grasping that if she didn't find shelter soon she was going to be in danger of becoming hypothermic. At that realization, panic started to set in. She had to find shelter before she lost her ability to reason.

Smoke winding its way up through the treetops caught her attention. Whether she was imagining it or not, she didn't know, but she had to hope it was real as she stepped off the road and started in that direction.

Despite it hurting worse and making her sick to her stomach, she shook her head to clear it as she wove her way through the trees. She was not going to give in to Mother Nature this close to potential salvation.

Please help me make it.

Right as she was beginning to doubt what she'd seen, Maya broke free of the trees and spotted a modest log home. The thought that she recognized the house managed to surface through the thick fog in her head. The old… Black…thorn place. Even her thoughts were shivering. She shook her head again, but it felt as if she were moving in water this time—sluggish, with the surrounding sound muted.

Her steps were slower too, her feet…what was the word? Started with an *H*. She blinked but almost couldn't lift her eyelids. The house was right…th-th-there. The next time she blinked, her lids refused to open and her legs seemed to freeze in place like mechanical gears seizing up in the cold.

In the next moment she was falling, but she didn't feel the impact with the ground.

AFTER SEEING TO his horse's needs, Gavin Olsen headed out of the barn. He'd check on his small herd of cattle again after the snowstorm passed, but for now he wanted a warm meal and hot coffee while surrounded by four thick, solid walls. Even though he was used to wintry weather, he also appreciated being able to retreat inside when his work was done.

As long as he didn't lose power, he planned to kick back and watch some TV after a long day that had started before dawn. When you worked outside, you structured your days based on the weather forecast as best you could.

A gust of wind had him tightening his grip on the barn door as he pushed it closed and secured it. Thankfully, he'd managed to complete the most important repairs to the structure before winter set in, so he was confident that Jasper would stay comfortable inside. Now it was his turn to move to warmer quarters.

He turned toward the house, but movement out of the

corner of his eye drew his attention. Had he been living out here alone with his thoughts and sorrow so long that he was now seeing things? Because it sure looked as if a woman was walking toward the house from the direction of the tree line. Actually, *walking* might not be the best description of what she was doing, because she was obviously struggling even though the snow wasn't deep yet.

Who was she? What was she doing here? Was she a hiker who'd somehow gotten lost and bewildered in the storm? How long had she been out in the cold? His pulse jumped when she stumbled. She appeared to try to right herself, but in the next moment she crumpled to the ground.

Gavin stood for a moment, battling the instinctual frustration that someone had invaded his private space, even if accidentally. But he wasn't so bitter that he would let her freeze to death. So he ran toward her, knowing he had to get this unknown woman out of the cold. There was no telling how long she'd been wandering around in this weather, and despite her winter attire she might be close to hypothermic.

Don't let her die on my front lawn.

He dropped to his knees next to her.

"Hey, can you hear me?"

No response, but thankfully she was still breathing. Not wasting any time because the storm was only getting worse, he placed his arms behind her back and knees and lifted her off the cold ground. He winced a bit when his boot slid on the snow, but he kept on his feet and quickly moved toward the house.

Once he managed to open the door and get her inside, he set her on the couch before hurriedly closing the front door. Facing her again, he sighed and knelt in front of her.

"Hey, can you wake up?" He knew he sounded curt, but that was how he felt most days. When she again offered no response, he shook her arm a bit. Even if he didn't want her here, he still possessed some basic human decency. "You need to get out of this coat and your shoes. They're wet."

She grunted a bit as if in response to pain. Had she injured her arm?

With another sigh, he realized he was going to have to help her out of her wet winter outerwear. He hoped she didn't wake up in the middle and totally freak out that she was being undressed by a man she didn't know.

As he got her out of her coat, gloves, shoes and socks, he noticed her wince. When he removed her knitted hat, he spotted a trickle of dried blood. It wasn't fresh enough to be a result of her tumble in his yard, so she'd already been injured somehow.

He hurried to get a wet cloth and washed away the blood, glad to see the injury was only a small cut. Still, it was concerning that she was still unconscious. What was worse than some strange woman freezing to death in his yard? Her dying on his couch.

Hoping once again that she didn't misunderstand if she woke up, he set about checking her limbs for serious damage that would require him trying to get her to the little local hospital despite the fact that it might be more dangerous trying to get down the mountain now than staying put. And with the rate at which the snow was falling, he doubted an ambulance could make it up here. He was just going to have to make do, no matter how much he disliked the situation.

Thankfully, nothing seemed to be broken, but he noticed a knot that was bruising at the edge of her hair on the left side of her forehead close to the cut.

After stretching her out on the couch and propping her head with a pillow, he covered her with two quilts. That accomplished, he crossed to the freezer and put together an ice pack. When he eased it against the bump on her head, she winced more visibly before settling. He really hoped she didn't have a concussion, because if she did wasn't he supposed to wake her up?

He'd just keep an eye on her because going out in the storm could end up doing more harm than good to his unexpected guest. Deciding hot food when she woke up would increase her chances of surviving, he strode back across the room to the kitchen area. It was probably a good idea to put distance between them anyway. He wanted it to be abundantly clear when she woke up that he wasn't a physical threat to her, even if he wasn't likely to be the friendliest of hosts.

If she had some sort of identification with her, he'd try to contact a relative. But he hadn't seen any purse or backpack, and there'd been nothing in the pockets of her coat.

He opened some cans of hearty chicken noodle soup because that seemed to be the accepted cure-all and dumped them into a pot on the stove. A great cook, he was not, but he got by. He doubted his guest would be too picky if what she was offered helped to warm her up.

He glanced over his shoulder, saw that the woman hadn't moved at all, then redirected his attention out the window above the kitchen sink. The snow was coming down so fast now that he could barely identify the trees. Seeing into the valley where his cattle were was impossible.

Why did this woman have to stumble onto his property of all places?

The quiet that filled his house now was exactly the opposite of what he wanted. Since moving back to Wyoming a broken man and buying a ranch in need of a substantial amount of work, he'd done his best to keep his hands and mind occupied with his to-do list. But his plan to turn on the TV to whatever would keep his thoughts off why he'd left Denver was put on hold. And thus his memories waltzed in and assaulted him. An unexpected—and admittedly unfair—wave of anger at the woman on his couch hit him. Her presence made the difficult task of forgetting even harder, though she'd had nothing to do with his loss.

He turned and stared at her prone form. He needed her to wake up and the storm to clear so he could get her out of his space. At least chances were she'd be totally on board with that. Then he could go back to the only marginally successful job of staying so busy that he didn't have time to curl in on himself and give up entirely.

CHAPTER TWO

WHO HAD HIT her in the head with a baseball bat? that was Maya's first question as she began to emerge into consciousness. Even before she opened her eyes, she lifted her hand and pressed it against her forehead, hoping to alleviate the pain. But this wasn't a sinus or tension headache where activating pressure points would work. The reason for the pain slowly came back to her. And—good news— if she had the queen of all headaches, she was pretty sure she wasn't dead.

As she opened her eyes to unfamiliar surroundings, she tried to remember where she'd been right before she'd evidently blacked out. She'd been meeting with someone for a story. No, that hadn't worked out, and that had led to her accident. She remembered crawling out of the car, walking through the snow, and... Oh, she'd turned toward the sight of smoke curling up from a chimney.

The mental images of weaving through trees and deepening snow were fuzzier. Even more so was the one of a cabin, almost as if she'd seen it through fog or water. She scanned the wooden ceiling above her, then realized she was lying on a blue couch, and finally that she was blessedly warm even if her head did feel as if it might explode at any moment.

"I take it you have a headache."

Maya startled so violently that pain pierced her skull

like a flaming arrow, making the headache of moments before seem like bumping a feather in comparison.

"Don't move too fast. It'll make it worse." The unknown man was saying the right words, but if he was a doctor his bedside manner needed some work.

"Duh," she replied without thinking while she tried to not throw up.

"Would you like some Tylenol?" Did he really sound begrudging, or was she just in a foul mood because she felt terrible?

Doing her best to not sound so rude to the man who'd evidently saved her from freezing to death in the snow, no matter how annoyed he sounded, she said, "Please."

In truth, she felt as if an entire bottle of acetaminophen didn't stand a chance against the throbbing in her head. Even blinking seemed to add to the ache. Thus, Maya didn't look up when the man returned from another room with a big bottle of "please, give me some relief" and a glass of water. She did notice he stayed on the opposite side of the sturdy coffee table, perhaps sensing that it was a good idea to have some sort of barrier between himself and the woman who'd found herself lying on a stranger's couch. Maybe that was why he didn't sound overly friendly. He didn't want her to get any wrong ideas.

"Thank you." She moved carefully as she sat up, swallowed two pills and drank almost the entire glass of water. "Sorry for being rude before."

He grunted acknowledgment from several feet away, making Maya realize that he'd created even more distance between them. "You've apparently had a not-so-great day." The way he sounded, the same was true for him.

Hey, buddy, I'm not thrilled to be here either.

"That is, quite literally, the biggest understatement I've heard in my entire adult life." She winced at a fresh throb of pain, and she reached up to gingerly touch what she knew had to be a substantial goose egg on the left side of her head. "I ran off the road thanks to a deer that was really impatient to see the scenery on the other side."

"That explains the cut and knot on your head and why you were wandering around in a snowstorm."

Whoever her savior was, he had a nice, deep voice with a rich tone that would be great at lulling you to sleep with a bedtime story. At least when he didn't sound irritated. Wondering what kind of face went with the voice, she eased her gaze up until she spotted him standing, arms crossed, where the living area flowed into the kitchen on the other side of the main room.

She blinked a few times to focus and was rewarded with a view of the handsomest man she'd seen in Jade Valley in…maybe ever. Nice build, a healthy tan, sandy brown hair, probably a bit over six feet tall.

"It's possible you have a concussion," he said, making her wonder if his words had been prompted by her staring at him too long.

Maya lowered her gaze to the coffee table and downed the rest of the water before replying.

"Maybe, but I woke up, so that's a good sign. Thanks for not letting me turn into human tundra in your front yard."

"Trust me, I didn't want that either." He sounded very much like he thought an ice brick of a body in front of his house would be incredibly annoying.

He seemed to be a matter-of-fact man of few words. Of course, he probably hadn't expected to have to carry a half-frozen woman into his house either. Her face heated at the thought of him carrying her, and she unconsciously pulled a quilt up and around her shoulders.

"Cold?"

"No, I'm fine." What a dumb answer. If she wasn't cold,

why would she be wrapping herself up? The knock on the head had evidently relieved her of any common sense she'd once possessed.

"I warmed up some chicken noodle soup."

"That sounds really good." She'd skipped lunch to make the interview that hadn't happened, and the granola bar she'd had for breakfast was long gone. Hopefully having something in her stomach would prevent the queasy feeling every time she moved her head too quickly. "What time is it, anyway?"

"Just after six."

She slowly turned and looked outside to see it had grown dark.

"I would have called your family, but you didn't have any ID with you."

"I—" She looked around for her purse but didn't see it. "I must have lost my bag along the way."

"You were pretty out of it, close to hypothermia, so that's not surprising." His tone made it sound like she'd willingly done something idiotic.

She bit down on a snappy comeback, reminding herself that maintaining a friendly attitude had served her better in the past than snark or rudeness.

"Maya," she said. "Maya Pine, that's my name."

"Okay. Do you want to call your family?"

"If I could make a couple of calls, I would appreciate it."

The man, who hadn't offered up his name, grabbed a cell phone from the kitchen counter and crossed the room to offer it to her. She was careful not to make contact with his hand as she took it. He might have saved her and was providing her with the things she needed, but she still didn't know him. And it was obvious he wasn't thrilled to have her as a houseguest.

"Where can I tell them I am?"

Instead of revealing his name, he offered up the address. "But I don't think anyone is making it up the mountain tonight. The snow hasn't stopped yet." He did not sound happy about this state of affairs.

So she was going to have to spend the night under the same roof as a man who had yet to identify himself. She was fairly certain she wasn't going to sleep a wink.

As her host went back to the kitchen and started scooping soup into a bowl, she called Trina Gray, her next-door neighbor, to have her check on and feed Blossom, her cat. After they hung up, she took a deep breath and called her mother.

"Hey, Mom. Just wanted to let you know that my phone went kaput in case you tried to call or text me, and I obviously won't be able to get a new one until this storm is over."

"Whose phone are you using? I don't recognize this number."

"Someone I met at work. Listen, just wanted to let you know. I gotta go."

"You're not getting out in this storm, are you?"

"Don't worry. My car isn't moving an inch." Her mom didn't need to know about the current location and condition of Maya's car, however.

When she ended the call and placed the phone on the coffee table, Maya felt as if she'd expended way more energy than she had. In the next moment, a steaming bowl of soup and a refilled glass of water were placed in front of her.

"Thank you." She attacked the soup as if she hadn't eaten in days instead of hours. Despite that she could tell immediately it was canned soup, in her current situation it was in the running for the best-tasting food that had ever passed her lips. The soup warmed her from the inside while the fire in the wood-burning stove and the quilts did the same on the outside. The hot food finally pushed away the last of the chill that had invaded her body during her wintry search for safety.

"I'm sorry I'm imposing on you like this," she said once she was about halfway through with the bowl of soup.

The man nodded once and uttered a simple, "Um."

So he didn't like having his space invaded, but he wasn't cruel enough to leave her to the elements. She was just glad she hadn't wound up in the home of someone creepy and dangerous.

"Do you mind if I ask your name?"

He hesitated in answering for several seconds, long enough that she wondered if he actually would answer.

"Gavin Olsen."

"It's nice to meet you, even if the circumstances are not ideal."

Again with the simple nod as a response. She was getting the distinct impression that this guy lived here alone and liked it that way.

"Would you like some more soup?" he asked.

"No, thanks. I'm not finished with this bowl yet." She noticed how he was standing next to the stove but not serving himself any of the soup he'd prepared. "You should have some too. I'm sure saving people from their own stupidity works up an appetite."

Maya saw not even a hint of a smile. She half expected him to decline for some reason, but in the next moment he served up a bowl of soup and seated himself at one end of the wooden kitchen table. Still keeping his distance.

She took her time finishing her soup, then slowly started to push to her feet, careful not to jostle her head too much.

"You can leave the bowl on the coffee table," he said.

"Actually, I need to use your bathroom."

"Oh," he said, looking more embarrassed than annoyed this time. "Door at the end."

He directed her down a short hallway. As she went down it, she noticed a door on either side. She caught a quick glimpse of a bed in one, and the other appeared to be used for storage. Before she returned to the main room, she took a few moments to straighten her hair and wash her face. The bump at the hairline of her forehead made it look as if she was on the verge of growing a horn.

As she was about to emerge from the hallway into the brightly lit kitchen, a wave of dizziness hit her and she reached out a hand and pressed it against the wall to steady herself.

Gavin was suddenly in front of her, seemingly ready to catch her if she passed out again.

She managed a smile as the spinning in her head receded. "I'm okay. Just a little woozy."

"You should sit."

"I think you're right." But instead of heading for the couch again, she pointed herself toward the kitchen table and claimed the chair opposite where Gavin had been sitting. When she glanced up, he appeared to be surprised by her choice.

"Don't you think you should lie down?" She couldn't tell if there was any true concern in his question or if he simply wanted to keep the original distance between them.

"I need to move around so I don't get any stiffer than I already am. For some reason, the human body doesn't like crashing into trees. Who knew?"

He didn't laugh at her attempt at humor.

Instead of sitting again, Gavin moved to the refrigerator and refilled the bag-type ice pack she realized he'd been holding. Even when he placed it near her on the table, she noticed that he fully extended his arm so he didn't come any closer than necessary. Was he shy? Was that why he lived alone and wasn't happy about suddenly having to share his space? Or was he only trying to make sure she knew he wasn't a threat?

She pointed toward his half-full bowl as she placed the fresh ice pack gently against her head.

"You should finish your soup before it gets cold."

After a moment of standing behind his chair, he pulled it out and sat. Instead of saying anything, he focused all of his attention on his soup. Maya barely suppressed a smile by pressing her lips together.

"I was glad to hear someone finally bought this place," she said, hoping to generate some more conversation to fill the silence and keep awkwardness at bay. "How do you like it so far?"

Gavin looked up from his soup and stared at her as if he couldn't identify her species.

"What?" she asked at the confusion on his face.

"You're awfully at ease considering you woke up in a stranger's house."

She tried to ignore the curt tone of his observation, like he thought she might actually be stupid.

"But you're not exactly a stranger anymore. I know your name, that you saved this place from falling into complete disrepair, and you rescue frozen wanderers." She pointed at his bowl. "And you warm up a mean can of soup."

He glanced down at the bowl before meeting her gaze again. "I wasn't expecting company."

Honestly, she doubted he ever had any. She tried to understand what it must be like for him, if he was used to being alone, to suddenly have a talkative guest.

"I sincerely don't mind. I think it counts as the most welcome bowl of soup I've ever consumed." She paused for a moment. "And I figure that if you intended me harm, you would have perpetrated it already. You wouldn't be making sure I stay warm, fed and supplied with ice for my goose egg. And you wouldn't be obviously keeping your distance."

"I didn't want to scare you or give you any reason to suspect me."

"Unless you start acting drastically different, you're safe from my suspicion. And thank you, again, for saving my life. If you hadn't found me when you did, I don't think I'd be alive right now."

"You wouldn't be."

The reality of that caused a shiver to run down her spine.

"You cold?" he asked her for the second time since she'd awoken on his couch.

She slowly shook her head. "No, it's nice and toasty in here. I was just thinking of all the stories I've heard of people dying of exposure due to hypothermia, and how close I came to becoming one of those statistics."

Gavin looked toward the front window, and quiet settled between them for several seconds.

"How long were you out in that weather?" His tone suggested that his desire to not engage with her had lost out to his curiosity, and he wasn't happy about it.

"I'm not sure. What time did you find me?"

"Shortly after noon."

"It must have been about an hour, then, but part of that I was knocked out in my car."

"Are you injured anywhere else? I only checked to see if there were any obvious broken bones."

"There doesn't seem to be anything other than what I'm sure is going to be a collection of colorful bruises. I got lucky."

Despite his kindness, albeit given reluctantly, Maya

was pretty sure Gavin Olsen did not share the same view about how his day had turned out.

GAVIN WOKE THE next morning hoping the previous day had been nothing more than a vivid dream. But when he heard the commode flush in the bathroom, he realized the memory that he had an unexpected houseguest was all too real. He had the urge to pull his covers up over his head as if he could hide from her, the same trick he'd tried to use to get out of going to school when he was a kid. It wasn't going to work now any more than it did back then.

Why was this happening to him? He just wanted to be left alone. He was no longer fit for human interaction.

When he finally forced himself out of bed and walked over to the window, he couldn't believe his eyes. It was still snowing. The weather people had gotten the forecast for this storm all kinds of wrong—the timing of its arrival, the amount of snowfall, how long it would last. He growled inwardly and ran a hand over his face. Looked as if his unwanted guest wasn't going to be able to leave today either. Thank goodness he had work he could do outside, because the idea of being trapped in the house with her all day made him want to take up residence in the barn.

Despite what she'd gone through the day before, she seemed to be one of those look-on-the-bright-side kind of people. He had no energy to deal with that, not to mention he thought those people were lying to themselves. Life was not all sunshine and rainbows. It was dark clouds and cold, pelting rain more often than not.

Putting off having to face her for a few more minutes, he retreated to his blessedly private bathroom to take a shower and shave. By the time he was finished and dressed, he figured if he waited any longer it would be obvious he was avoiding her. And though that was exactly what he'd like to do, he did realize that she'd not chosen to invade his solitude. He wanted to be able to blame her for being out in the storm in the first place, but she'd likely been surprised by the timing of its arrival the way he had. He hadn't talked to her long, but she didn't seem like the type of person to make stupid decisions, her bright personality notwithstanding. In fact, she came across as someone who thought things through and arrived at common-sense decisions.

If only *he'd* always possessed those qualities.

He reminded himself that Maya Pine wasn't a permanent fixture in his home. As soon as the road was clear enough for travel, she'd thankfully be gone—whether someone came to pick her up or he drove her into town. He'd prefer the former but would do the latter if it allowed him to reclaim his solitude sooner.

When he opened his bedroom door, he was hit with the smell of bacon. Unless he had unknowingly started cooking while sleepwalking, Maya had gotten hungry and taken it upon herself to raid a stranger's fridge. He bit down on instant annoyance until he reminded himself that he couldn't exactly starve her. And at least by her taking the initiative, he didn't have to cook for her again.

Despite his desire to flee the house, his stomach growled in response to the delicious scent. When he stepped into the kitchen, he was surprised to see that Maya either had a huge appetite or she'd cooked enough for him as well.

"Oh, good morning," she said with a wide smile that belied the fact that she'd wrecked her car and nearly frozen to death the day before.

"You cooked breakfast?" Obviously.

"Yes. I hope you don't mind." She gestured toward the spread gracing the table. "Call it a thank-you."

"This wasn't necessary." How messed up was he that her kind gesture made him uncomfortable? And suspicious.

"I'd say this isn't much considering what you've done for me."

His stomach growled again, louder this time. Maya laughed at his audible hunger.

"Looks as if I finished up just in time."

Even though he didn't typically make so much for breakfast, it looked and smelled great. He felt edgy and out of sorts, but maybe filling his stomach wasn't a terrible idea before venturing out into the cold. After all, food shouldn't go to waste. And no matter how hungry Maya might be, he didn't think she could eat everything she'd made.

When he took his first bite of scrambled eggs, it was all he could do not to moan in appreciation. Did she have some magical way of making eggs? Because his efforts never produced such stellar results. Not that he tried to do more than simply fill his belly when the need arose. As with most things, he hadn't taken much pleasure in food in a long time.

"I hope scrambled eggs are okay," Maya said. "I didn't know how you liked them, and I'll admit to not being the world's best cook."

"They're good," he said.

She didn't fish for more compliments, something else he appreciated. Compliments invited people to become friendlier and more talkative, and that wasn't what he wanted. He got the distinct feeling she'd deduced that he'd rather be alone and was doing her best to be helpful rather than a burden. Oddly, that softened him the smallest fraction toward her.

"How does your head feel?"

"About as well as can be expected." She lifted her hand

and pushed her hair away from the knot. "It's all kinds of pretty colors today. I'm thinking of changing my name to Rainbow."

He was unexpectedly tempted to smile at that, but it never made it past a slight tug at the corner of his mouth. He honestly couldn't remember the last time he'd smiled. Of course, he hadn't had anything to smile about since he'd lost his son.

No, he couldn't think about Max now. He didn't want to risk his pain showing on his face and Maya asking questions.

They ate in silence for a bit before Maya spoke again.

"I'm sorry to report that the snow hasn't seen fit to stop falling."

"I saw." Because none of this was her fault and he sounded like a jerk with his short, clipped replies, he added, "Feel free to watch TV. I'll be out of the house working most of the day. And there's a landline phone if you need to make more calls." He pointed toward the phone on the wall.

"Is that a *rotary* phone?"

"Yes. The previous occupant hadn't updated in quite some time."

"I'll say. But that's not surprising. If Ansel Blackthorn had told me he'd been living here before Wyoming gained statehood, I would have believed him. He was quite a character and averse to change, as you've gathered by his blast-from-the-past phone."

Gavin wondered if this place attracted hermits, because he'd sure been living up to that label since moving here.

"When he passed, no one in town could quite believe it. He seemed eternal somehow."

He gave a "hmm" and a nod in reply, and she seemed to take the hint and fell into silence as she ate. He wondered how difficult it was for her to stay quiet, because she seemed like a cheery, chatty person—the complete opposite of him. All the more reason to get her out of his home as soon as possible. But as much as he wanted her gone, he wasn't about to shove her out the door before it was safe to do so. Maybe if she lived nearby her departure could be sooner rather than later though.

"Do you live up the mountain?"

"No, in town. I was up here to meet someone to do an interview, but he didn't show up."

"A job interview?"

She shook her head as she ripped a piece of bacon in half. "An interview for the paper. I'm the editor of the *Valley Post*."

His breakfast threatened to sour in his stomach. Of all the damsels in distress to collapse on his property, it had to be a reporter.

He stood quickly, almost knocking over his chair in the process. "Work to do."

He retrieved his coat and hat and strode out of the house. When the door was closed safely behind him, he took a moment on the front porch to inhale a deep breath. The air was visible when he exhaled. He had the strangest thought that he wished he was a dragon so he could burn away the snow, making a clear path for Maya Pine to leave and occupy space anywhere else but his home.

CHAPTER THREE

MAYA STARED AT the front door for probably a full thirty seconds after Gavin walked out. She needed that long to process his sudden departure and the most likely reason for it—the revelation that she was a reporter.

She sighed. To some extent she could understand why people had a negative opinion of her profession. There were definitely journalists out there who wouldn't know truth and journalistic ethics if they slapped them upside the head. But they were the ones who were after big national audiences, and often weren't real journalists anyway. They weren't running little local papers on a shoestring budget like her. Some people didn't distinguish between the two, however. If you asked people questions for a living, some thought you were evil incarnate.

She bit into a slice of bacon more aggressively than was required, disappointed that there would likely be no chance of increasing the friendliness of the conversations with her host now.

After finishing her food, putting away leftovers and washing the dishes, she took some medicine for the dull headache that was still lingering. She wished her laptop was handy, but even if she'd had it with her, it would likely be buried in the snow somewhere alongside her purse.

Despite being stranded, she had to work every bit as much as Gavin did. So she used the ancient phone to call

Janie, her one and only staffer at the paper, to let her know what was going on.

"You're where?"

"The old Blackthorn place. The new owner, quite literally, saved my life."

"That should be the article you write to replace the one that fell through."

"Yeah, not happening. He's not a fan of reporters."

"So…are you in a bad situation?"

"No, nothing like that. He's just the quiet sort." And grumpy. "But he's not even here now. I'm sure he's out doing rancher things. Ranching waits for no one and nothing, not even a snowstorm."

Out feeding cows and probably wishing she'd fallen face-first in someone else's yard.

"So, what are the road conditions like?" Maya asked. If she and her car could be retrieved soon, that would probably be best for both her and her not-so-happy host.

"Terrible and getting worse. The crews are having a hard time keeping even the main roads somewhat passable."

So much for giving Gavin his privacy back.

Janie assured Maya that she'd get the weather story done for the front page and make sure the paper got sent to press on time if Maya could come up with something to fill the spot she'd been saving for the St. Michaels feature.

"I've got an idea, but I'll have to call you back later to dictate it to you."

"Okay, I'll get everything else wrapped up in the meantime."

"Thanks. You're the best."

"I know. Employee of the Month every month."

Maya laughed before hanging up and seeking some paper and a pen. When was the last time she'd written a story longhand? Probably three years before when they'd had a storm knock out the power and her laptop battery ran out.

As she sat at the kitchen table and got to work on a piece about the state's new infrastructure plans for the county, something she'd slotted for next week's issue, she mentally chewed out Benjamin St. Michaels again. She doubted a story about funding for roads and bridges was going to draw lots of extra purchases of this week's issue.

By the time she'd filled the first page of the small note-book, she had to stretch her hand. She looked down at the words scrawled across the page and shook her head. Her handwriting got worse with each passing year.

When she was satisfied with the article, she called Janie back and read it to her so she could type it in.

"You sure you're okay there?" Janie asked once they were finished. "I could ask Angie if there's a way to come get you."

"No, I'm fine. You said the road conditions were rotten. I'm not putting anyone else at risk simply because I find myself in an awkward situation. Besides, maybe I can convince him that all reporters aren't bad."

Though she wasn't going to bet her savings on that.

"Oh yeah?" Janie asked. "What exactly does this guy look like?"

"Janie! That's not what I meant."

"You didn't answer the question."

"Go do your work or you're fired."

Janie was still laughing at the absurdity of Maya firing her one and only staff member when Maya hung up the phone.

Maya scanned her surroundings, but it looked the same as it had when she'd taken it all in while waiting for Gavin to emerge from his room earlier. Simple furnishings, a few books on a shelf, a good-size TV, but no personalization such as family photos or mementos.

To be honest, it seemed somewhat odd that a man who looked like Gavin Olsen was living out here alone. A litany of possible reasons why ran through her head: he wasn't a people person (evidence pointed toward this), he was a workaholic with no time for relationships (maybe, but that didn't ring particularly true), he was unlucky in love (hey, it happened to people of all attractiveness levels), he was a serial killer (nope), or he simply hadn't found the right person (dude, you're not alone).

She could empathize with the last possibility. Dating in a small town was a challenge if it was even feasible once you discounted all the people you were either related to or who you knew way too much about. The fact that she'd never even seen Gavin in town added to the unlikelihood of him dating anyone local.

As much as she'd nixed her mother's matchmaking efforts and swatted away her best friend Sunny's teasing about her dating, it wasn't as if Maya wanted to spend the rest of her life alone. But her hectic work schedule combined with limited eligible bachelors made happily-ever-after more difficult.

Sunny had gotten lucky—the man who'd been head over heels for her since they were both teenagers was sitting right there on her family's ranch when she made the decision to come back to Jade Valley after years away. The only guys to cause a flicker of interest for Maya seemed to always be attractive tourists stopping at one of the two sit-down restaurants in town on their way through.

She shook her head, trying to clear away her wandering thoughts of romance. Even if Gavin Olsen was an attractive man, she didn't know enough about him to determine whether she could like him as more than her literal savior.

For that she'd always be grateful, despite his curt manner. And judging by his reaction to the news that she was a reporter, she'd venture a solid guess that she was way, way down his list of potential romantic partners. The best she could hope for was to convince him that not all reporters were the same. There were plenty who simply did their jobs reporting the actual news and shining a spotlight on worthy stories in their communities instead of capitalizing on people's fears for ratings and sales.

That gave her an idea for an article. She flipped to a fresh page in the notebook and started a bulleted list of points to cover. By the time she looked up from the pages she'd filled, she realized three things. One, this was more material than could fit into a single article. Two, this had the potential to be a series picked up nationally. And three, two hours had elapsed without her realizing how stiff she'd become while sitting on the hard kitchen chair.

She stood and stretched her aching muscles, some of the soreness caused by her accident. What she could really use was a massage, but that was nowhere on her horizon. But maybe a hot shower would suffice, and while Gavin was away from the house was the best time to take one. He hadn't given her any reason to be afraid of him, but it would still feel weird to take a shower in the home of a man she didn't really know.

She planned it to be a quick shower, but the moment she stepped under the stream of hot water she didn't want it to end. The warmth soaked into her aching muscles, giving her relief she hadn't fully been aware she needed. Gavin's shampoo didn't smell feminine, but it felt great to wash her hair, even if she had to be gentle with the area she'd injured.

Not wanting to use all the hot water, she reluctantly stepped out of the shower and made quick work of dry-ing off and putting her clothes back on. Thankful Gavin actually owned a hair dryer, she dried her hair and pulled it up into a knot.

Speaking of knots, she wiped the steam off the mirror and checked out her colorful goose egg.

"You sure don't do anything halfway, do you?" she asked her reflection.

With a gentle shake of her head, she left the bathroom. Judging by how quiet the house was, Gavin had still not returned. Since he'd obviously skipped lunch, possibly to avoid her, he was going to be starving when he finally came back for the night. Still conscious that he'd saved her and that he was stuck with an obviously unwanted house-guest, she went to the kitchen to see what she could make for dinner. She had to eat too, after all. And maybe her making something warm and hearty could begin to chip away at his preconceptions about the type of person she was based on her profession.

It would probably help if she was as good a cook as her mom, but you worked with what you had.

After examining the contents of the fridge, freezer and pantry, she decided on beef stew. It seemed perfect for the kind of cold, snowy weather they were experiencing, especially after Gavin had been out in the elements all day.

What had he been doing during all those hours he'd been absent?

The ancient telephone had a long enough cord that she was able to call and talk to Sunny while she was assembling the stew.

"Um, let me get this straight," Sunny said after Maya explained her current situation. "You are making dinner for a man you don't know, who resents you being there, while being trapped in his house?"

"Don't make it sound so sinister," Maya said. "He's

been a perfect gentleman, if not super friendly, and I have to eat as well. It's not as if I'm an invalid who can't fend for herself."

"What do you know about him? Have you called Angie to see what she knows?"

Maya rolled her eyes. "Have you been watching true crime shows or something? If he was planning to off me, do you think he would have let me use the phone? Or left me alone all day?"

Sunny hesitated before responding. "I suppose those are valid points."

"Thank you. I'm kind of known for having a good sense about people, remember?"

Sunny grunted her reluctant agreement in a way that made Maya laugh.

"So, how old is this Gavin Olsen? Where did he come from?"

"I'd say late twenties, but maybe early thirties. And I don't know where he moved from, but my gut instinct says he has ranching experience, because he didn't act like a hobby rancher."

She glanced around the room, noticing again that it wasn't fancy but rather comfortable in its simplicity.

"And this isn't the kind of place that someone who is playing at ranching would buy."

"You truly believe you're safe?"

"Yes, I have no concerns about that at all." It was honestly amazing how quickly she'd come to that conclusion about Gavin. "I get the distinct feeling that he'll actually be relieved when I leave."

"So he's a loner."

"Seems so, but there are lots of valid reasons for liking to be in only your own company. I mean, you and I are obviously not like that, but I realize that not everyone is a social butterfly."

She didn't divulge the information about Gavin evidently not liking reporters, and she wasn't sure why. Maybe she just wanted time to figure out on her own why he held that view and try to change it. At least help him understand that reporters weren't a monolith. Their views on how to convey the news varied widely.

A cry from the other end of the call brought Maya out of her wandering thoughts.

"Sounds like one of your wee people isn't happy."

"Liam hasn't been feeling well, and we're keeping him separated from his sister so Lily doesn't get sick too. Let's say neither of the twins is happy with this new arrangement. I better go and check on him before he goes into full meltdown."

"Kisses to the kiddos from Auntie Maya to your adorable niece and nephew."

"Call me immediately if anything changes and you need help. I'll send out a snowmobile brigade or organize an airlift or something."

"Seriously, stop worrying about me. You've got enough on your plate, woman." With raising her brother's two orphaned toddlers, a husband who was one part rancher and one part entrepreneur, and her own consulting business, Sunny Breckinridge Wheeler was one busy woman. But that was exactly how she liked it. Sunny was always so full of new ideas on how to diversify the ranch, expand her business's offerings, improve the community of Jade Valley or the twins' early education opportunities that Maya didn't know when she slept.

Sunny laughed. "You're not wrong there. I'll talk to you later."

After she hung up, the house around her seemed extra

quiet. Of course, when it was snowy like this, it seemed to put a hush on the world. If this were her home and she didn't always have work to do, she could imagine finding the weather relaxing—well, now that she wasn't in danger of dying out in it. But the thought of kicking back in a pair of soft pajamas, with an equally soft blanket, a good book and a cup of hot cocoa with plenty of marshmallows sounded fabulous.

But she rarely got that kind of time to relax. Not that she was complaining, not much anyway. She loved her job, but it wasn't one she could leave at five in the afternoon and not have to think about until the next morning. The news never stopped, even in a little town like Jade Valley. There were always accidents to cover, sports events at the schools, local government decisions, feel-good features about someone's cat that had come home after wandering for six months, or a blue ribbon won at the state fair.

Even while stuck in a stranger's house with no access to her computer and with an ugly, painful knot on her head, she'd been working. A little voice at the back of her mind kept whispering that if she stopped, everything she'd worked for would disappear. She wanted to make the *Valley Post* successful enough that she'd stop getting messages from the owners pressuring her to do more, sell more. But to reach that goal, she had to be innovative.

Once she had the stew on the stove, she visited the pantry again and found some little boxes of cornbread mix. That sounded as if it would go well with the stew, so she set about preparing that while she let her mind wander through ideas for the paper.

She was pouring the prepared mix into a pan when she realized her thoughts had drifted away from work and toward when Gavin might reappear. Sunny's questions about him had gotten Maya's own curiosity to spinning.

Was he a Wyoming native? Did he know anyone in Jade Valley? And if not, why move here? Or was not knowing anyone the reason he'd relocated here? Had he always been an introvert?

She reined in her runaway questions, reminding herself that he was not someone she was interviewing. He was the person who'd saved her life and was allowing her to stay in his home until she could safely leave. She needed to respect his privacy as much as sharing the same space would allow. Even so, she thought casual conversation would help to alleviate any awkwardness between them. She just had to find the right balance between encouraging conversation and not letting her inclination to find out about people go too far. There was definitely a line between interested and nosy, and Gavin wouldn't appreciate her crossing it. Or perhaps even getting within spitting distance of it.

With the stew on the stove and the bread in the oven, she returned to her notes and jotted down the names of other small-town journalists she planned to consult. If this series turned out how she hoped, she'd actually have Gavin to thank for the idea. Somehow she doubted he'd want any part of it though.

Unless she could change his mind. What an awesome twist ending to the series that would be.

When the door suddenly opened, revealing the man she'd just been thinking about, an uncharacteristic wave of embarrassment caused her face to flush. Why, she wasn't sure. It wasn't as if she was thinking about him in an inappropriate way.

He took off his hat and hung it on the peg next to the door, revealing his face was red too but from the cold.

"I take it that it hasn't suddenly turned spring outside," she said.

He looked at her with an expression that almost seemed

as if he'd forgotten she was there, though she doubted very much that was the case.

"Unless spring looks and feels like Hoth, then no."

He sounded incredibly exasperated, but she couldn't help but laugh at the *Star Wars* reference. When she did, he looked surprised yet again.

"What? I've seen all the movies, the animated series, and even read some of the books. And my brother's room is filled with model ships, droids, stations, you name it. I half expect to hear 'The Imperial March' when I step into his room."

If she wasn't mistaken Gavin almost smiled. Or maybe that was wishful thinking on her part. Whatever the expression had been, it disappeared when he glanced at her, but in its place was an unasked question.

"What?"

He shook his head.

"If you're curious about something, you can ask."

He seemed to weigh his curiosity against the likelihood that she'd ask something in return. Or possibly against the moral implications of tossing her out into the snow after he'd saved her from it.

"Don't worry, I won't launch into a thousand questions about you," she said, adding a smile to hopefully put him at ease. Not to mention herself. The impression that he didn't seem to like her very much bothered her, though she was trying to not let that show. She was the one who'd invaded his home, so she didn't have the right to expect him to be cheery about it.

"I didn't say you would," he said, his tone chilly but not completely frozen.

"You didn't have to. I picked up pretty easily on the fact you're not fond of my profession, but I won't ask why. Everyone is entitled to their opinions."

Did she hope by giving him an out that he might feel more comfortable sharing something about himself? Yes. She'd be lying if she claimed otherwise. But would she be offended if he didn't? No. Sure, she liked to dig until she found good stories, and the stories behind the stories, but she didn't drag them out against people's wills. Unless, of course, they were politicians or criminals (or both), and then all bets were off.

Gavin took his time hanging his coat on the peg next to his hat and slipping off his boots. Even when he was finished, he didn't immediately face her and she could almost feel the tenseness in his body, the tumult of his thoughts. Finally he slowly turned and hesitated a moment before exhaling an audible breath then asking, "So you have a brother who is a lot younger than you?"

He wasn't winning any awards for being warm and friendly, but at least this was progress.

She nodded. "Though Ethan's not a kid anymore, if that's what you're thinking. He's in college in Laramie. But he's still a big sci-fi nerd. I tease him about it, but I like it too. I'm a big believer in finding what you like and embracing it, no matter what anyone else thinks."

"Healthy attitude." He said the words, so why did it sound like he didn't quite believe them?

"Yes, but it's not always popular with the older or stick-in-the-mud crowd."

"Few things are."

There was a note of bitterness in his voice, but she pretended not to notice and laughed instead.

Gavin seemed to catch the scent of the stew. "You didn't have to cook again."

"Something else about me, I get bored easily. I have to have things to do or I go stir-crazy. Plus, again, there's that little fact of you saving my life. I'm pretty sure I could cook meals for you for the next decade and it wouldn't be enough."

As those words left her mouth, a strange wave of awkwardness hit her. She hadn't considered how…intimate they could be interpreted, and she hoped that Gavin didn't take them that way.

Thank heaven that possibility seemed to fly past him as he moved toward the kitchen.

"It smells good." His stomach growled, quite audibly, which must be common for him.

"Well, evidently your stomach agrees."

While Gavin wordlessly excused himself to take a shower, she pulled the bread from the oven and tried not to think about there being a naked man who she barely knew not that far away. She wasn't prudish by any means, but it still felt strange. So much so that she exhaled in relief when the shower shut off and he'd had enough time to properly clothe himself. Still, when he stepped out with damp hair, wearing a T-shirt instead of the usual long-sleeve work shirts, she wondered if the short amount of time she'd been stuck in Gavin's house was enough to make her lose her common sense. Because the thought that she didn't mind being snowbound with a surly man she'd just met flitted through her mind, laughing as it went.

She turned to spoon stew into bowls, glad to be able to have a few moments to compose herself before facing him again. Had she let her mother's matchmaking latch on to some part of her brain? She shuddered at the thought, then spoke before Gavin could ask her if she was cold yet again.

"I brought in some more wood earlier from the pile outside," she said, using the ladle in her hand to deliberately point his attention toward the woodbin behind the stove.

"You di—"

"If you say I didn't have to do that, I'm going to toss

it back outside into the snow." She turned and placed the filled bowls on the table.

He stared at her for a long moment, seemingly confused by her response, before nodding once. "Point taken. Thank you." He hesitated again before continuing. "If you feel bad or dizzy, don't push yourself. Don't cause problems we can't fix."

"Deal. Trust me, I don't want to face plant off your porch and smother in a snowdrift while you're out feeding cattle, causing you to come back to a human popsicle. That just seems rude after you saved me once already. Twice seems to be pushing it."

"You joke about that a lot."

"What?"

"How close you came to dying," he said, not mincing words. He looked at her as if he couldn't wrap his mind around her way of thinking.

She shrugged. "Maybe it's a coping mechanism, or maybe just my personality, but I've always been that way. I figure dwelling on negatives and what-might-have-beens doesn't do me or anyone else any good, so why bother? Be thankful or deal with it, as the case may be, and move on."

"It's not always that easy." Gavin pulled out his chair, seating himself in front of his steaming bowl of stew.

His comment made her wonder about his past, if there was something that he couldn't move beyond. Maybe it was why he was so distant and bordering on ill-tempered. But, true to her word, she didn't pry.

"That's true. Some things that happen are more difficult to navigate or get over than others." She placed the plate of cornbread muffins on the table along with a tub of butter and a knife before taking her own seat. "I'm just thankful that I survived, and I don't want to dwell on the fact that I almost didn't."

Maya hesitated as the full weight of what she'd gone through suddenly slammed into her, as if it had been waiting nearby for the slightest invitation. She stared at her stew as another shiver ran through her, for a very different reason this time.

"I won't lie. I was scared, especially when I started having thoughts some part of my brain was telling me I shouldn't."

"Hypothermia," he said, having still not touched his food.

She nodded, then took a deep breath and met Gavin's gaze. "Seriously, thank you for saving me. I don't think I would have lasted out there much longer."

He stared at her for several seconds before responding with a solitary nod. "You're welcome."

His response surprised her, but she was thankful for it all the same.

They both dug into their stew as if ravenous. How she was so hungry after not doing much all day, she didn't have a clue. But winter was like that. The short, cold days made you want to eat and sleep.

She swallowed a bit of her cornbread then stared at the muffin in her hand.

"You ever wonder if humans are part bear?"

"Um, no." His response sounded very much as if he wondered if she'd taken leave of her senses.

"Hear me out. Days like today," she said, gesturing toward the window, "make me want to eat all the calories, then burrow under about ten blankets and sleep like I'm hibernating."

"It's just the body's instinct for self-preservation. Staying warm and being well-fed are at the top of that list."

She didn't allow her next thought to attach itself to her voice, that it was easier to stay warm when sharing body heat. Yeah, her mom's attempts to find her dates and Sunny's newly wedded bliss were messing with her brain. Or her body chemistry. When was the last time she went on a date? And that disaster of an evening with the delivery guy who brought orders to both Trudy's Café and Alma's Diner each week one hundred and ten percent did not count.

She needed to stop thinking about dates and bodies and eat her dinner instead.

And find a safe topic of conversation.

"So, was everything okay when you went out today?"

He nodded again. "Yes."

Maya sighed inwardly. He was back to single-word answers.

"That's good. My best friend's family has a ranch in the valley. I know it's a ton of work in all kinds of weather. You have to love it to put up with being frozen to the bone in the winter and burning up in the summer." She tore off another piece of muffin and crumbled it up in her stew. "But I guess there are good and bad points to every career."

Even though she loved her job, it wasn't perfect. She could live without the pressure from the paper's owners and the requests for feature articles that were not-at-all-veiled attempts to get free advertising, and a vacation every now and then would be nice. More than once, she'd envied Sunny's posts from around the world before Sunny had moved back from Los Angeles. Maya had wondered what it would be like to explore places such as Singapore or Brazil or Ireland. The amount of stories Sunny could write about her adventures would fill volumes.

Maya noticed that Gavin didn't say anything in response. Her instincts told her that he had zero interest in hearing about her chosen field. Curiosity nibbled away at her, but she held it in check.

"Sometimes you just do what you know," he finally said, surprising her.

"You've ranched before?"

Again, a nod. "Grew up on a ranch."

Had she managed to create a small crack in his icy exterior?

Questions came to her quickly, one right after another. Did his parents still operate a ranch? If so, why didn't he work with them? Or had they passed? Maybe the ranch was gone instead. Why had he chosen Jade Valley?

Once again, she pulled the brakes on her mental query train.

The phone rang, startling them both. She'd bet her meager savings that Gavin didn't get a lot of phone calls. When he answered, Maya had to press her lips together to keep from laughing at how he looked as if the phone might actually bite him.

"She's right here." He extended the receiver, surprising her further.

Had Janie run into an issue with the paper? She realized the more likely caller as she answered. "Yes, I'm still alive."

She smiled when Gavin turned toward her with his eyes wider than normal, probably without thinking.

"Maya! He'll hear you," Sunny said.

"Definitely. He's about five feet from me."

Gavin Olsen looked as if he'd give any amount of money to have her stop talking and then get immediately out of his house.

Maya would swear she could hear Sunny's eye roll.

"Well, now that I've reassured myself you're still among the living, I'm going to go spend time with my incredibly handsome husband."

"This has to be the record for the shortest phone call we've ever had."

"Hey, you need to take that off," Sunny said, obviously talking to Dean.

"TMI! Goodbye!" Maya hung up the phone in dramatic fashion, then shivered in an equally excessive way. "Ugh, newlyweds."

During the remarkably short phone call, Gavin had evidently inhaled the rest of his stew since he was now rinsing his bowl at the sink.

"Sorry about that," she said. "My best friend is a little...overprotective."

"Oh," he replied without looking at her.

"I already told her earlier today that I was pretty sure you aren't an ax murderer."

"Well, that's good to know."

Maya laughed. "Be careful. That sounded almost like humor."

He glanced at her, his forehead knitted in question. She walked over and leaned back against the kitchen counter a couple of arm's lengths away from him.

"Listen, I know you'd rather I not be here. I'd a million times rather not have totaled my car and nearly frozen to death, but here we are, stuck for the time being. I figure the best way to get through situations we don't plan for is to make the most of them. In case you haven't figured that part out about me yet, I tend to do that with humor."

"How do you know I'm not an ax murderer?"

She barely resisted laughing because he looked so serious.

"Well, for one, I woke up this morning. And two, the ax has stayed outside. So, two points in your favor."

He looked out the window above the sink into the darkness. "Why is it always an ax?"

"Huh?"

He looked back at her. "Why is it always an ax murderer? I don't think there are that many Lizzie Bordens walking around."

Maya stared at Gavin for a couple of seconds before she busted out laughing. There was no holding it in this time. "I have no idea. Maybe baseball bat murderer is too long."

Why she found it so funny that he knew who Lizzie Borden was, she wasn't sure. Maybe because the historical tidbit seemed so random. Did he like to read about history? True crime? She glanced toward the books on the shelf. She hadn't examined the titles yet. She'd do that the next time he left the house. Perhaps it would give her a little more information about Gavin. Tonight she'd already discovered that he did have a sense of humor, even if he was hesitant to show it or it was rusty for lack of use.

She finished the last few bites of her own meal then brought her dishes to the sink. Gavin extended his hand for the bowl and spoon.

"I can wash them."

"No. You cooked, twice. I'll do the dishes." She couldn't tell if he was thankful or simply didn't want to be indebted to her, as if her cooking a few meals could ever repay him for saving her life. He nodded toward the living room. "Watch some TV if you want."

When she clicked on the television, she found it already tuned to the Casper news. Unsurprisingly, the weather was the top story. She watched as the meteorologist talked about snowfall amounts, additional accumulation and the frigid temperatures expected in the days ahead.

"I don't know whether to believe him or not," she said as Gavin surprised her by settling into the recliner opposite from where she sat on the couch. "The weather people don't have a good track record with this storm."

Gavin only grunted, a sound that seemed to communicate he agreed. Did he group weather people on TV in with all other reporters? That would be a tad extreme, but she still wasn't going to ask any questions tonight. They'd actually had a bit of a conversation. He had loosened up the tiniest fraction. If she was going to be stuck here for the foreseeable future, she didn't want to risk making him retreat again. Her instincts told her that she had to toe a fine line to have him talk to her at all.

As soon as the weather coverage was over, Gavin leaned forward and grabbed the remote control. He looked over at her as if silently asking if she minded him changing the channel.

Maya motioned toward the television. "It's your TV."

Gavin flipped a few channels until she spotted a distinctive opening text scroll.

"Wait," she said, then laughed when she realized they'd landed on the opening credits of the original 1977 *Star Wars* after talking about the franchise earlier. "What are the odds?"

They settled in to watch the movie, even though she'd seen it so many times that she couldn't remember an exact count.

"Too bad we don't have any popcorn," she said.

He didn't respond, and she didn't push him to. Being willing to watch a movie with her seemed like enough of a step toward him thawing toward her for the time being.

When the first movie ended, the second in the original trilogy started immediately.

"This one is my favorite," she said.

Gavin got up from his chair, and she thought he must be going to bed in preparation for another early day tomorrow. But he simply shoved a couple of pieces of wood in the stove before returning to his chair.

It was oddly comfortable watching a *Star Wars* marathon with Gavin. Though she was the chatty sort, she didn't like people to talk during movies. In this way, Gavin proved to be the perfect movie buddy.

When *The Empire Strikes Back* ended and *Return of the Jedi* started, she turned to ask Gavin if he wanted something to drink. But she discovered that the reason he'd been so quiet wasn't because he was engrossed in the movie. Because he wasn't snoring like her dad and brother did, she hadn't realized he'd fallen asleep.

She found herself staring at him the way she couldn't when he was awake. He appeared more relaxed than he'd been at any point in their short acquaintance. If she was being honest, he wasn't hard to look at. She almost giggled remembering how she'd told her mom that she wouldn't look the other way if a hot man crossed her path. She hadn't imagined collapsing in front of his house and him having to save her from freezing to death, but life was strange sometimes.

But, like any other good-looking man she'd encountered, there was a substantial obstacle standing in the way of it developing into anything more than a brief meeting. Tourists went home, and her savior would probably throw a one-person party when she departed.

Even so, she found herself grabbing one of the quilts she'd used the night before and easing over to drape it across him. She held her breath, hoping he didn't wake up and see her standing above him.

Or maybe she hoped he would.

She shook her head at the strange thought. What was wrong with her? Why was she so interested in this man who was less than interested in her? Wondering if she'd knocked something vital to proper reasoning loose in her head in the wreck, she retreated to the relative safety of the couch. She turned off the lamp, covered herself in the remaining quilt, and stretched out with her back toward Gavin.

Gavin's obvious desire for her to go home as soon as possible suddenly seemed like the smartest idea any human had ever had.

CHAPTER FOUR

GAVIN WOKE THE next morning with pain in his chest. As he came awake, he was already rubbing at an ache that couldn't be alleviated, a hole that couldn't be filled. The dream and its emotional effects still lingered like a thick morning fog. He missed his son every day. Knowing that he was only a state away but he couldn't see him…he wouldn't wish that on any parent.

As he blinked away more of the lingering sleep, he noticed things were not normal. For one, it was later than he typically slept. He also wasn't in his bed.

Realizing he must have fallen asleep while watching TV, he glanced toward the screen to see it had been turned off. And a quilt had been draped over him. He looked to his right and noticed Maya curled up on the couch with her back toward him. She looked cold, and although she was only a temporary guest that he didn't want, he nevertheless didn't like the idea of her not being warm enough, especially after what she'd gone through.

Even after he'd been cold toward her, she persisted in friendly and kind gestures. Either she wasn't very bright or she was a good-hearted person. Evidence pointed toward the latter, so she didn't deserve to be the target of his foul attitude. He didn't have it in him to be cheery, but maybe he could try to be less gruff.

As quietly as he could, he lowered the footrest of his recliner and returned the quilt to its proper place. Maya rolled over as he settled the quilt atop her, and he froze. The last thing a woman needed to wake up to was a man she barely knew standing above her, even if she had decided he wasn't an ax murderer.

He smiled a fraction, surprising himself. Despite his not liking the media as a whole, Maya Pine seemed like a decent person. And despite her being a reporter, she hadn't grilled him for answers about his past or anything else. He was one for giving credit where credit was due, and her restraint though she was probably curious deserved acknowledgment, even if it was only to himself.

When it seemed Maya had settled back into sleep, he eased away from her and headed for the bathroom. Afterward, to keep from waking her, he exited the house via the door off the laundry room. He was greeted with a gust of frigid air that had him turning up the collar of his insulated jacket.

Unbidden, his thoughts returned to the arguably more comfortable life he'd been living prior to returning to Wyoming. There had been no early mornings making his way through deep snow to feed animals and make sure his livelihood was safe. Keeping warm was a certainty as long as the electricity stayed on. Instead of living like a recluse, he'd had a family, friends, had been following his dream.

But now that family, those friends and that dream were all part of the past, no matter how much he'd tried to keep them all.

He trudged toward the barn, hoping the freezing weather would take over all his thoughts because thinking about the past couldn't change it. He knew that from lots of experience.

"Good morning," he said to Jasper as he entered the barn. He walked over to the stall and scratched between the horse's ears. "Sorry, buddy, but we need to go for a ride."

A few minutes later, as he rode among the snow-laden trees down toward his pasture, he enjoyed the momentary sunshine even though he felt no warmth from it. And he wasn't fooled that it would last for long, because already the wind was blowing in heavy gray clouds that promised more snow. At this rate, he was going to be stuck with a roommate until spring.

It struck him as odd that he didn't hate that idea as much as he had a couple of days ago. Had he been that starved for human interaction and fooled himself into thinking he didn't need it? Because if he had been home alone, he was certain he wouldn't have stayed up late watching a sci-fi movie marathon.

His stomach grumbled, reminding him that he had slipped out without eating breakfast. But he'd had no idea how late Maya had been awake watching TV and he didn't want to wake her.

He shook his head. How quickly he'd adjusted the way he did things because of a virtual stranger.

She wouldn't be a stranger if you talked to her.

Cattle. He needed to focus his thoughts on cattle, not the woman with shoulder-length black hair, pretty dark eyes and a smile that broadcasted her fun-loving personality. He actually laughed a little at the memory of her short conversation with her friend the night before, at her response to her friend's obvious and understandable concern for her safety.

Cows, cows, cows.

He lost count how many times he had to tell himself to refocus on his work and that the very last thing he needed in his life was a woman. The last time he'd been romantically involved had ended in a spectacularly bad fashion. He was not venturing down that road again. He'd be a fool to.

When he was satisfied the herd was safe and had everything necessary, he was in need of both food and warmth so he headed back uphill toward the barn and house. By the time he led Jasper into the barn and tended to the horse's needs, he'd almost convinced himself that there was no reason to be anxious about seeing Maya again. It wasn't as if they'd kissed or something. They'd simply watched movies together, fallen asleep in the same room, and she'd shown enough compassion to place a quilt over him so he wouldn't get cold. That was just basic human courtesy, something that he was out of practice offering.

He headed toward the house but halfway there stopped in his literal tracks.

"What in the world?"

He moved closer to the object that had not been in his front yard that morning, stopped to stare at it, and then couldn't help laughing though the sound was foreign from disuse. Staring back at him was a snowman wearing one of his older hats, a smile made from wood bark and a flannel shirt held wide open by the stick arms that made it look as if it was a flasher.

He couldn't remember the last time that something had made him laugh so much. In a way, it felt wrong. But he couldn't deny it also felt good.

MAYA SMILED AT the sound of male laughter. Glancing out the window, she noticed that laughter looked good on Gavin Olsen. He was a handsome man to begin with, but a smile made him even more so.

She might not know what existed in his past that may have made him quiet and withdrawn, but her gut instincts had been telling her that he hadn't always been that way and that he needed reasons to smile again. It wasn't her job to make him smile, but she was glad her little joke had done the trick.

When he headed up the front steps, she spun back around and stared at the notes spread out in front of her on the coffee table. She'd spent the day outlining every possible article she could think of that would make sense to run in the paper and then worked on writing part of the small-town press series by hand. She couldn't recall the last time she'd written so much that way, and she'd had to stop several times to massage the muscles and joints in her hand and wrist as a result.

She glanced up when Gavin walked through the front door and went through the already familiar pattern of hanging up his hat and coat and slipping off his wet boots.

"Sounded as if you found your new lawn decoration amusing," she said.

"If the sheriff could get up here, I think that snowman would be arrested for indecent exposure."

She laughed. "Angie would just laugh and save her citations for living, breathing criminals."

"Angie? That the sheriff?"

"Yeah. She's a friend."

"You friends with everyone in town?" Why did he sound a bit suspicious? Did he think that she only pretended to be friends with people so she could pump them for information when her job called for it? She couldn't deny that thought stung.

"Not everyone. And I know how to separate personal from professional." This time, she was the one whose reply was clipped.

Gavin stopped and stared at her for a long moment, as if he didn't know how to respond, before walking away toward the bathroom.

Perhaps she'd been too direct, but she was a straight-to-the-point kind of person. Surely he'd picked up on that by now.

That said, she also knew when to push forward and when to hold back, so when he returned to the living room she changed the topic of conversation.

"So, I hate to ask this, but do you happen to have anything I could wear while I wash my clothes? If I wear these much longer, you're going to kick me out into the jaws of winter."

"I'll see what I can find after I eat."

She started to stand, but he waved her back down.

"I can fend for myself."

But when he placed food on the table a few minutes later, there were two plates filled with ham, turkey and cheese sandwiches and plain potato chips.

"Come eat," he said without looking in her direction.

Maya pressed her lips together to keep from smiling at his standoffish tone because he was using it after having fixed her lunch. She joined him and noticed he'd cut her sandwich in half while his remained whole.

"It's nothing fancy, but it's food," he said.

"Thanks. I didn't know if you'd be back for lunch."

"It's not your job to cook for me." He glanced toward the living room. "You appear to have been busy doing your actual job."

"As much as I can without a computer anyway. I'll be lucky if I can read my own dreadful handwriting."

"You should run a terrible snowman contest and use yours as an example."

"Hey!" Before she thought about what she was doing, she swatted him on the arm. "I'll have you know I put substantial thought and effort into Snowy."

Gavin choked on the food he'd just swallowed and took a drink of his orange soda to wash it down.

"Snowy? Really? Why not just call him Flasher?"

"Oh, that gives me a great idea! The cousins of Santa's

reindeer." She held up a new finger each time she called out the name that rhymed with those of the original reindeer. "Flasher, Stupid, Honor, Necromancer."

"I doubt the locals are ready for a snow reindeer that raises the dead."

She sighed. "You're probably right. I doubt that would fly even for Halloween."

Maya caught Gavin staring at her as if trying to figure out a complex puzzle. Or perhaps trying to understand why he'd just allowed himself to converse with her in more than grunts and single-word replies.

"What?"

"You're unexpected."

"Because I'm a journalist with a sense of humor or because I don't seem like I live in a small town?"

He tilted his head a fraction. "Both."

"News flash, not everyone who lives in small towns fits the stereotype, although some around here no doubt find me odd. But I make friends easily despite that."

"I guess that helps with your job." He returned his attention to his food, shoving chips into his mouth.

"It does, but I don't use friendships to get stories. Well, except when I roped Sunny into doing travel pieces because she's been all around the world and I thought at least a handful of readers would find the articles interesting."

Gavin made a sound of acknowledgment that he'd heard her but one that telegraphed he had his doubts. She wanted so much to ask him what his beef with journalists was, but she held herself back. Those instincts of hers were communicating that doing so was not the right tactic in getting him to change his mind. Best to let him sit with what she'd said and continue to show him that she was a decent person.

Why do you even care what he thinks?

She pondered that question as she ate the rest of her lunch. Partly, she didn't like being lumped together with people whom she didn't agree with on how reporting should be done. She admired a lot of big-time journalists, but others who wore that mantle were little more than propaganda artists or were more concerned with their own advancement than with giving the public the unvarnished truth they deserved. Not all journalists were alike, just as not all practitioners of any profession were the same. There were good and bad elements in every field, even Gavin's. But she didn't voice those thoughts. She kept them stored away for potential later use.

She glanced across the room toward the window and saw fat snowflakes falling again.

"You've got to be kidding me," she said.

"Saw that coming."

"You don't happen to have skis or a snowmobile, do you?" She was only half kidding.

"Afraid not." He glanced at her before returning his attention to the fresh supply of chips he'd poured onto his plate. "Why did you schedule an interview when a snowstorm was due to move in?"

"Because I was afraid if I didn't do it then, I'd miss the opportunity. I was supposed to meet with the mystery author Benjamin St. Michaels. He has a vacation place near here. But he wasn't there and never showed up. Combined with the storm moving in earlier than expected and an unfortunate run-in with wildlife, it just wasn't my day."

"I'll say." Gavin paused for a moment before asking, "Did you reschedule for after the storm is over?"

Wait, what was that? Was Gavin asking her work-related questions without any disdain in his voice? Maybe she'd made a bit of progress changing his mind already.

"No. He didn't return any of my calls or texts when I

was standing outside his house, nor as I was driving away. And I don't remember his number. It's stored in the phone I lost. He hasn't called the paper either or Janie, my one staffer, would have told me."

"He seems rude."

Though she could legitimately level that accusation at Gavin as well, it wasn't the same. She hadn't had an invitation into his home as she'd had with St. Michaels. While some people were rude by nature, others had situational reasons for being so.

"There's always the possibility that something happened that prevented him from being there or responding." After she'd gotten over being upset, that thought had occurred to her.

"There's the possibility it didn't too."

"Oh well, that's just how it goes sometimes. Only most of the time I don't crash my car and nearly freeze to death as a result." She shrugged, again making light of what had happened because thinking about how close she really had come to dying made her want to throw up. She kept reminding herself that she wasn't someone who dwelled on the past, because it was a useless endeavor.

After lunch, Gavin disappeared into his room. A couple of minutes later, he emerged and extended some items of clothing to her.

"These will be huge on you, but it's the best I can do."

"Thank you. Your olfactory receptors will thank you too."

A hint of amusement appeared in Gavin's eyes. Even though it paled when compared with the wide smile he'd worn earlier when he'd encountered the snowman, she was glad to see it. He might still prefer she be gone from his home, but at least he seemed to be thawing around the edges a little.

WHEN GAVIN RETURNED to work, Maya did more of her own. But feeling guilty that the continual snow accumulation would make it more difficult for her to vacate the premises, she didn't only wash her own clothing. She hoped Gavin didn't see it as overstepping, but she washed his accumulated laundry too. And then she found herself cleaning house, which would make her mom hurt herself laughing if she wasn't freaking out about her only daughter cohabitating with a male stranger.

As if thinking about her mother prompted the universe to nudge her mom, the phone rang. Somehow Maya knew who it was before she answered, that her mother had obviously gotten the landline number from either Janie or Sunny. Maya took a moment to prepare before answering.

"Hello," she said, trying to sound cheerful but not overly so.

"Don't hello me. Where are you?"

Her mom wouldn't have driven from her home on the reservation into Jade Valley in this weather, so something else had led to her tracking down Gavin's number and the current tone she was using.

"At a friend's."

Friend was stretching it, but the truth would make this conversation go downhill fast. Her mom was likely to try calling out military air rescue.

"What friend? And don't tell me it's Sunny or Janie, because I've talked to both of them and know you're not at either of their houses. Obviously, since I called this mysterious friend's number."

"Mom, why do you sound as if you're freaking out? I told you my phone died."

"The one at the paper didn't, and yet Janie is always the only one there when I call."

Maya sighed. She was going to be forced to give her mom at least a slice of the truth. This should be fun.

"Listen, I'm perfectly okay, but I was up the mountain to do an interview and the storm came in faster than expected. I slid off the road but one of the residents has been nice enough to give me a place to stay until the road is cleared."

"What resident?"

"You don't know them."

"Them? So it's a family?"

Maya closed her eyes and asked the universe for patience.

"No, Mom, his name is Gavin Olsen and he's been a perfect gentleman the entire time I've been here."

A bit grumpy, but a gentleman nonetheless.

"You're staying with a man you don't know?" Her mom's voice held a hint of a screech that was begging to be released.

"He's not a total stranger now."

"What does that mean?"

"Mom, how old am I?"

"Twenty-nine, and before you say you're old enough to make responsible decisions, you will never be old enough for me to not worry about you."

"Like I told Sunny, if he had nefarious intentions, he would have acted on them already."

"You don't know that. He could be lulling you into a false sense of security."

Maya barely restrained herself from mentioning how she'd been totally vulnerable and at his mercy when she collapsed in his yard. That would only add gasoline to the fire of her mother's worry.

"Hey, weren't you the one who has been hoping I'd

meet a good-looking man, get married and start giving you grandchildren you can use for grandma clout?"

Whatever her mother said in response, Maya didn't hear it. Because when she turned around, Gavin was standing there. How had he come inside without her noticing him or the accompanying cold air when he opened the door? What she did know was that she was mortified. So much so that she nearly crushed the phone receiver in her hand.

She made a gesture, waving off what she'd just said, as she grimaced. In response, Gavin extended his hand for the phone. Maya shook her head, but he didn't retract his hand.

"Did you hear me?" her mom said in her ear.

"Hang on a moment."

"Maya Jane Pine!"

She lowered the receiver but didn't give it to Gavin. "You don't want to do this," she whispered.

In response, he reached forward and extricated the phone from her hand.

"Hello, this is Gavin Olsen. Am I speaking to Maya's mother?"

Maya really did feel as if she might throw up at any moment as she listened to one side of the conversation. Even that much told her that her mom was giving Gavin a grilling he didn't deserve. And as the conversation progressed, she began to think that her mom also should have been a reporter or possibly an FBI agent because she was getting Gavin to answer questions that Maya hadn't yet asked.

For instance, she now knew his parents ran a ranch near Sheridan but he wanted to make his own path. And that he was a year older than her.

After several minutes of him listening and answering as if he had been dragged in for police interrogation, he finally returned the phone to her.

"I am somewhat more comfortable with your situation," her mom said without prompting.

"So you believe a man you've never met over your own daughter, nice."

Her mom sighed. "I may have overreacted."

"You think?"

"Remember this conversation when you're a mother yourself."

"After this, I'm considering being single and childless my entire life. I'll adopt twenty cats instead. You can show your sisters pictures of them."

When she finally hung up the phone, she stayed facing the laundry room off the kitchen, not wanting to turn around.

"You don't have to be embarrassed," he said, as if he'd read her mind. Though, admittedly, it was probably glaringly obvious how she was feeling.

After blowing out a breath she faced him.

"I'm really, really sorry for all of that, and for what you heard me say before I saw you had come into the house."

"I was pretty sure it was said in jest. I'm not exactly a catch."

But he could be.

She mentally swatted that idea away. That he was handsome and had been kind to her was indisputable, but so was the fact that he'd shown zero interest in her and didn't like what she did for a living, something that was so much of her identity. Plus, she was aware that any positive feelings she might be having toward him were likely rooted in his having rescued her from death's doorstep. Once she was back home in her real world, around other people and able to move about freely, the temptation toward attraction would go away. That would be helped by her suspicion that she'd rarely, if ever, see him in town.

"You'll live longer if you have a healthy self-image," she said, trying to inject a bit of humor into the conversation while also letting him know in a roundabout way that he shouldn't have that kind of negative view of himself. Sure, he might be on the quiet and reclusive side, but perhaps he had valid reasons. As she'd been cleaning earlier, she'd been struck again by the complete absence of family photos, or photos of any kind. His walls were bare except for the hooks where he hung his jacket and hat and one utilitarian clock that was available at any low-cost retailer. The books had revealed themselves to be a dictionary, a couple of novels and, most notably, biographies of painters Frederic Remington and Frida Kahlo.

"I don't think that's a real statistic," he said.

"Maybe they just haven't done the research on the tie between longevity and self-esteem yet. I think I'm onto something."

"Don't reporters claim to base their reporting on facts?"

The way he said it left no doubt that he thought otherwise. "I'm not going to say some don't stretch the truth, and others flat out lie. The latter, in my opinion, shouldn't be able to call themselves journalists."

She hadn't meant there to be any heat in her words, but they came out that way nevertheless. Not wanting to potentially get into an argument with the person with whom she was being forced to share lodging, she turned and walked into the laundry room. After quickly folding the dry clothes, she took hers and exited the room.

To her surprise, Gavin was still standing in the kitchen staring into the fridge. After his last comment, she really didn't feel like fixing him a meal. He was obviously able to feed himself before she arrived, so he could do it again.

"Your clean laundry is on top of the dryer," she said as she headed toward the bathroom to change. Not in the mood to face him and wondering about how quickly her feelings had shifted, she stayed in the bathroom longer than was necessary. After changing, she sat on the edge of the tub and tried to dissect why his question had gotten under her skin when the same type of attitude hadn't bothered her overmuch whenever she'd faced it from other people. Normally she either allowed it to bounce off her and roll away or she was able to charm a change in attitude in the other person, an acknowledgment—if sometimes begrudging—that maybe every reporter in the country wasn't cut from the same cloth.

But it seemed as if despite them getting along fairly well for virtual strangers, Gavin's attitude about people in her profession hadn't changed. That made her one part angry, one part sad and one part intensely curious what had caused him to have that type of entrenched attitude. Had something happened to him because of reporting, or had he simply adopted beliefs held by his parents? She was well aware of how prejudices were handed down from one generation to the next, and not only those against her career choice.

But knowing that didn't make them any easier to swallow.

CHAPTER FIVE

AFTER GAVIN TOOK his clean and folded clothes into his room, he looked around his obviously cleaner house and felt like a complete jerk. Maya had been doing her best not to impose even though it was no doubt obvious that he was used to, and preferred, being alone. But what did he do? He didn't miss an opportunity to trash her career choice. Granted, he had legitimate reasons for not liking the media. They'd played a part in preventing him from seeing his son, after all. But she didn't know that.

Despite how he detested the power the media could hold over people's lives, sometimes ruining them, Maya didn't seem like that type of person. Sure, he didn't know her well, but she hadn't been pummeling him with intrusive questions. And he didn't think she had the money and power to destroy those around her. The one time he'd heard her on the phone talking to her coworker, the conversation had centered on an article about funding for bridge and road improvements. Not exactly yellow or vindictive journalism.

She deserved at least the benefit of the doubt. And he deserved a kick in the rear for taking his hatred out on someone who'd done him not a single wrong.

He noticed she was still in the bathroom, and he'd bet hard-earned money it was to avoid him in the only place she could. He wondered if it would be best to make a quick sandwich and leave the house, or wait until she came out so he could properly apologize.

He chose to split the difference.

Despite the cold and the fact that his grill was covered in snow, he grabbed a couple of steaks he'd pulled from the freezer the night before and wrapped two pre-baked potatoes in foil. Then he bundled up, grabbed the charcoal, lighter and matches, and headed out to the small back deck.

Though the sky was still lead gray with clouds, it had at least stopped snowing for the time being and the wind was calm. After firing up the grill and placing the food on it, he rounded the house and began splitting wood and carrying it to the front porch where it could better dry out before being transferred to the woodbin inside.

He ran gas heat too but supplemented with wood. Having two sources of heat in this part of the country was more than a good idea. And after what Maya had gone through, she shouldn't have to be cold again.

He'd still rather she not be stuck here, but what was the use of making himself even more miserable by staying upset about it?

Gavin stopped after several minutes of splitting wood and looked toward the forest through which Maya had trudged in a nearly frozen state. He wondered if her car had been totally covered by the snowfall as had the purse she'd evidently dropped between here and there. He also wondered when the road would be cleared. Well, first, it had to stop snowing. And despite the reprieve he was currently enjoying, more snowfall was predicted for later in the evening and overnight. Add that to the fact that the road that passed his place, winding up the mountain, was one of the lesser traveled and it could be days still.

If he didn't want those days to be uncomfortable and awkward, he needed to set aside his negative views and apologize.

After a flip of the steaks, he retreated to the barn to... what? Talk to his horse? Clean the tack that didn't need cleaning? If he had a dog, he could have a one-sided conversation with it. But he'd not gotten one because it reminded him of how Max brightened whenever he was around dogs, cats or literally any animal within view.

There were still some further repairs to be made around the place, but those would have to wait until the weather improved and at least some of the snow melted.

Acknowledging to himself that he was in full-on avoidance mode, he passed the next few minutes doing odds and ends that he couldn't even really remember once he'd done them. Bracing his hands against one of the stalls, he heaved a deep sigh. Why was he out here like a scared chicken when he could be warm and comfortable in his house?

Just apologize and get it over with.

Tired of being so tense and edgy, he returned to the back deck and scooped the steaks and potatoes onto a platter. After beating the snow off his boots, he stepped into the house.

As he entered the kitchen, he noticed Maya had resumed her spot on the couch and appeared to be hard at work judging by the scattered paper in front of her on the coffee table. She didn't even glance up at his entry.

"I made some steaks and potatoes," he said as he placed the platter in the middle of the kitchen table.

She looked up and seemed to be debating whether to decline his peace offering when her hunger evidently won out. As Gavin turned to retrieve plates from the cabinet, he found himself unexpectedly smiling. He didn't think Maya Pine was the type of person who could avoid food or talking for long.

He glanced at her a few times after she seated herself, noticing that she liked a lot of butter and pepper on her potato. Before taking a bite, however, she glanced toward the refrigerator.

"If there's something else you want, feel free." Being somewhat friendlier felt like stretching muscles that hadn't been used in months.

Needing no further prompting, she retrieved a bag of shredded cheddar cheese and covered the top of her buttery potato with it.

"Dairy fan?"

"Someday butter and cheese will catch up to me, but today is not that day."

He smiled at that though she was too busy diving into her food to notice. That was probably for the best.

After they'd been quietly eating for a few minutes, he paused before looking toward the opposite end of the table.

"I'm sorry."

Maya looked up, a bite of steak on her fork.

"For being a jerk earlier," he said.

Maya nodded. "Apology accepted." And then she shoved the piece of steak into her mouth.

"That's it?"

She finished chewing and swallowed. "You do remember what I said about not holding on to things in the past, right? You apologized, I accepted the apology, the end."

He leaned against the back of his chair. "I've never met anyone like you."

"That's because I'm one of a kind," she replied, then offered up a mischievous grin.

He couldn't hide the smile that felt oddly natural in response to her comment. Maya didn't seem to pay it much mind though as she went right back to cutting her next bite of steak. He found himself watching her, envious of her ability to let the past go so easily. He wondered if she'd been that way her entire life or if she'd cultivated that mindset in response to something in her own past that had hurt her. He hoped it was the former because, from what he'd seen, she didn't deserve to be hurt by anyone. That included him, so for the duration of her stay he was going to do his best to be more than a grudging host. Who knew? Maybe if he engaged a bit more he'd learn how to cultivate his own ability to live in the moment, to only concern himself with things he could change.

To not feel so hollow all the time.

MAYA AWOKE IN the middle of the night, jerked to consciousness by a loud noise. Her heart thumped hard in her chest, and it took her a few moments to realize it was because she'd been dreaming. But already the dream was fading and she wasn't sure if the bang she'd heard had been part of the dream or what had yanked her from it.

In the next moment, a howling gust of wind rattled the windows. She sat up and looked out the window. It was still dark, and even if the moon was shining tonight it was hidden well behind the clouds that were dumping more snow on the world outside. Even though she couldn't see far, she was able to make out the fat flakes of snow blowing nearly horizontal at a fast clip. She wondered if the wind had blown something into the side of the house, and that's what had woken her.

The way things looked and sounded outside, it almost felt as if a world beyond the blinding snow didn't exist. That the entirety of the world lay within Gavin's house. She shook her head at the strange thought.

The sound of his door opening drew her attention.

"The storm woke you up too?" he asked. As he walked into the area lit by the small night-light in the kitchen, her breath caught. It might be a blizzard outside, but he was dressed as if it was summer, in loose shorts and a T-shirt that did amazing things for his upper body.

"Uh, yeah," she said, belatedly remembering he'd asked her a question.

He crossed the room and bent slightly to look out the window, then shook his head.

"Makes a person consider moving to Texas or Florida."

She finally shifted her gaze away from him and forced herself to focus on the snow again. Maybe it would cool down her thoughts.

"I wouldn't be the least bit surprised if a yeti showed up on your front porch."

"Well, that would give you a big front-page story."

"If he didn't eat us for a midnight snack."

"I guess you wouldn't have to worry about deadlines, then."

Maya snorted a laugh. "Or the owners constantly pressuring me to increase revenues. It's not as if I can suddenly double the population of Jade Valley."

She noticed that Gavin didn't respond. When she looked up at him, his face had taken on a tense, faraway look.

"Are you okay?"

"Uh, yeah. Would you like some hot cocoa? I don't think I'm going to be able to go back to sleep."

What had just happened? Had he suddenly remembered he didn't like reporters? But if that was the case, he wouldn't be offering to make her hot cocoa in the middle of the night. She decided to let it go, nodding instead.

"That sounds good."

Though he didn't ask for help, she followed him to the kitchen and pulled two mugs from the appropriate cabinet while he retrieved milk and cocoa. When he pulled out miniature marshmallows, she was surprised.

"Those I wasn't expecting," she said.

"I got used to them a few years ago."

Why did she feel as if there was a story behind that simple statement? But she didn't ask about it, not wanting to give him a reason to abandon the hot drinks and her, disappearing back into his room. She didn't know why, but she didn't feel like sitting alone in the quiet of a snow-hushed night. Even though she was used to a lot of human interaction in any given day, thrived on it, she oddly hadn't felt deprived the past few days with only short conversations with Gavin. But maybe she had reached her max of alone time and just wanted to be in the presence of another person, even if he wasn't the most talkative guy ever.

"Good thing because hot cocoa tastes exponentially better when topped by marshmallows."

Although they were both quiet as he made the cocoa and poured it into the mugs she'd set out, it wasn't an uncomfortable silence. Quite the opposite. If she didn't know better, she'd swear they'd known each other long enough to be content to be in each other's presence without the need for conversation.

After Gavin topped both drinks with a generous amount of tiny marshmallows, he took his mug and headed for the living room. To her surprise, he sank onto the couch. He'd not sat there since her arrival in his home, and she was left wondering if she should sit in his recliner or act as if nothing was different and sink onto the opposite end of the couch. She decided on the latter, as much to convince herself that Gavin's very male presence didn't bother her as for any other reason.

"Umm, this hits the spot," she said after taking her first drink.

He made one of those sounds of agreement he tended to use more often than actually speaking. It was interesting to her how quickly she'd grown used to them.

But then he did say, "Seemed like a better idea than coffee at this hour."

"Yeah, though you're probably going to need a lot of coffee in a few hours."

"Yeah."

"What do you think the noise was?"

"The wind's pretty fierce right now, so it probably caught something that wasn't secured well and tossed it against the house."

Maya suddenly remembered the clothing she'd borrowed for the snowman and spun to look out the window as if she could actually see it.

"What little he was wearing is long gone now."

"I'm sorry. I should have brought the shirt and hat back in after you saw it."

"The loss of an old shirt and hat are worth the laugh I got out of your efforts."

"I'm glad." She paused, questioning whether she should voice her next thought. But now, in the quiet, dimly lit middle of the night, might be the only time he'd actually answer. And the more time she spent in Gavin's home, the more curious she became about him. Like why he had biographies of painters on his shelf but no paintings on his walls.

"I hope you don't mind me saying this, but it seems as if you don't laugh often."

She held her breath, hoping her observation didn't anger him or cause him to leave the room.

"Sometimes life doesn't give you a lot to laugh about."

"That's true."

He looked toward her, wearing an expression that said her response hadn't been what he'd expected.

"Don't look so surprised. Despite my delightful personality, I have not lived my twenty-nine years in unending bliss. Everyone's life has its sad or dark times. The death of grandparents, not having enough money, living in non-white skin in a country that doesn't have a good history with people who look like me."

Gavin took a drink of his cocoa and sat quietly for a few seconds afterward.

"Sorry. I must seem really self-absorbed."

She shook her head. "Everyone deals with the stuff life throws at them in different ways. Though I do believe in airing it, whether that's publicly exposing wrongs or talking through problems with friends."

Gavin grinned the slightest bit. "Subtle."

"That is one thing no one has ever accused me of being."

"I'm shocked."

Maya laughed and relaxed. While she hadn't known Gavin long, at the moment she felt as if she was hanging out with a friend. Granted, he would win the title of Best-Looking Friend, but a friend nonetheless. Or at least it felt as if they were on the road to friendship.

"Is that why you became a reporter, exposing wrongs?"

Maya knew she had to tread carefully with this topic because she still heard the doubt and suspicion in his voice. He didn't totally trust her, but he was at least making an effort. She respected that.

"Kind of. It was a mix of reasons. Writing was the part of school that came most naturally to me for one. And I find it easy to talk to people. My mom has always said I could get scarecrows to talk to me."

"That also would be front-page news. That or the plot for a horror movie."

Maya laughed. "My friend Sunny said something very similar once."

"She's the one who called to make sure I wasn't an ax murderer."

"Yeah. And the one whose family runs a ranch." Now that she thought about it, she'd bet that Gavin and Sunny's husband, Dean, could be friends. Dean wasn't a hermit, but he also wasn't a social butterfly. Sunny had pulled him out of his shell some, but he was also fine with his own company despite having been quite popular in high school.

Maya stirred her cocoa and took another drink. She glanced out the window at the frigid night before continuing.

"But, yes, I've used my writing to focus on topics such as injustice and corruption. I mean, I run a small-town paper, so it's not the same as covering national politics or corporate wrongdoing, but I have written about the time the former principal at the high school was caught embezzling and about BIA decisions and how they affect the reservation."

"Did you grow up on Wind River?"

"Yeah, and lots of my friends and family still live there."

"I knew a guy in high school who used to live there. I heard a couple of stories about encounters he'd had with people after he moved to Sheridan, the names he was called and how he was treated as less than." Gavin shook his head. "I don't understand people most of the time."

"I suppose how some of them act is a point in your favor for staying away from them."

He nodded once while staring at his mug. She got the feeling that while his body was seated not far from her, his mind was somewhere else entirely.

"I wasn't always this way," he said, surprising her and quite possibly himself.

Maya quickly tried to determine how to respond that wouldn't cause him to back out of saying anything further.

"We all change over time in response to things that happen around and to us."

"I guess so." He paused before continuing. "I was married before, but it didn't work out."

"I'm sorry." So many questions bombarded her mind. Despite Gavin being incredibly handsome and accommodating to her, she didn't automatically assume his ex-wife was the one at fault for the demise of the relationship. Maybe he hadn't paid her enough attention. Or he'd been grumpy then too, and his wife had grown tired of it. Perhaps they got married too young and grew apart. Marriages ended for a whole host of reasons, from the relatively simple to the spectacularly awful. Offering her condolences over something that obviously had affected him, even if he'd been at fault, seemed enough for her to do.

He glanced at her. "You're not asking questions."

"This isn't an interview. I'll listen if you want to talk, but it's your personal business."

He stared at her as if he'd stumbled upon a species of creature long thought extinct.

"You're staring and I know for a fact that I am not at my most stunning in the middle of the night." She punctuated her words with a little laugh, attempting to hide the sudden fluttering in her middle.

"I don't know. Don't they give models deliberate bed-head looks for fashion shoots?"

"Maybe if they're advertising lingerie." Did she really just mention lingerie while sitting in half darkness with an incredibly attractive man who had an equally attractive voice? Thank goodness the dim light would hide the unusual heat that had rushed up her neck into her cheeks. Maybe a hot beverage wasn't the best thing for her to be consuming at the moment.

He looked away, perhaps feeling awkward at the direction the conversation had taken. She resisted the urge to apologize, to bring more attention to what she'd said.

"Turns out my parents were right that she and I were too different." She recognized what the tone in his voice meant.

"Annoying when our parents are actually right, isn't it?"

The laugh that burst from him seemed at odds with the quiet of their surroundings, but it made her smile. Laughter helped get one through tough times and difficult conversations.

"You have no idea."

She mentally held her breath as she asked the next question, not sure how far she could go before he shut down or grew cold again. He was harder to read in some ways than many people she'd come across. Maybe that was one of the reasons he intrigued her.

That and, oh yeah, the hotness.

Stop thinking about how hot he is!

"Is that why you don't live near your parents?"

He nodded. "I know I made mistakes, but I really don't need to hear them saying 'We told you so' all the time."

"Yeah, salt in wound and all that."

"Bingo."

"Do you mind me asking how long you were married?"

"Three years. Been divorced for a little over a year now." Gavin shifted in his seat, and she thought he was about to stand and end the conversation. She noticed him wince as if he was in physical pain. But he stayed on the couch, and she wasn't sure if she should keep going forward with the conversation or change the topic altogether.

"I'm going to admit that I don't know what the correct response is to that," she said, hoping he appreciated her honesty.

"Better to say that than a lot of what I've heard from people."

"Things of the platitude variety?"

"So many platitudes."

"I personally think they should be outlawed."

"I'd vote for that."

She drank the last of her cocoa and set the empty cup on the coffee table.

"Do your parents know why you decided to live this far away from them?"

"I've never come right out and said it, but they have to. Not that I talk to them that much. They've made their disappointment abundantly clear on more than one occasion."

Though he was the kind of strong, hardworking man she was used to seeing toiling on ranches all over the valley, she also heard a vulnerability in his voice that she'd bet a substantial sum he didn't know was there. She hesitated only a moment before she gave in to the impulse to reach over and place her hand over his where it was splayed atop his leg.

"I'm sorry," she said, echoing herself from before.

When Gavin looked up at her, there was something new reflected in his eyes. Some emotion she wasn't sure if she should ignore or be afraid of.

Or perhaps lean into.

CHAPTER SIX

As MUCH TIME as Gavin had spent working outdoors, in all kinds of weather, he had never been struck by lightning. But he wondered if it was anything like the sudden shock that jolted through his body as his gaze connected with Maya's in the middle of their dimly lit conversation. He barely restrained the urge to pull her into his arms and kiss her, which made zero sense considering he'd just been telling her about how his last relationship had ended. Plus, he barely knew her. Not to mention that he'd spent most of his time since meeting her wishing she wasn't there.

From somewhere among his scattered thoughts he remembered he should respond to what she'd said.

"Thanks." Then he shifted his gaze away, purposefully looking at the clock on the wall. "Well, I think we should both try to get some more rest. Hopefully the warm drink will do the trick."

His speaking seemed to remind her that her hand was atop his, and thank goodness she removed it before he had to awkwardly extricate himself. Her hand had barely ceased contact with his when he shot to his feet, too quickly. To try to cover up how quickly, he extended his hand.

"I'll take your cup if you're finished."

"Oh, thanks, yeah." She lifted the cup, which still had a few sips of cocoa in the bottom, no doubt cold now.

Was he imagining that she sounded every bit as awkward as he felt? Best not to think about it. Pretending that moment between them hadn't happened was definitely the wisest course of action, especially considering they were basically trapped together for at least a while longer.

He made sure not to walk toward the kitchen quickly enough to further give away how startled he felt. Instead, he tried to affect a sense of normality as he made for the sink and then as he dumped the remains of Maya's cocoa down the drain and rinsed the cups, leaving them in the sink to wash later.

Before he turned back around, he planned to say a simple good-night on the way to his bedroom. But Maya had already stretched out on the couch, covered herself with a quilt, and presented her back to him.

Had she seen his thoughts in his eyes? Had it freaked her out, especially after all the claims that she was perfectly safe under his roof? He shook his head. Hadn't temporarily losing any semblance of common sense once before taught him anything? Starting now, he needed to keep himself better in check. Maya Pine was not a permanent fixture in his life, so giving in to a momentary desire was a giant no-no. As the saying went…been there, done that.

He retreated to his room, but instead of lying down like Maya had, he sat on the edge of his bed thinking about how he'd spilled more details about his past to her than he'd meant to. But for some reason, she was easy to talk to. And he was beginning to acknowledge that she was not a heartless journalist digging into his life to satisfy some belief in her investigative skills.

The fact was he knew that all journalists were not the same, not even the ones associated with his ex-wife's family. No doubt their own livelihoods had been in danger if they hadn't done as they were told.

He lifted the framed photo of Max laughing while on the toddler swing at the playground. The hole inside Gavin's heart gaped wider. How he missed that smile, the sound of his little boy's laughter. He'd never forgive those who'd taken his son away from him.

After placing the photo back on his nightstand, he stretched out under his covers. The last thing he needed to think about if he hoped to get any sleep before dawn was Rinna, her family or what he'd lost. He was only beginning to reconstruct some sort of life for himself. Not exactly a happy life, but one that at least was his own and free from the influence of others.

The memory of the few times he'd laughed since Maya's arrival tempted him to believe he could actually live again instead of simply exist, that maybe he could find a new happiness. But he needed to brutally cull that idea from his thoughts. People were never what they first appeared. Maya might seem harmless, friendly and fun-loving, but there had to be something lurking below the surface that would eventually ruin their tentative pseudo friendship.

Did you tell a not-quite-friend about your sad past? Granted, he hadn't told her the worst parts. After all, it was far from uncommon to meet someone who'd gotten a divorce.

Gavin rubbed his hands down over his face, wishing he could take back everything he'd divulged—the revelations about his marriage, his estrangement from his parents and especially that moment of attraction that had almost gotten the better of him. Maya hadn't even had to drag it out of him. He'd volunteered everything under the influence of hot cocoa, dim lighting and the novelty of having someone to talk to during a long winter night.

The only positive was that none of what he'd said was fodder for a news article. Not that he thought Maya would use anything he'd said to her advantage, but he was grateful none of the information he'd shared would be a temptation. After all, he wasn't famous, unlike the guy she'd been up on the mountain to interview.

If Gavin was Maya, he'd give that author an earful if she ever got to talk to him again. Because the man hadn't lived up to his end of the bargain, Maya had crashed her vehicle, nearly lost her life and ended up stuck in a stranger's house. A stranger who needed her to leave before she presented any more temptation.

He rolled onto his side, punching one of his pillows into submission and reminding himself that he was strong enough to resist temptation. If nothing else, all he'd have to do was think of Rinna and what she'd taken from him. He was never going to allow himself to be in that type of vulnerable position again.

Maya barely slept the rest of the night. Her mind had been too filled with a single question circling her brain like a satellite in orbit—had she really seen interest in Gavin's eyes or had she imagined it? Maybe it had simply been the way the faint light from the kitchen had lit his eyes and face because there was no way he'd be interested in the person who had invaded his home without warning. Right?

She shook her head as she rolled onto her back on the couch and stared at the ceiling that she'd begun to get used to seeing when she woke each day. It was best to pretend she hadn't noticed anything since there had likely been nothing to notice.

Then why had he retreated from the couch, the conversation and the room so quickly?

Ugh, this was one bad part of being an inquisitive person—the tendency to even grill yourself for answers.

No matter if there had been something in Gavin's eyes

or not, the best course of action remained the same. So she got to her feet and began Operation Pretend Nothing Has Changed by folding the quilts and placing them at the end of the couch where Gavin had sat the night before when he'd—

Stop it!

She was allowing cabin fever, shared space with a good-looking man, her lack of a dating life and her mother's matchmaking efforts to erode her common sense. Gavin was her host out of necessity, nothing more.

When she wanted to avoid thinking about something, she focused her mind and hands elsewhere. So after setting coffee to brew and whipping up a couple of omelets, she parked herself back on the couch with her work spread out in front of her. By the time Gavin emerged a full half hour later than normal, she had eaten half her breakfast and was hard at work drafting her first piece on small-town journalism.

"This omelet is good," Gavin said a couple of minutes after he entered the kitchen.

"I'm glad you like it," she said, barely looking up from her work.

She noticed Gavin stayed in the kitchen, eating standing up at the counter instead of sitting at the table. He didn't approach the living room, and she couldn't help but wonder if he was in the midst of his own efforts to pretend nothing had shifted between them the night before. Even if she'd imagined the attraction, he might be regretting having shared bits of his past with her. Probably best if she didn't bring up any of the revelations either.

"Did you sleep at all?" Gavin asked after a long silence.

"A little, but my mind started spinning with work stuff so I decided to get an early start."

"You're going to hit a wall later."

"Nah, I'm good. When I get on a roll, I can work for a long time."

Was he buying any of what she was saying?

"Well, I'll leave you to it, then."

Apparently he was.

As soon as she heard his boots crunching in the snow outside, she let out a long exhale and collapsed against the back of the couch. She hadn't realized how tense she'd been until Gavin was no longer under the same roof as her. But the fact that he had acted as if nothing was different between them was a good thing. By the time he returned, she was determined to have all crazy thoughts purged from her mind.

Gavin didn't return for lunch, so she snacked on some cheese, crackers and part of a can of peaches she found in the small pantry. After checking the rest of the contents of the pantry, fridge and freezer, she decided to make spaghetti for dinner. But that could wait awhile. She returned to her work, fighting yawns and heavy eyelids throughout the afternoon.

To wake herself up, she bundled herself into her winter gear and went outside. A gust of cold air whipped around the end of the house, feeling like a slap comprised of ice crystals. How could Gavin stay out in this kind of weather all day? She knew ranchers and other people with outdoor jobs did it all the time, but despite being a Wyoming native she didn't think this weather was fit for man or beast.

She stared toward the barn but didn't see any sign of Gavin. When a twinge of worry tightened in her chest, she told herself to stop being silly. He was a grown man used to working in harsh conditions. And living alone, he likely was conscious of not taking undue risks. Grabbing the shovel she'd seen Gavin use to clear off the front steps and the short path to the woodpile, she got to work following the footprints he'd made earlier. The snow had finally stopped, at least for more than the short breaks they'd had so far, so she was able to see pretty clearly the route he'd taken to the barn that morning. The wind had partially filled in the prints, but they were still visible. By the time she'd shoveled only to the point even with the end of the porch she was already breathing heavily, and her nose was running.

"My nonexistent kingdom for a snowblower." Evidently Gavin didn't own one or he would have used it by now instead of trudging through snow.

She looked up at the sky and saw more clouds moving to blot out the earlier brightness. It felt very much as if she'd done something to really tick off Mother Nature.

"Tell me what I did and I promise never to do it again," she called out while shaking the shovel at the sky as if that would do any good.

Receiving no answer, she sighed and returned to her task. She'd managed to carve a path halfway to the barn when she ran out of the strength and willpower to go on. Plus, after her near-death experience, the cold held no appeal. While shoveling she'd been thinking how sitting poolside on some tropical island with a fruity drink sounded great right about now. They needed reporters on islands, right?

But Gavin wouldn't be there.

Maya made a sound of frustration as she tossed the shovel down onto the snow in front of her. Why did she keep thinking of Gavin like he was a man?

Well, he is a man.

A very appealing man who had actually opened up to her the night before. Of course, he had seemed to regret it, so she needed to not put too much weight on his revelations. Or that might-not-have-actually-been-there look in his eyes as he'd held her gaze for a few moments longer than what occurred during a normal conversation.

New snowflakes started drifting through the air, causing her to shiver at the memory of the day she'd arrived. Was it just the fact that he'd saved her life that had her thinking of him in romantic terms? She didn't think so because her feelings had shifted gradually, at first without her realizing it. Sneaky little things.

And you can sort out your feelings inside the warm confines of Gavin's house instead of standing out in the snow, you fool.

She retrieved the shovel and returned it to its spot on the porch, then carried in enough wood to replenish the supply in the box inside. She felt sweaty after all the activity, so she decided to take a shower while Gavin was still away from the house.

Again she borrowed the clothes Gavin had let her use before while she tossed her dirty ones into a small load of laundry. While she waited for the wash cycle to complete, she returned to the couch to resume her work. She should really call the office to see how things were going, but she couldn't muster the energy to walk to the phone. Despite her outdoor time and the shower, she quickly started getting drowsy again. Maybe all she'd succeeded in doing was making herself even more tired.

She tried concentrating on her notes, deciding which section of her article to work on next, but her eyes kept drifting closed. Maybe if she rested for a few minutes, it would give her a needed boost. But as she leaned against the back of the couch and shut her eyes, she felt sleep pulling her toward its depths.

GAVIN SPENT MORE time away from the house than necessary. He'd made his check on the herd more leisurely than one in their right mind should considering the weather, then he'd ridden the property line just because. When the day began to wane and yet more snow started falling, he began his trek back up to the barn. Once inside, he also didn't rush in taking care of Jasper, who deserved some pampering, or the tack before he put it away.

Yeah, he was full-on avoiding Maya and the unexpected temptation he'd felt the night before. And tonight he planned to use the excuse of not having slept much last night to go to bed early. If he hadn't skipped lunch, he'd bypass dinner in favor of retiring even earlier. But his stomach had been growling audibly for a couple of hours, and there was no way he'd be sleeping without filling it.

Before exiting the barn, he paused in front of Jasper's stall, his hands gripped atop the door.

"You want a roommate for the night, boy?"

Jasper snorted and shook his head as if to say, "You're on your own, buddy."

"Well, you're no help at all."

Unbothered by Gavin's problems, Jasper lowered his head and began to nibble on the fresh supply of hay.

"Guess I'm not the only one who's hungry."

With a sigh and a renewed determination to act as if no suspended moment of staring had happened between Maya and him in those quiet middle-of-the-night hours, he headed out of the barn. Halfway to the house he stopped and stared at the path she'd obviously shoveled. Why in the world had she gone through that effort? Why would she even want to be out in the cold after what she'd gone through?

A twinge of concern had him following the new path the rest of the way to the house. He knocked the snow off his boots on the steps before crossing the porch to the front door.

When he stepped inside, however, he didn't find Maya in the kitchen or even with her head bent over work. She'd evidently hit that wall he'd mentioned that morning because she was out like a light on the couch, though at what looked to be an uncomfortable angle likely to leave a crick in her neck. He eased the front door closed and slipped off his boots beside it.

As he looked at Maya again, he couldn't help smiling. He imagined she'd fought falling asleep because her hand still held a sheet of paper and a couple more lay on her stomach. He wouldn't have been surprised to find them covering her face.

Despite his earlier determination to keep his distance, he found himself moving toward her. She was obviously a grown woman and could take care of herself, but a protective instinct that had been dormant for a while poked at him, even more so than when he'd found her nearly frozen to death in his front yard.

Well, she'd been a complete stranger then. And now... what exactly was she? More than a stranger, more than an unexpected or unwanted guest. An acquaintance bordering on friend? He sat on the sturdy coffee table facing but not touching her. Everyone looked a bit silly when they were sleeping, but if he was being honest she was pretty. Really pretty.

It was her bright personality and the way she looked at the world that made her even more attractive. Maybe that was what he'd been responding to the night before, the way she'd simply listened to him talk about his past without asking too many questions. To be truthful, although he regretted doing so it had felt good to say the words out loud, to let what he'd gone through exist somewhere outside of his head.

He should really move away and let her be, but a part

of him he didn't want to examine too closely wanted her to rest in a more comfortable position. Would he be able to help her lie down without waking her? It was no doubt wiser to either leave her be or wake her just enough to tell her to shift to a position less likely to give her a neck ache later. Instead, he found himself standing and removing the papers she held, setting them aside on the coffee table, and then gently nudging her shoulder so that she slid down the back of the couch onto her side, her head against a pillow. Next he carefully lifted her legs by her ankles, aiming to stretch her legs out so he could drape a quilt over her.

Suddenly, she jerked awake and he stepped back so quickly that he tripped over the coffee table. He barely kept himself from tumbling backward onto his rear, but he winced when his calf struck the corner of the table.

"Are you okay?" Maya asked, moving as if to grab him to keep him from falling.

"I'm fine," he said. "I didn't mean to startle you."

Maya dropped back onto the couch and rubbed a hand over her face. "I…" She looked at the clock on the wall. "I didn't mean to sleep so long."

"You obviously needed it, but you were sleeping at an awkward angle when I came in. I was just trying to help you avoid a crick," he said as he pointed toward his neck.

In response, she rubbed her own. "Oh, uh, thanks."

He had stayed away all day to avoid awkwardness between them, so what did he do as soon as he came back? Put them in another awkward position. And if he retreated now as he had the night before, it would be even more obvious in the light of day, waning though it might be. Instead, he pointed toward the front door.

"So between your sleeping position and your sudden need to take up recreational snow shoveling, you must be angling for a trip to the nearest chiropractor."

Maya stopped rubbing her neck and looked up at him. "Hey, I was trying to do a good deed. And, well, I might have been going a little stir-crazy. With a dose of trying to stay awake thrown in."

"Why didn't you just go back to sleep this morning?"

"That doesn't seem particularly fair, does it? You go out into the dreadful weather to work and I lounge around in the warm comfort of your house, snoozing away."

Gavin crossed his arms. "You're not my employee, you know? You are not obligated to do anything here though I'd prefer if you didn't freeze to death in my front yard."

"Trust me, that will not happen. When I can go home again, I'm thinking about packing up a couple of bags and moving to Tahiti."

Gavin laughed. "I might have imagined a sunny beach in Mexico a few times lately."

"Probably a little beach bungalow where you don't have any uninvited guests."

"That's not what I meant." Okay, why had her comment bothered him? Didn't he want her to leave so he could have his solitude back?

"I know. I was just teasing."

Teasing. When had been the last time someone had teased him for fun?

He knew the answer to that, but he didn't want to think about Rinna right now. Or about...

No.

"Are you okay?"

He jerked out of his thoughts to find Maya looking at him with a concerned expression.

"What?"

She made a circular motion toward his face. "You looked as if you suddenly went somewhere else."

"Sorry. Probably hunger and my own lack of sleep catching up to me."

She shifted her gaze toward the kitchen. "I slept right through when I was going to make spaghetti."

"How about I toss a frozen pizza in the oven?"

"Better yet, I'll do that while you go shower."

He grinned a little. "Are you saying I stink?"

"Well, I didn't want to say anything…"

He let his mouth drop open in dramatic fashion, which resulted in Maya laughing. He couldn't say it out loud, probably shouldn't even admit it to himself, but he really liked the sound of her laughter. He didn't want to think about how he was probably going to miss it when she left.

CHAPTER SEVEN

EVIDENTLY ALL IT took to get past their awkwardness was some good-natured teasing and a dinner of cheap frozen pizza, for which Maya was immensely glad.

"I didn't think to check when I was outside earlier," she said in between pizza slices. "Did you figure out what caused the bang last night?"

Gavin shook his head. "Whatever it was has probably blown halfway across the state by now."

"Thank goodness it didn't hit a window."

"Yeah. Maybe I'll figure out what it was if something comes up missing."

The phone rang, startling them both. Only this time it wasn't the house phone but rather Gavin's cell, which was probably the least used cell phone she'd ever been near. Gavin froze when he saw the identity of the caller, his entire body going rigid. Without a word, he got up and stalked to his bedroom and closed the door behind him.

For several seconds, Maya simply stared in that direction. Not once since she'd met Gavin had she seen him that tense or with that kind of tight, stony look on his face. Even after she'd first arrived and he'd barely grunted at her, he hadn't looked as if he was wound so tightly he was on the verge of breaking.

Had it been one of his parents calling him? An unexpected call from an estranged family member might lead to the type of expression that had taken over his face the moment he saw who was calling.

Whatever the caller's identity, it was none of her business. And yet she found herself not only curious but hoping he was okay. Thinking about how alone he seemed to be in the world made her realize how much she took being close to her family for granted. So she ate her last couple of bites of pizza then walked over to the house phone to call her parents, to make sure they were faring okay after the storms.

"I hear you're stuck at Hotel Stranger," her dad said when he answered the phone.

"How much has Mom been driving you crazy with worrying about me?"

"Enough to send me out for more than one walk in this mess."

"Sorry, but I'm really okay."

"I trust you," he said. "You've got a good sense about people, and I figure if he posed a threat you'd simply knock him out with the nearest heavy object."

Maya laughed, then stopped herself. It felt wrong to laugh on one phone while Gavin was very far from laughing on the other.

"I was just calling to see how you all were doing."

"We're fine. Other than worrying, your mom's been cooking as if she thinks the apocalypse is on final approach."

After finding out her mom was next door at Maya's Auntie Fran's house, Maya had a good chat with her dad about the latest goings-on on the reservation, her idea to write about small-town journalism, and the latest good books her dad—a high school English teacher—had read.

"I'm not going to read any more by that St. Michaels guy though after he stood you up."

"Yeah, he's not high on my to-read list anymore either." Though, when it came right down to it, she would probably continue to read the series to hopefully get answers to her pressing questions. She'd just check them out from the library instead of buying them unless he contacted her with a really good explanation. The last time she'd talked to Janie, he hadn't yet called the office.

When she finished her call with her dad, ending with his promise to give her mom the full accounting of their conversation to help alleviate her concerns, Gavin was still shut away in his room. Considering he also hadn't gotten a lot of sleep the night before, it was possible he'd simply gone to bed. With that in mind, she quietly did the dishes and retreated to her usual spot on the couch.

But no matter how much she tried, she couldn't concentrate on work. Her gaze kept wandering to Gavin's closed door, wondering if he was okay. She resisted the urge to move closer, not to hear what he was saying but to simply know if he was still on the phone. Part of her wanted to knock on his bedroom door and ask how he was, but they were not close enough for her to do something like that.

And what if he wasn't okay? It wasn't as if she could comfort him without it seeming awkward at best. Or worse, weird and intrusive.

Unable to stay still, she crossed to the phone again and called Janie to talk about the next issue of the paper. Of course, the big story would be the weather, and she found out that there had been one house fire, a shed collapse from the weight of the snow and half a dozen car accidents, not including her own.

"April has been helping out where she can," Janie said, referring to the editor of the high school's paper who did some interning at the *Post*. "Nothing that puts her in any dangerous situations though."

"Good. The last thing we need is a liability claim."

"One other thing," Janie said, hesitation in her voice.

"What is it?"

"Mr. Clarke called and said he expected the storm coverage to improve our circulation numbers."

Maya sighed. "He realizes this storm won't last forever, right?" Though sometimes it felt as if it might. "No one is going to buy a subscription based on the coverage of one storm. At most we'll get a one-week bump in sales numbers."

"You know how he is. I just listened and 'ummed' in reply at appropriate points."

"I know it's not your job to deal with him. Does he know I'm out of commission at the moment?"

"I simply said you weren't in the office and you were having some trouble with your cell. Thankfully, he didn't press for further details."

"I'll get back as soon as I can."

"Don't put yourself in danger. April and I have got things covered. I'd tell you to use this as a break, but I know you. I'd bet a substantial sum that you were working on something right before you called me."

"You make me sound like a workaholic."

"You *are* a workaholic. I sometimes worry for poor Blossom, that you'll forget to feed her."

"I would never. I love my kitty." Thankfully Trina had been willing to care for her cat while Maya was stuck away from home.

Janie chuckled. "Perhaps I was exaggerating a bit, but not much. You are always working. I bet you do interviews and write articles in your dreams."

The mention of dreams reminded Maya of something she'd forgotten. During her unintentional nap that afternoon, she'd dreamed about that moment on the couch with

Gavin the night before, the one when she'd imagined him looking at her lips and wanting to kiss her. She'd dreamed that he actually had, and the memory of what his kiss had felt like in the dream sent heat rushing through her body.

She gasped a little and brought her fingers to her lips.

"What's wrong?" Janie asked.

"What? Oh nothing. I just…stubbed my toe." She winced at the lie. Not only did she hate lying, but it had been a pitiful one on top of that.

Before Janie could question the truth of her statement, Maya made a quick exit from the phone call. After hanging up, she turned so that her back was to the wall beside the old phone. How had she forgotten that dream? Maybe the way she'd come awake so suddenly to find Gavin next to her had startled the dream right out of her memory. Well, at least for a while, because now it kept replaying in her head.

She had no idea what kind of kisser Gavin was in real life, but in dreamland he was phenomenal.

To avoid having him come out of his room and find her cheeks on fire, she hurried to the bathroom and washed her face with cold water. Maybe she should have gone outside and stuck her head in the nearest snowbank instead. She shivered at that thought, of how she was never going to look at snow and approach winter the same way again. She had a whole new respect for how quickly it could snatch away a person's life.

As she stood looking at herself in the mirror, she realized she didn't hear Gavin's voice. Maybe she'd been right that he'd simply gone to sleep after his call. She hoped her phone conversations hadn't bothered him. Working on the premise that he was asleep, she eased out of the bathroom and back to the couch. But instead of returning to work, she sat looking out the window at the inky blackness of the night and the faint white of the snow under a cloudy, moonless sky.

She thought back over her conversation with Janie, deliberately shoving aside the part about Mr. Clarke. That was nothing new. What had struck her, however, was Janie's comment that Maya was a workaholic. That wasn't exactly news. After all, she didn't have much of a choice if she wanted to keep the paper going on limited resources.

Even knowing that, hearing it now had somehow hit her differently. Was she missing out on a lot of what life had to offer because she was always working?

She shook her head. Why was she thinking this way? She liked her life. Her job was one she enjoyed and believed in. She had good friends, a small and modest home at a decent rental price, and the most adorable kitty to come from the litter born on Sunny's ranch. And she'd survived her brush with death, fortunately rescued by someone who didn't have any ill intentions toward her. Even if her life had its frustrations, like everyone's did from time to time, she was fortunate.

And yet…

She glanced toward Gavin's closed bedroom door. Had she brushed off her mother's matchmaking and Sunny's teasing not because of her busy schedule but rather the fact that she was somehow unaware that maybe part of her life was empty?

And why was it occurring to her now? Here, in this place removed from her normal, everyday life? When she was forced to live each day in close quarters with a man who despite his proximity felt so very far away?

Maya wasn't sure she wanted to know the answers to those questions. She wasn't sure she was ready for those answers.

GAVIN SAT ON THE side of his bed for some unknown amount of time, feeling hollowed out all over again. He'd at first panicked at seeing Rinna's number show up on his phone, terrified that something had happened to Max. But when he heard her say she'd called simply to find out the name of a book his son had liked being read to him because "he just won't stop crying about it" and then she refused to let him speak to Max, he'd nearly crushed his phone into a pile of plastic and metal molecules.

He missed Max more than he would one of his own body parts if it suddenly disappeared. No matter how many times he went over and over things in his head, he still couldn't believe that he might never see his son again. At least not until he was an adult, and Max might very well hate him by then or not remember him at all. Who knew what kinds of thoughts Rinna was filling his head with?

As much as he hated to admit it, his parents had been right about her. He'd just been too blinded by her beauty, by her carefree nature, by her pretty words of support for him and his dream to realize none of it was real. But by the time he had come to that realization, it had been too late.

Noise from the bathroom reminded him that he wasn't alone in his house, that Maya's mind was probably spinning with questions regarding his abrupt departure from dinner. He was surprised by his urge to walk out of his room and confess everything to her, to see if it brought any semblance of the kind of relief he'd felt after he'd told her he'd been married before and about his rocky relationship with his parents.

But this was too personal, too raw. So he stayed in his room, avoiding her the way he had after thinking about kissing her the night before. He needed the snow to stop, to melt, so he could get her out of his house and out of his head.

THE ENTIRETY OF the next two days, Maya did her best to be invisible. She didn't speak to Gavin unless he addressed her first, but that was as rare as it had been that first day after he'd saved her. Her instincts told her that her peppy personality would not be appreciated in the aftermath of that phone call he'd received. And while she thought he might feel better if he talked out whatever was bothering him, she didn't broach the topic.

Instead, she focused on work, doing everything she could by phone to help Janie and April. Everything would be so much easier if she had a laptop and an internet connection, but she had to make the best of the situation. On the plus side, it had finally stopped snowing and the days were clear if still frigid. Even if nothing was melting, hopefully the county crews would soon be able to clear the road and she could make it back to town. Gavin would no doubt be glad to see the last of her and to reclaim his solitude.

As soon as she thought that, however, doubt pecked at her. She wasn't sure being out here alone was good for him. She knew that some people preferred it, but something deep inside her was saying it wasn't the best option for Gavin. Only the reality that they were not close friends prevented her from telling him exactly that.

Even without a computer, she was able to complete a lot of work while Gavin was out fixing a leak in the barn's roof. She'd gone outside once to make sure he hadn't fallen off, but watching him up there made her too nervous and she'd retreated back inside.

When she was satisfied with the work she'd completed, she busied herself fixing the spaghetti she never got around to making before. There was no garlic bread or even seasoning, so they would have to make do with toasted sandwich bread to accompany the main dish.

As if he could smell dinner from outside, Gavin came into the house about five minutes before the meal was ready.

"Great timing," she said, trying to be friendly but not over-the-top chipper.

"It smells great in here," he said, sounding more like the Gavin she'd gotten to know before he'd received the mysterious phone call.

"It's almost ready."

"I'll take a quick shower unless you need some help."

"No, I've got everything covered."

With a nod, he headed into his room for fresh clothes, and a few moments later she heard the water in the shower turn on. It struck her how very domestic they seemed even though they were not a couple in any way.

As they ate dinner, Maya was glad to see that both Gavin's tenseness and the invisible barrier that had been between them since that phone call had eased. He was a bit more talkative, so she felt comfortable engaging him in more conversation.

"I'm glad you didn't fall off the barn today," she said, trying to make the true statement, a subject that had caused her worry, sound light and teasing. "I don't think I could have carried you to the house like you did for me. At best you would have gotten dragged through the snow."

"Snow down my collar as well as breaking my neck, sounds awesome," he said before taking a bite of bread.

The tone of his response was so unexpected that she snorted a laugh, then immediately covered her nose and mouth.

Gavin looked up from his plate. "Nice."

Then he gifted her with a smile that made her insides do somersaults. His smiles were like spotting a rare bird species. They made her feel as if the universe had allowed her to see something precious that few were ever fortunate enough to witness.

"What?" he asked, making her realize she'd likely stared at him too long without saying anything.

"You have a really nice smile."

The smile faltered and the fact that he looked flustered by her compliment was so cute that a flock of butterflies joined the somersaults. She should be embarrassed, but she wasn't. She was someone who believed in and told the truth as a rule, and what she'd said was the absolute truth.

"Um, thank you," Gavin said as he focused his attention on his plate again, spinning spaghetti onto his fork but not bringing it up to his mouth.

Realizing that he wasn't going to say anything else, she returned to eating her own dinner.

"Thank you," Gavin said again several moments later.

"You said that already."

"No, I meant for not asking."

She knew he was referring to the phone call and his reaction to it.

"You deserve your privacy, at least as much as I can give you while forced to stay here." It would have been easier to do so if she didn't have to sleep on his couch, but the house's second bedroom didn't have any furniture.

By him bringing up the topic of the phone call, she thought he might finally share who had called and why it had upset him so much. But he didn't, and she allowed the topic to drop. It wasn't her natural curiosity that made her continue to wonder about it, however. She found she was still concerned about him, about how he seemed to keep so much locked away inside himself. That wasn't healthy, but it was not her place to tell him that. If it was Sunny or Janie, sure, but not Gavin.

He was only a temporary fixture in her life. Now that the sun had replaced the snowy skies, it was only a matter of time until she was back to waking up in her own home each day. She loved Blossom, but her furry feline companion couldn't hold a conversation over the dinner table. Couldn't smile at her.

Couldn't make her feel as if her heart was ready to expand to include someone else.

CHAPTER EIGHT

HE'D BEEN WRONG about Maya. Gavin paused in his efforts to replenish the supply in one of the hay feeders and looked up at the clear blue sky. Common sense kept telling him that he was allowing himself to focus too much on the simple compliment she'd paid him, as if she'd been offering water to him after he'd crawled across a desert. But there was a part of him that really wanted to toss common sense into the nearest canyon.

The fact that she'd restrained what must have been a lot of curiosity about his behavior when Rinna had called and in the days afterward earned Maya a lot of his respect. What she'd said to him, about him deserving his privacy, had seemed one hundred percent authentic. So much so that for a moment he'd considered telling her everything. But he'd reined in that impulse, remembering that she wasn't a permanent part of his life. With the break in the weather, soon the road would be cleared and one of her friends or her mother would show up to whisk her away.

When she'd first awakened on his couch after collapsing, nearly frozen to death in his front yard, he'd wanted nothing more than his solitude back. Now there was a twinge of something uncomfortable in his chest when he thought of her leaving. It was a bit like coming out of a dark cave, experiencing sunshine like what shone overhead now, then being tossed back into the depths of the cave again.

He shook his head at that silly thought and refocused on his task. Now that the storms had moved on, the cattle had ventured out of the sheds along the edge of the tree line. Thankfully the temperature had not dropped into the danger zone for them. After all, they were hardier than humans when it came to surviving the elements.

A shiver ran through him as a gust of wind reminded him of that fact. His thoughts circled back to that day he'd seen Maya stumble then fall into the snow, and he shivered again. If he had not been where he was at that exact moment, she would have no doubt frozen to death. It was enough to make a person believe in fate or divine intervention.

As he went about replenishing the other feeders and ensuring the water supply was accessible, he really tried to focus on something other than the woman he'd come to expect to see at the end of each workday. It wasn't her cooking or cleaning that he appreciated most, though he did appreciate that she undertook those tasks even though he'd told her she didn't have to. Rather it was simply her presence.

She brought a brightness to his daily existence that he hadn't thought to ever experience again. And if he was being honest, he was attracted to her. He'd recognized she was pretty from the moment he'd placed her on his couch and worked to warm up her frigid body to save her. But as he'd gotten to know her, her kindness and laughter and way of looking at the world had made her even more beautiful.

The surprising truth was he was going to miss her when she left. He even wondered if he might find himself venturing into town more often on the off chance he might see her.

You could ask her out on a proper date.

He shut that thought down so fast he'd swear he heard

the slam of the mental door. What Rinna and her family had put him through, what they'd taken from him was enough to ruin anyone on romantic relationships. What started out as great, what you could never imagine ending, did indeed end—and in a very painful way. Inviting that kind of experience into one's life again would be like escaping a wildfire only to jump into an active volcano.

No, it was for the best that once she left, he should make no effort to maintain contact, for her sake as well as his. Though he'd had preconceived notions about her based on her career choice, she'd proven herself to be a kind, respectful and fun person to be around. Fun. Yeah, he could admit that for the first time since his and Rinna's marriage had started crumbling, there had actually been some fun moments in his life following Maya's arrival. Watching movies, her streaking snowman, even her reaction when she'd realized he'd overheard her talking to her mother. He laughed a little at the memory of how big her eyes had gotten when she'd turned around and noticed him standing behind her a moment after she'd been teasing her mom about possibly dating him.

But then he remembered her mentioning grandchildren and his heart seized up. He missed Max so much. His little-boy laughter and smiles, the way he'd crawl up into Gavin's lap so he could read him a story, how his weight had felt against Gavin's chest when he fell asleep there. It still didn't seem real that he was no longer a part of his son's life. The thought of Max growing up thinking his father had abandoned him made not only Gavin's heart ache but his very soul.

He was never giving a woman the opportunity to do that to him again. There was no way he'd survive it. As it was, he trudged through his days only because he knew Max would never want for anything. Rinna's family had enough money and influence to take care of countless children, so Max would never be hungry, never be without shelter, would go to the best schools and be able to start out his life several steps ahead. What could Gavin offer him other than a life of endless work and struggle? Certainly not a role model who'd been able to chase his dreams until he achieved them.

He shook his head, trying to clear it of the past as well as a future that could never be. Soon, Maya would be gone back to her proper place, and he could resume his life of putting one foot in front of the other as one day bled into the next.

GAVIN HAD GOTTEN used to his house smelling good when he came in after a day of work, but today the aromas were extra appealing because he smelled baked goods.

"Don't tell me you ran out of things to write and you've decided to start a bakery on the side," he said as he hung up his coat.

"No, today we're celebrating," she said as she spun toward the table with oven mitts on her hands and carrying a familiar-looking frozen package. "I hope you don't mind. I found this cobbler in the freezer, and since I didn't have anything to make a cake I baked this instead."

"Um, it's not my birthday." Not that she'd know when his birthday was considering he hadn't told her and hadn't left his driver's license out where she could easily see it.

"Nope, it's mine."

"It's… I'm sorry."

She looked at him with a slightly startled expression. "Why are you sorry? You couldn't possibly know when my birthday is."

"I'm sorry you have to spend it here, with me. I'm sure you had plans."

"I did not, in fact, have plans. I mean, I might have made some in the past few days if I was home, but I would have just as likely been working." She paused, as if remembering something. "I guess Janie was right. I am a workaholic."

"You even made your own birthday dinner. That doesn't seem fair."

"I got to stay inside this nice, warm house while you were out in the cold, so I'd say it's a good trade."

"Well, I guess my present to you will be to go remove the smell of cattle from myself before sitting down to dinner."

"Best present ever."

"Hey!"

Her laughter soaked into him as much as the heat filling his house. Wanting to evade that dangerous thought, he grabbed clean clothes and headed for the bathroom. Why, after everything he'd been through, was he allowing himself to be tempted by her? Especially after he'd reassured her and her mother that she was safe from any advances.

Still, he couldn't stop thinking about her and how cheerful she was, how she had been that way almost from the moment she'd awakened in an unfamiliar house. Maybe there were people like her in the world to offset the ones with negative attitudes about everything. He wasn't naturally a negative person, but the past couple of years had certainly chipped away big chunks of his ability to be positive.

He turned off the shower and ran his hand back over his head, sluicing water out of his hair. Though nothing could come of it, he realized how much Maya had given him something to look forward to each day. Just having someone with whom to share meals made him…happy.

When she left, was it going to feel as if something else

had been ripped away from him? He pressed his hands against the wall of the shower in front of him. Why had he allowed himself to grow so used to her presence?

To be fair, he hadn't intended to. It had simply happened, little by little, escaping his notice until the knowledge that her leaving was going to create another hole in his life made itself known.

While Gavin was in the shower, Maya finished setting the meal on the table and topped it off with her hilariously bad craft project results. Granted, she'd had limited supplies, no more than pen and paper and a roll of clear tape she'd found in a drawer, but the little party hats made her smile.

She'd already received birthday calls from her parents, Sunny, Janie and even Trina, who assured her that Blossom was faring well and seemed to be perfectly fine having total reign over Maya's house.

"She has that on a normal day," she'd told Trina.

"And whose fault is that?"

"Guilty as charged."

When the water shut off in the shower, a surge of excitement went through Maya. Even though she knew it was unwise allowing herself to think of Gavin in any sort of romantic way, she couldn't seem to help it. And it wasn't simply how attractive he was, though that fact was so obvious it induced heart racing all on its own. No, it was more the way he'd taken care of her when she most needed it, how he didn't push her to leave before it was safe to do so even though he liked his privacy, and that he'd gradually warmed up to the point where they could even share laughter.

And that smile of his was like bright, warm sunshine. She got the feeling he hadn't showed it to anyone in a long time, so the fact that she'd been gifted it filled her with...

how could she describe the feeling? She made her living with words, and yet she wasn't sure which ones could appropriately convey the warm, full, fluttery feeling that overtook her when Gavin smiled at her.

"Please don't tell me I have to wear that," Gavin said as he appeared a few minutes later.

Maya picked up the hat she'd made for him and held it in the palm of her hand as if it were a luxury item on display.

"It's a special, one-of-a-kind birthday hat," she said. "Not just anyone gets one of these, but I'll let you off the hook and you only have to wear it during dessert."

She placed the hat back next to his plate and took her own seat.

Gavin pulled out his chair, thanked her for making dinner as he did every time she did so, and started cutting up his pork chop.

"I'd forgotten these were in the freezer," he said.

"I had to chuckle when I saw them. They reminded me of my friend Sunny. It's a big joke that one day her dad will disown her because her family owns a cattle ranch but she's not much of a beef fan. She prefers pork."

"A brave viewpoint." In between bites, Gavin picked up his party hat and examined the little doodles she'd drawn on it.

"Pardon my amateurish artwork," she said. "My creative talents do not lie in visual art."

Gavin looked up at her with a questioning gaze, almost as if she'd said something surprising. She smiled in response.

"Not that I expect you to frame it or anything. If I had access to a computer and printer, I could have done a better job."

She took a bite of her mashed potatoes, then looked up to find him still staring at her.

"What?"

He shook his head. "Nothing." Returning his attention to the hat, he turned it slowly and examined each image. She knew the moment he got to the stick figure of him falling off the barn roof with a circle drawn around it and a line running diagonally to create the universal "don't do this" sign.

"Maybe it's not gallery-level artwork, but it's amusing," he said. "You should start your own comic strip in the paper."

"Hey, not a bad idea." She ran her hand through the air, palm forward, in the shape of a rainbow. "We'll call it the Bad Art page, and readers can submit their own work."

Gavin chuckled. "That seems like inviting disaster."

"You never know. Maybe it'll help get our subscription numbers up so the owners will stop bothering me every five seconds. Thanks, by the way, for allowing me to escape that for a while."

"Happy to serve here at Olsen's Retreat from the World."

"I like it. That's what Sunny and Dean should have called their place."

Gavin looked confused. "I thought you said they ran a ranch."

"Oh, they do. It's been in Sunny's family for ages, but when she married Dean—he's the ranch foreman and now part owner—he had lots of ideas for diversification to help provide a financial buffer against bad weather years or herd problems. And Sunny is like a geyser of business ideas. She's also a business consultant. Honestly, I don't know how they do it all and raise two little ones."

"It does sound like...a lot."

There it was again, that sound of distancing in Gavin's voice. Was he remembering his failed marriage?

"I'm sorry. I should be more careful what I say."

"Huh?"

"I didn't mean to bring up bad memories for you by talking about my friend's marriage."

He made a dismissive motion with his hand. "You didn't."

She wasn't sure she believed him, but she let the topic drop. When they'd finished the main course, Gavin surprised her by dishing up a generous helping of cherry cobbler for her.

"Too bad I don't have any ice cream on hand," he said.

"It's fine. If I ate that, I'd have to shovel your entire front yard to get rid of the calories."

Gavin snorted.

"What was that for?"

"Nothing."

"Oh no," she said. "You're not getting out of it that easily. Spill."

"Respectfully, you are nowhere near needing to lose weight."

"Yeah, because I didn't have buckets of ice cream at my disposal." Despite her making light of his comment, it had caused her skin to tingle and grow warmer than could be attributed to the house's heating. "Now remember, you have to wear the hat for dessert."

Gavin gave a dramatic sigh before placing the sad little conical hat on his head.

"I'm not singing though. No one wants to hear that, and we'd probably end up with wolves on the front porch."

"Deal."

"Not bad for a frozen cobbler," Maya said, drawing Gavin's attention from the stick figure rendering of Streaky the Snowman on his hat. Without any sort of elastic or tie, the hat had refused to stay on his head and Maya had given her permission for its removal. He smiled a little at the memory of how she'd sounded almost like some fictional queen granting her subject's request.

"I'm glad I hadn't eaten it before now so you at least have something sweet for your birthday. Sorry about no cake or presents."

"Don't worry about it. I'm alive to see another birthday because of you, so I can't think of a better present than that. And as far as cakes go, I'll just be all pitiful when I go into Trudy's Café next time and she'll make something delicious for me. If I play my cards right, I might get one from Sunny and my mom too."

"What was that you said about gaining weight?"

"Hush. I didn't ask you to make sense."

Gavin laughed then took another bite of the cobbler. As they finished off the entirety of the small dessert, he tried to think of something he could give her. But he had very little because of a combination of design and financial necessity. And the thought that he could give her a birthday kiss was all kinds of wrong. He didn't need that complication, and it went against his assertion that he posed no threat in that way.

While she might be friendly and tease him, he got the impression she was like that with everyone. She'd shown no interest in him other than as her savior and possibly as a friend.

Or had she? That night on the couch when he'd looked at her in the dim light... No, that had been all him. His attraction. His imagination. His almost mistake.

He insisted on clearing the table and doing the dishes. While doing so, he kept racking his brain for something at least remotely special to give to or do for her. He didn't think washing the dishes counted since they were his dishes in his house, after all. As he looked out the window over the sink, thankful to not see snow falling, an idea popped into his head.

After finishing the dishes, he went into his room and started digging through the boxes stored in his closet. Things he'd never unpacked after moving.

There it was. He grabbed a long box and heaved it over the other boxes, then pulled out the telescope. Even though it had been a gift from Rinna when they were dating, when she'd still liked romantic ideas such as looking at the stars under the wide-open Wyoming sky, he hadn't left it behind or gotten rid of it. He'd considered doing so but then stubbornly kept it, telling himself that while it was nothing compared to his son he wasn't going to let her rob him of one more thing.

He let out a sigh, shoving aside the telescope's origins, and carried it out to the living room.

"I don't have ice cream or birthday gifts, but how about we take advantage of the clear sky?"

"Oh, that sounds fun, even if it is freezing."

He retrieved an extra stocking cap and a hoodie for her to wear under her coat.

"Thanks."

Once they were both bundled up against the cold and Gavin had turned out the house lights, he carried the telescope outside to the end of the partial path Maya had shoveled.

"I really should finish this," she said.

"No, you really shouldn't. Just stay inside where it's warm."

"Says the man who ushered me outside at night as a present."

"We can go back in." He started to lift the telescope again, surprised by how good it felt to tease her. He'd once been that kind of person, quick to smile and prone to teasing. It angered him how much the past couple of years had changed him. Was it possible to reclaim some of the person he used to be?

But every time he wondered anything along those lines, he'd immediately feel guilty. How could he be happy and carefree when he couldn't even see his son?

"You okay?" Maya asked.

"Yeah." He had to remember how observant she was, guard against showing too much. She'd been respectful of his privacy so far, but there was always the possibility that she'd change the way Rinna had.

No, Rinna had always been self-centered and spoiled. But his infatuation had prevented him from seeing her for who she really was.

Enough of dwelling in the past. His life might never be the same again, but at least for tonight he could enjoy looking at some stars with a pretty woman. Even if nothing could come of it.

He found Polaris first, then Ursa Major, giving Maya a turn at viewing them before shifting to a new point of astronomical interest. When she was ready, he shifted the telescope to Cassiopeia.

"When I was little, I used to think this one was just a *W* and stood for Wyoming," she said. "It was about the time we were learning the states. But my dad's best friend set me straight. He taught an extra astronomy class at the high school we could get college credit for, so I took it when I was old enough. Dad's an English teacher. I don't think I ever told you anything about my family other than that Mom is overprotective and my brother is a *Star Wars* fan."

Gavin wasn't sure why she was telling him now, but he found himself asking if her mother taught as well.

"No, not unless you count teaching people how to do

home rehab or how to take their blood pressure. She's a home health nurse."

"Really? So is my aunt, Mom's sister. She lives up in Missoula." Why was he so willing to divulge personal information all of a sudden? Was the cold freezing his brain?

"Oh, that area is really pretty. I've only been there once, but I liked it."

Was the fact that Maya so easily shared information about herself what made him willing to do the same? Was breaking down metaphorical walls her superpower? That would certainly come in handy in her line of work.

But it also could pose a danger for her if she was too open with the wrong person, especially since she lived alone. At least here, with him, she was safe.

He jerked his attention away from her at that startling thought, thankful she was looking up at the sky and not at him.

After they'd located and viewed a few more celestial objects, he noticed Maya shifting from foot to foot and hugging herself.

"Cold?"

When she looked up at him, she wore an apologetic expression.

"Yeah. As nice as this is," she said, pointing at the telescope and then the sky, "I think I'm done. Another cup of hot cocoa sounds great right about now."

"Okay." Gavin only barely kept his voice from breaking at the sudden memory of the last time they'd indulged in hot cocoa. How many times had he replayed that moment in his mind, wondering what it would have been like to give in to his urge to kiss her?

He could do this. All he had to do was not sit beside her, not stand too close to her. If there was more than an arm's length between them, he'd succeed in resisting any unwise temptations.

"Great!" she said, sounding like a kid who'd been given permission to eat ice cream for breakfast.

Her joy made him huff out a single laugh. "Go on in. I'll be there in a bit."

Not only did he need to pack up the telescope, but he could use some time alone to shove all the romantic thoughts about Maya into some hidden corner of his brain where he'd forget about them and they'd dissipate for lack of attention.

But as Maya bounded up the steps and into his house, he was afraid that the attraction he felt had boarded a train that didn't stop at any stations and wasn't prone to derailment.

He sighed, his breath coming out in a visible fog. He didn't remember rational thought being something he had to part with in his divorce settlement, but it sure seemed he'd left it far behind.

CHAPTER NINE

CONSIDERING THE SITUATION, Maya thought it had turned out to be a pretty good birthday. She didn't have to cover anything for the paper, had enjoyed a good meal, gotten to do some stargazing and had heard more laughter from Gavin. She didn't examine too closely how she felt as if she'd received a burst of serotonin each time he laughed or, even more thrilling, smiled at her.

If she didn't know he had gone through what she gathered was not an amicable divorce, she might try out her rusty flirting skills and angle for a birthday kiss. Instead, she would be satisfied with sharing hot cocoa with him again.

He took a while coming back inside, and she figured he must have gone to the barn to check on his horse. She realized she had no idea if there were any other animals in the barn. She'd seen no evidence of such, and considering Gavin lived alone she doubted he had more than one horse. Despite what he had said, maybe she'd work off that cobbler the next day by finishing the path to the barn and then check out the only other building on the property. Exploring a barn wouldn't exactly be a great adventure, but it'd be something different.

When Gavin returned, she extended a warm mug toward him.

"Just put it on the table," he said. "I'll get it in a minute."

He disappeared into his room to put away the telescope,

an item she'd honestly been surprised he owned. But lots of people had hobbies, and who knew? Maybe when she wasn't here he routinely pulled it out and watched the heavens.

He'd told her that he was different than he used to be, so maybe he hadn't enjoyed that particular hobby since his marriage had dissolved. She hoped he'd been able to enjoy their night of astronomy as much as she had.

Again, he took longer to return than she anticipated. Maya began to wonder if he'd fallen asleep, though she hadn't heard his door close. Curiosity almost got the better of her when she considered going to the bathroom to perhaps see more of the bedroom she'd only glimpsed once before. But she kept herself firmly in the kitchen, guessing that the bedroom was as sparsely furnished and decorated as the rest of the house.

She had no idea why, but something told her that even his bare walls were at odds with the Gavin of the past. In the wake of his divorce, anything bright or pretty probably didn't match his mood. Home decor was probably way, way down his list of concerns, if it made the list at all.

When he walked out of his room, he grabbed his mug and strode over to stand by the stove. She noticed he didn't make eye contact with her, once again seeming to put distance between them and not just the physical kind. The way he acted around her was a bit like a pendulum, swinging from quiet and distant to more open and fun, then back again. Was that part of his personality, or was she saying or doing something to cause the shifts?

Trying not to think about it too much, she carried her mug over to stand next to the stove as well. At least he didn't move away again.

"This is nice," she said. "A warm fire and hot cocoa are perfect for a night like this. Very cozy."

"Umm." Gavin's response reminded her of that first day she'd been an uninvited guest in his house, when he'd seemed like an antisocial hermit.

Maya didn't know how to respond, and that was so unlike her. But it suddenly seemed as if they had come to the end of available conversation, and that felt so odd. She almost always had something to say, or at least had a response at the ready. But now? Nothing. So she found herself staring at the stove, taking drinks of the cocoa, and feeling the awkwardness between them grow with each passing moment. How was that possible when they'd been laughing and enjoying the stars only a few minutes before?

She glanced at Gavin's profile and it struck her again how incredibly handsome he was.

"Hey, let's take a picture," she said out of the blue, surprising herself as much as she appeared to surprise Gavin. "There are always pictures taken at birthday parties."

"I don't think two people make a party."

"Of course they do. All the best parties have two people."

What in the world was she saying? It was as if random words were attaching themselves to each other and launching from her mouth in an effort to make the situation even more awkward. She genuinely felt as if someone else had inhabited her body.

Rather than admit to the possible interpretation of what she'd just said, she acted as if everything was fine…until she remembered that she didn't have a phone anymore.

"Oh." She looked around the room as if a new cell phone might magically appear. "Never mind."

Instead of pretending his guest had not temporarily taken leave of her senses, Gavin retrieved his own phone from his room. But when she realized how close she'd have to stand to him for a photo, her pulse accelerated. She'd evidently left all her marbles out there under the snow with her bag and phone.

Gavin looked around the living area and the kitchen. "Sorry, I don't really have a good spot for a photo."

"Anywhere's fine." Maya moved closer to him, and she thought she detected his body growing more rigid. But it was too late to back out without it seeming extra weird.

She was careful, however, not to touch him. She was afraid actually making contact would allow for some supernatural transfer of her thoughts to him, and among all the current chaos in her head he might be able to detect how she was becoming more attracted to him each day.

When Gavin lifted the phone and focused the camera on them, she did her best to look her normal cheerful self, one hundred percent the fun-loving birthday girl. She deliberately focused on her image on the screen because if she looked at Gavin she would almost certainly reveal too much.

"One, two, three," Gavin said, then snapped the photo.

He did not snap a second one, prompting Maya to move away from him quickly. She barely resisted fanning herself because she felt really hot. She wasn't sure if the heat originated from him, the stove or from within her addled self. If Sunny could see her now, Maya would never hear the end of it. They would be doing crafts at the nursing home decades in the future and Sunny would still be cackling about how discombobulated Maya had gotten by simply standing close to a hot guy.

"Well, uh, thanks for a nice birthday," she said, not looking at him. "I think I'll turn in. All the festivities have made me tired."

Did her excuse to get away from him sound as fake as she thought it did? For someone who didn't like lying, she'd sure been tossing out some fibs to hide the truth of her changing feelings. If Gavin noticed, he thankfully didn't say so.

"Yeah, me too. Good night."

"Good night." She nearly dropped her face into her hands at how her voice squeaked.

This was one of those times she really wished the small bedroom across from Gavin's held something other than a few moving boxes.

As she lay stretched out on the couch a few minutes later, wide-awake, she mentally made her to-do list for the next day. It contained exactly one item.

Gather her scattered wits before Gavin realized that in her eyes he'd gone from the hermit who saved her to the handsome man she wanted to kiss.

SUNLIGHT BROUGHT SANITY. Or at least more of it than Maya had been able to muster the previous night. It helped that Gavin left the house extra early, before she'd even risen. She was going to consider the previous night a glitch in her system. Even though nothing had happened between them, the air had seemed thick with…wanting.

Wanting to know Gavin's full story. Wanting to understand what caused his mood swings. Wanting to figure out if she was really attracted to Gavin or whether the fluttery, heart-racing way she sometimes felt around him was simply a product of them being snowed in together.

And, yes, the wanting to kiss him that had sent her fleeing as far as the confines of his house would allow.

She rubbed her face vigorously with both hands. She didn't know if he would have attracted her so much if she'd met him in the normal course of her days. Doubtful since he would have probably just grunted a greeting and been on his way.

But by having to share his house, she'd had the time

and limited space to get to know him better. At least as much as he'd allow.

Frustrated by her meandering thoughts, she tossed back the quilts and hurried through what had become her morning routine here—brush teeth and hair, make breakfast, eat breakfast, check in with Janie. She skipped the shower and any reporting work because she was getting out of the house for a while despite the cold. At least it was bright and sunny now, enough that the snow on top of the house was beginning to melt and drip off the icicles that had formed at the edge of the roof overnight.

She bundled up, including the hoodie and extra hat Gavin had given her to wear the night before, and headed outside for some wintry exercise. Before tackling the path, she used the shovel to knock off all the icicles she could reach so they didn't cause any damage.

Maya wouldn't say her shoveling task was fun, but it quickly had her warm enough that she didn't mind the cold so much. And it helped to clear her head. By the time she finished the path to the barn, she felt both accomplished and farther away from whatever had possessed her mind the night before, whatever had made her speak and act as if her neurons were misfiring. Her fondest wish was that it had not seemed as strange to Gavin as it had felt to her when it was happening.

She turned and looked back at the path. Parts of it had been covered in a thin layer of white from blowing snow, but it was much more passable than trudging through the fallen snow. She'd gotten warm while shoveling, but now that she was standing still the air made her shiver. She leaned the shovel against the side of the barn and hurried inside.

Since Jasper wasn't currently in residence, the barn was quiet. It was also surprisingly warm. Of course, the protection from the wind alone was a big plus. As she wandered through, she noticed things one would typically find in a barn—tools, horse tack, some hay bales, but no machinery.

During one of his more talkative evenings, Gavin had told her there was a shed down by the pasture where he kept a tractor and other equipment needed for taking care of his small herd of cattle. He'd admitted he hoped to gradually grow his operation and thus his income. From what he'd said, she gathered he was very careful with money and not prone to take on debt that wasn't absolutely necessary. It was a practical viewpoint, but like everything else about him she'd gotten the feeling there was more to the story. But she hadn't probed for more details. Letting him gradually become more comfortable with her and thus share details on his own, if he so chose, had seemed the better plan.

She paused at what was obviously Jasper's stall and considered all of her conversations with Gavin since she'd unceremoniously collapsed in front of his house. She had an innate sense of when to push for more information and when to back off, but she'd done more of the latter than typical when it came to Gavin.

It was strange how despite sensing there was so much more to his past, she'd felt protective of him instead of trying to get more information. She couldn't point to one thing that made her feel that way. It was more an accumulation of little things—how withdrawn he got at times, the occasional faraway look, what felt very much like a wall he'd built around himself, that phone call he'd received.

She spotted a wooden ladder leading up into the loft and decided to check out what she could see from the upper level. When she reached the top, she noticed miscellaneous, dust-covered detritus that she'd bet old Ansel

Blackthorn had left behind and Gavin hadn't bothered to clear out.

Maya crossed to a window at the back of the barn and looked out. Unsurprising but nonetheless a bit disappointing, the view it afforded was simply more trees and snow. Oh well, at least it was a different vantage point. And to tell the truth, it was pretty. She wished she still had her phone for a lot of reasons, the ability to take photos among them.

That reminded her of the photo Gavin had taken of them the night before. She'd been too flustered in the aftermath to ask him to email it to her. Maybe it was best that she not have that photo when she left. She doubted very much that being able to get back to her normal life included looking at Gavin's handsome face every five minutes.

When she turned away from the window, she spotted a thick cloth covering something next to the far wall. Since it wasn't covered by years of dust so that it looked gray, she assumed it must have been put there by Gavin. Curiosity drove her toward whatever lay underneath the cloth. She told herself taking a peek wasn't a big deal. It wasn't the same as snooping around his bedroom. It shouldn't be super private if it was stuck in the loft of the barn, and she was putting off going back to the house even though she could work on her article series or try to drum up some advertising for the paper. But today, she just wasn't feeling it.

Maybe because sitting in the house reminded her too much of all the little moments shared with Gavin and the temptation to assign way too much meaning to them.

She lifted away the cloth and was stunned by what she found. In this most unlikely of places was a painting with a deep blue background filled with twinkling stars and a shooting star so bright white it felt as if it might actually fly off the canvas.

When she pulled it slightly forward, the next canvas

revealed a scene of dusk with a sky filled with blues, purples and a sliver of orange with a solitary dot of white to denote Venus.

In love with this artist's style and subject matter, she flipped to the next piece. The stars of Ursa Major stared back at her against an inky sky, and the painter had included a fine white line to illustrate the Great Bear around the constellation.

Maya experienced a pang in her heart. Had Gavin's divorce affected him so much that he didn't even want to hang these beauties in his home? Did they hold some sort of special meaning to him that brought up bad memories? If so, why had he kept them at all?

Though she was glad he had. She hated the idea of these paintings being thrown out in the trash.

Maya had her hand on the fourth painting, about to take a look, when she heard Gavin's voice. She quickly covered the paintings and walked over to the top of the ladder to find Gavin staring up at her. When he glanced to the right, toward where the paintings were stored, his expression told her she'd made a mistake.

"What are you doing up there?" His voice was the harshest she'd ever heard it, enough to make her tense.

She pointed toward the window on the opposite end of the barn from the paintings.

"I came up to see what the view was like from up here."

His steely stare told her he knew, without a doubt, what she'd been looking at when he arrived. She had to navigate her way out of this like a ship exiting a rocky harbor in a storm.

"These paintings up here are really pretty. The comet one would—"

"Please come down."

Despite the look he wore, she was surprised by how

abruptly he'd cut her off. But she'd been living off his kindness so she complied, wondering what she could say to make amends.

"I'm sorry. I didn't know they were something so private."

"The fact they were covered up in the barn loft should have been a clue."

Maya startled so much that it caused Jasper to sidestep. Gavin was quick to soothe the horse while not making eye contact with her. She had to press her lips together and inhale a shaky breath, then blink a couple of times against sudden and uncharacteristic tears. Gavin was obviously angry, and she had no one to blame but herself.

"I apologize." She wanted to say more, but the words refused to pass by the lump in her throat. Instead, she turned and hurried out of the barn and straight to the house.

When she stepped inside and leaned back against the door, she honestly thought she would give her next year's pay to have somewhere to escape to until she could figure how to turn back time or make things right.

GAVIN STOOD IN the same spot until he heard the door to the house open then shut. As he went about removing his saddle and tack then undertaking Jasper's after-ride care, he tried to calm down. He didn't know why he was so surprised that he'd found Maya snooping in his things. She was a reporter. He should have expected it. Now he wondered what else she might have gone through while he was away from the house.

He shook his head. No, she wasn't like that. Or was she just really good at convincing him that she wasn't the kind of journalist who stuck her nose where it didn't belong? Was he destined to be a fool over and over again?

When Jasper was settled in his stall, Gavin knew the

time had come for Maya to leave. He'd gotten used to having her around and so he hadn't checked on the status of the road, but he planned to correct that now. Bypassing the house, he walked to the end of his entrance drive to the road. He discovered that the lane going up the mountain had been plowed, which meant that the county snowplow would be coming back down the mountain in a while.

Perfect timing.

Even thinking that, he hesitated to return to the house, because he didn't know what Maya might say and how he would react. Instead, he headed back toward the barn. He grabbed the shovel Maya had left behind and started clearing enough of the snow in the driveway to allow his pickup to pass through to the road.

He half expected Maya to come outside to offer to help as a further apology, but she stayed in the house. That was probably best for both of them.

After he'd been shoveling for probably half an hour, he stopped to catch his breath and rest. In the distance he heard what he thought was the snowplow making its way back down the mountain. He glanced toward the house. Still no sign of Maya. She might very well be digging through his belongings while he was outside, sensing her last chance to do so.

You know that's not true.

Did he?

He closed his eyes and heaved a sigh. He wanted to believe he'd been right that Maya was different, that she was every bit the fun and kind person she appeared to be. Why had she found those paintings and replanted the seed of doubt in his mind?

Why had he kept the paintings? They were a painful reminder of what might have been but now would never be. He'd nearly burned them on more than one occasion, but something always stopped him. He guessed there was still enough of that once-held dream to have him shoving them into the hayloft of his barn rather than onto a burn pile.

It was fully dark by the time he reached the end of his drive and cleared it enough to be passable, including the pile of snow caused by the snowplow that had passed by earlier. He was bone-tired and frozen despite wearing proper winter gear, and he suddenly didn't know if he had the energy to walk back to the house. But then he remembered the day Maya had arrived, how her steps had faltered and she'd collapsed, not able to move one more inch despite lifesaving warmth being within sight.

With that in mind, he trudged toward his house. When he came into view, he saw the lights filling the windows and Maya pacing the front porch. He stopped and stared. Was she worried about him, or was she waiting with another apology, hoping he'd forgive her trespass?

Could he? Maybe with time, but right now it felt as if she'd reinjured an old wound. It was time for her to go back to her world and leave him in his.

He knew the moment she noticed him, because she stopped pacing and stared straight at him, though she couldn't possibly make out more than his dark shape against the white of the snow. Having had enough of cold for the day, he continued toward the house.

"Go back inside," he said as he drew near.

To her credit she didn't argue and headed for the front door, leaving it unlatched for him. When he stepped inside, she was across the room scooping up bowls of what appeared to be vegetable soup.

"You should eat something and warm up. You've been outside for hours, and it feels like Jack Frost's posterior out there."

He heard the struggle in her voice to be amusing, but he wasn't in the mood for…well, mood lightening.

"I'll be taking you home in the morning," he said. "I don't want to chance the road being slick tonight, but the plow came by today."

"Oh, okay. Good."

Without saying anything further, he headed for the bathroom for a shower. As the water began to warm his skin and then his inner chill, he tried to let go of the anger that had gripped him when he saw Maya in the hayloft and realized she'd seen the paintings. He knew she'd been about to say he should hang some of them in the house to cover his bare walls, but that wasn't happening. Keeping them at all was as much as he could bear.

I should have never encouraged you.

The memory of Rinna's words when he'd been declined yet another opportunity to hang his work in a gallery stung as much now as it had when she'd said them.

Your work is mediocre at best, but hot guys love to be complimented.

He sighed. What had he ever seen in her? How had she managed to fool him when she'd acted as if she loved him as much as he loved her?

He'd fallen hard and fast almost the moment he'd met her, and look where that had gotten him. As things now stood, he was really glad he hadn't given in to any of the urges to kiss Maya. But his judgment of people had to be questioned. Best to stay away from them as much as possible.

After his shower, he considered going straight to bed but his stomach felt hollow from hunger and a hot bowl of soup sounded good. He didn't plan to linger in Maya's presence, however. Beginning to sever that temporary tie was a wise move at this point.

Maya had covered his soup to keep it warm, but he resisted thanking her. That would invite conversation he didn't want.

"Gavin—"

He held up a hand. "If you're going to apologize again, don't. It's not necessary."

"I think it is because you're obviously angry and have every right to be. I'm truly sorry I let my curiosity get the better of me. And since I'm sure you've wondered if I've dug through anything else of yours, please believe me that I haven't."

Despite his upset and his war with doubts, he did believe her. He nodded once then picked up his bowl of soup and a tablespoon.

"I would like to say one more thing and then I'll leave you alone," she said, staring into her own bowl of soup that she seemed to have not touched. When he didn't object, she continued. "I won't ask you to reveal anything to me, not about your past, the paintings, anything, but if you ever want to talk, you can contact me. I know that probably won't happen, but I have to make the offer. And this has zero to do with my job. It's me wanting to be a friend, even though I've probably ruined any chance of that."

She didn't wait for him to respond, either because she didn't expect him to or didn't want to hear a negative reply. Instead, she ate a spoonful of her soup then carried the bowl to the coffee table. He watched as she gathered the various papers she'd had spread out there, the only things other than her shoes and clothing that belonged to her. There was nothing to pack for her departure.

A pang of guilt hit him. She hadn't asked to stay here, hadn't intended to wreck and lose everything she'd had with her. On the whole, she'd been a good houseguest. They'd almost parted on good terms.

Feeling confused by his back-and-forth feelings, he wordlessly carried his soup into his room and shut the door. He needed the barrier between them until he could have his home all to himself again. Needed the closed door to remind him not to make any more mistakes.

CHAPTER TEN

MAYA DIDN'T SLEEP a wink. She tried, but even dozing proved elusive. Her brain simply wouldn't shut down and let her rest. Instead, it kept repeating how she had ruined what had felt like an early friendship. All the thawing that Gavin had done toward her, how they'd grown able to laugh together, that was gone.

On the surface, what she'd done might not seem like a huge offense. But she'd still invaded a space that wasn't hers, and those paintings obviously embodied a story that Gavin did not want to share.

Giving up a few minutes before daylight started making an appearance, she moved quietly to the kitchen and made coffee and toast. She didn't think she could stomach anything else, but she needed the caffeine if she was to get through the day. It wasn't as if she could go straight to bed when she got home, not when she'd been away from the office for way too long.

She considered making breakfast for Gavin, but she wasn't sure he'd appreciate it anymore. If she thought there would be any passing vehicles at this hour, she would simply walk out to the road and hitch a ride to town. She'd never be able to tell her mother that or she might find a bunch of relatives dragging her back to the reservation where she would be guarded like an errant teenager prone to making bad decisions.

When Gavin emerged from his room a while later, Maya

felt more awkward than she had that first day she'd awakened in a strange house with a man she didn't know. If only she hadn't crashed that day she could have saved both of them many uncomfortable and tense moments.

But she might never have met Gavin otherwise. Maybe that would have been a good thing.

"I'll be back after the sun has had time to hit the road for a while," he said before putting on his winter outerwear and stepping out the front door without breakfast or even a cup of coffee.

Maya sank onto the familiar couch and lowered her head to her arms that lay atop her knees. She hated so much that she had likely undone every positive step she'd made toward convincing Gavin that she wasn't like the type of journalists he disliked so much. She didn't even know what had caused him to look at her profession with such derision. There was so much she didn't know about him and now never would.

Her remaining time in his home crawled by with agonizing slowness, to the point where she thought she might go mad. If only she had a computer and internet access, she could occupy her time. But she was left with pacing, staring at the clock and mentally naming every resident of Jade Valley she could remember.

After about an hour of sloth-speed time passage, she decided to write Gavin a letter. There was a lot she still wanted to say, but when she was facing him and his stony expression she couldn't form the words. She wasn't sure he'd stick around to hear them anyway.

Ripping one more page from the notebook she'd been using to work, she sat at the kitchen table and stared at the blank page. Where to start?

After taking a while to consider what she wanted to say and how she should say it, she put pen to paper. When she finally finished, she folded the letter and slipped it under the loaf of bread on the counter. She didn't want him to find it until after she left. She honestly wanted to avoid seeing his reaction as he read her outpouring of regret and thankfulness.

Despite how she wanted to get the parting done and over with, it still felt as if it came too soon when Gavin returned to the house.

"The road appears to be safe now."

She didn't hesitate to stand up or put on her coat and gloves. They didn't speak as they walked to Gavin's truck, nor as he turned onto the road and headed down the mountain toward town. She'd never felt so uncomfortable in her life, so she stared out her window and tried to think of other things—seeing her cat again, how many long hours of work she had ahead of her after being gone for days, when she might be able to have her car retrieved and the damage assessed.

The silence between them was only broken when they reached town and she had to give him directions to her house. Too soon and yet not soon enough, he pulled into her driveway. Instead of immediately getting out of the truck, however, she sat for a moment with her hand on the door handle.

"Thank you for everything. And again, I'm sorry."

She didn't wait to see if he might say something in response. Whether words she didn't want to hear or silence, she'd rather not know. But as she stepped out onto her snowy driveway, she didn't hurry. The last thing she wanted to do at this point was fall, resulting in embarrassment at best and injury at worst.

After how he'd acted toward her since the day before, she was surprised he waited until she was at her door to put his truck in reverse. If she had not looked at those paintings, in this moment she would turn around and wave a goodbye. Because of that one error in judgment, she instead unlocked the door and slipped inside. She didn't even allow herself to look out the window to watch him drive away.

Her entrance woke Blossom from a nap atop the ottoman that was her favorite sleeping spot.

"Did you miss me?" Catching her unaware, Maya's voice broke at the end of her question. She pressed her lips together and blinked to keep from crying, but it didn't work.

She picked up Blossom and held her close as tears spilled.

"Why am I being this way? It's not as if we were in a relationship and broke up?"

But Blossom didn't have an answer to Maya's question, and neither did she.

AFTER PICKING UP some groceries and a pizza from Little Italy, the small carryout pizzeria, Gavin headed to his blessedly guest-free home. He would be able to kick back and relax the way he'd intended to do the night Maya had ended up on his couch nearly frozen to death.

He tried his best not to think about how dejected she'd looked as she'd walked from his truck to the front door of her little house. He told himself that he'd done nothing wrong and therefore didn't have to feel guilty.

Then why was his brain telling him that wasn't true? She was the one who'd gone snooping through his things, dredging up the past he was trying and failing to move beyond.

He hoped that the more distance he put between them, the less he would think about her. And once she was back in her normal routine, she'd likely forget about him too.

When he stepped into his quiet house, he realized that maybe distance wasn't the answer to getting Maya Pine out of his thoughts. More likely it was time because at the moment the quiet he'd wanted seemed too quiet. He'd gotten used to Maya's bright chatter, her laughter, her—

Stop thinking about her!

He dropped the pizza box on the coffee table then took off his coat and boots. After retrieving a soda from the fridge, he kicked back in his recliner to watch TV.

As he flipped channels, he came across an old Bob Ross painting show. Of course he did. Did he burn down a village in a former life? It sure felt as if the universe delighted in poking him with sharp sticks.

He finally landed on some basketball highlights, but he found it difficult to pay attention. His thoughts kept drifting to Maya, to how she was no longer a fixture on his couch. There would be no more coming in from working all day to find her with papers spread out from one end of the coffee table to the other. No more sharing meals with her. No more unexpected funny moments like the snowman she'd built or silly birthday hats.

Having his space back was what he'd told himself he wanted, but now that he had that privacy it felt incredibly empty.

MAYA DIDN'T HAVE time to think about Gavin for the rest of the day, and yet she did. In between an interview with the head of the county road department about the state of snow removal, going to get a new driver's license, replacing other things she'd lost, and assuring her mother that she was back home safe and sound, memories of her time with Gavin assaulted her. The first time she'd heard him laugh, the way he'd fallen asleep in his chair while watching movies with her, how he'd pulled out his telescope to celebrate her birthday.

He must like astronomy a lot to have a nice telescope and paintings depicting the night sky. It seemed strange that he'd share one with her but the other drove a wedge between them.

She was so tempted to do an internet search on him, but she resisted. Her curiosity was what had ruined their budding friendship. So she focused on work, and when her thoughts strayed she dragged her attention back to work.

"Aren't you going home?"

Maya looked up at Janie's question. "Huh?"

"Home. I'll give you a ride since you don't have a car."

Maya looked toward the glass front door of the newspaper office and saw it was dark.

"I'm okay to walk."

"It's below freezing outside, and after what you went through—"

"It's okay, really. I want to finish up some things before I call it a day."

"Okay. Be careful going home. The way your luck's been lately, I feel like you might slip and crack your skull."

Maya laughed a little. "That sounds about right."

Though she did manage to get some writing and interview prep done, Maya wasn't anywhere near as productive as she would normally be. Fatigue and the inability to focus finally got the better of her. She logged off her computer and bundled up to head home.

When she opened the door, a blast of wind caused her to gasp. Though there wasn't any additional snow in the forecast, it certainly felt as if it could dump a few more inches. But the air didn't smell right for that, so this time she thought the meteorologists were actually correct. At least if a snowstorm came now, she wouldn't be stuck at a stranger's house or risk running off the road, seeing as how her car was still probably buried under snow up on the mountain. Tomorrow she'd have to check on that.

After what she hoped was a solid twelve hours of sleep.

But as she was locking the door, someone pulled into the parking lot. For a moment, she had the crazy idea that it was Gavin. Maybe he'd found her note and had come to apologize.

No, he didn't have anything to apologize for. He wasn't the one to go snooping through her personal belongings.

When she turned around, she found her best friend waving at her to get in her truck.

"What are you doing here?" Maya asked as she slid into the passenger seat.

"Girls' night!"

"Okay, I appreciate the thought but I'm way too tired for a girls' night. I could manage some takeout and a bit of chatting before I collapse in my bed though."

"You should have taken a break before coming back to work."

Maya laughed. "I've been away from the office for over a week. The last thing I needed to do was take another day off."

"Fine, takeout from Trudy's and a bit of necessary catch-up."

"What, do you need to tell me you're pregnant or something?"

"No! Whew, I think taking care of the twins, my job and helping Dean around the ranch is quite enough on my plate, thanks."

"Looks like I'm not the only workaholic around."

"Okay, I do work a lot, but I also know when to take some time off and enjoy life."

"Enjoy life." Maya snickered. "Is that what they're calling it these days?"

Sunny reached across the truck and swatted her, then pulled away from the newspaper office for the short drive to Jade Valley's little downtown area. Considering dining options were limited in a town of five hundred, it was no surprise that they'd opted for Trudy's Café.

"They should really open a place with drive-through service in this town so that tired people don't have to get out of their cars to buy dinner."

"Come on," Sunny said. "Stop being so pitiful. Who knows what interesting tidbits you might pick up while waiting for your order?"

Maya stuck her tongue out at Sunny but mentally acknowledged the truth of what she'd said. Trudy's Café and Alma's Diner, which sat directly across the street, were the hubs of gossip in Jade Valley. Trudy and Alma themselves provided some of that gossip via their longstanding feud. Maya figured her ultimate victory as a journalist would be to break the story of what had led to said feud because no one seemed to know and the feuding parties weren't telling.

She stifled a yawn as she got out of the truck and followed Sunny into the restaurant.

"Well, look who returned from the snowy wilderness," Trudy said as Sunny and Maya approached the front counter to order.

Maya laughed, unsurprised that word had gotten around about her predicament.

"I wasn't exactly roughing it in the wilds," Maya said as she grabbed a menu even though she could probably recite it. "The kindness of strangers is alive and well."

Even if that former stranger didn't think very highly of her now.

"You girls not eating here tonight?"

"No. Maya is a party pooper," Sunny said.

"I'm tired and will be lucky if I don't drop face-first into my dinner."

After Trudy took their orders and disappeared into the kitchen, Sunny turned and stared at Maya.

"So, why exactly are you so tired?"

Maya wasn't in the mood for the kind of teasing her friend was dishing out, but she also didn't want to act in a way that attracted the wrong questions.

"I didn't sleep well last night wondering if my car is salvageable and, if so, how much it's going to cost me."

"Are you sure that's all you were thinking about?"

"I'm sure I thought about something else at some point." Technically, Maya wasn't lying, because she had worried about her transportation issue. Getting around town she could do on foot or by riding with Janie, but she needed wheels to go farther afield for work.

Sunny placed her phone, screen up, on the counter in front of Maya and pointed at it.

"Is he part of the reason you couldn't sleep?"

The picture staring up at her looked like Gavin and yet it didn't. Instead of ranch attire, he wore jeans and a suit jacket paired with a pale blue dressy T-shirt beneath. He stood next to a familiar painting, the one of the falling star streaking across the night sky.

Though she didn't want to give Sunny any further fodder for thinking there was more between Maya and Gavin than there was, she picked up the phone and scanned the article that accompanied the photo.

The paintings were his.

Out of all the possibilities that had run through her head regarding why her uncovering the paintings had upset him so much, Gavin being the painter had not been one of them. The article was short, basically just one of many quick features on budding artists at an art show held in a hotel ballroom.

How had Gavin gone from aspiring artist to a rancher who hid away his work? Was it somehow tied to his divorce? Whatever the reason, it caused a tight knot in her middle.

"I take it by the look on your face that it's the right Gavin Olsen."

Maya handed the phone back to Sunny.

"Yeah, that's him. I won't even ask why you were looking him up."

"If the roles were reversed, you would have done the same thing."

"Probably, but then I also might not have had time because Dean would have found a way to get to you so you didn't have to stay in the house of someone you didn't know."

"Surely you got to know him over the course of your stay."

"Enough to say hello if I see him, but I wouldn't say we're besties."

"Of course not. That's my title."

"I was fortunate that he saved me and was kind enough to let me stay until it was possible to get back home."

Sunny was quiet for a moment while Maya examined the offerings in the pie case, wanting to take a pie to Trina as a thank-you for taking care of Blossom.

"What aren't you telling me?"

Maya feigned ignorance as she met Sunny's gaze. "What do you want to know?"

"Like how well did you get to know him? Did you all talk a lot?"

"He's not the talkative type." She had to give Sunny

something or she would keep pecking away, but she didn't feel right sharing too much. "He's originally from up near Sheridan, is divorced, likes living alone and doesn't much like reporters."

"But you said you were getting along fine when I talked to you before."

"We were." No need to tell her that was no longer the case, especially since there wasn't likely to be any further contact between Maya and Gavin.

Trudy returned with their orders, and Maya took the opportunity to exit the conversation by pointing at the pie case.

"I'd like both the chocolate meringue and the cherry pie."

"Whole or slices?"

"Whole."

"Okay, someone came home with an extra sweet tooth."

"The chocolate is for Trina for cat duty, but I fully intend to consume the cherry by myself. Call it self-pity for crashing poor Blueberry."

She really hoped her little blue hatchback could be fixed because she loved that car, the nicest vehicle she'd ever owned.

As Sunny drove them to Maya's house and they hurried inside out of the cold, Maya managed to keep the topics of conversation on anything other than Gavin. How the twins were doing, Sunny's latest business undertakings, the continued frustration of trying to keep the *Post* afloat and the owners happy.

"If anyone else were at the helm, I'm certain the paper would have shuttered long ago," Sunny said.

"Every community needs an actual news outlet to separate fact from fiction."

As they stepped inside, Sunny stopped to coo over the precious Blossom.

"Who's a beautiful girl? You are," she said to the cat.

"I'd think you get enough baby talk at home," Maya said as she dropped to the couch and tried to muster up enough energy to open her take-out container and the plastic utensils.

"Nope. I talk to the cows this way too."

Maya snorted. "Of course you do. For someone who not that long ago said she was an LA girl, you sure have rediscovered your love of ranch life. Of course, a certain good-looking rancher had a lot to do with that."

"That he did. And speaking of good-looking men…"

Maya pointed a seasoned French fry at Sunny.

"Stop. There is zero between Gavin Olsen and me. There will continue to be zero between us. Remember how I said he liked to be left alone? Yeah, that."

"Would you like there to be something?"

Maya sighed. "You've got romance on the brain."

"Hey, pickings are slim around here, so when there's a hot new guy who is also an artist—"

"He's not an artist. At least I saw no evidence of that." Which was true because while there were paintings tucked away in his barn, there had been no empty canvasses, no painting supplies, nothing to indicate he was actively still engaged in art. He'd probably tried his hand at it as a hobby but got busy with the business of making a living and set it aside.

But that didn't explain his reaction when he'd found her in the barn. That fact kept spinning in her head long after Sunny took pity on Maya for yawning so much and headed home.

The part of her that felt compelled to find answers warred with the part that didn't want to invade Gavin's privacy anymore and the substantial part that could no longer keep her eyes open. Still, as she drifted toward sleep, she thought of how Gavin was smiling in that news photo while standing next to the painting he'd created. She wondered where that smile had gone, and if there was any way of getting it back.

CHAPTER ELEVEN

GAVIN WAS GLAD to have his solitude back, but the problem with being alone was that he couldn't escape his thoughts. Despite knowing it was for the best that Maya was no longer a fixture in his house, it felt odd to step inside and not find her there.

But the end to their unexpected time as housemates was as necessary for her as it was for him. She had things to do, even if he didn't want to think about them, people who depended on her. Family and friends had worried about her while she was forced to stay with him.

He had none of those things, and it was a miracle his attitude hadn't siphoned away Maya's sunny personality. Instead, she had managed to cause his exterior to begin to thaw like the snow surrounding his house.

But had it all been part of a plan to soften him up? To get him to reveal more of his past?

Another part of his brain asked, to what end? He wasn't someone famous. No one would care about what he'd said or done in the past. Any damage that a journalist could do to him had already been done. What he cared about most had already been taken away from him.

He crossed to the kitchen. Not feeling like cooking, he started pulling out the makings for a sandwich. When he lifted the loaf of bread, he disturbed a folded piece of paper underneath. He stared at it for a moment though he knew who'd left it there for him to find. And the fact that Maya had hidden it instead of leaving it out in the open meant she'd wanted him to find it after she left.

Gavin placed his hand on the paper, considering throwing it in the stove without reading it. What purpose would it serve?

Still, he couldn't resist opening the paper.

Gavin,
I don't really know where to start other than to say again that I'm sorry. I shouldn't have invaded your privacy the way I did. I let a weak moment of curiosity get the better of me, and I understand why that upset you after you had been so kind to me despite my intrusion into your life and home. It was not a way to pay you back for saving my life. I don't think I'll ever be able to pay off that debt. I know that I'll likely never hear from you again, and that's understandable. But if you ever need anything, you only have to ask. I owe you that. I wish you all the best, and remember that you deserve happiness.
Maya

He reread the last few words—*you deserve happiness.* They didn't make sense. He'd been angry at her, was kicking her out of his house, and yet she had taken the time to write that to him. He stared at the paper, trying to unearth the hidden agenda. But the longer he stared at it, the more his brain told him that the words were genuine.

That still didn't change anything. They'd gone their separate ways, and there was no reason for them to interact in the future. But even knowing that, he couldn't seem to erase her from his thoughts.

Frustrated, he slapped together the sandwich and ate it while staring out the window at the waning daylight. He wondered when memories of Maya would fade. After all, they'd not had a relationship like he and Rinna had. But she was every bit as beautiful as Rinna, more so because of her personality. If Rinna had never entered his life and he'd met Maya instead, he might have asked her out. He wouldn't have had the baggage of hating her career choice. He wouldn't have so little to offer.

He sighed, wondering if he would always feel the same sense of emptiness that seemed to be a permanent part of him now. A void that for a brief time Maya had begun to make him think he could at least partially refill. Now that she was safely away from him, he finally admitted that a part of him had actually liked having her around—the part of him that remembered when he'd been more outgoing, had smiled more, had laughed. The part that Rinna and her family had damaged so much.

LIFE WAS BACK to normal. And normal meant Maya had spent the past week on the go from the time she woke up until she fell into bed at night. She and Janie covered their normal array of stories plus some spawned by the recent winter storms. She managed to wedge in necessities such as canceling the credit card she'd lost and ordering a new one, arranging for the recovery of Blueberry at the earliest available opportunity, and a quick trip out to Sunny's ranch for dinner.

It seemed Lily and Liam had grown exponentially in the short time since she'd last seen them. It made her wonder how much her aunts' grandchildren had grown since she'd been over to Wind River to visit family.

That was another thing she'd had to do, promise to visit the moment she had transportation again. Her mother had threatened to bring the whole family to Maya's house if she didn't, and she was certain not all of them would fit inside.

As she got off the paper's phone after talking with Angie about the total number of traffic accidents caused by the storms, her cell rang.

"Hey, Maya," Theo Kent said. "We can try to get your car now, but I need you to go with me to show me where to find it."

Since she didn't have any more appointments scheduled for that afternoon, she agreed to meet Theo in front of the office in five minutes. It only took about three before the tow truck sporting the faded text Theo's Towing and Repair pulled off the road outside.

"Do you think enough of the snow has melted to get to my car?"

"Depends on where it's at, but I'm a bit of a miracle worker at towing." Theo gave her a big grin that made her laugh.

As they ascended the mountain road a few minutes later, however, she didn't feel much like laughing. She'd done her best not to think about Gavin, but it hadn't worked very well. It annoyed her, frankly, that someone she'd spent so little time with had affected her so much.

She was used to living alone as well, with only Blossom for company, and yet she'd found her house too quiet. It was as if it'd always been that way but she'd never noticed, hadn't minded. What was she supposed to do with the fact that she found herself missing someone who was glad to see the last of her?

Maya shook her head, trying to get rid of the nonsensical thoughts. She hadn't known Gavin long enough, didn't know him well enough to miss him. So why was her brain telling her that she did?

"Something wrong?" Theo asked.

"No, nothing."

But it was definitely something because her heart beat

faster as they passed Gavin's driveway. Carrie Mason, the mail carrier for this route, was stopped at the end of his driveway, depositing that day's collection of mail. Maya deliberately shifted her focus to the road ahead so that she didn't miss where her car had slid into the trees. She hoped she could remember the right spot.

It didn't take long for them to approach a familiar-looking curve.

"Slow down." She looked down the slope on her right until she spotted a streak of cobalt blue against the white surroundings. A lot of the snow had melted in the valley, but at this elevation and in the shade a good bit of it remained. Still, enough had disappeared that her car was visible. "There it is."

"You sure are giving me a challenge today," Theo said as he eyed the curve ahead and how close it was to where he'd be working.

"I'll walk up above the curve and make sure anyone coming the opposite way eases around," she said.

"Thanks. That'll be safer."

With an orange flag in hand, she walked up the road a couple of minutes later as Theo maneuvered his truck into position.

"Be careful," she called back before she rounded the curve.

Theo waved and called back, "Always am!"

Maya didn't relish standing out in the cold, doubted she'd ever enjoy cold weather again after her near-death experience, but she also wanted her car back in hopefully a fixable form. So she danced from one foot to the other to keep warm, even did a few jumping jacks since there were no vehicles within sight.

She wished she could see how things were going with her car, but she needed to stay where she was to ensure

Theo's safety. She didn't want anyone rounding the corner, seeing the tow truck in the middle of the road and sliding off the edge in the same spot she had.

The sound of an approaching vehicle from the other direction caught her attention, but it never appeared around the corner. Maybe it was someone who knew Theo and had stopped to see if they could help out.

A few moments later, she made use of her flag for the first time, slowing down a shiny black SUV, the driver of which she didn't recognize. Must be another owner of a vacation home, which reminded her that she should try again to get in touch with Benjamin St. Michaels. She'd honestly forgotten about the man in the flurry of work she'd been tackling since her return to the office. But she should at least call and leave a message about why she'd not been reachable by cell in case he had tried to contact her. A little part of her wanted to send him her towing and repair bill.

She began to pace to stay warm, mentally going through her to-do list. When she turned to head the other direction, her feet and brain stopped functioning. Gavin stood facing her, and she wondered why until she noticed her purse in his hands. How had he found it? Had it been somewhere in his yard the whole time, covered up with snow?

He started moving before she remembered how. In fact, she stood still until he reached her.

"I thought you'd want this back," he said.

"Oh yeah, thank you," she said as she accepted the bag from him.

"I didn't look through it, but I assumed no one else's purse would be in the woods at the end of my property."

"I didn't think you had. Looked through it, that is." She lowered her head, embarrassed all over again about how they'd parted. She had no trouble digging for information when the situation warranted it, but his private life hadn't.

"If you're about to apologize again, don't."

Her heart sank because he had to have found the note by now, and evidently it hadn't helped.

Well, at least she had her belongings back, and if things went how she hoped, Blueberry would be fixed soon. She supposed that was about all she could expect.

Gavin turned so that he stood facing the opposite side of the road. Man did he have a great profile.

"I read the note you left." He paused for a moment, and she realized she was holding her breath. "Thank you."

She didn't know if he meant for leaving it at all, for what it had said, or if he only referred to one part of what she'd written, but she didn't ask. For someone who communicated for a living, presently she was without not only appropriate words but any words at all.

Gavin turned his head at the change in sound from around the corner.

"Sounds as if he's winching your car up now." He glanced back at her for a moment before looking straight ahead again. "You were lucky you weren't really hurt. Your car slid in between a lot of trees before it finally hit one."

"All things considered, I had a lot of luck on my side that day."

He only acknowledged her words with a single nod, but he had to know that she included his carrying her into his home as part of that luck. Despite the cold air, her face warmed at the thought of him carrying her in his arms. It was a strange thought as she'd been unconscious and frozen at the time. She wondered what it would feel like if she were aware.

"Good luck with your car." With that, Gavin turned and started walking back down the road.

Maya started to lift her hand in some subconscious effort to bring him back. For what reason, she didn't quite understand. All she knew was that there was an ache in her chest as he left. It didn't matter that the ache made no sense. It was there nonetheless.

He either managed to turn around in the middle of the road or backed the whole way to his driveway to avoid driving past her. That knowledge caused a pang of sadness.

Maya was still hugging her purse to her chest long after Gavin disappeared and Theo drove around the corner with poor dented Blueberry loaded up. She hurried around to the passenger side of his truck and got in quickly.

"I take it that was the guy you were staying with," Theo said, a teasing grin on his face.

Oh no, she had to nip this in the bud before the story got out of control.

"He was kind enough to give me shelter until the road was clear and I could get back home." She looked back at her car. "I would have rather not wrecked at all than have to impose on his hospitality." She made the entire thing sound as uninteresting and decidedly unromantic as possible.

"Seemed like a decent guy." Theo nodded at her purse.

"Yeah. I lost this that day while wandering through the snow, trying to find a place to get out of the storm. He found it once some of the snow melted."

"Lucky."

Maya made a sound of agreement then focused her gaze out her window as Theo climbed up the mountain in search of a good place to turn around. If only it was as easy to turn time around so that she didn't even try to meet with St. Michaels that day. If she hadn't been trying to race a winter storm, she wouldn't have had an accident, wouldn't have almost frozen to death, wouldn't have invaded the private world Gavin had built for himself.

And she wouldn't be wondering if she might have started falling for Gavin a little without realizing it was happening.

GAVIN THOUGHT PERHAPS he'd lost his mind. Instead of simply putting Maya's purse in the tow truck as the driver had indicated he could, he'd instead taken it to Maya. After escorting her out of his home at the first available opportunity, why wasn't he continuing on the path of avoidance? Why in the world had he wanted to see her?

When he'd spotted her pacing against the cold, he'd wanted to usher her back to his truck so she could get warm. He'd had the very protective thought that he didn't want her to ever be cold again. Almost dying of hypothermia filled her lifetime quota of being cold, in his opinion.

He'd had to walk away before he said something that would invite her back into this life. He didn't want to cave to a weak moment, to what-ifs, and make even more mistakes.

When he reached the house, he didn't go in. Instead, he sank onto the edge of the porch at the top of the steps. He stared out across his property, trying to identify exactly what he was feeling and why. Was it frustration that he'd let a few days in the presence of a pretty, cheerful woman tempt him to try living again when he knew all too well how that had turned out before? Or was it that he'd tried to convince himself that he was fine with being alone, away from any regular human interaction, but he wasn't? Would he feel this same way if any other woman had collapsed in his front yard, leading to the same progression of events?

Had he been so angry at Maya for looking at his paintings because she'd uncovered something he'd hidden away or because it was her who'd found them? Again, would he have been as upset if someone else had discovered them?

He shook his head at his inability to answer any of the questions. Ironic that when he'd met Rinna and fallen fast, he'd thought he had all the answers without asking questions. Now all he seemed to have were questions with no answers.

CHAPTER TWELVE

"WHEW, ANOTHER ISSUE put to bed," Maya said as she leaned back in her office chair after sending off the latest issue of the *Valley Post* to the printer.

"I feel like a celebratory milkshake," Janie said from her own desk.

Maya laughed. "It's about twelve degrees outside, and you want ice cream."

Janie looked at her phone. "I'll have you know it's actually fifteen degrees."

"Oh, my bad. It's a veritable heat wave." At least with the blast of arctic cold, there wasn't any snow predicted.

The front door opened, sending a gust of frigid air through the office, making Maya shiver. An attractive, well-dressed woman holding the hand of a little boy stepped inside looking not the least bit happy. Whether that was because of the weather or because the boy was fussy, or for some other reason, Maya didn't know.

"Can we help you?"

The woman fixed her gaze on Maya. "I certainly hope so. Do you know Gavin Olsen?"

Hearing Gavin's name unexpectedly sent a jolt through Maya.

"Yes."

"Thank goodness. Where is his house?"

Maya stood and rounded the end of her desk. "Can I ask what this is about?"

The woman pointed at the little boy. "I'm here to give him his son."

His son? Was this woman his ex-wife? Maya had been in the woman's presence for all of thirty seconds, and already she couldn't imagine Gavin married to her.

"Uh, he lives several miles up the mountain on the other side of the valley."

The woman sighed. "You've got to be kidding me. He said he lived in Jade Valley, so I assumed his house was somewhere in this town."

The way she said "town" made her dislike of Jade Valley evident, as if it was beneath her. Maya knew nothing about Gavin's ex, but she pegged her as a snob. What had he seen in her? Had he become estranged from his parents over this person? Maya had so very many questions.

The boy fussed even louder.

"Can you be quiet for one minute? Good grief."

Maya was horrified by how the woman talked to her son. No wonder the kid wasn't happy. Even at his young age, he could probably tell his mother saw him as a nuisance. Without thinking, Maya stepped forward as if she might somehow rescue him.

To her complete surprise, when the boy saw her he reached out his arms for her to take him. And before she could fully register how odd that was for a kid to prefer a stranger to his own mother, the mother in question had basically shoved the boy at Maya.

"Here, maybe he'll be quiet if you hold him."

On instinct she picked him up, and he promptly put his head on her shoulder. Maya was liked by her aunts' grandkids and Sunny's niece and nephew, but this little boy's reaction was completely unexpected. She couldn't have been more shocked if the CEO of the biggest company in the country had walked through the front door and told her they were building a new headquarters in Jade Valley.

Maya reached up and patted the boy gently on the back.

"Listen," the woman said as if she was used to ordering people around and having them do her bidding, "since you know him and where he lives, and Max obviously likes you, can you drop him off for me?" The woman reached into a large designer bag and pulled out a legal-size envelope, then extended it to Maya. "Here are all the legal documents giving Gavin custody."

"What? Wait." Maya felt as if she was having a truly wacky dream. She looked at Janie, who looked every bit as stunned by what was happening as Maya felt. "Call Angie."

"Who's Angie? Does Gavin have a girlfriend?"

"Angie Lee is the local sheriff. I can't be responsible for a child being dumped at my place of business."

The woman made a face as if she was incredibly offended. "I assure you everything is perfectly legal. Goodness knows my legal team costs enough to make sure of that."

"Still—"

"I have a long way to go, and the sooner I leave the sooner I get back to some semblance of civilization." With that, Gavin's ex-wife spun and headed out the door.

Maya started to move to stop her. But what was she going to do, tackle the woman? She couldn't exactly do that while holding a child who had begun to sniffle as if fully understanding that his mother didn't want him anymore.

"Angie will be here in a minute," Janie said as she hung up the phone. "She's just down the street."

Since the boy's mother had to take the time to remove several suitcases and the car seat and place them in front of the building, Angie had time to intercept her. The woman looked as if she might be the type to report Angie to the higher-ups for questioning her, but the joke would be on her. The mayor wouldn't like her superior attitude any more than Angie would. She'd picked the wrong place to try that attitude.

While Angie carefully read through legal documents, Gavin's ex, who Maya had now ascertained was named Rinna, called a member of her expensive legal team. She evidently heard something she didn't like from them as well and gave the person an earful.

Wanting to protect the innocent child from as much as she could, Maya carried him into the tiny kitchen and checked out what food they had on hand that would be appropriate for a kid his age. She turned back around.

"Is he allergic to any foods?"

Rinna gave her an exasperated look. "No."

Maya's jaw clenched against the not-nice comeback that begged to be set free. Instead, she walked farther into the kitchen and eyed the bowl of fruit on the counter.

"Hey, Max, do you like bananas?"

He lifted his head, and his sad eyes broke her heart. But when he nodded slowly, she smiled and peeled the banana. As she broke off small sections and handed them to him, the tense conversation continued in the other room.

"Of course he wants him," Rinna said. "I don't think he fought for custody so hard for funsies."

Maya's heart hurt for Gavin. Now she was almost certain that phone call he'd received while she was staying with him had been from Rinna. And having witnessed the woman's attitude, it was no wonder Gavin had been in a foul mood afterward. This was why he'd basically gone into seclusion. He'd lost not only his wife but also his son. And after losing that battle, the victor now didn't even want the spoils of war.

Okay, terrible to think of a child that way, but sometimes ugly custody battles seemed to view them as such.

Although Maya was usually pretty happy and easygoing, when someone hurt a person she cared about she got really mad really fast. And even though she didn't have any sort of relationship with Gavin, at least not anymore, she did care about him. So it was all she could do not to walk out of the kitchen and give Rinna a hot, flaming piece of her mind. But she reminded herself that she did not, in fact, know the whole story, and she might do more harm than good by opening her mouth right now.

Instead, she did what she could to soothe and distract Max while Angie talked to Rinna and made a succession of phone calls, no doubt to other legal types and probably Gavin. Janie stayed out front to take care of any customers who came in. Maya hated that the newspaper office was likely going to be the center of the day's gossip around town. The fact that Max was evidently the child of the man Maya had been snowbound with for several days and now that man's ex-wife was visibly upset at Maya's place of work…that's what you called fodder for some monster gossip sessions over the tables at Trudy's and Alma's.

Maya felt a headache forming.

When Max finished the banana, she tossed the peel in the trash can and gave him a drink of water. She turned her head toward the doorway as Janie stepped inside the kitchen.

"How's it going out there?" Even though Maya could hear a lot of it, some wasn't clearly audible, especially Angie's phone conversations.

"That woman is a piece of work," Janie said, obviously referring to Rinna. "But it seems everything is legit."

"How could she get all of this settled without even telling Gavin?" Maya was pretty sure this hadn't been the topic of the phone conversation that had upset him so much.

Janie lifted her hand and rubbed her thumb and fingers together to indicate money. Rinna certainly had the look and attitude of the worst kind of rich people. Certain types could buy whatever they wanted, and the rules didn't seem to apply to them.

Again, she wondered how in the world Gavin had ever been married to that kind of person. Granted, she hadn't known him long nor super well, but she trusted her gut that it was not a good match. Obviously, since they'd gotten divorced.

Angie stepped into the doorway a few minutes later, rubbing her hand back over her black hair, which was pulled into a ponytail. She shook her head as if she couldn't believe what she'd just gone through. Which was saying a lot considering her job brought her into contact with all types of people.

"Is she gone?" Maya asked.

Angie nodded. "As weird as this all seems, it's legal."

"Well, she's certainly not winning Mother of the Year," Janie said, keeping her voice low so she didn't draw Max's attention to the fact he'd just been abandoned by his mom.

Thankfully, he now seemed content playing with a promotional plush bear toy given out at the fall festival a couple of years ago. Since then, Maya and Janie took turns dressing their kitchen guardian in seasonally appropriate outfits. The little guy still wore a birthday hat and a tiny T-shirt with a cake on it for Maya's birthday, which she had ended up not even spending at the office. Or at home, for that matter.

"I can't reach his dad," Angie said.

"He's probably outside working."

"Which begs the question how he's going to care for a small child alone while running a ranch."

Maya's heart lurched at the idea that child protective services might get involved.

"I'll make sure he has help."

Angie and Janie both stared at Maya, surprise on their faces.

"I didn't realize you were that close," Angie said, her expression and voice full of unasked questions, not all of them professional.

"I just think someone has been through enough, don't you?" Maya pointed at Max's back.

And so she found herself a few minutes later securing Max into his car seat in the back of Angie's sheriff's department SUV while Angie loaded the suitcases filled with Max's things. Maya noticed the luggage was not the cheap kind you bought at a discount store. Neither were the clothes that Max wore.

Thank goodness the kid wasn't old enough to be spoiled by brand names yet because Maya very much doubted that Gavin could afford them.

Glad she'd been able to finish that week's issue of the paper before Rinna had arrived, Maya tried to think of a plan to help Gavin as Angie drove them toward his house. She didn't know if he'd welcome her help or tell her he'd figure it out on his own. He'd have to hire a babysitter, and she could already imagine how uncomfortable he'd be bringing yet another stranger into his house.

Maybe it would be different if the person was hired by him instead of being foisted upon his hospitality, someone who didn't take up residence on his couch.

One thing was for sure—he couldn't take a preschooler with him as he worked with cattle, climbed atop barn roofs and such. Maybe Max would learn how to do those tasks from his dad one day, but he was still too young now.

As Angie turned into Gavin's driveway a few minutes later, Maya took a deep breath, attempting to bring a sudden attack of the nerves under control. This was not about her and Gavin. It was about the innocent little boy beside her and what was best for him and his father.

GAVIN MOVED THE blade of the chain saw, setting it against the log again. He'd felled the tree the day before, but he'd lost daylight before he could cut it into sections and then chop it up to add to his firewood pile.

Though spring was not far away by the calendar, it would still be plenty cold at this elevation for a good while. Movement out of the corner of his eye had him turning as he let go of the throttle.

Surprised to see a sheriff's department vehicle sitting in his driveway, he set the saw down and removed his safety glasses. A dark-haired woman got out of the driver's side and headed toward him. Maya had told him the local sheriff was a woman, and he suspected this might be her. But then he wondered why she was here. Had someone else gotten lost on the mountain and she was checking with the residents to determine if the person had been seen?

But when Maya exited the vehicle, his curiosity morphed into concern. His brain worked frantically to figure out what could possibly bring both of these women to his doorstep, at least one in her official capacity. Surely... He swallowed hard at the insane thought that entered his head. What if Maya had accused him of something? Theft of some item out of her purse or, worse, that he had made unwanted advances while she was a guest in his home.

That didn't seem like something she'd do, but how well did he really know her?

"Mr. Olsen, I'm Sheriff Lee."

"Is there something I can do for you, Sheriff?"

He glanced at Maya, but she was leaning into the opposite side of the SUV. It was hard to focus on what the sheriff was saying when his mind was screaming for an answer to what Maya was doing, why she was here with a police escort. When she stepped back, he couldn't believe his eyes. He was afraid to blink, afraid that if he did Max would disappear.

"I take it from the look on your face that you know the boy."

"It's—" He had to stop speaking to clear the sizable lump that had formed in his throat, and he blinked against tears. "My son, Max."

Maya stood still, holding Max where Gavin could see him, seeming to talk to Max while pointing at Gavin. Was she identifying him as Max's father? Had his son already forgotten who he was? That he even existed?

And why was Maya here at all?

"How?" It was the only word he seemed to be able to form.

As Sheriff Lee told him about what Rinna had done, he finally pulled his gaze away from his son. Even after everything Rinna and her family had put him through, what they'd taken from him, this felt surreal. And of all the places for Rinna to stop to find out where he lived and of all the people to leave Max with, it ended up being the newspaper office and Maya. He thought he might laugh if he wasn't so incredibly stunned by the turn his afternoon had taken.

"I checked all of the paperwork, made the necessary calls, and to my surprise all the t's seemed to be crossed and the i's dotted."

Gavin couldn't keep himself from his son any longer

and started walking toward Maya. Sheriff Lee didn't stop him, probably figuring that any further necessary discussion could wait. Whether it could or not, it was going to have to.

As he drew close to Maya and Max, however, his son hid his face in Maya's neck, clinging to her like a koala. Despite knowing that Max might have forgotten him, Gavin wasn't prepared for the intense pain caused by his son's reaction to him, especially when he seemed to prefer the comfort and protection of a stranger.

But he reminded himself, yet again, that he was a stranger to Max now too. If he had memories of Gavin, it might take a while for them to resurface. His body filled with anger that Rinna had not even considered this possibility. He wanted to scream at her, but he was honestly afraid to initiate any contact for fear she'd change her mind and take Max away from him again.

"I'm sorry."

Maya's soft words drew his gaze to hers. He wasn't sure if she was sorry about what Rinna had done, what had happened in the past or the fact that Max preferred to stay with her rather than go to his father, but it didn't matter. In that moment, he was just thankful she'd brought Max to him and that she was taking care with his scared son.

"Thank you."

Maya's eyes widened a bit in surprise as she rubbed Max's back to soothe him.

"Maybe you could get his stuff out of the car while I take him inside and get him some milk?"

Though Gavin wanted nothing more than to pull Max into his arms, to hold him tightly, he managed to nod. As he retrieved the luggage and large bag of toys, Sheriff Lee extricated the car seat then followed him inside.

Once everything was shoved into a corner of the living

room on the other side of the couch, he offered the sheriff a soda, which she accepted.

"Are you okay?" Sheriff Lee asked.

He watched as Maya helped Max drink a glass of milk.

"I still can't fully believe he's here. I feel as if I'm going to wake up from a dream any moment."

"I gathered during my checking on the validity of everything that you and your ex-wife did not part amicably."

"You could say that." He turned his attention to the woman. "How much detail do you need to keep from taking him?"

"Mr. Olsen, I have no right to take him unless I feel he's in danger. Considering the legality of all the paperwork and the fact that Maya vouched for you, I don't see any reason to question why Max shouldn't be with his father."

Maya had vouched for him? Even after how he'd treated her following the incident with the paintings? Had he been wrong about her? Jumped to conclusions based on past experience?

Remembering the question the sheriff had asked him, he sighed.

"I made a mistake marrying Rinna, getting involved with her at all, but I was blind to that fact for a long time. And by the time I realized it, we had Max. Let's just say that Rinna has spent her life always getting her way, no matter if she was in the right or the wrong, and when it came to custody she got her way again."

"I won't ask you for anything further," Sheriff Lee said. "The way you reacted when you saw him versus how your ex-wife treated him tells me enough to believe he is better off here with you."

"Thank you. I appreciate that."

Her radio crackled to life and she headed out to the porch to respond. That left Gavin alone with Maya, the woman he'd kicked out of his home, and his son, who was now playing with a toy train engine that Maya had evidently retrieved from the bag of toys.

Gavin simply stared at Max, marveling at how he'd grown since he last saw him, saddened by how much he'd missed. Maya looked up and caught him watching but didn't seem surprised. She motioned for him to come closer but carefully, as if he was approaching a skittish kitten.

He wanted to race to Max, but he had to hold that impulse in check. This reintroduction to his son had to be done right, even if Gavin wanted nothing more than to hold Max close so that no one could ever take him away again.

"Hey, Max," Maya said gently, as if she dealt with children every day. "Do you remember your daddy?"

Max looked up at her, but when he caught sight of Gavin again Max moved closer to Maya, sticking to her side.

When Maya met Gavin's eyes, she had an apologetic look on her face.

"It's okay," he said, though it wasn't true. He'd fantasized so many times about reuniting with Max, having his son's eyes light up and his little legs carry him toward Gavin with as much speed as he could muster. That the fantasy didn't become reality hurt, but at least Max was here. They'd take all the time Max needed.

How he was going to manage taking care of Max and his work as well, he didn't know. But he'd figure it out.

Out of Max's line of sight, Maya motioned for Gavin to sit on the floor. He did so, thinking that perhaps if he didn't tower over Max it would help the situation.

"Hi, Max," Gavin said with a smile. "I like your train."

Max didn't respond other than to keep staring at Gavin.

"Can you say thank you, Max?" Maya prompted.

Instead, Max turned and hid his face between Maya's side and the back of the couch. Maya reached up and smoothed her hand over his arm.

"Sweetie, there's nothing to be scared of. You might have forgotten him because you haven't seen him in a while, but this is your daddy and he loves you. This is his house. Isn't it nice and warm in here? What a nice place to play with your toys."

Gavin's heart swelled and his throat clogged with emotion. As he watched Maya try to bridge the gap between father and son, he knew without a doubt that she'd meant every single word in that letter she'd left for him. And he'd questioned if she'd had a hidden agenda.

The front door opened and Sheriff Lee stepped back inside then looked at Maya.

"I have to go on a call and can't take you back right now," she said.

Maya waved to indicate that it was okay.

"We're fine here. Go do your thing, and be careful."

"Nice to meet you, Mr. Olsen," the sheriff said.

"You too, and thank you."

"Just doing my duty." With that she hurried out to her SUV and left.

"I hope you don't mind me staying until I can arrange for someone to come pick me up."

"No hurry, or I can take you home." He thought about the last time he'd delivered her to her house and how cold he'd been toward her. "I'm sorry about before."

"How about we agree that we're done with the back-and-forth apologies?"

"If that's what you want."

"It is."

He nodded.

"So, how about a tour?" Maya said in a chipper voice directed at Max. Without waiting for an answer, she stood and placed Max on his feet despite how he seemed to want to stay glued to her side. She did allow him to hold her hand as she led him around the combined living area and kitchen, pointing out the chair "your daddy likes to sit in" and telling Max that he must stay away from the stove so he doesn't burn himself.

Max put out one of his hands toward the stove, but not to touch it. When he felt the heat, he jerked his attention to Maya with an amazed expression on his face.

"It's hot."

"Yes," Maya said, nodding. "It's why you should never touch it. Don't even get close. If you are playing, don't forget, okay?"

When Max nodded, Gavin's breath caught. By agreeing, did he understand that this was where he'd be staying now?

Gavin's hope continued to build as the tour continued, then as he made dinner and the three of them ate. Max still stuck close to Maya, eyeing Gavin warily, but at least he ate and didn't seem overly scared. Small steps, Gavin supposed.

After dinner, they moved to the living room and Gavin scanned through the channels until he found the channel with animated content. He'd seen it before but had always flipped past it without noting the channel number.

He felt as if luck might finally be with him because the program that was on he remembered as one of Max's favorites. Was it still? The answer to that question came quickly as Max scrambled off the couch and sat instead on the end of the coffee table nearest the TV so he could be closer to the little cartoon bears on the screen.

When Max laughed, it was the happiest sound Gavin had ever heard. He glanced at Maya, who was also smiling. She gave him a thumbs-up, but what he really wanted was to hug her, to thank her from the bottom of his heart for bringing his son back to him.

The day must have been a lot for Max because after the program was over he crawled back up onto the couch and laid his head on Maya's lap. She looked over at Gavin with that apologetic look again.

He smiled, trying to let her know it was okay. He wanted Max to be comfortable here, and if Maya helped to clear that particular path, then he was grateful to her. It didn't take long for Max to fall asleep.

"I should have taken you home before he fell asleep."

"It's fine. We can go later. He'll probably stay asleep the entire ride there and back." She smoothed Max's hair in the way a mother would do, and the action caused a strange tugging sensation in Gavin's chest.

"Why did you come here today?" he asked.

She nodded at Max. "He was very upset earlier when Rinna came into my office. For some reason he reached out to me, and I found myself wanting to give him some comfort. It felt as if his little heart was breaking, and…" She paused and took a deep breath. "Honestly, if I hadn't been trying to soothe him, I might have said or done something I shouldn't have."

"I'm sorry."

She smiled a little. "I believe we agreed to nix the apologies."

"You're right, but I feel I owe you one. I can't believe Rinna showed up where you work. What are the odds?"

"Well, considering there aren't too many options of places to stop in Jade Valley, the odds weren't that bad. They increased by virtue of the newspaper office being one of the first buildings you encounter when coming from that direction."

"I guess that makes sense." It still felt somehow cosmic that his ex had left their son with the woman who was tempting Gavin to open up, to maybe try really living again. Good thing Rinna didn't know that.

Maya grew quiet but he could guess the question uppermost in her mind—how he and Rinna had ever ended up married. Despite all Maya had done for him, he wasn't sure he was ready to share what an utter fool he'd been. Maybe someday he could have that conversation, but it wouldn't be tonight.

MAYA HAD HOPED that Max would warm up to Gavin as the hours passed, but it appeared that process was going to take longer than a single day. How did she know this? Because Max refused to let go of her as they all sat in Gavin's truck outside her house.

"Max, sweetie, it's going to be okay. Your dad will take good care of you." She glanced at Gavin, who sat with his head lowered in the driver's seat. She reached up from her spot in the back and gripped his shoulder in support. This had to be hard on him, having his own son forget him and cry at the thought of being left alone with him. But he seemed prepared to give Max the time and space he needed.

While that was admirable and showed he was a good father, it was going to have to be a delicate balance. Enough time and space to allow Max to gradually settle into his new living arrangements but not so much that the adjustment period dragged on too long. The sooner Max accepted his new life, the better for everyone.

But she also didn't want to further traumatize Max or send Gavin off with a wailing child. Who knew what Max had been through prior to his arrival that afternoon? For that matter, she didn't know the extent of what Gavin had experienced either. Her heart hurt thinking about how he had lost his son, what he must have endured leading up to that.

"Gavin?"

"Yeah?" He turned his head to look at her.

"How would you feel if I stayed at your place tonight? Help through the first night and while you go out to work tomorrow, and then help you arrange child care for after that?"

"You don't have to do any of that. You've done so much already."

"But I want to if you don't object to me being there. Maybe tomorrow I can talk to him more, make him understand. Everything is new today. Maybe after he's slept there, it will feel more normal. We can have you spend more time with him tomorrow, do something fun to show you aren't a threat."

Gavin finally agreed, looking more tired than she'd ever seen him in their short acquaintance.

"Let me feed my cat and grab a few things." Then she turned her attention to Max, who had quieted somewhat to sniffles. "Max, you see that house right there?" She pointed out the window at her home, and Max nodded. "That's my house. I'm going to go inside for a few minutes to get some things I need, and then I'll be back, okay?"

Max looked as if he might get upset again, and it was all she could do not to pull him from his car seat and into a comforting hug. Instead, she pointed at Gavin.

"I bet your dad can find some music on the radio for you to listen to until I'm back. Maybe if you're really good he'll even sing to you."

Gavin snorted. "No one wants to hear that."

Maya laughed, partly because it was funny and partly to show Max that Gavin was a good person, not someone he should fear.

"Can you be a good boy for your dad until I come back?" She resisted offering him a treat for good behavior. That could lead to a negative cycle of a child only being well-behaved if there was some sort of gift or sweet treat as a reward. Even if that might be the way Rinna had parented, even if Gavin might be tempted to do the same to win over his son, it was a bad precedent to set, especially when Max wasn't her child and she wouldn't be responsible for him long term.

There was hesitance in Max's eyes as he glanced at Gavin, but then he nodded. Hurray for small victories.

Maya hurried inside, where she first fed, watered and gave Blossom some love.

"Sorry, girl, I'm going to have to be gone overnight, but I'm sure you'll rule your queendom well while I'm gone." As if to assure Maya that she, indeed, would be fine alone, Blossom only accepted a few head scratches before she strolled away.

Hoping that Max was still okay outside, she quickly gathered some clothes, toiletries and her laptop. When she returned to the truck, she was glad to see that Max was still okay. His little feet were even bouncing along with the music coming from the radio.

"Ta-da! I'm back," she said as she climbed in beside him, though part of her wanted to sit up front with Gavin, maybe even hold his hand to help give him strength to get through this.

That's not the only reason you want to hold his hand.

In the privacy of her own mind, she could admit that. When she'd seen him earlier, watched the raw need to hold his son but the strength he displayed to give Max the time he needed to hopefully remember him, her heart had filled with a lot of different emotions. But one of those was affection. And definite attraction.

No, she couldn't think about that now. At the moment, the most important thing was helping to reestablish the father-son bond. She'd never imagined being in that type of position, but for whatever reason existed in Max's mind she was his current safety blanket. His father had saved Maya's life, and this was the way she could help to repay Gavin.

By the time they reached Gavin's house, Max was fast asleep.

"Why don't you carry him?" Maya wanted Gavin to be able to hold his son, even if the first time was when the boy wasn't aware.

"What if he wakes up?"

The question hurt her heart.

"Then you soothe him, show him that you care about him and are a safe place."

"How do you know all this? You seem like a mother."

She smiled. "Watching my own mom, aunts and cousins with their kids."

She'd never felt left out by not having children of her own, satisfied with her single life and career, but now she experienced a little twinge of…what was that? Maternal instinct? The first tick of the supposed biological clock?

Or was she just in her feels because a cute kid had been taken away from everything he knew and then thrust into a situation he didn't understand?

What she soon realized was that she'd not been prepared to see Gavin holding his son for the first time in more than a year. Though it was dark outside, she'd swear she saw the glimmer of tears in his eyes. Thankfully, Max continued to sleep, because Gavin might actually fall apart if his son woke up and became upset by being held by him.

Maya blinked several times, holding back her own unexpected tears. This was like when she saw those reunion photos of military families that had been apart a long time. They punched her in the emotions every time, and she couldn't help tearing up.

She grabbed her bags and followed Gavin into the house. When she stepped inside, he stood still in the middle of the living room.

"What's wrong?" She kept her voice soft so she didn't disturb Max's sleep.

"I know I should put him to bed, but I don't want to let go."

Maya placed her palm against his upper arm. "Just go in and stay with him. As you must remember, I know my way around."

He smiled at that. If the man only knew what power his smile held.

As Gavin disappeared into his room, Maya turned to stare at the couch.

"Hello, old friend." She chuffed out a small laugh, then tucked her bags away next to the suitcases holding Max's belongings.

After retrieving a glass of water, she opened up her laptop and worked some more on her small-town journalism series. She'd sent out a set of interview questions to other journalists she knew across the country—former college classmates and editors of weekly papers she'd met at a conference in Las Vegas a couple of years before. She was happy with how the first article was coming together.

Typically she was able to lose herself in her work, but she kept glancing toward Gavin's bedroom. He'd left the door open, but from her angle she couldn't see him or Max. If Gavin had closed the door, she would have assumed he'd curled up in the bed with his son and fallen asleep.

Probably twenty minutes went by before Gavin emerged but left the door halfway open. He moved into the living area and instead of sitting in his usual chair, he sank onto the opposite end of the couch from where she sat.

Maya set aside her laptop.

"Don't let me interrupt your work," he said.

Maya waved off his concern. "We sent this week's issue to the printer shortly before Rinna showed up, so I'm fine. How is Max? How are *you*?"

"He's still fast asleep, but I had a hard time pulling myself away. I'm still afraid I'm going to wake up to find this was all just a very realistic dream."

"It's real."

More like surreal, but he didn't need to hear that.

"Thank you for taking care of Max, especially after how I treated you."

"You had every right to be upset and to want your home back to yourself. I overstayed my welcome."

Gavin was shaking his head even before she quite finished speaking.

"No, I overreacted." He sighed. "Full disclosure, the paintings are mine. As in I painted them."

"Full disclosure, I know. But I didn't go digging myself, just so you know. Sunny did and found an article about a painter with your name at a Denver art show at a hotel."

"Ah yeah, I remember that day. I think I spent more on lunch than I made."

"What? How is that possible? Your paintings are great."

Gavin showed her a hint of a lopsided grin. "You don't have to say that."

"I'm not just saying that to be nice or supportive. I think they're beautiful."

"Too bad that was not a widespread opinion, especially after…" He trailed off, as if he didn't know whether he wanted to continue with what he'd been about to say.

"You don't have to reveal anything more." She said the words, even believed them, despite the fact that she was so curious her brain felt as if it was itching.

"But I feel this sort of combination of I want to and I need to." He looked toward her. "If you're willing to listen."

She nodded.

He shifted his focus to his lap, appearing to stare into the past.

"I don't know where to start for everything to make sense."

"The beginning is always good."

He seemed to think about that for a few moments before nodding. "That makes sense."

Still, he didn't immediately launch into any sort of "Once upon a time there was a boy who met a girl."

"When did you start painting?" she asked, helping him with a prompt.

"First painting was in high school, in art class. To be honest, I took the class for an easy A since the teacher was known to be a breeze. But I ended up liking it, and when I had time I kept painting. My parents didn't understand, so even when I started thinking I might want to do it for a living I didn't tell them, not for a long time. It was a hobby as far as they knew, one they said I had to fund with my own money."

Gavin picked at the edge of the couch arm for a moment before continuing.

"It's how I met Rinna. I went with a friend to Denver. Even though I was an adult, I was still living with my parents and working on the ranch. They thought we were going to a rodeo, and we did go to one, but I also went to an art show I'd seen people talking about online. I'd really had no exposure to that world in person, and I wanted to see whether it seemed like a good fit or if I felt horribly out of place and it would always be nothing more than a hobby."

"And Rinna was at the show?"

He nodded. "She was the most beautiful woman I'd ever seen in real life."

"She is indeed beautiful." Physically anyway. Her personality left a lot to be desired.

"She gave me no clue what she was really like then," he said, as if he'd read Maya's thoughts. "The combination of her looks and her telling me my paintings were great turned me into an idiot, and we eventually got married. Much to both sets of parents' displeasure, I might add. Mine knew what she was like the one and only time they met her, and hers let it be known that their daughter married way beneath her."

Gavin sighed and leaned his elbow against the armrest and his head against his palm.

"It's embarrassing to admit to all this."

"Love blinds people. You're not the only one and won't be the last."

"I'm supposed to take comfort in that, I gather."

"Yep," Maya said with a smile, trying to make this conversation easier for him by lightening the mood a tad.

He did smile, so mission at least partially accomplished.

"I guess all parents of daughters probably think the men who become their sons-in-law aren't up to their standards," she said.

"That was certainly true in my case. After all, I was a rancher and mediocre painter from small-town Wyoming."

"Sheridan's not that small."

"Compared to Denver it is, and not just as far as population goes. Rinna's family is wealthy, really wealthy. Ever heard of Zachary Communications?"

Gavin looked at her right as the stunned expression must have hit her face because he nodded as if acknowledging what she was thinking.

"Yeah, that's them."

"That's why you don't like reporters?" The Zachary family owned a media empire made up of newspapers, radio and television stations, and internet communications companies under their huge corporate umbrella. If media royalty was a thing, they would be the reigning monarchs, at least west of the Mississippi River.

"Not because they own newspapers, but what they did to me using all that ability to sway opinion. And though I can't prove it, I'm certain they paid off people to get the result they wanted when Rinna and I divorced—me completely out of her and Max's lives."

Maya turned more fully toward Gavin, pulling both of her legs up onto the couch and sitting crisscross.

"Explain what you mean by that." She winced inwardly at how she sounded a bit too much like a reporter in that moment.

But as he proceeded to tell her how an art show he'd lined up at a small gallery had fallen through at the last minute, how he'd had not one but two attorneys abandon him during the divorce and custody process, how a reporter had contacted him to supposedly do a piece on his artwork but it had really been a fishing expedition for information to use against him, Maya felt her anger building. Her hands formed fists as if she could punch those responsible for hurting Gavin and Max.

"I cannot prove any of that, but I know in my gut that Rinna's family was behind all of it. They did what they could to build a case against me getting custody of Max, not even partial, saying that I couldn't provide a financially stable environment that would afford him the opportunities that they could."

"Rinna agreed to all this? From what you're saying, you did nothing to warrant that treatment from her."

"I got her pregnant."

"What? She wasn't happy about having a child?"

"You could say that."

"Then why did she fight so hard to keep Max from you?"

"I never said she did, at least not at first. Rinna is spoiled. She's used to getting what she wants, and she said having a kid would cramp her lifestyle. But then when Max was born, she saw how cute he was and she went wild buying him little outfits and toys, taking pictures and posting them on baby social media places. I told her that I didn't want Max's face and identity splashed all over the internet for anyone to see, but she waved it off as me worrying for no reason."

"She treated him like an expensive doll she could show off to all her classmates who couldn't afford one."

Gavin fixed his gaze on Maya for a few moments before saying, "Exactly."

"Until she got tired of the new toy." How could a mother have so little love for the child she'd borne?

"When I dared to point out any of Rinna's faults as a mother, however, that just made her family more determined to be rid of me. And they made sure their money and influence made that happen. Literally no one was on my side. I didn't even feel like my attorney was, though he went through the motions."

"Gavin, I'm so sorry. Sorrier than I even know how to express." Maya glanced toward the bedroom before refocusing on Gavin. "How did she manage all the legal maneuverings to grant custody to you, then? It doesn't sound as if her parents are the type to change their minds or admit they were wrong about anything."

"I don't have any idea, and I honestly don't care as long as I have full custody now. They may have paid for everything to go her way before, but she was the only one granted custody. Not them."

"So she was the only one who could legally change that."

He nodded. "I guess they didn't count on her going against them at any future point."

"That's good news, then." And yet anxiety twisted inside her. She wondered if it did for Gavin as well.

Maya opened her mouth to ask one of the questions running through her mind, but then stopped herself.

"Go ahead," Gavin said.

"I don't want to be too intrusive." She was keenly aware now of why he disliked the media, and her career hadn't changed in the past hour.

"If I don't want to answer, I won't. But you can ask."

"Why did Rinna marry you?"

If her question was rude, he didn't act as if he thought so.

"Did she ever love me, you mean? She did a good job of convincing me she did, but then there was that whole love-making-me-blind thing. I think it was a combination of physical attraction and wanting to try out rebellion against her parents."

"Rebelling against people who give you everything you want doesn't make any sense at all."

"I can't disagree, but I've come to realize I don't understand a lot about how Rinna thinks."

Maya sighed and pulled one of the quilts off the back of the couch, balled it up in her lap, and only barely resisted punching it repeatedly. If she had known any of this when Rinna showed up at the newspaper office... No, it was better she'd not known, because she would have had a difficult time holding her tongue. By not knowing, she may have saved Gavin extra heartache.

Silence stretched between them as Maya let everything he'd told her soak in. She wondered if he was regretting opening up to her. He'd said more to her during this one conversation than during the entirety of their acquaintance prior to this. It was a good thing she was on the opposite end of the couch because the urge to hug him was strong.

"So, you gave up painting?"

He nodded. "Hard to put yourself in front of a canvas when no one wants your work and when your wife tells you that your paintings aren't very good."

"Count that among the things Rinna got dead wrong. I really liked the ones I saw."

"Maya—"

"I'm being completely truthful. I know different people are attracted to different kinds of art, but I think they're beautiful."

Just like the man who created them.

CHAPTER FOURTEEN

GAVIN COULD NOT believe what he was hearing, that some-one actually liked his paintings. The work he'd almost burned in his rage and brokenness. But in Maya's eyes was an honesty so fierce that it jarred every cell in his body.

"You mean that." It wasn't a question because he al-ready knew the answer. But he was still so stunned that he had to say it out loud.

"Don't act so surprised. I mean, I've seen some art that I think is hideous auctioned for crazy amounts of money. I like yours loads better. It's simple and yet really beauti-ful. The telescope makes perfect sense now."

"Yeah, I've always liked watching the stars. That was a benefit of growing up on a ranch, and living here. Wide-open sky without many lights."

"It's one thing my friend Sunny said she missed a lot when she lived in LA."

"Rinna didn't have any interest in astronomy."

"Yeah, well, Rinna's an idiot, and she doesn't know good things when they're right in front of her. Your paint-ings, Max," Maya said, starting to tick off items with her fingers. "You."

She didn't look at him when she said the last word. Was she embarrassed?

His heart fluttered, though not the same way it had with Rinna. That had been fast and all-consuming, but he had fought his attraction to Maya from the beginning. He knew that not all women were like Rinna, but he'd used the fear of making another mistake as a personal barricade against relationships. And though Maya was a journalist, she wasn't the type who would deliberately hurt people for a story or allow herself to be forced into doing so by higher-ups.

"You're…" He wanted to tell her she was awesome, but he still hesitated to say something so revealing. "Thank you. I appreciate you saying that."

Coward.

"Just telling the truth." She uncrossed her legs and spun so that she could stretch them out beneath the coffee table. "One more question."

"Shoot."

"Rinna was the one who called you when I was here before, wasn't she?"

The mere memory of that conversation caused his jaw to clench for a moment before he answered.

"Yes. I hadn't heard from her in months, and she called to ask what storybook Max was referring to that he wanted her to read to him. He was upset and crying, and she doesn't deal well with that. She knew I used to read it to him and called to find out the name." He leaned his head against the back of the couch. "After I told her, she still refused to let me talk to Max. She said it would just make him cry more, and if her parents found out she'd never hear the end of it."

"Yeah, I really, really don't like your ex."

Gavin actually laughed at that. "You're not the only one."

When Maya yawned, he realized how late it had gotten while they were talking. He couldn't remember the last time he'd talked so much. Even when he'd been married, before things had gone bad, he'd never had such a long conversation with his wife.

"We should get some sleep."

Maya nodded. "Good idea. It's been one wild day."

After taking a quick shower, he headed to his bedroom. He noted that Maya was already stretched out on the couch asleep. Before stepping into his room, he paused a moment to look at her. He'd felt more relaxed around her tonight than he had since they'd met. She was such a kind, caring and funny person that he didn't want to keep her at a distance anymore. Her willingness to help with Max, to listen as Gavin poured out the details of his past, made him acknowledge that he liked having her in his life.

What that meant exactly, he wasn't sure. But for the first time he thought perhaps he was willing to find out.

Gavin eased into his room and slipped into bed opposite Max. Though he was exhausted, he tried to keep his eyes open a while longer so he could watch Max sleep in the dim light shed by the night-light that had been left behind by the previous owner. He didn't want Max waking up to the type of darkness he wasn't used to in his bedroom back in Denver.

Though he knew Max was right in front of him, Gavin was afraid to go to sleep. That thought about this being a dream wouldn't leave him be, even with common sense telling him that dreams were never this long, detailed or realistic. Despite that, a part of him that had lost Max before was afraid he'd open his eyes in the morning and find that Max was no longer there. Had never been there.

No matter his fears, sleep started to claim him. As he finally surrendered, he mentally whispered a prayer that his son would still be with him when he woke again.

And that he could figure out exactly how he felt about Maya and what, if anything, he was going to do about it.

MAYA JOLTED AWAKE, much like she had the night something had hit the side of Gavin's house. But this time, there was no storm blanketing the world with white outside. It took her a few moments to discern that it was Max crying. She jumped to her feet and hurried to Gavin's door but then stopped. Max was not her son, and Gavin's room was his personal space. She couldn't continue to be the shoulder Max cried on. He had to get used to being with his dad again.

As she was about to turn around and return to the couch, the door opened and she gasped. Gavin startled too.

"I'm sorry," he said.

"Don't apologize." At the helpless look on Gavin's face, she took pity on him. "Do you want me to help?"

"Do you mind?"

"Of course not." She reached out and squeezed his upper arm, then stepped into the room when he moved out of her way.

Max sat in the middle of the bed, tears streaming down his face. Maya's heart hurt wondering how long it would take for father and son to be comfortable with each other again. Even if Rinna's parents had been the driving force between separating Gavin from Max, Rinna was ultimately at fault and was the root cause of this middle-of-the-night meltdown.

Maya didn't want her anger at the other woman to show on her face, so she approached Max with a bright smile.

"Hey, what's all this fuss about?"

Max tried to crawl into her lap as she sat on the edge of Gavin's bed, but she didn't let him. Instead, she faced him and held his hands with hers.

"Max, there is nothing to be scared of, okay?" She pointed at Gavin. "It's been a while since you saw him, but he's your daddy. He used to read stories to you, play with you, and he loves you a lot. He just had to be away for a while, working here to make a cool place for you to stay together. Did you know he has a horse named Jasper?"

Max wiped the tears off his cheeks and stared at her for a moment, then at Gavin, then at her again.

"Really?"

"Yes, really." She glanced at Gavin and smiled. "Why don't you tell him about Jasper?"

Gavin stayed where he was at first as he began to tell his son everything he could apparently think of about Jasper. As he drifted into talking about the cows, Gavin gradually moved closer. When he sat on the edge of the bed too, Max moved closer to Maya but didn't cling or cry. That was progress, especially when Max asked a couple of questions, like if he could see the cows.

"Sure, and as you get older I can teach you to ride Jasper. Someday you can have your own horse too."

Max's eyes went wide at that, and Maya would swear she could feel the happiness radiate off Gavin in waves.

It was nearly four in the morning by the time Max drifted back off to sleep again.

"I think that went pretty well, all things considered," Maya said softly as she stood and stretched. Her back had been aching for a while, but she'd dared not move for fear of breaking the tentative connection between Gavin and Max.

"I can't thank you enough." Gavin speaking in a soft voice sent tingles running from her scalp all the way down her arms and spine.

Yeah, time to vacate the man's bedroom even though his kid was sleeping only a couple of feet away.

"You better try to get some more sleep," she said. "Can't have you falling out of the saddle into cow patties tomorrow. Well, I guess technically today."

Good grief, was she babbling?

"Anyway, good night. Again."

Get out of the room, woman.

She obeyed her inner voice and eased out of the room, closing the door behind her. Needing some hydration, either to drink or possibly pour over her head, Maya made for the kitchen for a glass of water. Maybe she should stick her head in the freezer instead because she felt way warmer than the wood heating should cause.

When she finally did return to her familiar spot on the couch, she knew she wouldn't be sleeping anytime soon. Might as well get some work done. It wouldn't be the first time she'd worked in the wee hours when insomnia struck. Granted, this was the first time she'd done so because of a man, but there was a first time for everything.

By the time the sun rose, she was finished polishing her first article in the small-town journalism series. She was quite proud of it, if she did say so herself. Her plan was to let it sit for a while though, until she had finished at least two more articles. She didn't want there to be any lag in content once she started publishing them.

Her lack of sleep was making its presence known, and since she didn't hear any stirring from the bedroom she curled up on the couch to grab a few winks.

When she woke up again, the house was flooded with sunlight and the smell of bacon frying made her stomach growl. She rolled over and spotted Gavin in the kitchen. Her heart beat a bit faster at the sight of his broad back covered by a Henley shirt above loose track pants. It was so unlike what she usually saw him wearing, but she liked it. He looked somehow at ease in the outfit, and he perhaps deserved to be at ease more than anyone she knew.

While he was still unaware, she resisted offering to help him and allowed herself to watch him instead, the way he moved, obviously trying not to make any more noise than necessary. She smiled at his consideration and realized she was probably falling for him. She couldn't help but wonder what he would think if she admitted that out loud. Would he push her out of his life again? She wanted to think the answer to that question was no, but she wouldn't blame him if it was yes.

Before, she'd wondered if it had only been their forced proximity that had caused her to be attracted to him. But after time away from each other, time in which she thought about him every day no matter how busy she was, it had become obvious that the proximity had only been the catalyst and not the sole reason.

As if her thinking about him caused Gavin to become aware that she was awake, he half turned to look in her direction.

"Did I wake you up?"

"Maybe, but that's okay." She lifted herself to a sitting position and smoothed her sleep-mussed hair. "Need some help?"

"No, I'm good."

He looked good too. The hard angles of his face had eased, and only now did she realize why they'd been there before. He'd been carrying his loss not only in his heart but within his entire body.

She glanced at the clock and noticed it was after ten. Luckily, she'd remembered to text Janie to hold down the fort once again.

After she took a quick shower and changed, she returned to the kitchen to see Gavin had prepared what seemed like a feast complete with bacon, eggs and pancakes. He caught her eyeing the array of food.

"Max likes pancakes. I used to make them and he'd

gobble up the few bites I gave him. He'd end up a sticky mess, but grinning ear to ear."

She didn't have to be super intelligent to figure out that he wanted nothing more than to see his son happy again. And she wanted it for him, for both of them.

"I hope you don't mind that I didn't wake you up earlier," he said. "I thought you could use the rest."

She placed her hands on the back of one of the chairs at the kitchen table. "So could you."

"I slept."

"Not enough."

He smiled, causing that fluttery feeling in her chest again.

"I've lost sleep for way worse reasons."

"I suppose that's true."

She heard the sound of little feet about the same time Gavin looked beyond her and smiled.

"You hungry?" Gavin asked.

Maya turned to watch Max, to see how he would react to his father now that it was daylight and he'd slept. For several seconds, he just stared at them. Maya held in her laughter despite the fact that Max appeared as if his wee mind was buffering. Finally, he nodded.

"You still like pancakes?"

Max's eyes lit up for a moment before he said, "Nana says I can't eat them."

Even though she wasn't looking at him, Maya sensed Gavin going rigid.

"Well, it'll be our secret," he finally said, revealing none of the anger he had to be feeling.

Within a couple of minutes, they were all seated and digging in. It wasn't long before Max was indeed sticky though he was older than the last time Gavin fed him pancakes.

Maya laughed when Max picked up a napkin and it

stuck to his fingers. While Gavin freed his son from the napkin, Maya got up and went to wet a washcloth. When she returned to the table, she wiped the syrup off Max's mouth and hands.

"The pancakes are good, aren't they?" she asked him.

He grinned and nodded, then went back to eating. She smiled and patted his head. Max seemed like a different little boy than he'd been the day before, but she was still there as a buffer. She hoped he didn't melt down when he was alone with Gavin.

Maybe she could help prevent that.

She shifted her attention to Gavin, who she found looking at her as if he sensed she was about to address him. Even so, his eyes on her made her super aware of his attractiveness again. Oh, who was she kidding? She was always aware of it.

"So, um, I assume you need to do some work. Maybe when you're ready, someone could make a fun visit to the other building on the property?"

Good thing she had practice speaking in front of her cousins' kids in a way that kept them from knowing what she was talking about.

"Don't you need to go to work too?"

She pointed toward her laptop. "I came prepared this time."

"And bonus points for not passing out in the front yard."

Maya snorted a little laugh. "If you'd baked biscuits, I'd be tempted to throw one at you."

"Never waste a perfectly good biscuit."

As they cleaned up after breakfast, working together with an ease that belied how long they'd known each other or the status of their relationship, Maya couldn't help but notice how comfortable she felt. She needed to rein in those feelings before they went galloping too far ahead and right off a cliff.

"Thank you for helping out today," Gavin said, glancing over his shoulder to where Max was sitting at the table, now with a couple of toy cars instead of sticky pancakes. "I'll figure out something so that you can get back to your life. Again."

"If you don't think it's too much of me sticking my nose in your business, I think I can help out with arranging child care for you."

When he looked at her, he wore that expression she'd seen from him before, the one that said he couldn't understand why she was saying or doing the things she was.

"That's not your responsibility. You've already done so much."

"Remember how you said that I probably had a lot of connections in town? Well, that comes in handy for more than my work."

"If you know a good babysitter, I'd appreciate a name. But—"

"But nothing." She grabbed his arms and turned him toward the front door. "Go do what you need to, and let me work my magic."

It wasn't really magic, just years of getting to know people, caring about them, being friendly. Whatever you called it, in between playing with toy cars on the floor with Max, reading him a couple of the books that were in one of his suitcases and finding the cartoon channel for him, she made a flurry of phone calls and sent a good number of texts. By the time Gavin returned midafternoon, she couldn't wait to tell him what she'd mapped out for him.

As if he had forgotten who Gavin was during the hours he'd been absent, Max abandoned his toys and crawled up onto the couch next to Maya when his dad came in. The way Gavin's face fell caused Maya's heart to ache. They couldn't go backward.

"Hey, Max," she said. "Remember when your dad told you last night that you could meet his horse, Jasper, today?"

Max's eyes lit up as he looked at her. "Yeah."

She pointed at Gavin. "Why don't you ask him if you can go do that now?"

"Are you going?"

She glanced at Gavin over the top of Max's head before answering.

"Sure, we can all go."

After Max and she bundled up against the cold, Maya led Max to the barn, following Gavin down the path she'd shoveled. When they stepped inside the barn and approached Jasper's stall, Max's eyes went wide.

"Whoa," he said in amazement, drawing chuckles from both Maya and Gavin.

"Would you like to pet him?" Gavin asked.

Max nodded, but he hesitated when Gavin lowered himself and offered his arms to give Max a lift. A glance at Jasper, however, had the desire to pet a horse winning out over any lingering fear of this man he didn't remember.

When Gavin took Max into his arms and lifted him, Maya had to bite her lower lip and look away for a moment so she wouldn't cry. The look on Gavin's face, a mixture of heartbreak dispelled and the purest happiness she'd ever witnessed, was powerful. And though it was the wrong time to have such a thought, Gavin suddenly seemed a hundred times more attractive even though she would have sworn only a minute ago that wasn't possible.

In that moment she considered she might have made a mistake by including her mother in her child care plans for Gavin.

Gavin opening the gate to Jasper's stall drew her attention. First, he showed Max how to rub Jasper's forehead and between his ears. When Max giggled, Gavin's smile could have lit up the darkest point in outer space. She moved to the edge of the stall and let Jasper sniff her hand, then rubbed his forehead as Gavin lifted Max up and placed him gently on Jasper's back, never letting go of him.

It probably wasn't the first time an animal had served as a bridge between people, but watching it play out in front of her was like witnessing a flower blooming after a rain shower following a long drought. Jasper caused Max to open up, to ask every question his young mind could form. And Gavin answered them all, not seeming to tire of them. In fact, she'd never seen him look happier. That filled her heart with joy.

To her surprise, Max didn't fuss or protest when Gavin said it was time to go back to the house for the night.

"Can I see Jasper again tomorrow?"

"Sure. He likes you."

"I like him too." Max patted Jasper's head gently, the way Gavin had showed him.

It had to be one of the most precious things Maya had ever seen.

Throughout dinner and his bath afterward, Max was a little chatterbox. She could hear him clearly through the closed bathroom door. It was amazing how much progress Gavin had made with him, considering how afraid Max had been when he arrived. The fact that he didn't ask about his mother, however, worried Maya. Would he suddenly break down at some point and cry with missing her, or was it possible for a four-year-old to understand enough to know that he was now with the parent who wanted him more? Children sometimes had better instincts about people than adults did.

While Gavin put Max to bed Maya finished washing the dishes and turned out all the lights except the night-light that Gavin kept on in the kitchen. As she headed to the couch to stretch out, tired from a full day despite the later start, she noticed Gavin had quietly come out of his room. He stood with his head lowered and a hand covering his eyes. Thinking things had taken a negative turn with Max, she stepped up to him and placed her hand on his forearm.

"What's wrong?"

In the next moment, he pulled her into his arms for a firm, warm hug.

"What is it?"

"Thank you," he said next to her ear, causing a shiver to run down her back.

For a frozen moment, she didn't know how to react. But then she remembered that if he was any one of her other friends in a similar situation she would hug him back, so that's what she did.

"I'm glad things are working out."

"Thanks to you." He pulled away but didn't let her go.

Being face-to-face while still held in his arms made her heart thump harder and her skin feel as if it were buzzing. As he lifted a hand to her cheek, she'd swear time slowed. When he caressed her skin with his thumb, she found herself entranced, unable to look away from him.

Again moving at a pace that would allow her to protest and step away if she wanted, he looked at her lips and then began to lower his own toward them. She did not want to protest or move away. Instead, she sank into the kiss the moment his lips touched hers, feeling as if she'd been waiting for this moment half of her life.

She had the oddest thought that she felt as if she'd been floating in the ocean alone in a life raft for a very long time, so long that it had become her norm, something she didn't think about. But when Gavin had pulled her close, she'd just found land with flowers, fresh water, food and the most beautiful music she'd ever heard.

Gavin gradually ended the kiss and put a little distance between them though he didn't break contact. He still held her lower arms lightly.

"I should probably apologize," he said.

"Why?"

Her question seemed to surprise him.

"Because that's not why you came here."

She looked into his eyes for a moment before deciding to be more open and honest than she had been—not completely, just more.

"Do you hear me complaining?"

His lips tipped up slightly at the corners. "No."

She swallowed before admitting the next part. "I like you, Gavin."

"I like you too." He smiled. "Who would have thought that when I was being a jerk, huh?"

This time she was the one to lift her hand to his cheek. "You weren't a jerk. You've been hurt, and it's natural to build walls and lash out after that."

He took a deep breath then exhaled slowly. "This scares me."

"I know. But I'm not Rinna."

"Thank goodness. You more than proved that today alone." He slipped his hand down to hold hers. "You've proved it from the moment I met you, only I refused to see it at first."

"The past is the past. Live in the moment."

His smile took on a bit of a devilish look. "I think that's what I just did."

"And how is living in the moment?"

He closed the distance between them again. "I like it. I like it a lot."

So did she.

CHAPTER FIFTEEN

IT WAS A good thing Sunny showed up at Gavin's house bright and early the next morning, because Maya needed a buffer between her and Gavin. After they'd kissed the night before, it had felt a different kind of awkward being in his house. A good, tingly awkward, but awkward nonetheless.

Gavin looked at her as he was lifting his coat from where it hung next to the front door, the uppermost question in his mind obvious: *Who is pulling into my driveway?*

"That's my friend Sunny," she said. "Sorry, I didn't think she'd be here this early. I might have arranged a series of trusted babysitters for when I can't be here because of work. Basically my best friends and family for now."

He looked stunned, but thankfully in a good way.

"I hope you don't mind. I kind of took the ball and ran with it."

"You're amazing."

The compliment surprised Maya. It did not seem like the type of thing Gavin Olsen said, but then she had a feeling the real Gavin was only now beginning to emerge. The one she'd met and gotten to know had been only an outline of who he really was and not a full-color picture.

She smiled. "You might want to save the compliment, see if you still feel that way after you meet all the friends and family members."

With that she hurried outside to help Sunny with the

twins. They'd thought maybe having a couple of other kids around, albeit ones younger than Max, might help him relax more into his new environment.

"This is a nice place," Sunny said as she looked at the forest surrounding Gavin's house and barn. "So different from ours."

The Breckinridge family had started their ranch in the valley alongside the river, so the acreage was pretty flat in comparison to Gavin's property.

"His cattle are in the valley," Maya said, pointing toward the path Gavin took when he went to tend his herd.

When they stepped inside, Maya's heart jumped again at the sight of Gavin holding Max in his arms. He looked like the ultimate protector, a man who would literally fight a grizzly to keep it away from his family.

Maya made the introductions, including telling Max the twins' names.

"Babies," he said as he looked at Gavin.

"Yes. It seems like yesterday you were that small."

Max found that funny and laughed.

"They do grow fast. I feel as if I blinked and these two went from newborns to keeping me chasing after them. I think they sometimes strategize going in opposite directions to keep me on my toes," Sunny said.

After a few minutes of chitchat to get to know each other, Gavin thanked Sunny and excused himself so he could get to work. He paused, looking at Maya for a moment longer than he probably should have. She imagined he wanted to ask if she'd be there when he returned, but he refrained in front of Sunny. Smart move.

"Janie's coming to pick me up in a while. Duty calls."

"Okay. Thanks again, for everything."

Maya's skin warmed as she wondered if their kisses were included in that "everything."

Once he was out the door, Sunny wasted no time shooting Maya a smirk. "Well, *he's* definitely more attractive than the picture I saw led me to believe, and he wasn't exactly ugly in that. And what was that look I saw between you two?"

Maya didn't feel like pretending nothing had happened, and she was dying to talk to someone other than her own overexcited brain.

"Yes, he is. And yes, we kissed last night."

Sunny squealed so loudly that all three of the kids jumped where they sat together on the floor playing with an assortment of toys ranging from cars to dolls to a punch-the-shapes thing that was filled with lights and sounds.

"Ignore the loud lady," Maya said, and motioned for the kids to go back to playing.

The loud lady pushed Maya toward the couch. "You must tell me everything."

So for the next hour or so, that's what Maya did. She left out parts that were too personal on Gavin's end, but it felt good to have someone to talk to about her unexpected feelings.

"Were you attracted to him from the start?"

"I recognized he was attractive, but I wouldn't say I was attracted at first. He was so quiet and withdrawn that it was hard to get to know anything about him."

"Understandable if he went through a bad divorce." Sunny glanced at Max. "I cannot believe what she did."

"Yeah, good thing she wasn't standing next to the river when all this went down or I would have been tempted to push her in for a good soaking."

"Probably better that the newspaper editor not get arrested for trying to drown someone."

"I would have chosen a shallow spot."

Sunny snorted.

After a moment she asked, "You really like him, don't you?"

"I do, but if you tell my mother that I'll disown you. She'll be here grilling him so much Angie will try to hire her as an investigator."

"You better not let her see the two of you together, then, or the cat is going to be way out of the bag."

That thought stayed with Maya the rest of the day as Janie came to pick her up, as she started work on the next week's issue of the paper, as she talked to her mom about what time she'd arrive at Maya's house later in the day. She was half-afraid her mom would be able to tell she'd kissed Gavin simply by listening to her voice. She managed to escape the call with her mom none the wiser. But how long would that last?

"DID YOU ENJOY playing with Lily and Liam?" Gavin asked Max as they ate dinner. Like Maya before her, Sunny had made herself at home in his kitchen and left behind a delicious lasagna and garlic bread.

Max nodded as he stuffed a bite of lasagna in his mouth, decorating the area around his lips in tomato sauce. Gavin couldn't help but laugh as he took a napkin and wiped Max's mouth. When Max grinned at him, Gavin wanted to thank Maya all over again for helping him reconnect with his son.

That thought brought back memories of how he'd thanked her the night before. He hadn't come out of his room meaning to kiss her, but he couldn't resist with her so close and his emotions so heightened. When she'd told him that she liked him—despite that incident with the paintings, despite knowing all that he'd been through and how it had changed him—he'd swear he had felt pieces of hard shell breaking and falling away from his heart. He liked her too, maybe more than liked. Even though he'd sworn never to put himself in a vulnerable position again, he realized he was already falling for her. It scared him but also filled him with an excitement he hadn't felt in a long time.

Gavin noticed Max staring at the front door, and he hoped things wouldn't backslide when he realized Maya wasn't coming back tonight. Maybe he should head that concern off before it was voiced.

"Maya will be back tomorrow, and she's bringing her mom to meet you."

If Gavin was being honest, he was nervous about meeting Maya's mother. He'd talked to the woman that one time on the phone, but facing her when she knew how many times her daughter had stayed overnight in his house was entirely different. He wondered if she would be able to tell by looking at him that he'd kissed her daughter, and more than once.

"Will she bring her cat?"

Gavin detoured away from his thoughts to answer Max's question.

"I think she'll probably leave her cat at home."

The sudden pouty bottom lip didn't bode well.

"Can we ask her?"

Gavin considered the question for a moment. "We can ask, but you can't get upset if she says no, okay?"

"Okay."

He hoped Max could keep his promise as he called Maya after dinner, trying not to think about how he'd used his son's request as an excuse to hear Maya's voice. He couldn't believe how quickly he'd gone from wanting her out of his house to never wanting her to leave.

"Hey, is everything okay?" Maya asked as soon as she answered her phone.

"Yeah. Max has a question for you."

Max stood next to Gavin, hopping up and down with his hand extended toward the phone. Gavin ruffled Max's hair, grateful to have things to laugh and smile about again.

The phone looked so big in Max's little hands as he brought it up to his ear. "Bring your kitty."

"Ask, Max. Don't tell."

"Oh," he said with a nod of understanding. "Can you bring your kitty?"

Max listened to whatever Maya said, and judging by the excited reaction he must have gotten the response he wanted. Max then proceeded to tell Maya about his day with Sunny and the twins. He was so animated in the telling that Gavin let him go on for several minutes.

"Okay, Max. Save some to tell Maya tomorrow."

Max didn't argue and after saying goodbye to Maya he handed the phone back to Gavin. This was the good-natured kid he remembered. Maybe both he and his son were recapturing who they used to be.

As Max traded conversation for playing with his toys, Gavin sank onto the couch and put the phone to his own ear.

"You still there?"

"Yeah."

"He's a bit chatty tonight."

"That's good though. It sounds as if things are going well."

As he watched Max chattering away, creating a conversation between his teddy bear and a plush dolphin, he said, "Yeah, the one-eighty has been surprising."

"Has he mentioned Rinna?"

"No. Why does that make me angry? Not at him, of course."

"Because the fact that he hasn't asked for his mother tells you that she wasn't being very motherly to him. He's in a better home now, I don't care what her family says about money and opportunities. Neither of us came from wealth, and we turned out just fine."

"Well, you did anyway."

"You did too. Listen, I want to ask you something, see what you think."

"Okay."

"I know the owner of the little art center here. What would you think about me asking if she'd like to do an exhibit for you? I know it's not a fancy gallery in Denver, but I think people would really like your paintings."

"I don't paint anymore, Maya."

"But you could."

"I have a ranch to run and a son to raise. I don't have time for it."

"Then you could just display the ones you already have."

A twinge of the old desire flickered deep inside him like an ember looking for the slightest bit of wind to flame to life, and here was Maya creating a breeze. Maybe it would be okay. Like she said, it was only a little local art center. There wouldn't be any nasty art critics, and she ran the local press so he felt certain he had no concerns there.

"You really think people would bother to go see them?"

"Can't know until you put them up, but I think so. If nothing else, *I* will go every day and appreciate them. The art center is handier than climbing into your barn loft."

Amazing that her finding those paintings had caused a rift between them, but now he found himself laughing a little at her comment.

"Well, I guess I have nothing to lose, then."

He felt very much as if he'd gained the world.

"WELL, YOU'RE CERTAINLY a good-looking young man," Maya's mom said the moment she met Gavin.

Maya hid her face in her hands, not the least bit surprised that her mother had tossed Maya's request to behave herself right out the window into the melting snow.
This meeting could have gone two ways—suspicious interrogation or matchmaking mama—and it appeared her
mom was going with the latter option.

"Thank you, ma'am. And I see where Maya gets her
looks."

"Oh, a smooth talker too. I'm not sure how I feel about
that, but since you think my daughter's pretty I guess I'll
have to let it go."

"Mom!"

When Gavin laughed, Maya pointed a finger at him.
"You are not helping the situation."

But man did that smile make him look better than any
dessert. She was going to have to be careful not to melt
right there in front of her way-too-observant mother.

Max came running into the room. He pulled up short
when he saw Maya's mom but then started forward again
the moment he spotted Maya. He barreled into her legs and
wrapped his arms around them, acting as if he hadn't seen
her in ages. She still didn't know exactly what had caused
Max to latch on to her, but her heart went soft every time
he showed his affection. Not in the same way as when his
father showed his, of course. The latter was more as if her
heart was going to beat right out of her body.

Her feelings for Gavin had felt very much like easing
down bunny slopes in the beginning. But now it was as if
she'd started tumbling head over heels down a black dia-
mond trail, the world going wonky around her as she tried
and failed to right herself.

"Did you bring your kitty?" Max asked, looking up
at her.

"Oh, so it's not me you wanted to see but Blossom," Maya said. "I see how it is."

"If it helps, he's now more interested in Jasper than his own father." There was no hurt in Gavin's voice or expression, but rather a happiness that glowed so brightly it almost seemed he wasn't the same man as the one who'd saved her from a wintry demise.

"Max," Gavin said, drawing his son's attention. "Say hello to Maya's mother, Mrs. Pine. She's going to be staying with you while I go to work."

"Hello. Do you have kitties too?"

Maya and her mom both laughed.

"I do," she said. "Two of them, and a dog."

Max responded with a sound of awe, as if Maya's mom had told him that she lived in the middle of a zoo.

"Sorry, he seems to have a one-track mind," Gavin said.

"No need to apologize. It's perfectly natural for little ones to be fascinated by animals."

Max was indeed fascinated by Blossom, and the feeling seemed to be mutual. As soon as Maya let her out of the carrier, her little black and white fluffball curled right up in Max's lap and started to purr.

"I think it's a love match," Maya said, then regretted it when she spotted the look on her mom's face. "Well, I have to get to work. Thanks for letting me use your car, Mom."

She'd just pulled into her parking space outside the newspaper office several minutes later when her phone dinged with a text.

You left so fast this morning you left scorch marks.

She laughed at Gavin's text and responded first with a GIF of the Road Runner cartoon character.

Her phone rang then and she stayed in the car to talk.

"What was up with the quick departure?" he asked.

"Don't tell me you didn't notice my mom was in match-making mode. And if you want to keep anything private, she is not the person to be around."

"Things like the fact we kissed?"

Despite the cold seeping into the car now that she'd turned off the engine, her body temperature rose a few degrees.

"Where are you right now?"

"Standing in my living room with your mom."

"What?"

Gavin laughed on the other end of the call. "Nice screech of panic."

Maya dropped her forehead against the steering wheel.

"I need to craft some excellent payback for the heart attack you gave me."

"I can think of a nice payment plan."

She lifted her head. "Seriously, who are you and what have you done with Gavin Olsen?"

"Nothing. You just found him again."

Maya thought about Gavin throughout the day at the oddest times. It was a startling feeling to be interviewing the pastor of the nondenominational church about the trip he'd taken to Jerusalem and have a memory of kissing Gavin pop into her head.

On her way back from the interview, she stopped by the art center to see Eileen Parker. As Maya had expected, the director was thrilled at the idea of having an exhibit to showcase a local artist.

"Do you need to see a sample before you say yes?"

Eileen shook her head. "I trust you, dear. If you say they're good, then they're good."

"Oh, they are."

When Eileen gave her a curious look that wasn't too

dissimilar to Maya's mom's, she made the excuse that she had to get back to the office and zipped out the door.

Was she projecting some sort of bright announcement board that said she'd kissed Gavin Olsen and liked it?

By the time she returned to Gavin's at the end of the day to pick up her mother, she'd mapped out in her head how to extricate her mom before there were any too-obvious looks between her and Gavin. But that was torpedoed the moment she stepped through the front door to find her mother placing a wide array of food on the table while she shooed Gavin out of his own kitchen.

"Mrs. Pine, I appreciate this, I really do, but don't you think this is a bit much for me and Max?"

She waved off his concern. "You can have leftovers. Besides, Maya and I can stay and help you eat a bit of it tonight."

"Mom—"

"Good idea," he said before Maya could voice anything that might change her mom's mind.

Maya met his gaze, and she saw pleading there. And it wasn't because he needed help eating what looked like a feast worthy of the holidays or a family reunion. He looked as if…he'd missed her.

She wasn't sure what to do with that knowledge or her own feelings. They were all so new to her, and she didn't know how to gauge if their mutual attraction was going somewhere or was a passing infatuation, one fueled by gratitude on Gavin's side.

Somehow they made it through dinner without her mom maneuvering Maya and Gavin into a marriage proposal, but that hadn't stopped her mom from sharing embarrassing childhood stories about Maya or telling Gavin he should bring Max to one of Maya's family gatherings.

"Are you trying to overwhelm the man? Our family is a lot to handle when we're all together," Maya said.

"What? We're delightful."

Gavin laughed. "I'm sure that's true."

Maya looked at Gavin. "Don't let her strong-arm you into anything you don't want to do. You are under no obligation."

"Well, he has to meet everyone at some point," her mom said. "Might as well do it all at once."

Maya stared at her mother, quite literally open-mouthed.

"Why are you looking at me as if you're in shock? It's obvious you two like each other."

"Mother!" Maya's complexion wasn't going to be able to hide how heated her face had to be in that moment.

To Maya's surprise, Gavin started laughing. She shifted her stunned gaze to him.

"You were right when you said she was observant," he said.

"I feel as if I'm about to prove that, yes, someone can indeed die of embarrassment."

"What's to be embarrassed about?" her mom asked. "You're two nice, attractive young people. And it's about time you had a life outside of work." She pointed at Maya as if there would be any doubt who she was addressing with her last comment.

When her mom got up to retrieve a cake she'd baked, Gavin reached over and squeezed Maya's hand. The way he was looking at her, all soft and caring, made her suddenly willing to endure any embarrassment if she could have him in her life.

After dinner, her mom tried to clear the table.

"Absolutely not," Gavin said. "You made a feast fit for a king. I will do the cleanup. You've had a long day. I hope you're staying at Maya's tonight instead of driving home."

Her mom reached over and patted Gavin on the forearm. "I am, and thank you for your concern. You're a good man." Then she ran her hand over Max's hair. "And you have a charming little boy here."

"I'll agree with the second half of that," he said.

"They're both true, so you might as well agree with all of it."

"Yes, ma'am."

When Maya started to retrieve Blossom to put her in the carrier, Max looked as if he might cry. Maya kneeled in front of him.

"What's that, Blossom?" She leaned close to Blossom's face as if the cat was speaking to her. "Oh, she says she had fun with you and looks forward to seeing you again. But it's time for her to sleep in her favorite spot on my ottoman while you have fun with your dad."

Remarkably, Max seemed to accept this as he petted Blossom's head one more time. Maya gave him a hug, and it warmed her heart how strongly he hugged her back.

Once the cat was in her carrier, Gavin reached past Maya and lifted it, brushing Maya's hand in the process.

"I'll take this out for you."

"Oh…uh, thanks."

Great way not to be obvious about how he affects you.

After Gavin put Blossom in the back seat of the car and secured the carrier, he turned to Maya and immediately kissed her. Her body grew so warm she forgot she was standing on what was left of the previous snowfall.

Winter? What winter?

"I've been wanting to do that all night," he said when he lifted his lips from hers.

"If we're not careful, our mouths will freeze together out here."

He chuckled, his warm breath brushing her face.

Did this mean they were officially a couple now? It certainly felt that way. She didn't want to see anyone else, and she was pretty sure he felt the same. She had the funniest image pop into her head of the two of them as gray-haired grandparents telling their grandkids about how they met.

She imagined Gavin saying, "Well, you see, your grandma was so struck by my handsomeness that she passed out in my front yard."

Maya laughed at the crazy progression of her thoughts. She was getting way ahead of herself.

"What's so funny?" Gavin asked.

She shook her head. "Nothing."

After another delightful kiss, they walked hand in hand back to the house, only breaking contact right before stepping inside.

Maya hadn't even reached the end of Gavin's driveway a few minutes later before her mom started laughing, only half-heartedly trying to hide it.

"Out with it." Might as well invite her mom to say whatever was on her mind instead of waiting for it to trickle out.

"You, my dear, are in love."

"Well, I think it's a bit premature to say that."

"I don't. You know I fell in love with your dad about thirty seconds after I first saw him."

"I'm not you."

"You're part of me. It's not out of the realm of possibility you might take after me in some ways, especially with a man that handsome and caring."

Gavin was, indeed, both of those things, even if the caring part had taken a while to fully reveal itself.

"I know you pride yourself on being an independent, hardworking career woman, and that's great. But that doesn't mean you can't also have a relationship that fills the other parts of your heart."

Long after her mother had fallen asleep in Maya's bedroom, Maya lay on her own couch thinking about her mom's words. Was she in love with Gavin? Could it really happen that quickly for her?

Yes and yes.

She might be a grown woman with a well-established career, but that didn't prevent her from feeling like a teen-age girl with a big ol' crush on the most handsome boy in class. Even more thrilling was that the handsome boy seemed to like her too.

CHAPTER SIXTEEN

GAVIN LOOKED AROUND at all the people filling Maya's parents' house, wondering how they had all fit inside the small home.

"Are you sure you want to do this?" Maya asked him. "We can still make a run for it."

He smiled at her, amazed again by how he'd grown used to her being there at his side.

"It's fine."

"Well, say the word at any point and we'll leave."

He reached over and quickly squeezed her hand.

"I saw that!"

Maya rolled her eyes. "I hear the geek."

Gavin looked toward the younger man approaching them, the college-age brother he'd heard a lot about.

Ethan Pine was taller than his older sister, but when he tried to ruffle her hair she put him in a headlock instead until he cried out for mercy. It was a funny and loving scene at the same time. Gavin wondered what that was like, having a sibling. Not only was he an only child, but so was Rinna. So was Max.

But maybe he won't always be.

Gavin mentally shook his head, needing to not get ahead of himself. But yes, he and Maya were a couple now though there had been no verbal "Do you want to be my girlfriend/boyfriend?" conversation. They'd simply fallen into the relationship. How natural it had felt to do so continued to surprise him, as did how happy he felt. It scared him sometimes because he'd been happy before and it had all come crashing down. He couldn't help feeling it would happen again, even though Maya wasn't like Rinna in any way.

No, he needed to stop borrowing trouble. Things were finally going well for him. He couldn't ask for anything more. He had his son back, a relationship with a woman who had chipped away at the barricade he'd built around his heart and his paintings were going to be in a solo exhibit. Sure, it wasn't a fancy, highly trafficked gallery in a big city, but even if only a handful of people saw and liked his paintings, that was enough.

Maybe he'd eventually carve out a little time to return to painting as a hobby. Anything was better than the canvases rotting away in his barn, a hidden reminder of the horrible experiences he'd gone through.

"This is my annoying little brother," Maya said when she finally relinquished her hold on Ethan.

"That much I figured out."

"Are you sure you want to date my sister?"

Gavin grinned at Maya. "Positive."

"What did you do to him?" Ethan asked Maya, as if she'd bewitched Gavin.

"Boy, do you want some more?" Maya raised her knuckles in Ethan's direction, eliciting a snicker from the young man.

Ethan lowered himself so that he was eye to eye with Max. "Hey, little man. Would you like to see some spaceships?"

"Yeah!"

"And they're off to a faraway galaxy," Maya said as they watched Ethan lead Max down the hallway.

Over the next several minutes, Gavin was introduced to a parade of relatives he hadn't already met in the rotation of babysitters Maya's family had recently sent his way. Every time he mentioned getting a permanent babysitter, Maya had informed him that her family might disown her. It did seem that her mom, aunts and cousins had adopted Max as one of their own. It was as if they'd adopted Gavin too, if he was being honest. It was a strange feeling after the strained relationships with his family and then Rinna's. Strange but wonderful.

"You must be the young man I keep hearing so much about."

Gavin shifted out of his thoughts to see a man who appeared to be in his mid-fifties.

"Dad, this is Gavin. I hope you behave better than Mom."

Mr. Pine smiled at his daughter. "Don't I always?"

The man extended his hand to Gavin, so he shook it. "Nice to meet you, sir."

"I saw some pictures of your place. Looked really nice."

"Thank you. I like it."

Sometime over the past few weeks, he'd gradually come to realize that his ranch was no longer a place to hide out from the world and the past. He was happy to discover that even in his darkest time, he'd picked well. It honestly felt more like home than any place he'd ever lived, but he thought that was in part because of the happiness that had been building there recently. Between Max gradually remembering a few things from when Gavin had lived with him before and Maya being a frequent visitor, his house had become a home.

He'd even had Maya pick her favorite of his paintings, and he'd hung it on the wall. He'd been afraid it would bring back bad memories, but the opposite ended up being true. It was as if he'd reclaimed something that had brought him joy before it had been tarnished by his life falling apart.

The sound of Max's laughter drew Gavin's attention.

"It appears Ethan has found an appreciative audience," Mr. Pine said.

"Boys and their toys," Maya said with feigned long-suffering.

A few minutes later, everyone started filling their plates from an array of food that made the feast Maya's mom had made at Gavin's house look like a snack.

"Here, you have to try the fry bread," Maya said, placing some on his already full plate. "Don't tell Mom, but Aunt Sylvie's fry bread is the best."

"Your brother will inherit everything," her mom called out from across the room, prompting laughter.

Gavin's heart filled to overflowing. This was what family was supposed to be like.

"Are you okay?" Maya asked him.

He nodded. "Thanks for bringing me and Max today."

"This crowd didn't leave me any choice."

"You didn't want to bring us?" A sliver of panic shot through him.

Maya looked up at him. "Of course I did." She placed her hand on his lower arm and gave him a reassuring squeeze. "Don't worry."

He knew her words and touch were meant to remind him that she was not Rinna and wouldn't hurt him the way his ex-wife had. And Maya's family was so different from Rinna's parents that it was almost as if they were from a different universe altogether.

As the meal progressed, it was not the quiet and dignified affair that he'd had to sit through at the Zachary home. It was loud and rowdy and he loved every minute of it.

"So, when are you two getting married?" Ethan asked, a mischievous grin on his face.

Before Maya could toss her brother into the nearest deep body of water, Gavin decided to have some fun.

"I don't know," he said, then looked at Maya. "Should we do it now?"

For a brief moment, Maya looked surprised but then evidently picked up on what he was doing and played along.

"Sure, that sounds good. Won't even have to send out invitations since everyone is already here. We'll have to wait until Sunny and Dean can drive over though or she'll never forgive me."

"We can do that. Will give us time to write our vows."

"You two are no fun," Ethan said.

"And you," Maya said, pointing at her brother, "are just as annoying as you were when you were ten."

Ethan grinned ear to ear as if he'd been paid the biggest compliment ever.

MAYA DIDN'T THINK her heart could feel any fuller. She'd been a bit nervous bringing Gavin and Max to her parents' anniversary party. That they both seemed to be having a good time made her happy.

She admitted to herself that part of her wanted to contact his parents, tell them what they were missing with their son and grandson, but that wasn't her place. Even if she realized she was already in love with Gavin, that she loved Max as if he was her own child, any reconciliation would have to be initiated by Gavin or his parents. She really hoped it happened at some point though, for all of their sakes.

"Why don't you two go for a walk?" her mom said to her after the meal was over. "The weather is finally nice enough you won't freeze or blow away."

"I can help with the cleanup," Maya said.

Her mom waved off her offer. "We have plenty of hands here for that and watching little Max. Take advantage of that."

Maya glanced toward where Gavin was chatting with her great-uncle Roy. It would be nice to do something alone together, even if it was a simple walk around the paths of her childhood. They'd not had any alone time since Max had arrived, not since they'd become a couple.

She leaned over and gave her mom a kiss on the cheek. "Thanks, Mom."

When Roy got distracted by something his son Cal said, she slipped her hand into Gavin's and led him out of the house, grabbing their coats along the way. He looked back at the house when it became obvious they weren't only stepping out onto the porch.

"Don't worry about Max. He has a houseful of my relatives to watch him and spoil him rotten."

It made her happy that after a moment's hesitation, he didn't seem worried about leaving Max in her family's care.

"Where are we going?"

"The grand tour," she said, waving her hand around dramatically.

Gavin smiled. "Sounds good."

She had another of those visions of the far future, of how she could be eighty years old with Gavin's smiles still making her heart flutter.

They passed by the school she'd graduated from, the little restaurant where she'd worked for a couple of years, the house where Mr. Eagle still lived. She told Gavin the story of when her car was stolen and placed in Mr. Eagle's yard.

"That car served me well despite its ugliness. It had

more than three hundred thousand miles on it before it went to the great junkyard in the sky."

"My dad has an old truck like that he uses around the ranch. He's had it since before I started school."

For a moment she considered whether she should take the conversational opening he'd given her. She decided to forge ahead, if carefully.

"Do your parents know you have Max now?"

He shook his head. "I've thought about calling them, but I want to enjoy my life as it is for a while longer."

The way he squeezed her hand and looked at her made it obvious that she was part of what he was enjoying. The feeling was definitely mutual.

Grinning, she veered onto a dead-end street, keeping a firm grip on Gavin's hand. At the end of the street, she led him through a stand of trees and down a slope toward a little creek. Because it was shaded, more snow still clung to the shadows.

"What are we doing here?" he asked.

"This, Mr. Olsen, is where all the kids come when they want to sneak kisses without the entire reservation seeing and spreading the news lightning fast."

Gavin lifted an eyebrow. "You brought me to a make-out spot?"

"That sounds so tawdry. Let's call it the smooching spot instead."

"Well, I guess we're obligated to help it live up to its new name."

"I think that's an excellent idea."

MAYA WALKED INTO the sheriff's department office a couple of days later, whistling.

"Someone sounds happy," Sadie, the secretary and dispatcher, said. "Gee, I wonder why."

Maya was almost certain all five hundred residents of Jade Valley knew about her and Gavin dating now. If Maya wasn't the editor of the newspaper, it would have probably already made headlines in at least one issue.

"What's not to be happy about? Life is good." She looked around. "Angie in her office? I need a quote about the wreck north of town this morning."

"No, she's in the conference room with some suits from Denver. Not sure what their business is."

Denver. Sudden concern knotted up inside Maya.

No, there could be any number of reasons for lawyers— she assumed they were lawyers—to have traveled to Jade Valley from Denver.

"I'll go wait for her."

But instead of seating herself in Angie's office, she paused outside the open door to the small conference room.

"You must agree that the child would be better off with his grandparents. They can give him a better life than he could ever get—"

"If you say 'in a place like this,' I'm afraid you're going to force me to not look too favorably upon you, Mr. Springer," Angie said.

Panic surged up in Maya like a volcano erupting. She had no doubt who "the child" or "his grandparents" were, and she couldn't let this happen. She stepped into the open doorway and made immediate eye contact with Angie. The look in her friend's eyes told her she was right.

"I'll be done here in a few minutes," Angie said.

But Maya didn't leave the room. Instead, she looked toward the two men who wore suits that looked expensive, the kind of expensive that was paid for by clients such as the Zachary family.

"This is about Max, isn't it?"

"And you are?" one of the men asked in that misogynistic way some well-off, self-confident men had. He might as well have said, "Why is this brown peasant talking to me?"

"I'm the editor of the local newspaper and a friend of Gavin Olsen's."

"Oh, you're the one Miss Zachary imposed upon to take care of the child."

"The child has a name, and she didn't impose upon me. I was glad to give comfort to Max, who'd obviously had none given to him in quite some time."

"Maya," Angie said in a warning tone.

Maya took a deep breath, trying to bring her anger under control. But she couldn't totally back down. No one had ever fought for Gavin, but she planned to. For him and for Max.

"Gavin is a great father, and Max is really happy. And, since you work with the law, you should understand what it means when a mother signs over full custody of her child and a judge approves it. You should also make sure your clients know that."

"You seem very invested in a family that isn't your own, Miss…"

Maya didn't give him the satisfaction of offering her surname. He could make the effort to find it out himself, which he no doubt would. She should probably shut up now.

"I'm sure Mr. Olsen is a fine person, but the opportunities… Max could be given by his grandparents far outweigh what his father could."

"Not everything a child needs can be bought with money, and there's not a person on this planet who could love and care for Max more than Gavin. And Max has already been tossed around enough. He's happy, he's thriving, he has a lot of people who care about him. That's enough."

She could tell the men didn't agree, and she suddenly

felt sorry for any children either of them might have. When they left a few minutes later, she was still fuming. Angie met her gaze.

"That was quite the speech you gave. If I hadn't been in uniform, I would have given you a standing ovation."

"Can they really take Max away from Gavin?" She didn't think he'd survive that.

"I want to say no, especially after what Rinna did, but people with that kind of money often get whatever they want."

Maya felt as if she might throw up.

"Why did they come see you instead of Gavin?"

"Probably because they wanted to plant the seed with local law enforcement that Gavin wasn't the right person to have custody. They wanted to play on the instinctual need to make sure children are protected. Little did they know that they were barking up the wrong tree and I don't like being manipulated or talked to as if I don't have a brain."

"Are they headed to Gavin's now?" Maya pulled her phone from her pocket, needing to warn him.

But Angie shook her head. "I doubt it. I might have stressed how people around here don't take kindly to others trespassing on their property or showing up at their front doors unannounced."

Of course, that's exactly how Maya had arrived in Gavin's life, but she wasn't going to bring that up at the moment.

"I could seriously kiss you right now," Maya said.

"I would prefer you didn't. Save those kisses for someone else."

No matter if the lawyers were heading back to Denver, she still needed to warn Gavin.

"Can you send Janie a quote about the wreck this morning? I need to go."

Thankful she'd gotten her car back a few days earlier, she hurried out to Blueberry and slid into the driver's seat. She didn't want to chance another accident so she didn't drive as fast as she wanted to on the way to Gavin's. When she arrived, it was her mom who greeted her. If Max got taken away, it would break her mom's heart too. Maya and Gavin might not be married, and Max might not be her son, but her mother already thought of him as her grandson. She'd not said so out loud, but Maya could tell.

The same way her mother could tell something was wrong the moment she saw Maya.

"What is it?"

"Maybe nothing, but maybe something." Before she could share the details, Gavin came into the house. He must have been nearby, possibly in the barn, when she arrived. Maya glanced at where Max was watching a cartoon that matched some of the toys he had. She motioned for her mom and Gavin to go toward the kitchen.

"I just came from the sheriff's office. There were a couple of lawyers there representing his grandparents," Maya said, with a nod back toward Max.

All the color drained from Gavin's face, and he gripped the back of one of the kitchen chairs so tightly that she half expected the wood to dissolve into dust. She reached out and placed her hand on his arm.

"We won't let you lose him again. You have a lot of people on your side this time," Maya said.

She told them everything she'd heard and the details of her conversation with Angie.

"If you'll excuse me," Gavin said, his tone an odd mixture of angry and distant, "I need to make a phone call."

Helplessness rushed over Maya as she watched Gavin walk toward his bedroom. When he closed the door, Maya sank onto one of the chairs. Her mom patted her hand.

"Don't worry. Like you said, he has a lot of people in his corner now."

Maya would do whatever she could to prevent Max being ripped away from Gavin again, for both of their sakes, but she couldn't deny a significant amount of worry. Would the entire state of Wyoming be enough to triumph over people with the kind of money, power and influence the Zacharys had if they truly decided to fight? She wondered if they cared about Max at all, or if they simply couldn't stand the thought of someone with their blood living the kind of life they considered inferior to their own.

Max abandoned the TV and walked over to the kitchen. He moved close to Maya, putting his hands on her leg.

"Was Daddy sleepy?"

Maya ran her hand gently over Max's hair. "No, sweetie. He had to make a phone call and didn't want to bother your cartoon watching."

"It's done."

"Do you want a snack?" Maya's mom asked Max.

Thankfully, Max was at the age where snacks were a good way to draw his attention away from other things. Maya wished it were that simple for her. Instead, she resisted the urge to pace, not wanting Max to pick up on the fact that something was wrong. He deserved to live in blissful ignorance of the disagreements between his relatives.

It seemed to take forever, but Gavin finally emerged from his room. Maya again had to restrain her instinctual response to jump up and hurry to his side, instead waiting for him to come to her. He sank onto the chair at the end of the table, looking as if he'd aged a decade since she'd arrived.

"What happened?" she asked gently.

He glanced toward where her mom and Max were fixing a tray of snacks, half of them healthy and half of them of the cookie variety.

"I talked to Rinna. She said her parents were furious with what she did, told her she still hadn't grown up. I can't disagree with that last part. In many ways, she's like a spoiled child."

"She still had the legal right to do what she did." A sudden horrible thought occurred to Maya. "They wouldn't go so far as to have her declared incompetent or something, get the ruling overturned?"

Gavin didn't immediately answer.

"I don't think so," he finally said. "They'd think that would reflect poorly on them."

Thank goodness for small favors, she supposed.

OVER THE NEXT few days, Gavin only did the work that was absolutely necessary for the safe running of the ranch. He couldn't stand to be parted from Max for too long, irrationally afraid that someone from Rinna's family would come snatch him away while Gavin wasn't at the house.

He'd consulted an attorney, a local one Maya had recommended. It seemed even a town as small as Jade Valley managed to have a couple of lawyers, one of whom specialized in family law. It had been Mr. Bancroft's advice to do everything he could to prove that Max had a stable, safe home environment. To that end, Gavin had installed a variety of safety measures including a gate around the stove, childproofing the lower cabinets, getting new bedroom furniture and fixing up the extra bedroom for Max. He also hired a regular babysitter instead of depending on the kindness of Maya and her family and friends.

Max had at first fretted that he didn't get to see his variety of adopted relatives, but after a couple of days his friendly nature won out and he and Mrs. Grimes were getting along. Gavin's attorney had approved of the new child-care situation, saying it looked better to have consistency and to be bringing a middle-aged, married woman into his home to care for Max instead of his girlfriend.

Gavin had been offended at first at the implication about Maya, but Mr. Bancroft had told him in no uncertain terms that if he wanted to ensure he kept Max he had to think like the other side. He had to eliminate any situation that could be used against him.

That thought had bored deep into his mind to the point that he'd distanced himself a bit from Maya. When she offered to come out to the ranch to help him with preparing for the art exhibit—the farthest thing from his mind at the moment—or just to see him and Max, more than once he'd declined. He hated the idea that he might be hurting her, but the voice in his head kept saying that the Zacharys might insinuate inappropriate things were going on under the same roof where Max was living. He couldn't take that chance. But he needed to find a way to tell Maya that in a way that wouldn't hurt her feelings. Did that way even exist? She'd done so much for him that he felt horrible even thinking about pushing her away, plus he'd miss her like crazy.

He was trying to stay positive, but it was difficult to silence the voice that told him he should have known he was too happy. That, at best, he would only get to keep one part of his life that brought him happiness. He couldn't have his son, his creative outlet and the woman he loved.

Gavin reined in Jasper on his way back toward the barn and looked up at the blue sky. Spring was around the corner even if the air was still crisp and cold.

And, yes, he could admit, if only to himself, that sometime in the past weeks he'd fallen in love again. It wasn't the fast-to-flame, banish-all-rational-thought kind he'd experienced in the early days with Rinna, but this felt more solid, more real, deeper. And here he was afraid he'd have to let it go, at least until he was certain it wouldn't contribute to having to suffer through another custody battle.

He closed his eyes, took a deep breath of the clean mountain air. It must not have dispelled enough of his agitation though because Jasper fidgeted, so Gavin urged the horse forward.

When he arrived back at the house, he noticed Maya's little blue car in the driveway and his heart sank. He really didn't want to have the necessary conversation, but he also wanted to be completely honest with her. And the sooner the better.

She'd taken over for Mrs. Grimes with Max, who was thankfully taking a nap when Gavin stepped inside the house. Maya's bright smile almost caused him to reconsider what he'd come to say.

His mood must have been visible on his face because Maya's smile faded away.

"What's wrong? Have you heard something?"

He walked straight to Maya and pulled her into his arms. His heart urged him to tell her he loved her, but that wouldn't be fair considering what he was about to ask of her.

Maya was the first to pull away.

"Tell me." She was a smart, observant woman, so it was no surprise that she knew he had something to say.

"I need to ask something of you that I don't want to ask."

"I think at this point you know you can ask me anything. I'll help however I can."

Needing to break contact to get through this, Gavin took a couple of steps back so that Maya's hands fell away from him. The momentary flash of panic and confusion in Maya's eyes almost derailed him.

"When I talked to my attorney, he said I needed to do everything I could to make sure it appeared to anyone looking that Max was living in a safe, happy, and...wholesome environment."

Maya nodded. "That's all true. We all understood why you hired Mrs. Grimes."

She didn't really. Well, only part of the reason.

"Yes, having a married older woman as his caretaker looks good to anyone who might question the moral environment."

Maya tilted her head ever so slightly, and he could almost see the gears turning to figure out what he was really saying. He couldn't stand this dragging out, so he plunged ahead.

"For now, I think we should hit pause on our relationship."

He watched as the confusion gave way to a hurt he hated to see. But then Maya, being the person she was, nodded.

"Because we're not married, you're concerned the Zacharys might turn our relationship into something it's not to convince a judge to give them custody."

Gavin seriously wanted to cry, but he forced himself to reply. "Yes. I know it's not fair—"

"Stop." Maya took his hands in hers. "I understand. I don't have to like it, I might even think it's going a bit overboard, but after what you've been through I do understand."

"Why are you so awesome?"

Maya released him and framed her face with her hands, as if she was a pretty flower in a pot, and smiled.

"Just born that way."

He wanted to kiss her so much, but that would only make things harder.

Her smile changed to one of sympathy, but she didn't touch him again. Instead, she grabbed her coat from the couch.

"I should get going."

She didn't say to let her know if he needed anything as she usually did before leaving, and that perhaps hurt more than anything. Not that she hadn't offered to help him— she'd already given him so much—but that she wasn't hesitating in fully pulling away.

CHAPTER SEVENTEEN

MAYA SAT ACROSS from Sunny at Alma's stuffing crinkle-cut French fries into her mouth. She preferred going to Trudy's, especially since she adored the older woman, but Trudy knew that as the editor of the paper Maya had to spread her business around. Also, Alma's fries were better, not that she would ever tell Trudy that.

She looked up to find Sunny staring at her.

"What?"

"You don't have to consume those at the speed of light."

"I'm hungry. And busy. Lots of work to do."

Granted, she was way ahead on material for future issues of the paper and had made a lot of progress on the follow-up articles about small-town journalism. She was probably going to run the first one the following week if something hugely newsworthy didn't require the space.

"Okay, I've lived in Jade Valley for a big chunk of my life, and I know there isn't enough news to keep you as busy as you've been the past week," Sunny said. "You are working to forget your pain."

"Pain? If you're talking about the situation with Gavin, I told you I understand where he's coming from."

"You can understand and still be hurt."

Sunny's direct hit on how Maya was feeling erased her appetite, and she dropped the fry she was holding into the ketchup on her plate.

The truth was she missed Gavin and Max a lot. And

while she really did understand why Gavin was distancing himself, she couldn't deny that a little part of her was angry at him for it too. She kept reminding herself that they'd made no promises to each other, hadn't even said the three simple but important words that would take their relationship to the next level.

She wasn't certain Gavin would ever be able to say those words again. She didn't doubt he cared about her, but that didn't mean he'd ever be able to commit to a long-term relationship. In a not-so-little corner of her heart, she was afraid that this time apart would become permanent, that away from her he'd remember why he'd chosen to be alone before. That the happiness of having his son back would be enough.

"You love him, don't you?"

"Yes." No sense denying it when Sunny knew her so well.

"And you haven't told him."

"It seemed too soon to take that step."

"I don't believe in timelines when it comes to confessing one's feelings, at least not anymore."

Maya knew that her friend was probably thinking about the mother she'd lost, the brother and sister-in-law who'd died too soon, leaving Sunny to raise their children.

"We're not guaranteed tomorrow," Sunny said, confirming Maya's guess.

"I know, but there's a lot more to consider here than if it was just Gavin and me and none of the other factors involved."

"That's true, but I don't want you to sacrifice your happiness either."

"It's temporary—we're just putting things on pause." At least she hoped so.

Feeling a little sorry for herself, she ordered a big slice

of banana cake. Caving to the allure of dessert, Sunny ordered a slice of strawberry pie. While they waited for the infusion of calories and sugar to arrive, Maya's phone buzzed. She sighed when she saw the text was from Mr. Clarke, the owner of the paper.

"Oh joy. I wonder what he could be pestering me about today." No doubt it was of the same "Get the circulation numbers up" or "Sell more ads" variety.

But when she clicked on the message and started reading, her heart sank.

"What's wrong?"

Instead of answering, Maya kept reading. When she got to the last vital piece of information, not only did she lose her appetite for dessert she also thought she might be sick.

"Maya?" Sunny's voice was full of concern.

"The paper's been sold…" She looked up and met Sunny's gaze. "To Zachary Communications."

It took Sunny a moment to connect the dots.

"As in Rinna's family?"

Maya nodded.

"This does not feel like a coincidence."

The nauseated feeling in Maya's stomach intensified. "No, it doesn't."

Did her encounter with Rinna lead to this? Or was it those lawyers for the Zachary family she'd unloaded on? She pressed her hand to her stomach.

Please don't let this hurt Gavin and his custody of Max in any way.

"I need to go call and find out more," Maya said. "You take my cake, give it to Dean or your dad."

Though it was a short walk back to the newspaper office, she didn't wait to place the call to her boss. Well, former boss, it seemed. But he wasn't available or was simply avoiding her call.

Janie was on the phone, her own lunch in front of her, when Maya stepped inside the office. Maya wished she knew more before she had to break the news. When Janie got off the call, she looked up at Maya.

"Um, why are you staring at me like that? Do I have pasta sauce on my face or something?"

Instead of answering, Maya pulled up the message on her phone and handed it to Janie. She watched Janie read it and imagined the changes in her expressions mirrored what Maya had gone through a few minutes before.

"Did you know this was going to happen?"

Maya shook her head. "Not even a clue. I mean, they were pressuring me to get circulation and ad revenue up, but they've always done that."

"What does this mean?" Janie knew as well as Maya did that media consolidation often didn't bode well for journalistic freedom or even unbiased reporting. Or job retention.

Maya thought about how Gavin had looked at her when he found out she was a reporter and how he had gradually come to realize that she was honest and fair in her reporting.

She knew she couldn't abandon her beliefs and integrity simply to keep her job.

"I don't know, but I intend to find out."

While working on the layout for the next issue of the paper, Maya kept trying to reach her former boss. Evidently he wanted to be rid of her, because he finally sent a text that pointed her toward a contact at Zachary Communications. Maya wanted to reach through the phone and strangle the man.

Instead, she took a couple of deep breaths and called the number he'd given her. After being transferred to three different people, she was told that she would be receiving an official letter from the company shortly.

It seemed no one was willing to talk to her on the phone. Her thoughts went back to that day in the sheriff's department conference room. Had those suits gone back and told their bosses that she was difficult to deal with? That she wasn't the type to simply nod and comply?

A bad feeling settled in her middle, and late in the afternoon she found out why. The universe had been preparing her for a sucker punch.

When a registered letter arrived from the legal department at Zachary Communications, she and Janie looked at each other as if doom lay inside the envelope.

"This can't be good, can it?" Janie asked.

Maya didn't answer. Instead she ripped open the envelope, thinking that, based on the timing of its arrival, whatever message was inside had been in the works before the sale of the paper had been finalized. Would it be the same types of demands about circulation and ad revenue that she'd been working to address for a while? Or was she being replaced by someone from Zachary?

This letter is to inform you that Zachary Communications has taken ownership of the Valley Post newspaper operation, building, and all equipment, files, and property previously owned by Clarke Communications. Let this letter also serve as notice that the operation of said newspaper is to cease immediately. All personal belongings must be removed and any keys to the building left with local law enforcement by the end of the business day on March 15.

The next day.

For a few moments, Maya stared at the letter, rereading it, stunned. Then the significance of the day hit her. Her own, personal Ides of March.

GAVIN OPENED HIS mailbox to retrieve his mail, but the week's issue of the *Valley Post* he'd been expecting wasn't there. After he and Maya had started dating, he'd subscribed so he could read her articles.

How he missed her. He'd lost count of how many times he'd almost called or texted her, especially since he'd heard nothing more from Rinna's family. Of course, that made him nervous that they were planning to weaponize some other part of his life to get what they wanted.

When he returned to the house, Mrs. Grimes left for the day. He spent the evening feeding and playing with Max, then getting him into bed. He ended up reading him three stories before Max started drifting off. Even after Max fell asleep, Gavin couldn't pull himself away for several minutes. He sat and watched his son sleep.

He could not lose him again, and not just for his own sake. Based on how Rinna and her family acted, and a few things Max had said, he'd become convinced Max was better off with him. He firmly believed that most objective observers would think the same. Even if the Zacharys did love Max, Gavin thought they also didn't want to lose out to someone they considered lesser than them. What a toxic mindset to have. How could anyone be happy with those kinds of thoughts? Maybe they weren't. He hadn't been around them enough to know if they ever looked genuinely happy.

Finally leaving Max to rest, he left the room and retrieved the laptop that until recently had lived in a box in his closet. When he'd finally let Maya and other people into his life again, he'd started to reconnect with the world—setting up internet service, talking a bit more with people when he had to go into town, subscribing to the paper. Each day it had felt as if he was discarding another layer of his solitude. Even now, he'd not totally backslid.

No, you just pushed away one of the two most important people in your life.

Had he made a mistake? Would it actually look better for him to be in a committed relationship?

He shook his head, not wanting to think that way. Maya was not a vehicle to help him secure custody of his son. She had her own space in Gavin's heart. And despite her saying that she understood his actions, he couldn't help but worry that he'd let his fear of losing Max lead him to losing Maya instead.

Trying not to worry, he logged on and searched for the *Post*'s website. When the site loaded, however, he didn't see articles or an image of the front page of the latest issue. Instead, there was a "Notice to Our Readers" message.

Thank you to those who have faithfully read the Valley Post, whether you were a newer subscriber or your family has been getting your local news from us for decades. The most recent issue of the paper was its last. We are sorry for not giving you notice, but this sudden change came as a surprise to staff as well.

Gavin stared at the screen, not quite believing what he was reading. He knew Maya's boss was always pestering her, but she'd never indicated that the paper closing down was a possibility. He couldn't imagine how she was feeling.

He picked up his phone. He was done with pushing people away, especially the ones who cared about him. He'd done nothing wrong regarding Max, and he had to believe that if his son's custody ended up in court again he'd be able to prove he was the right parent to raise Max.

And if she would have him, would forgive him for letting his fear get in the way, he wanted Maya to be there beside him.

His concern grew when he couldn't reach her by calling or texting. Though it went against her personality, he imagined her sitting at home alone with her phone off, wondering how she was going to make a living in a town without many job opportunities.

His heart lurched at the thought that to keep pursuing her career, she would likely have to leave.

He wanted to hop in his truck and race to her house, but he couldn't. Max was asleep. And no matter how Gavin felt about Maya, his son would always come first. As much as it pained him to not be there for her, she was an adult capable of taking care of herself. Max was a child who could not.

Still, he had a difficult time quieting his mind and heart enough to sleep. And even after falling asleep, he didn't stay that way for long. His worry for Maya invaded his dreams. His rest was so fitful that he gave up and rose even earlier than normal. As soon as Mrs. Grimes arrived to watch Max, he informed her that he had to go to town and only barely kept himself from running to his truck.

When he reached Maya's house, her car wasn't there. Even so, he knocked a few times. Next he drove to the newspaper office in case she was there cleaning out her desk or something, but that was a bust as well.

Sitting outside the darkened building, he tried calling her again. When he still didn't reach her, he called Sunny.

"Are you searching for Maya?" she answered instead of saying hello.

"Yes, she's not answering calls or texts, and she's not at home. I know right now I don't have the right to be upset about any of that, but I heard about the paper and I'm worried about her."

"I'm glad to hear that."

"Huh?"

"It means I was right, that you feel about her the same way she feels about you."

The same way she feels about you.

"What did she say?"

"You need to hear that from her, not me. She's at her parents' house."

Thankful he knew the way and that he trusted Mrs. Grimes to take care of Max while he was gone, he headed immediately to the Wind River Reservation. All the way there, he had the hopefully irrational fear that she wouldn't be there either, that she would have disappeared to start her life anew somewhere else far away. So when he made the turn onto her parents' street and saw Blueberry sitting in their driveway, he breathed a huge sigh of relief.

She stepped out onto the porch before he could even cross the distance between his truck and the front door.

"Gavin, what are you doing here? Is something wrong?"

He bounded up the steps and pulled her into his arms, planting a kiss atop her head.

"Gavin?" she said against his chest.

"I'm sorry," he said, his throat thick with emotion. "For everything."

Maya pulled away enough to look up at him but not completely out of his arms.

"I guess you heard about the paper."

"Yeah. I can't believe they shut it down."

Maya did slip out of his arms then and sat on the edge of the porch, her feet on the middle step. She patted the porch next to her, and he sat too. Alarm bells were tolling in his head, but he didn't say anything. Instead, he waited while it seemed she was collecting her thoughts or figuring out how to say whatever she needed to.

"They actually sold out and the new owners immediately shut us down."

"What? That doesn't make sense. Why would someone buy a business only to close it?"

She turned her head to look at him. "It was Zachary Communications."

Maya might as well have punched him in the sternum. It took all of two seconds for him to figure out why they'd done it. It was to punish her for siding with him. White-hot anger rushed up in him like the water in one of Yellowstone's geysers, but in the next moment Maya placed her hand on his arm.

"Don't say or do anything. You keeping Max is more important."

Gavin took her hands in his. "Yes, Max is important, but so are you. I shouldn't have pushed you away. That wasn't fair."

"I underst—"

"Don't. I know you understand, that's the kind of person you are, but you shouldn't have to. They shouldn't be able to instill that kind of fear in me, and I refuse to let them do it anymore. Everything I've done shows I'm the more stable parent. I've done nothing to indicate Max would be better elsewhere, and that includes being with you. If anything, it should be beneficial because you're kind, well-respected—"

"Jobless."

"You weren't until they made it that way, which I am more than willing to point out to a judge if they dare to make your employment status a point in their favor." He looked out toward the small house across the street, at the multicolored whirligig blowing in the breeze. Listened to the wind chimes as he tried to calm himself at least a fraction.

He tried to think of what the best next step would be to ensure that everything turned out the way it should. Well, first things first.

Gavin shifted his gaze back to Maya, let his gaze roam the hair tucked behind her ear, her pretty dark eyes, the lips he'd kissed. She was a huge, important part of the new happiness in his life, and he'd missed her terribly since he'd pushed her away.

"Can you forgive me?"

She didn't even hesitate before giving him an understanding smile. It was amazing how well she could read him.

"There's nothing to forgive. I won't lie and say it didn't hurt, but life and feelings are rarely as black-and-white as lots of people like to think they are. We do the best we can in the moment and deal with the consequences, good or bad or somewhere in between, after the fact."

He framed her face with his hands and kissed her, not caring in the least who saw.

After the kiss, they remained sitting next to each other, hand in hand. He never wanted to let her go again.

"What are you going to do now?" he asked.

"I don't know yet. It's difficult to get a job in journalism now, especially in rural areas. I'll probably try freelancing."

"Why not start your own news site? Be your own boss. Sure, it wouldn't be the same as the paper, but I bet a lot of the locals would subscribe for a small amount. And you could publish things you never could before." He hesitated a moment, considering the wisdom of what he wanted to say next. But he'd determined he was through with living in fear of what might happen and under the shadow of the past. "I think you should publish the first article in the series you were writing, but include what just happened, the reality of the control the big media companies have over honest journalists trying to cover local news."

"Gavin, I don't want to do anything to endanger your custody of Max."

"That's what people like the Zacharys bank on, that everyone will cower and bend to their will because they're rich and powerful. But by selling the paper, they also freed you to say whatever you want. So say it. Contact every other editor you know to see if they'll run the piece too. At the same time, I'll prepare to hit back legally regarding custody. Sunny told me earlier that she knows a big-time attorney in LA who has done some high-profile custody cases and who owes her a favor. If it becomes necessary, she said he would absolutely help out my current attorney and wouldn't even flinch taking on the Zacharys."

"I sometimes think Sunny knows half of LA and half of those owe her a favor. She told me she wanted to send one of your paintings to a gallery owner friend of hers once your exhibit here is done."

"She's a good friend."

"She is indeed."

Maya waved as a couple of older ladies walked by.

"You two sure are a good-looking couple," one of them called out.

"Thanks! I think so too," Maya said, then surprised Gavin by stealing a quick kiss, much to the delight of their audience.

Much to his delight too.

CHAPTER EIGHTEEN

MAYA WATCHED AS Gavin talked with one Jade Valley resident after another. At first he'd seemed anxious and looked as if he might bolt at any moment, afraid that he'd be hurt again because of his creative passion. He'd looked a mixture of relieved and nervous when the first couple of people had entered, then increasingly stunned as more and more people filled the art center.

He'd seemed genuinely surprised that attendees were praising his work. At one point, he'd even glanced across the room at her as if to ask if she'd put them all up to it. Marveling at her ability to tell what he was thinking, she'd shaken her head and smiled at him.

After that, he'd relaxed more. She loved seeing his conversations becoming more animated as he chatted about a mixture of art and ranching. Maya realized that both jobs had strong ties to the natural world—earth and sky. And watching him like this was akin to witnessing the first buds of spring, a rebirth.

Her heart so full she wanted to stride across the gallery and tell him she loved him, she instead turned and passed through the doorway on the opposite side that led to a room that had been converted to a little hands-on art space for children. There she found Max with Sunny and the twins making what she thought were small animals out of modeling compound. Three other children, siblings

from another ranching family, were painting brightly colored pictures at another child-size table.

"How's it going out there?" Sunny asked.

Maya sat on one of the miniature chairs. "Pretty well.
He's loosened up and is chatting more now."

Sunny smiled. "So, when are you two going to admit
how you feel about each other?"

"We have."

Sunny's eyes widened.

"Not how you're thinking. We haven't literally said
those words yet, but..." She glanced at Max, who seemed
to be pouring all of the concentration in his little body
into creating an orange-and-green creature of some sort.

"I know why you're both hesitating, but if you love
someone you should tell them."

Behind Sunny's words was the always-present loss of
the three people she'd loved and who'd been taken too
soon. A shot of fear arrowed through Maya's middle. The
thought of losing Gavin the way Sunny had lost her mom,
brother and sister-in-law caused a pain in her heart that had
her pressing her palm against her chest. Ranching wasn't
a profession without dangers. Disease and car accidents
claimed lives every day, the lives of people who had family and friends who wished they could have one more day
to tell them how much they meant to them.

Sunny reached over and placed her hand on Maya's
shoulder.

"Don't wait to live life to the fullest. Don't hold back
words that need to be said for a better time."

When the last of the guests had left the gallery and Dean
had taken the twins out to secure them in their car seats,
Sunny accompanied Maya and Max to where Gavin was

talking with Eileen Parker, who was thrilled with how well the exhibit opening had gone.

When Gavin spotted them, he smiled at Maya in a way that filled her with joy. She was going to tell him tonight.

Sunny pointed at the painting behind him, one of those with a midnight blue background filled with little points of white light, the ones making up the Pleiades constellation the brightest.

"This is the one my friend in LA wants you to send him. I'll text you all the information tomorrow." Sunny gave Maya a meaningful look before she also headed for the exit.

Maya reached out and entwined her fingers with Gavin's.

"How do you feel?"

Gavin caressed Max's head with his free hand and scanned the gallery around them, seeming to soak in the fact that his paintings were, indeed, hanging on the walls of a gallery and that people liked them.

"Happy." He turned to face her. "Thanks to you."

He was lifting his hand to her face, causing her heart to start thumping harder, when the front door opened behind her. Gavin glanced in that direction, and the happiness drained from his face.

She quickly turned around to see Kevin Bancroft, Gavin's attorney, standing there. The man wasted no time approaching them.

"What's wrong?" Gavin asked at the same time his hand gripped hers a bit more tightly. She squeezed back to give him strength, to let him know again that she was there for him.

Kevin glanced at Max, who was leaning against Gavin's leg, obviously tired.

"The Zacharys would like to have a meeting. Their lead

attorney suggested in the afternoon two days from now at the company headquarters."

No, they couldn't have the home court advantage.

"They can come here." She hadn't meant to say it out loud, but her anger at Max's grandparents overrode her understanding that this was Gavin's decision, not hers.

"Maya's right. Let them bear the expense of the travel." He glanced down at Max, who was thankfully unaware of the content of the conversation. "His home is here, and I'm not taking him back to a place that I believe holds bad memories."

Poor Max had experienced a few nightmares after he arrived, but according to Gavin they had thankfully become less frequent.

Kevin nodded. "I'll make it happen."

"Thank you."

After they were alone again, Eileen having gone into the kids' room to clean up, Maya faced Gavin.

"Are you okay?" She hated that his wonderful evening, the recapturing of this part of his life, had been tarnished again by Rinna's parents.

"I will be when this is over."

MAYA SAT IN the waiting room of Kevin Bancroft's law office, Max on her lap. He'd finally fallen asleep after initial upset at seeing his grandparents. Max had clung to Gavin and then Maya, saying he didn't want to go. It would be the grossest of understatements to say it had been difficult to refrain from expressing her opinion when she saw the annoyance on the Zacharys' faces at their grandson's reaction.

She looked down at Max and was glad to see his face was free from worry now. How she wished she could say the same for her own. Gavin had been in the conference room with Kevin, the Zacharys and their attorney for more than an hour, this after Kevin had met with Max to ask him how he liked living with his dad and carefully inquired about his mother and grandparents. Maya did not believe any of them had ever abused Max, but she didn't think they'd given him much in the way of warmth and affection either. Even if they did actually care for him, they hadn't done a good job of showing it.

Maya had wondered, still did, about the wisdom of her being there, especially since during the two-week delay for the Zacharys to arrive in Jade Valley her article had been published and had gained more attention than she'd ever imagined.

Small media outlets across the country—at least ones not owned by Zachary Communications—had shared it with their readers. She'd been extra careful to stick to only the facts, not tainting the article with personal feelings or the vindictive reasoning behind the Zacharys' actions. The truth was giant media companies were a bit like kings who moved the pieces across the chessboard however they liked and sometimes swiped them off the board entirely. That was not unique to Zachary Communications, and she'd added some other journalists' stories of it happening to them to show that.

Gavin had asked that she be there though. One, because she'd done nothing wrong and had, in fact, been wronged. Two, it would be good for Max.

Though Gavin hadn't said it, she'd gathered that having her there would help him too. Despite not being so legally or even in name, she couldn't deny that they felt like a family. And the residents of Jade Valley had rallied around them, sending droves of letters in support of Gavin keeping custody for Kevin to have at his disposal.

She'd seen tears in Gavin's eyes when Kevin had told him about the letters.

When the door down the short hallway opened, it startled her from her thoughts. Max grunted in his sleep, so she caressed his head to help ease him.

Mr. and Mrs. Zachary were the first to appear and they gave her only the briefest of looks before settling their gazes on Max. Unconsciously, Maya hugged him a little tighter. But then she saw something she hadn't earlier, a hint of sadness. While she was still processing her surprise, Max's grandparents turned and walked out the front door without a word.

Maya sat staring at the closed door. Did their departure mean what she thought it meant?

A few moments later, their attorney followed them out, not even sparing her a glance.

When Gavin finally came into view, all of her questions must have been written in bold, all-caps print across her face because he smiled.

"It's over." He looked at his son in her arms. "He's not going anywhere. They agreed to not contest my full custody again as long as they can have supervised visits at least twice a year."

Instant tears pooled in her eyes. She looked up at the ceiling and blinked so they wouldn't fall.

"I love you, Maya."

Gavin's admission in the middle of a law office waiting area surprised her but also didn't. When had anything between them been conventional?

So she smiled and said, "About time you said that out loud. I wasn't sure how much longer I could hold it in."

Gavin looked as if he'd been poleaxed, which caused her to laugh.

"If you love me, doesn't it make sense that I love you too?" she asked.

He stared at her for a heartbeat before he smiled again. "I guess it does."

GAVIN COULDN'T TRUTHFULLY say he was more nervous than he'd ever been in his life, but that did not negate the fact that he was so nervous his stomach was twisting itself into knots.

In the two weeks since Rinna's parents had assured him that they would not seek custody of Max, he'd been busy on his secret project when Maya wasn't around. Today, it was finally ready. He was ready.

He heard her car pulling up outside a moment before Max hollered, "Maya!" while looking out the window.

The fact that his son loved Maya had helped Gavin to make his decision. He'd been impressed by how Max had been able to keep the secret Gavin was about to reveal. Of course, his son only knew half the story.

As Maya came inside, gave him a quick peck, then sat down next to Max to hear about his day, Gavin thought he might expire from the need to spill his surprises. But he'd waited this long, so he could wait a while longer. It wasn't until Max had been tucked into bed for the night that Gavin was finally able to take hold of Maya's hands and begin the big reveal.

"I have something to show you."

"Oh yeah? Wait, did you finish the new painting you've been working on?"

"I did." He'd told her she couldn't see it in progress because he didn't like for anyone to see his paintings until they were finished. That was only partly true.

He led her through the kitchen, to the closed door of the small room off the laundry room. He'd fibbed and told her he'd been using it to paint. Again, only partly true.

"Go in," he said, motioning toward the door.

"Well, this is all very mysterious." When she opened the door, it revealed not a former storage room turned artist's studio but rather a freshly painted, furnished and decorated office. "I don't underst—"

Her words faltered the moment she saw the nameplate on the desk.

Maya Pine, Editor-in-Chief.

"Gavin?"

He stepped up behind her and pointed over her shoulder at the desk.

"It's not fancy, and it's not as big as what you had before, but it's a start."

She had begun to pick up some freelance work, but it wasn't yet enough to pay all her bills. But if she accepted the second surprise, she wouldn't have to worry about rent anymore.

"I... I can't believe you made an office for me." She slowly moved toward the desk, ran her fingertips across the smooth surface, then looked up and saw the painting on the opposite wall, the colorful spiral of the Milky Way galaxy. "Oh, Gavin. It's beautiful!"

"Not as beautiful as you."

She laughed a little. "I don't think I can compare to a celestial wonder."

"You can in my eyes."

"Thank you, for everything."

"There's one more surprise. Open the top, right-hand drawer."

"Don't tell me you went crazy with office supplies too." She opened the drawer and simply stared at the one thing it contained.

Gavin's heart beat a furious tattoo in his chest as he waited for her reaction.

"Yes."

Her single-word response surprised him.

"I haven't asked anything."

She lifted her gaze to his.

"Unless engagement rings mean something else I don't know about, then you did ask the question." The teasing lilt in her voice was one of the many things he'd grown to love about her. He decided to tease her back.

"You don't know that an engagement ring is what's inside the box."

She lifted a brow. "Am I wrong?"

He shook his head slowly.

"Then come over here and ask me properly."

He complied, rounding the desk and opening the box. He met her gaze.

"Thank you for coming into my life. I love you, and if you'll have me I want to spend the rest of my life with you. Will you marry me?"

She looked up at him with obvious love in her eyes. "Are you sure?"

He knew what she was asking, whether he was truly ready to let go of all the doubts and pain from the past and believe in a forever kind of love again.

"Yes, completely."

"Then my answer remains the same. Yes, I will marry you. Now, I think these types of things are usually sealed with a kiss."

He slipped the ring on her finger, grinned then pulled her close. "Happy to oblige."

Maya might have entered his life on a rush of frigid winter, but as he kissed her he felt nothing but soul-filling warmth. She'd given him a second chance at sharing his creativity with the world, a second chance at believing there were good people and kindness in the world, a second chance at raising his son.

A second chance at love.

* * * * *

The Paramedic's Forever Family
Tanya Agler

MILLS & BOON

Tanya Agler remembers the first set of Harlequin books her grandmother gifted her, and she's been in love with romance novels ever since. An award-winning author, Tanya makes her home in Georgia with her wonderful husband, their four children and a lovable basset, who really rules the roost. When she's not writing, Tanya loves classic movies and a good cup of tea. Visit her at tanyaagler.com or email her at tanyaagler@gmail.com.

Visit the Author Profile page at millsandboon.com.au for more titles.

Dear Reader,

I chaperoned my twins' field trip to the local botanical gardens and was awestruck at the exhibits, ranging from structured gardens to colorful topiaries. Out of that trip came Lindsay Hudson, a horticulturist who is clawing her way back to life after mourning the death of her paramedic husband in a line-of-duty crash.

Dedicated to his job, Mason Ruddick is a free spirit who relishes jumping on his motorcycle at a moment's notice. The last thing he ever expected was to fall for his best friend's widow, who also happens to be his next-door neighbour. While fighting those feelings, he makes room for some unexpected houseguests in the form of his grandfather and a lovable dog.

This book touches on a subject close to home for me—childhood asthma. My older daughter was diagnosed with asthma, and I'm forever grateful to the pediatric pulmonologists who helped her face this disease with a sense of calmness and encouraged her to live in awareness but not fear.

Please visit my website at tanyaagler.com, where you can sign up for my newsletter, or follow me on social media.

Happy reading,

Tanya

DEDICATION

For Carrie, my bright, artistic daughter,
who sees the beauty of life all around her.
Her messages to me on her whiteboard bring
me joy and smiles, as do her hugs that greet
me in the morning. Her happiness and quiet
strength inspire me every day. This one's
for you, Cupcake!

CHAPTER ONE

ONE MORE MINUTE on hold and Lindsay Hudson would scream so loud the spring wildflowers in bloom outside her office window would wilt. Since she'd pressed the Speaker button so she wouldn't miss out on a live customer representative, she had answered her morning emails, restructured the volunteer orientation and counted the number of jellybeans on her desk. There were five fewer than there'd been when she agreed to hold eighteen minutes and forty-eight seconds ago. She popped a cherry jellybean into her mouth. Make that six.

A knock almost prompted her to end the call, but she had to speak to someone at the Premier Bronze Engravers today. The door opened, and her best friend popped his head in. "Want to have lunch with me?"

"This is Angela. Is this a prank call?" A voice finally crackled over the speaker. Lindsay groaned at her friend Mason's timing.

Mason must have taken her grunt as a sign to enter. Lindsay held up a finger and grabbed her phone, taking it off Speaker. "No! I've been on hold for nineteen minutes. Don't hang up. I need to speak to someone about the proof for the memorial plaque that was sent to the Holly-dale Botanical Garden."

"One moment, please." The familiar sounds of Muzak played once more. As much as Lindsay loved Beyoncé, she much preferred belting out the singer's tunes in her trusty truck than listening to the instrumental version of her top hit.

"Lunch with me would remove those pesky thoughts of tossing your phone out the window." Mason's rich laugh filled her tiny office.

She wrinkled her nose, guilty, as her next-door neighbor knew her too well.

"That new deli downtown has two-for-one pimento cheese sandwiches today."

Considering how often he teased her about being a lifelong North Carolinian who shuddered at the mere smell of pimento cheese, he knew she despised the spread. "You want me along so you can have both for yourself?"

"That's what best friends are for." He shrugged and the light from the afternoon sun bounced off his thick ginger hair, making it almost glow. "I'll buy you a Reuben."

As hard as it was to resist that invitation, her workload prevented her from accepting his offer. "Could you bring it back here for me?"

Angela came on over the line. "If this is a bad time for you, I'd be more than happy to talk to another customer."

"Not at all." Where did her boss find this place? "Are you the person to speak to about the proof for the botanical garden?"

"I handled this requisition myself. A simple email would have sufficed to okay the order. If that's all?"

The representative's smugness took Lindsay by surprise. "No, that's not all. You've misspelled several of the names."

"That must have been a mistake on your part. That will result in a delay of two to four weeks for the new proof and the finished product. Send me the correct spellings, and I'll email you the updated version in which it was received in the queue." Angela's well-modulated, even voice gave no sign she was the guilty party.

Lindsay shuffled papers until she came upon her original document. "If the mistake is on your end, I expect we can still receive the plaque at the scheduled time. Its unveiling for the memorial garden is a major event. Just today we had confirmation of attendance from the mayor and a prominent state representative."

"We are not responsible for others' mistakes. We fulfill our orders with what we've been given."

"I didn't spell my last name wrong." This argument was going nowhere fast. "I have my invoice here, which I personally scanned and faxed to you. Somehow, someone, I'm not saying it was you, swapped the *d* and the *s* of one of the paramedics' last names. It's Hudson, not Husdon."

Lindsay stole a glance at Mason's genial face. A muscle in his firm jaw twitched, so imperceptibly that someone who didn't know him as well wouldn't have noticed. Tim had been his partner prior to the accident that claimed her husband's life two years, two months, and six days ago. Not that she was counting.

"Um, I see your point. However, spring is our busy season, and we can no longer guarantee our original date."

"Do you know what this order is?" Lindsay cut to the chase. "The Hollydale Botanical Garden was chosen as the site for a monument to the first responders who've lost their lives in western North Carolina. My boss, who's on vacation at the Outer Banks, chose your company based on your competitive bid. If there's no plaque during the dedication ceremony…"

"It was an honest mistake on our part. We'll rush the revised proof back to you."

"You do that. Have a nice day." Lindsay ended the call. Mason folded his arms and leaned against her office door, the twinkle in his blue eyes more mischievous than his relaxed stance would suggest. "Remind me never to argue with the head botanical horticulturist. She's feisty."

"*She's* also hungry, but I don't have time for lunch downtown." Lindsay rose from her chair and donned her green blazer. "Before you head out for the sandwiches, I want to show you the memorial site."

He shook his head and straightened. "I know better than to stand between you and your Reuben. I'll be back in a few."

He opened the door, but she ran ahead of him.

"Hmm. It's getting late. Don't want the deli to close before I place my order."

"You don't wear a watch when you're off duty." Pointing out the obvious, she grabbed his arm and tugged him toward the employee exit.

His indigo tie-dyed T-shirt and jeans were rather casual compared to the average wardrobe of the garden's visitors, but he'd have stood out in a crowd whether he wore a dress shirt or his black-and-blue paramedic jacket.

"It'll only take a couple of minutes. You're coming to the dedication ceremony, aren't you?"

Mason halted, and the door almost collided with her forearm before she scooted out of the way, leaving them inside the administrative building. "I haven't thought much about it."

"You have the same expression as Evan when he's lying." Lindsay faced Mason and folded her arms, beaming the same glare she'd give her four-year-old son.

"I'm not lying. I volunteered to work that day so other paramedics could attend."

"What? I can't believe you'd do that without talking to me first." Her mouth fell open and she marveled at him standing there so cool and nonchalant. "Why didn't you tell me this sooner?"

"Because I knew you'd respond like this."

"You don't know everything about me, Mason Ruddick. You don't know the half of how upsetting this is." She pressed the metal bar with a little too much force and the door flew open.

Bright April sunshine didn't match her mood at this second. No one else could aggravate her as much as Mason. She needed a new best friend, someone who'd keep her patience on its usually even keel. A field of wildflowers in bloom drew her attention, and she walked that way, appreciating a minute of beauty before she resumed her day.

"What type of flowers are they?" he asked. She'd sensed Mason had followed her even before his low, husky voice had called to her.

Lindsay remained where she was, resolute she wouldn't give in and turn around. Mason needed to get it through his head how important his attendance at this memorial was, and she needed a minute so she'd come up with a logical retort rather than get distracted by his charm.

A visitor to the garden arrived and echoed Mason's question, leaving her no choice but to turn around and answer. "Those blue-lavender stems are crested dwarf irises while the light purple flowers are wild geranium. The white trilliums are particularly striking."

"Those fragile-looking ones? Are they easy to grow? My husband and I just downsized and moved into a new home. I finally have the time to start the garden I've always wanted."

Lindsay faced the visitor, whose green visor shielded her eyes while she held out a notebook and pen, waiting for the answer. "We should be past the last frost of the year, although that's been recorded here in the mountains as late as May. It's important to triangulate the best place in your yard with access to sunlight and a good water source. If you join our annual membership here at the garden, you can show that pass at Farr's Hardware in town for a ten percent discount, the same for Jasper and Jules's Garden Center."

Mason cleared his throat and, despite herself, Lindsay glanced his way. "So those of us who want to impress our neighbors, the ones who are adept at gardening, should grow trillium to get back in their good graces?"

"Notice the other flowers in that field. They balance out the smell. Trilliums are beautiful, but there's a distinctive odor to them, a bit like rotting meat." Lindsay kept her smile calm and determined.

The woman shoved her notebook in her handbag. "Thanks for your help."

She scurried away, and Lindsay glared at Mason. "I wish I could say the same to you."

"What did I do?" His eyes widened, and he flashed that boyish grin that always sent her twenty-month-old daughter Chloe to the moon.

"That woman was excited about gardening and I let my emotions get the best of me." Lindsay headed for a nearby wooden fence that led to a shortcut to the greenhouse. She intended to spend her afternoon there checking on the progress of the petunias and other summer bedding plants and fixing the ancient irrigation system.

Mason's footsteps beside her proved he wasn't giving up yet. "Do you want extra Russian dressing on your Reuben, like always?"

"Are you coming to the dedication? Tim would have been there for you if the situation had been reversed."

He shoved his hands into the pockets of his jeans, his jaw clenched. "I don't deal in 'what-ifs.' I'll see you later."

Lindsay watched him walk away. Mason rarely made up his mind with such vehemence. What was going on in that head of his? Somehow, she'd find out the answer, while taking care to make sure their friendship remained intact. It was one of the few things that had kept her from staying in bed for the past two years.

MASON FLICKED ON the kitchen light in his rental home and trudged over to the refrigerator. He placed the to-go box holding two pimento cheese sandwiches next to the storage containers of chopped carrots and bell peppers. He hadn't liked the abrupt way he'd ended it with his next-door neighbor and all-around best friend, Lindsay, earlier today, and that uneasiness had carried over to his solitary lunch, where he hadn't been able to savor his one weakness to his organic lifestyle.

Now he had dinner, but no appetite.

Would she still appear tonight at the fence separating their adjoining yards, monitor in hand in case either Evan or Chloe got out of their beds? If so, he'd mend, well, fences with her. Somehow, they'd get through this. He'd work during the dedication ceremony so others in the department could witness her cutting the ribbon, doing double duty as the horticulturist in charge of the garden and the widow of one of the paramedics listed on the plaque.

Problem was, he couldn't bear seeing Tim as just another name and statistic. His throat tightened. This was too much to consider tonight. He took a deep breath and tried to clear his mind. Time with his future chopper would help. Building a motorcycle from the ground up had always been his perfect antidote to the worries lingering within. This was exactly what the paramedic ordered.

Mason ran upstairs, eager to change into his old clothes. Halfway up the stairs, his phone rang, and he checked the screen in case the chief needed him. *Hmm*. What did Bree want to discuss at three in the afternoon Nashville time, four here? She should be at work.

He answered as he reached his bedroom closet. "Hey, sis. Can I call you back? It's my day off and I want to finish part of the bike's electric panel."

He switched to Speaker and threw the phone on the bed, shrugging out of his tie-dyed shirt and replacing it with a long-sleeve shirt already stained with oil.

"Do you have a minute now? This is important," his sister said.

The wobble in Bree's voice was unlike her feisty and fun self, and he sat on the edge of his mattress. Mason reached for the phone and switched off Speaker. "Bree? What happened? Are you okay? Was Tris in an accident or something?"

"Tristan's fine. It's the *or something*." She paused, and he held the phone pressed next to his ear.

"You don't sound happy."

She and Tristan were married four years ago, with college graduation one day and their wedding the next.

"Bree?"

A sniffle turned into wailing, and his brother-in-law came over the line.

"Hi, Mason." Mason heard his sister still crying in the background. "Bree found out she has thyroid cancer. The doctors think they discovered it early."

Mason's heart stuttered, and a wave of nausea roiled his stomach. He clenched his phone and listened to his brother-in-law trying to sound optimistic while outlining the course of treatment, but the worry in his voice came through. Mason's mind wandered, knowing too well what Bree was facing. Most likely, they'd remove her thyroid and then scan to see if the cancer had spread.

Bree came back on the line, and Mason composed himself, tamping down the concern for her sake. "Have you told Mom and Dad yet?" They'd lost one child to cancer already. How they'd take this development was beyond him.

"I've only told Grandma Betty and you." Bree blew her nose, and he waited for her, itching to do something when he was three hundred miles away.

"Do you want me to fly to Nashville? It might be easier to deal with this if I'm at your side." This meaning all of it: telling Mom and Dad, the surgery, the recovery. He hadn't asked for any vacation time this year. He could pop to Nashville for a couple of days to start with, and no one would miss him.

"I love your visits, but no, I'll be okay for now. We'll visit later. I've got the treatment to get through and…when I'm on the road to recovery, that's when I want to see you." Bree sounded more like her usual self the longer she kept talking. "I'm glad I could get the words out. Thanks for listening. Really glad you answered. I'll talk to you again soon. Love ya."

"Right back at you, sis."

He held onto his phone and sat there remembering the day she was born and the day he served as an usher at her wedding and many of the days in between. He couldn't bear to lose someone else close to him. Everything blurred, and he forced himself not to drive to Nashville that second. The prospect of deserting his next shift and his new partner held him back.

He didn't know how much time had passed when he eventually tugged on his oil-stained shirt. Mason headed for the garage; an image of Bree laughing merged with the faint memory of his other sister Colette during her brief battle with leukemia from so long ago.

He switched on the light and stared at the motorcycle.

Processing Bree's news with a wrench in hand might be for the best. After Tim died, he'd dismantled the original bike until little piles of parts surrounded him. Since then, he hadn't even cracked the door to his workshop for six months. Tonight, though, he couldn't wait to install that breaker box underneath the transmission. Ever since he'd finished constructing his first bike way back in high school, he'd been hooked. Too often, on the online loops for fellow enthusiasts, he read about bikers starting similar projects only to give up and move on to easier pastures. He hadn't put the past eighteen months of his life into this for it to grace someone else's garage or be scrapped for parts.

Mason gathered the pieces for this next step, a welcome distraction until he'd talk to Lindsay later tonight. He stopped and breathed out the shakiness from Bree's news. Once his fingers were no longer trembling, he started working on the electrical system.

Perhaps this would be his therapy in light of Bree's diagnosis. Motorcycle sessions, along with confiding in Lindsay, the steadiest woman around, kept him together in a profession where burnout was legendary and stress propelled many paramedics into other careers.

He'd lasted eight years already.

Putting the thought aside, he concentrated on the intricacies of the panel. Mason crossed the length of his garage and picked up his drill, giving it a whirr for good measure. He examined the circumference of the bit and found it too wide. He rifled through the box until he located a smaller bit and then tightened the chuck. In no time, he'd mounted the breaker box and examined the plans tacked to the wall of his garage. The gray lines of the sketch reminded him of the charcoal flecks in Lindsay's serious eyes.

Those eyes had reflected hurt at his decision not to attend the dedication ceremony. While Tim was alive, they'd shared barbecues and birthday cakes, her on Tim's arm and him squiring a different woman every couple of months. Back then, she'd been gracious and greeted each of his dates as a long-lost friend. Then came the helicopter crash that rocked both of their worlds.

He regretted not being the person who informed her of Tim's death. Instead, he'd been the one who held her while the baby still inside her kicked lively unaware she'd never lay eyes on her father. About six months after Chloe was born, he'd spotted Lindsay on her patio trying to uncork a wine bottle with a screwdriver, muttering to herself. That was their first real one-on-one conversation. Since then, he'd come to appreciate how much of an open book Lindsay was, much more than himself. He let people see what he wanted them to see, whereas she wore her heart on her sleeve.

Mason found the signal flasher and checked the plans again. This was a tricky part, requiring he use his welding skills for sure. After donning his protective gear, he installed the rest of the switch housing hardware and stepped back, blinking at the quiet surrounding him. How long had he been lost in his work, anyway? He searched for his phone and couldn't find it anywhere.

His neck ached, and he rubbed it. The garage windows no longer had light flooding in, and he crossed the path leading to his house. Entering the back door, he then found his phone on his bed with four text messages waiting for him. If one of them was his boss...

Nope. They were all from Lindsay, wondering where he was, a sign she was still upset with him since she'd normally have knocked on the garage door. Checking the time, he winced. He should have been on his side of the fence thirteen minutes ago.

His stomach rumbled, and Mason stopped at the fridge.

He tucked a bottle of beer and Lindsay's favorite Riesling under his arm before grabbing the to-go container of pimento cheese sandwiches and heading out the door, closing it afterward with his foot.

He hurried to the fence and found Lindsay going inside, about to close her patio's sliding door.

"Wait!" Mason ran up to the fence separating his yard from hers.

Lindsay halted, raising her head so her short honey-brown hair framed her face. She came forward to open the gate for him and then retreated to her patio.

Seconds ticked by as she seemed to be composing herself. She stood, a good eight inches shorter than him, the difference more pronounced since she wore her flip-flops while he was in his work boots.

"When you're done counting to twenty, I could use a chat with my best friend." Mason kept his voice soft enough so as not to possibly wake Evan and Chloe.

Lindsay sent him a slow-burn glare. "Best friends don't ignore text messages."

"I forgot to bring my phone in the garage with me. I left it upstairs in my room."

"What if you'd hurt yourself while you were working on your bike?"

That slow burn became a forest fire, and he squirmed.

He placed the container and beer bottle on her patio table flanked by two yellow Adirondack chairs, his last anniversary gift to her and Tim.

"But I didn't." He held up the Riesling. "Are we sitting tonight instead of talking at the fence?"

She disappeared and returned a second later with a corkscrew. She twisted it until the cork came out with a soft pop.

"I should take this bottle inside with me and share it

with Aunt Hyacinth, who's reading Evan and Chloe bed-time stories." Lindsay pursed her lips together, but then her expression relaxed. "I sometimes lose track of time, too, while I'm gardening, but I'm out in the open. No one would have seen you if the motorcycle had fallen on you... or something."

She scooped up the bottle and her glass and took two steps toward the sliding glass door. He jumped to his feet.

"Bree has cancer."

Once again, she halted. Slowly, she returned and placed the wine with his offerings. She hugged him then, her lavender and freesia scent a change from the oil and other stinky fumes of his garage. He melted into her softness. As soon as he realized what he was doing, he jerked back. He had no business finding Tim's widow soft, even if Lindsay was his closest friend.

"How long have you known?" Her pink lips formed an O. "Was that why you wanted to have lunch with me today?"

"No. I didn't find out until I arrived home and got lost in the garage so to speak." Speaking of food, his stomach grumbled again, loud enough for her to arch her brow. "Sit awhile?"

"Of course. It'll help to talk to someone about your sister. She's my friend, too."

While she poured the Riesling, he devoured one of the sandwiches. Once he swallowed it down with a sip of his stout, he updated her on Bree's condition until a bark interrupted him.

He glanced at Lindsay, who paused with her glass halfway to her lips. "Did your aunt bring her boxers with her?" he asked.

"Her dogs are at her house." She rose and scanned the area. "The noise sounded like it came from your driveway."

Out of nowhere, a small black dog appeared and snatched the second sandwich from the to-go container.

"Goliath!"

His grandfather's voice reached him, and then he came into view, puffing and holding a bright green leash. "There you are."

"Grandpa Joe?" Mason reached in his pocket for his phone.

"Nine thirty. You really should start wearing a watch on your days off," Lindsay said.

Grandpa Joe boomed out a hearty laugh and clipped Goliath to the leash. "That'll be the day."

Yeah, the day I settled down, which would be never. "What are you doing here this late?" He frowned. "Does Grandma Betty know you're running out to the store for a pint of ice cream again?"

Ever since Grandpa Joe had a touch of angina last year, his grandmother had placed him on a strict diet of heart-healthy foods. But every other week, Grandpa Joe showed up with a pint of butter pecan from Miss Louise's Ice Cream Parlor for himself and rainbow sherbet for Mason. Mason still hadn't worked up enough courage to tell his grandfather that nine-year-old Mason loved the stuff while he only consumed it now to not hurt his grandfather's feelings.

"Your grandmother is the reason I'm here."

Mason folded his arms and huffed out a breath. "Your concern is really kind, Grandpa, but I'll be fine, and Bree will be fine. I'm not four anymore."

"Exactly. That's why Betty sent me here after we talked to your sister." His grandfather glanced at Lindsay, then at him. Mason could have sworn he saw a glimmer of a smile, but it must have been the moonlight that was throwing him, especially since the corners of Grandpa Joe's mouth now turned downward. "My wife is overly worrying of me and thinks I can't live without her."

That sounded ominous to Mason on several levels. If his grandparents, who'd celebrated their fifty-sixth wedding anniversary last June, were splitting up, what hope did any couple have of making it in this world? Just one more reason he stayed the course of being a confirmed bachelor.

"Where's Grandma Betty, and why aren't you with her?"

"After she arranged for a leave of absence from the community center, she caught the first plane to Nashville to be with Bree. I stayed behind for my job and for Goliath, but she's worried something might happen to me, so she made me promise to stay with you until she returns." Grandpa Joe came over and slapped him on the back, the impact of which sent Mason stumbling. "I bought groceries. Nachos, pizza and ice cream. It's going to be great. It'll be like I'm thirty again, until Betty comes home. We'll be bachelors together."

Lindsay let out a sudden burst of laughter. She held up her glass in Mason's direction. "Two bachelors out on the town. I'm glad I have a front-row seat. I wouldn't miss this for the world."

CHAPTER TWO

LINDSAY ENTERED FARR'S HARDWARE STORE, the next-to-last stop on her morning of errands. A quick visit with brief contact with others suited her fine. Then she'd go home and construct the trellis, which had been on her long list of gardening tasks for her backyard.

The smells of paint and peat enticed her as they entwined with the heavy scent of oil soap. The Farr family had used the soap ever since they opened the homey shop in the fifties. She grabbed a metal platform dolly and headed toward the lumber stored in the back.

Fabiana Ramirez waved to her enthusiastically and strode toward her. "You're just the person I wanted to see." Fabiana's long salt-and-pepper hair curled around her shoulders. Lindsay braced herself for the inevitable matchmaking ploy that always came from the well-meaning woman. "Someone is attacking my lettuce."

"Someone or something?"

"There are little holes in my leaves. Roberto is in the pesticide aisle, but perhaps you know something that won't hurt my daughter's new puppy when she brings her over for a visit? That dog's big brown eyes are almost as lethal as my Roberto's." Fabiana winked and laughed.

"Sounds like you have aphids. I have a recipe for an organic, all-natural garlic oil pesticide that will help." Lindsay extricated her phone from the front section of her purse and had Fabiana type in her email address. "I'll send that to you tonight."

Lindsay seized the dolly and began pushing, only to have Fabiana hold her arm. "One more thing. My son Carlos is coming home for Easter. You two would make such a cute couple."

And there it is.

She faced Fabiana, the gleam in the empty nester's dark brown eyes too diabolical for Lindsay's taste. "This is the busy season at the botanical garden. I'd hate to make plans and disappoint him."

"If your adorable children need a babysitter while you and Carlos go out on a date, let me know." Fabiana nodded.

"You're so sweet to offer, but…"

"But nothing, Graciela is an angel with dogs and kids, and Carlos would make such a loving father." She nodded more. "My older daughter Gisele is also taking her sweet time finding someone. I want my three kids to be happy. That isn't a crime. Don't forget to send me that recipe so I can get rid of those nasty aphids." She sped off, leaving Lindsay speechless.

Making haste since Tim's parents had driven into Hollydale and were watching Evan and Chloe for her, Lindsay hustled over to the cedar planks. *Eight ought to do it*, she thought.

"Need any help?"

Lindsay jumped at the sound of Mason's low husky voice behind her. "You scared me."

"Sorry about that, but you're just the person I was looking for."

Oh no, not again. Her jaw clenched, and she loaded a plank on the platform with a thud and quickly added the rest. "Not you, too? Let me guess. There's a new paramedic or firefighter in town, and you're convinced he'd be perfect for me. No thank you. Even if I wanted to get involved with someone again, and I don't, I would never date a first responder."

Even one as handsome as Mason.

Today's red tie-dyed T-shirt brought out the auburn glints in his thick wavy hair. She caught herself and blinked away that pesky thought.

"How many more planks? Can I do anything to make your life easier? Say the word and it's done." Mason pulled out another plank, and she stopped his hand with hers.

"I also need gravel, which is in a different aisle. See you at the fence tonight."

She glanced behind her and found him following but he soon disappeared. Lindsay hurried toward the bags of gravel on the other side of the store, but Mason arrived at the display two seconds ahead of her. "Do you want the twenty-or thirty-pound bag?" He flexed his arm muscles and grinned. "Or one of each?"

She tapped her watch. "Tim's parents drove here from Wilmington this morning to take Evan and Chloe to the new nature preserve, and I'm running out of time to finish my errands. I'm finally building that trellis I've been talking about for months." After stepping around him, she loaded her favorite brand of pea gravel on the empty side of the dolly. "So, whatever's on your mind, just ask."

"You're right about one thing. There is a male involved in my request. Actually, two males."

"No."

"Hear me out. You have a guest room. How would you like a boarder?"

"While moving in with me might keep the matchmakers at bay, Evan and Chloe would get the wrong idea." A gallon of exterior deck stain was next on her list. Some preferred to let the cedar planks weather, but she liked the rhythm of painting the trellis and the shiny finish afterward. She started for the paint aisle.

She'd loaded her preferred brand and noticed Mason steadying the cart for her. "Not me. Grandpa Joe and Goliath on the nights when I'm at the fire station for my twenty-four-hour shifts."

Lindsay remembered too well the small area designated for paramedics at the station.

"With Evan's asthma, a dog in the house wouldn't be such a good idea." A stop at the pharmacy for her son's new inhaler and spacer with a mask was next on her list.

"Studies show early exposure to a pet may decrease a chance of allergies or asthma. Goliath might be more help than a hindrance to Evan. You know I'd never ask you to do anything that would endanger Evan or Chloe."

Lindsay wasn't worried about him endangering her kids as much as her sense of well-being. She needed to stem this one-sided attraction before it grew. "Nice try, but he'll be more comfortable at your house without two young children underfoot." Lindsay made her way to the checkout counter. He continued to tag along and so she faced him. Something was wrong with this picture, but what? "You're empty-handed. You always buy something when you shop at Farr's."

She wasn't so predictable that he knew where to find her on her day off, was she?

They reached the front of the cashier line, where Mr. Farr's well-known granddaughter Missy checked out customers. "Mason!" Missy held up her index finger. "Grandpa said to look out for you. We have your special order at customer service. I'll only be a sec."

Missy hurried away, and Mason pulled out his wallet. "I ordered a new planishing hammer for the metalwork on my motorcycle. That's why I'm here."

Lindsay examined the side display of batteries, key chains and energy bars as if her life depended on a new LED flashlight. "That's nice."

Missy returned and rang up his purchase. "Thanks for the special order. We're trying to expand this service so we can keep up with the times but still provide that extra touch for our customers."

The young woman handed Mason's credit card back, and Lindsay caught herself staring at the lingering touch of Missy's fingers on Mason's hand. Lindsay blinked and turned her attention toward her purchases. In no time, she transported her paid order out to her truck, where Mason helped open the tailgate.

"Can I hitch a ride home with you?"

She glanced at him, picking up the cedar planks as if they were Lincoln logs rather than long, heavy pieces of wood. Her gardening clogs allotted her an extra inch of height, but he still had a good six inches on her average frame. "Where's your car?"

"I drove Grandpa Joe into town, and he bought me lunch at the Holly Days Diner since he wanted a piece of lemon meringue pie. Some of his buddies were heading to Sully Creek. When I saw your truck in the parking lot, I told him to go ahead in my SUV."

Lindsay slammed the tailgate shut. "Pretty sure of yourself, huh? It'd serve you right if I made you walk home, especially after eating a big lunch," she teased.

"Take pity on me. This planishing hammer's big and heavy. I can't lug it home by myself." He jutted out his lip and raised his hands as if surrendering. "Besides, Goliath hogged my side of the bed, and my three-day shift starts tomorrow. I'm exhausted."

She busted out laughing at his plaintive expression. "He's a slip of a dog."

"Chiweenies are long and feisty. He curls up right in the middle, and I can't tell him no."

"Oh, you poor thing. Tsk, tsk. If you get dark circles under your eyes, how will you keep your title of Hollydale's Most Eligible Bachelor?" She waited while he loaded his hammer next to her purchases, then jerked her thumb toward the passenger door. "This ride will cost you."

He turned toward the retro diner across the street. "I'll run over right now and buy you a slice of lemon meringue pie, if they're not sold out already."

"That's not my price." Although she wouldn't have minded a piece of pie from the Holly Days Diner. Lemon meringue happened to be her favorite, as Mason well knew. "I have one quick stop before heading home. I hope that's okay with you?"

"Beggars can't be choosers. Thanks for the ride." He settled into the passenger seat.

Lindsay started her truck, and the speakers began blasting a Taylor Swift tune. Her hand touched Mason's as they both rushed to turn down the music.

He chuckled as she reversed out of the spot. "Pumping up the volume when the kids aren't in the car?"

"I can listen to what I like as loud as I like when I'm alone. My kids prefer the newest Disney tunes, especially Chloe, who sings along much to Evan's dismay." She hated her defensive tone as she passed the brick storefronts of downtown. It wasn't about leaving her music on full blast and all about becoming more predictable than bees pollinating the spring flowers.

"I can't believe she's old enough to sing already," Mason said. "It seems like yesterday I thought you wouldn't make it to the hospital, and I'd have to deliver her."

There'd been five minutes where she'd been mortified Tim's former partner might have to deliver Chloe. They were waiting for her aunt to arrive to take care of Evan in the middle of the night after Lindsay's water broke. Fortunately, they'd made it to the hospital in the nick of time, and Mason stayed in the waiting room.

"She and Evan are even old enough to argue now. Evan complains about her music, and they bicker."

"Sisters can be the biggest pains, but big brothers will do anything they can on their behalf. Evan will step up. You'll see."

Without a doubt, Mason must be thinking about his own sister. "Any update on Bree's prognosis?"

Mason tapped his fingers to the beat of the song playing on the radio. "Bree got through her initial shock and reaction, she's regrouped and is ready to kick cancer to the curb and beyond. Having Grandma Betty there for moral support helped when they called our Mom and Dad together."

Stopped at one of four traffic lights in Hollydale, Lindsay let Mason's words sink in and she focused on the lush purples of the petunia planter on Cobb Realty's upper level. Chloe would especially love the shades from lavender to violet.

Next door, the personality of the outfitting store was on display with spring succulents gracing the window box. Still, the tulips surrounding the gazebo were her favorites, their long stems and bright variety of colors marking the transition from the muted stark browns of winter to the rainbow surrounding them.

The light turned green, and she found a parking space on Main Street in front of the pharmacy. Mason waited in her truck while she paid for Evan's inhaler.

On the way home, Mason read Evan's prescription label. "How's Evan doing since his asthma diagnosis?"

"Better now that we know the cause of his breathing issues."

She turned onto their street and backed into her driveway so it'd be easier to unload the wood.

"So, what's your fee for the ride? Unloading the wood? Buying your next bottle of wine for our nightly talks? Your wish is my command." Mason performed a mock bow from the passenger side of the truck. "Except for gardening, of course. I'm not big on standing around and waiting for something to sprout and grow."

"In that case, I'll have to do something to change your mind about my favorite hobby." She used the remote control on her key chain and raised her garage door. She hopped down and opened the tailgate, then removed the first plank.

"Come on, Linds." Mason grabbed two planks at once, and she rolled her eyes at his showing off. "Anything but gardening. Double the usual babysitting?"

"But I thought you love spending time with Chloe and Evan." She paused near the grid lines she'd drawn on the garage floor with chalk before plopping down the first cedar plank and leveling a look at him. "You care about them, don't you?"

"Lindsay." All traces of levity disappeared, and his gaze bored through her. "I'd never lie or joke about that. Chloe and I bonded the minute I first saw her and she held my finger. I love Evan and Chloe as though they were mine. As a matter of fact, they're my beneficiaries."

He laid his two planks near hers, muffling out her shocked "What?"

Mason wiped his hands and moved toward her shelves crammed full of fertilizer, buckets with gloves and trowels, loppers and other gardening tools. "Do you want the gravel inside or outside?"

Dumbfounded, she stood there, her feet planted to the concrete. "Repeat what you just said."

"Do you want…"

Lindsay shook her head. "About Evan and Chloe being your beneficiaries."

"It makes sense, plus, I'm too ornery for anything to happen to me." He headed outside and wiped his brow with the back of his muscular forearm. "Hey, if I'm going to help you garden, the least you can do is offer me a glass of water."

Mason wasn't getting off this lightly, she thought.

"Why didn't you tell me? You have a sister, parents and grandparents, not to mention a legion of cousins scattered here in North Carolina and out in Colorado."

Her question came as he gripped the first bag of gravel. He dropped it on the driveway, and Lindsay stared him down.

"A straight answer, please."

The muscles of his jaw clenched as seconds ticked by. "Because I didn't want it to be awkward between us…like it is right now. If something happened to me, you'd have found out then. I live in the present. It's easier that way."

Easier than what? Letting go of memories wasn't her style, but maybe he was right. There hadn't been this type of uncomfortable silence between them since Tim had introduced them, and they milled about while searching for common ground.

She scuffed the driveway with the tip of her clog. She wasn't sure how she felt about his revelation but let the beneficiary matter drop for now. "Gardening isn't all about planning for the future."

A bit of the challenge and spark she always associated with that chin tilt of his returned. "How is something that takes forever interesting? It takes forever for seeds to grow to fruition."

Lindsay tugged on his hand and led him to the side

yard that bordered her other neighbor's house. Bright sunshine warmed the deep pink peonies flourishing in the
rich brown mountain soil, unlike the red clay that pre-
dominated most of the state. "I transplanted those when
they were fully grown last year." She looked down, her
hand still holding his, she released him. "Sorry about that."

"You don't have to be embarrassed for caring about
something you're passionate about. I've put people to sleep
at parties talking about my favorite brand of motorcycle
helmets. One thing's always puzzled me, though."

Lindsay almost sighed with relief since he'd assumed
she was flustered about her hobby. Talk about awkward.
Her stomach fluttered when she dropped his hand as if
she was making some sort of mistake in letting him get
away. "What's that?"

"How can you spend all day at the botanical garden
and then come home and relax by doing the same thing?
There's no way I could finish a three-day shift and then
only read medical thrillers. I'd get bored if I didn't have
my motorcycle."

"Help me build the trellis for my new morning glories
then, instead of digging in the dirt as payment? Your electric saw will make quick time of those planks."

Mason waved his arm with a flourish along the length
of his torso, the bright sunlight turning the red locks of
his hair into burnished gold. "That's the deal? You could
have asked for anything from me, and you want my electric saw?"

"Driving you home wasn't that big of a deal." Unlike
the tingles still pricking her fingertips.

This was Mason, she reminded herself, her husband's
partner and her best friend. She'd already lost too much
to also lose her cool over a man who'd kept her together
after Tim died. Everyone else, including her parents, had

coddled her and thankfully taken care of Evan while she hid in bed, until one afternoon when he stormed into her room, opened her drapes and let the sunshine in.

"Your wish is my command." He smiled and turned, marching toward his garage with that determined gait of his, the one that made women in Hollydale stop and take notice. Just as attractive was the respect he'd earned from his fellow first responders.

Flicking her fingers, she absorbed the spring warmth and willed all thoughts of him as anything other than a friend aside while reviewing her strategy for building a trellis.

IN LINDSAY'S GARAGE, Mason drilled the screws on the back side of the cedar plank. Constructing this trellis was right up his alley. Give him a project that involved building something or his tools, and he was content.

Lindsay understood that, and that was why she was his best friend. Although in the past couple of months he'd caught himself wishing they were more than friends. The delicate arch of her eyebrows when she was animated. The lush pink of her lips when she finished her one glass of wine. The soft sway of her hips as she slid the door closed at night. These were not attributes he should notice about Tim's widow. Losing her as a friend? He'd do anything to prevent that from happening. Even tamping down his feelings while spending the day with her.

Lindsay came into the garage, and he pushed his safety goggles atop his head. She deposited a gallon of exterior stain at his knees, her hands stained with dust and dirt. "When's your grandfather coming home?"

"My best guesstimate is sunset." He exhaled at the mention of his grandfather. Right now, Goliath was safe in the confines of Mason's backyard, chewing on a beef bully stick. For the next three days, Mason would work twelve-hour shifts, something that must have slipped Grandma Betty's mind when she entrusted his grandfather's care to him. "About Grandpa Joe..."

Before he could ask Lindsay about Grandpa Joe moving in with her, car doors slammed in the driveway. Evan ran up to them with a container of plastic birds. "See what I got?"

Lindsay smoothed his fine blond hair plastered to the sides of his face. "Nice."

Chloe bounded over to Mason in that toddler run of hers, clutching a stuffed turtle. "Pick Chloe up?"

The way she uttered her name sounded so much like the way Colette had said *Coey*, his pet name for his first-born sister. He obliged and grinned. "I like your turtle."

He touched it, and she snatched it away. "My turtle."

"You won't share?"

"Your cheek feels funny so Chloe share." She rubbed the stuffed animal's green fur against his stubble and then giggled. He couldn't imagine loving a daughter of his own more. Lindsay's family was his family.

Tim's father headed his way and reached out his hand. "Mason, good to see you again."

Mason gently lowered Chloe, and she went over to show Lindsay her new toy. "Mr. Hudson."

He accepted the handshake.

"Call me Tom. Donna stayed in the car. She's feeling a bit wound down after a day with the kiddos, and it's a long drive back to Wilmington." Tom's blond hair was now liberally streaked with gray. Tall and still lean, he was the image of what Tim would have looked like in thirty years. "It's hard on her since Evan's the spitting image of Tim at that age. Sorry we can't stay, Tim talked so highly of you. We'll catch up more at the dedication ceremony."

Despite Tom's comment, Mason had no intention of making an appearance. "Maybe, maybe not."

A long blast of the car horn prevented Tom from asking the questions written on his face. He patted Mason on the back. "It's a relief for us both to know Lindsay has Tim's partner looking out for her. You're a good man, Mason."

Tom's throat bobbed, and he hurried away. Lindsay came over, and Mason cringed at whatever she was about to say. He spoke first. "I'm still not coming to the ceremony."

"I have a feeling you'll be there." She turned toward Evan after he threw a smooth stone between the slats of the trellis lying on the ground. "What are you doing?" she asked.

"Playing hopscotch. This is great, Mom!" He jumped and hopped the length of the trellis and back again.

"Fun is over." She faced Mason, her pretty features a mottled shade of pink, the same as her peonies. "I'll take the kids inside, could you move the trellis to the backyard by the fence?"

She tapped her chin, leaving a smudge of dirt, and he had the funniest urge to wipe it away and kiss the clean spot.

He quickly cast the thought aside. "Sure, but what else is on your mind?"

"I have another question, but I'm not sure I want to know the answer."

He glanced over at Evan dumping out the container of birds and Chloe plopping beside him with her turtle. "They're keeping busy."

He tried his special smile, the one reserved to calm patients, especially female patients. However, Lindsay, typically patient herself, was having none of it. "That'll only last for about a minute."

Seconds ticked by, the air growing thick between them. He started to panic. Something was changing between them. At the very least, something was changing in him. Every day when he woke up, he counted down the moments until he'd see her again. *No.* He couldn't be attracted to Lindsay. He'd keep this moment light, keep the friendship bond between them.

"C'mon. Tell me. I'm all ears." He used his fingers to wiggle his ears.

She leaned in close enough for her lavender scent to catch him and drive him crazy. "Earlier you said something about two males. Were you matchmaking?"

"Never." That wasn't quite what he expected, but he'd take anything right now to break the tension. "I need help with Grandpa Joe and Goliath while I'm working my three-day shift."

"Just help? At Farr's Hardware, it sounded like you wanted Joe and Goliath to move in with me until your grandmother came home." That intense gaze saw through him every time. "Don't forget who you're talking to."

"Okay, then." His palms became sweaty, not a result of the physical labor but because of this woman who sometimes knew him better than he knew himself. "The fact is Grandpa Joe doesn't listen to me."

"What're you talking about?" She looked at Evan, who was hopping around, making the plastic birds swoop and fly, and Chloe, who toddled over to her brother and picked one up under Evan's careful brown gaze.

The similarities between himself and Evan at that age, when he and Colette did everything together, struck him, and he fought the urge to flee. "Grandpa Joe does what he wants to do and won't accept my advice."

"That's not true. Why would you think that?"

"His diet, for one thing. He doused my low-fat turkey

chili with sour cream, guacamole and cheddar cheese." He shook his head remembering how his grandfather's first of three servings had resembled a heart attack in a bowl.

"Is that the recipe you tried out on Evan and Chloe last week? The one where you snuck in carrots and zucchini?"

He nodded and kept watch over Evan and Chloe, seeing how they were the closest he'd ever come to having kids. "Anything two kids under five demolished that fast has to be good."

"True. But it's sweet you're worried about him so I'll invite him to dinner for the next couple of nights. I'm glad he's staying with you. You need this time with him. Someday you'll realize just how much."

He opened his mouth to protest he already appreciated his grandpa's visit, but one look at Lindsay's resolute face told him to save his breath. Instead, he just smiled. "What time should I tell him to arrive tomorrow night?"

She narrowed her eyes and stared at him. "Was that a compromise or your intention all along?"

He smiled again, a genuine one that had everything to do with the way she made him feel. "I shared my chili recipe with you and Grandma Betty. I'll let you stew over this one and decide."

Lindsay groaned and threw her gardening gloves at him. "With puns like those, I don't know why I keep you around."

Sometimes he wondered the same thing.

CHAPTER THREE

GLEEFUL SHOUTS OF JOY from the Children's Play Zone carried over Sully Creek and the tree-lined bridge, which separated the heart-shaped Hollydale Botanical Garden into two halves. Lindsay knelt in Sycamore Station, testing the soil for pH levels one last time before the flower planting commenced. She reveled in the Carolina sunshine, the wide brim of her canvas hat shielding the harmful effect of the rays but not the caress of the breeze on her cheeks. Spring days like today made her job as head horticulturist seem more like play than work.

Sycamore Station with the center's most famous tree was in the southwestern quadrant where she'd lobbied for this memorial. The noise from the children's area was the primary reason she supported this section over Rose Blossom Way, where four squares of roses and gardenias converged upon a fountain into which visitors tossed a penny and made a wish.

She stood and stretched. Where were the volunteers she was expecting? A glance at the chart confirmed they were running late, but she groaned at the sight of the name of Heather Schmidt, her boss's gossipy wife, as one of the morning helpers. Nothing she could do or say about that. Finishing her stretch, Lindsay drank in the peaceful sight until something amiss with the sycamore caught her eye. Her focus narrowed in on the spot.

Her boots imprinted into the loamy brown soil as she examined the leaves of the sycamore, one of the few planted in the state from seeds taken up to the International Space Station. Visitors to the garden were always asking to see the space tree, as many referred to the garden's most famous landmark. Folks often claimed they traveled here for the sole purpose of having a look at it. Some leaves appeared as though they'd been covered in baby powder when in actuality the tree had powdery mildew fungus.

"You noticed that blight, too." Lindsay's boss, Phillip Schmidt, came up behind her.

"Fungicide should clear it up in no time." Lindsay released the limb. "No doubt the cool, wet spring is the culprit. Before I leave today, I'll apply the first dose."

As well as check the weather forecast again and take any precautions if the expected storms showed signs of worsening. This morning, the meteorologist had predicted only a soaking rain for later tonight, but this close to the mountains the forecast often changed.

While she had been buckling in Evan and Chloe for day care, Joe and Goliath had met her in the driveway at the end of their walk. Joe confided his rheumatism was a sure sign tonight's storm would be a real whopper before shuffling away, muttering how much he missed Betty. Right there, she'd invited him over for dinner for the third night in a row.

"Now that I'm back from my vacation, I talked to the plaque company." Phillip wasted little time in getting to the point.

"I thought my report showed that I'd handled that." She removed one glove, then the other, while counting to ten. She went to her rolling cart and dumped the gloves in a bucket.

Phillip tucked his clipboard under his arm. "The president of the company called me personally."

Lindsay grabbed her reusable water bottle that Mason had given her last Mother's Day, the one with flowers and the slogan "You're never too old to play in the dirt." She took a long swig of water. "They spelled *Hudson* wrong and then had the audacity to insist the order would take longer than promised."

"I'm friends with the president. He apologized and guaranteed the plaque would be here two weeks sooner and reduced the price by ten percent. I went ahead and contacted the media outlets, along with our web designer and moved up the opening. Several local celebrities who were unable to come with the original date said they'd attend."

The water went down the wrong pipe, and she coughed at her boss's sudden announcement. Every perennial on her site rendering and every detail on her meticulous chart had involved realistic preparation time. She'd allowed for five built-in days for delays, but not fourteen.

After her coughing attack subsided, she stared at her boss as if he'd sprouted branches and dogwood flowers. "You didn't consult me first to make sure this is even possible."

"You've worked here since your graduation. Your projects always come in on time and under budget."

But none of her previous projects had measured this high of a magnitude. Stunned, she sipped more water, only to have it follow the same path. Another coughing fit marred this beautiful afternoon. She wiped her mouth with the back of her hand. "As it was I left little margin for this significant of a change. Some of the flowers are set to arrive two days before the original opening."

Phillip pursed his lips. "It's done, Lindsay. You'll adjust and make our botanical garden the talk of the state. Last year our attendance numbers were down, and we need this publicity as a selling point."

"Tim and the others aren't a tourist attraction." She whipped out a clean pair of gloves and donned them. "We didn't bid so we can drum up business."

"The mayor rejected the gazebo, and it came down to a few other sites."

Mayor Wes made the right call in the end. The gazebo, located in the heart of historic downtown Hollydale, was a romantic spot and she preferred keeping it that way. Tim had proposed to her there, and she knew couples married on its steps, including her friend Georgie, who'd wed the town's sheriff, Mike Harrison. Now she had to get everything perfect in a mere ten weeks instead of the original twelve.

Tim and the other first responders deserved nothing less.

"I'll be busy with this afternoon's budget meeting, but I trust you'll handle the new date." It was a statement rather than a question, and Phillip walked away without waiting for her reply.

Shaking her head, she gulped down another few sips while keeping a lookout for those volunteers. *No-shows.* Lindsay frowned, knelt by the cart and glanced at the plats of cannas and cosmos flowers awaiting transfer into the prepared bed of soil. Needing little care, these plants would thrive in the area to the left of the sycamore. She checked her watch. She'd have to start without Heather or the others. It wasn't a big deal, just time-consuming.

She examined each plat and considered the order in which she wanted to plant the showier yellow-and-orange cannas and the daintier white cosmos tinged with the lightest of lavender.

"Of course, Phillip brought up Lindsay before they awarded the contract. Why else do you think we got it?" Heather's high-pitched voice caught Lindsay's attention.

From her low vantage point behind the cart, she saw she wasn't the only one staring at Heather and the other volunteers. People near the sycamore gawked in that direction. Boss's wife or not, Lindsay wouldn't let them gossip about the garden in full sight and sound of visitors, possibly Hollydale residents.

Lindsay popped up and motioned to the two volunteers. "Ladies." She silently counted to twenty as she ushered them behind a chained-off area for employees only. "This is a public area, and you're wearing the special green T-shirts that designate you as official volunteers."

Heather pulled to her full height, a good four inches taller than Lindsay's smaller frame. "May I remind you my husband is the director here?"

"And may I remind you people post cell phone videos online?" Lindsay refused to be intimidated. "Are you ready? We have a lot of work ahead of us."

Unsurprisingly, Heather didn't look shocked when Lindsay brought up the revised timeline and dates. After that the morning passed by in no time, and the flowers were transferred to the first arc while others would follow in the coming weeks, completing the circle that would always have one plant or flower in bloom. Already the area looked more colorful, a fitting tribute for the men and women who'd lost their lives serving others.

Heather and her friend left, and not a moment too soon as far as Lindsay was concerned.

She removed her gloves, and noticed her fingers trembled. She gripped the cart and rolled it back to the southern shed.

"Lindsay? Are you okay?"

Lindsay halted and found a very pregnant Natalie Murphy approaching her.

She smiled and nodded. "Natalie, I can't remember the

last time we talked." Her friend's wedding to Aidan perhaps. Come to think of it, she'd cut herself off from quite a few of her friendships after Tim died. "When are you due?"

"Not until June though Aidan originally told some people I was due in May. I've asked my obstetrician to make sure I'm not carrying twins, being one myself. But she assures me there's only one Murphy baby in there, who's destined to be as tall as his or her father, I'm sure."

Natalie's husband, Aidan, was the new city manager, having finished serving in the army before finding the position here and marrying her friend.

Should she ask Natalie if Heather had spoken the truth, and the garden received the contract because she was Tim's widow? If that was the case, she'd quit on the spot.

Natalie laid her hand on Lindsay's shoulder. "You look stressed. Do you need to sit down?"

"I should be the one asking you that."

"I could rest for a minute. My mother told me to enjoy some time alone before the baby comes while she watches Danny at the Children's Play Zone. He loves the annual membership Aidan gave him for Christmas, although, at the time, he scrunched his nose like the present was a pair of stinky socks." Natalie laughed, her bangle bracelets chiming like music. She headed for the nearest bench. "Do you have a few minutes to catch up?"

Lindsay glanced at the cart and considered the many afternoon duties awaiting her. Maybe a chat with an old friend would help her tackle that list with more enthusiasm. "I shouldn't, but I will."

They settled on a bench donated by Lindsay's aunt in memory of her husband, Craig Hennessy. "I'm sorry I can't attend the ceremony." Natalie patted her stomach. "Baby Murphy is limiting my engagements."

"You have the best of excuses."

"Speaking of excuses, you haven't responded yet to the baby shower invite from Becks and Georgie." Becks was Natalie's twin sister, and Georgie was her sister-in-law.

"I don't know if I'll be able to attend. Phillip just moved the dedication date up two weeks."

"Is that why you're pale?" Natalie rubbed her baby bump and stretched her back. "Or does it have to do with the reason for the memorial garden itself?"

"Thanks for your concern, but I'm okay." She'd kept herself relatively isolated, so her friends had no idea she'd come to terms with Tim's death. "It's the prospect of extra work to get everything ready in time. I'll start calling vendors this afternoon, but it's just…"

If Lindsay didn't want Heather to gossip about the way the garden's bid was accepted, she best keep what she overheard to herself. With attendance already down, the last thing she needed was people getting wind of negative talk like this and then staying away.

Natalie nudged Lindsay. "I might be overreaching here, but if you ever need a good listener, I'm available. I know how close you and Tim were. I still think about my best friend Shelby whenever her son Danny laughs a certain way. The hard truth is it took some time after she died for Danny to laugh again. Even though Aidan and I officially adopted him, Shelby will always be his mom in my eyes. I know talking to me won't be the same as talking to Tim, but the offer stands."

"Thank you."

Natalie swept her red hair away from her face and pushed off with her other hand on the armrest and stood. "Time with friends and family. That's the best thing to do as far as I'm concerned. I'm so happy I ran into you."

Lindsay walked alongside her with the rolling cart,

the matter of the bid still unsettling. "Natalie, did Aidan ever...?"

Natalie faced her. "Did Aidan ever what? Jump the gun? Act a mite stubborn? Plan everything about this baby to the nth degree, even though I told him the baby won't come with a day planner? Yes, to all of the above."

The redhead laughed, but then winced, placing both hands on her lower back. "The baby must be more like my husband than I thought. He didn't seem to like that."

"Are you okay? You're not going into labor, are you?" Lindsay thought about Evan born six weeks premature but relatively healthy, despite his recent asthma diagnosis.

"Braxton-Hicks, that's all. The hospital's the place where I want this wee one to be born, even though the garden might be my new favorite spot in Hollydale. Such vibrant colors. That butterfly enclosure is simply divine, but I should be getting back."

"There's an employee shortcut to the children's area. Let me take you that way." Although Natalie protested, Lindsay insisted.

Outside the entrance to the Children's Play Zone, Natalie hugged Lindsay goodbye. "At first, Aidan had his doubts about this being the right selection for the memorial though this was the lowest bid, but he's come around."

Lindsay's ears perked. They'd won the bid on its merits. "I'll do my best to attend your baby shower."

"If Becks and Georgie don't end up cancelling the party first, since they can't agree on much," she laughed jokingly. "Except how much they love me, of course." Natalie waved goodbye and passed through into the kids' play area.

There was no use dwelling on the bid process when Lindsay had vendors to call and fungicide to mix. More than ever, she looked forward to comparing notes with Mason tonight at their fence.

WITH ANOTHER SHIFT in the books, Mason shrugged on his jacket. Beside him, Jordan, his new partner of two months, his fourth since Tim died, stared off into space. No doubt the man's mind was still at Timber River and the scene from a few hours ago after a group of teens had flipped their raft. Everyone had made it out, but one teen was in critical yet stable condition in the ICU at Dalesford General while another had already been discharged.

Mason slammed the door of his locker shut and snapped the lock, ready to sleep in his own bed after this long three-day shift spent on call at the station. "Earth to Jordan."

Jordan blinked and shook his head. "How do you handle the stress of the job, Mason? How have you kept at it this long?"

"Because of things like today… we arrived in time, stayed calm, did our job and they survived. The teen with the concussion is already home and expected to make a full recovery, and the girl in the hospital can thank her lucky stars her boyfriend kept performing CPR until we arrived."

Jordan closed his locker but stayed where he was, his chest noticeably rising and falling. Mason worried and wondered if he'd have yet another new partner by the next shift. Burnout was a factor in this profession, and Jordan's hollow eyes told the story of why, even though Mason considered today a success. Days like these did take a toll.

"I'll lay it on the line for you." Mason tapped his partner's shoulder until the younger guy met his gaze. "Your grandparents run the best pizza joint in town, right?"

"I could start working there tomorrow." Jordan's voice sounded cool and distant, and Mason imagined the guy was already drafting his resignation letter.

"Maybe it's better you find this out when you're twenty-one instead of thirty-one, like me." Not that Mason was going anywhere.

"Except." Jordan placed one sneaker on his foot, tied it, then did the same with the other. He looked down and swore. "Wrong feet." He shucked off his sneakers and started over. He huffed out a breath. "I love this job."

"Remember that and take the successes where and when they come. Those can keep you in check and motivated during the hard losses." Mason sat beside him and softly elbowed Jordan. "If you do that, we'll make a good team, partner." He grew somber and handed his partner his other sneaker. "Are you prepared for the day when it turns out differently? We can't save everyone."

Jordan accepted the sneaker and slipped it on his foot. "I know. This is the first time we've handled a call with people younger than me. Is it hard the first time someone really young dies on your watch?"

"Yeah. But it's always hard when that's the outcome. Can you handle that?"

"I'm not sure. I hope so."

"Take the next couple of days and know so." He patted Jordan's shoulder. "Your instincts are good, some of the best I've seen."

Mason waited until Jordan was feeling better. By the time he got to his SUV, dusk surrounded him. The rain started picking up in intensity, and the wind made it almost impossible to open his door. He exerted extra force until the door blew open and then almost slammed shut on his leg. He sat there motionless, raindrops running down his face. Today's scene at Timber River was one that would stay with him for a while, a fun day for a group of teens cut short by circumstances beyond their control.

The rhythm of the rain on his car roof subsided, bringing him out of his memories. He inserted his key in the ignition and waited for his hands to stop shaking. His phone rang, and he wanted to ignore it, except it was Grandma Betty. He never ignored her.

"Hello, Mason. Can you hear me? This is Grandma Betty Ruddick." The lilt in her voice at her usual greeting, a running gag with her five grandchildren, always let him know she was in on the joke.

Only a handful of people lifted his spirits like his grandmother, and most of them resided next door to his house. "Excellent timing. My shift just ended ten minutes ago."

"I know. I timed it so I could check on that roguish husband of mine, who sounded very chipper on the phone today. How's Joe really?" That type of concern proved what fifty-six years of marriage and an abiding love could do for someone.

At moments like this, he wanted that same type of commitment. Then images of Colette and Tim flashed in his mind. He'd seen his parents mourn Colette. Same with Lindsay after Tim's death. He'd never want to cause anyone that kind of grief. The bachelor life was for him.

"As much of a rascal as ever." Somehow, he kept his voice casual. Enlightening her on Grandpa Joe's dietary downslide, however, would only cause her to worry, so he skipped that detail. Somehow, he had to corral his grandfather.

"That's my Joe. I miss him, you know?"

He could only imagine. "He's lonely without you, too, but Lindsay agreed to have him to dinner while I worked my long shift. She's probably spoiling him."

"You make Joe sound more like a dog than Goliath." She chuckled.

Mason heard Bree in the background, and he waited while Grandma Betty relayed everything to her. "How's Bree?"

"Why don't you ask her yourself? By the way, expect some surprises tomorrow."

Shuffling noises came over the line, and the rain seemed to be tapering off so now was as good a time as any to venture forth. He switched to the hands-free speaker for the drive home. He exited the lot, but Bree still hadn't come on the line.

"Bree?" he repeated her name. "Did we get disconnected?"

"I moved into another room so I could talk to you in private."

He braced himself. "I'm driving." As far as he was concerned, he could keep driving until he hit Nashville. "Do I need to call you back? Is this more bad news?" Had the scans showed advanced cancer? How would she cope? He couldn't bury another sister.

"Nothing like that, so stop worrying. My scans were clear. It's localized, and my long-term prognosis is good." With those simple sentences, Bree lifted that iron weight off his chest. "I wanted to talk to you about Grandma Betty."

He smiled. "So, she's driving you to distraction? Some days Grandpa Joe is happy to be on his own, and others he's ready to get on a plane and join her."

"Huh? That's not where I was going at all." Bree's serious tone was unlike his gregarious sister. "I don't know what I'd have done without her for the past week. Thanks to her, Mom and Dad managed to hold it together, although Mom still cried on the videoconference call. Grandma Betty even persuaded them not to fly home from Australia. You know how long they've waited for this opportunity at the university in Adelaide. Mom's hard at work on her doctoral thesis while Dad's loving teaching geology and studying the rift formation nearby. They'll visit over their winter break."

"Hold that thought. I'm almost home." He turned onto

his street, his smaller rental next to Lindsay's bigger, homier Cape Cod. Even the rain couldn't diminish the spring colors on full display in her front yard. He parked in his driveway. "So, I'm guessing the great news is Grandma Betty will reunite with Grandpa Joe soon?"

"That's why I wanted to talk to you in a different room. Tristan landed a major coding project, and he wants to turn it down since it will involve extensive travel over the next month, but Mason, you ought to see his eyes light up when he talks about the intricacy of the assignment and the challenges."

He knew where this was going. "And if Grandma Betty stays for a little while longer, Tristan wouldn't have to say no because she'd be here, and Mom and Dad can keep working in Australia." He glanced at Lindsay's windows, lights blazing, the picture of happiness. "Has she told Grandpa Joe she's extending her visit?"

Bree inhaled and exhaled. "I was hoping you could do that."

He'd be a heel if he refused this smallest of favors for his little sister. "Good thing he's at Lindsay's. That might lessen some of the sting of hearing it from me."

"My surgery's next week. After that, my doctor will finish planning my next course of treatment. Grandma being here is making all the difference. We're really bonding. I so appreciate you and Grandpa Joe banding together." Bree's yawn came through loud and clear.

"Go get some rest," he told her.

"Okay, love ya."

"Right back at you." He sat there, staring at his dark house. Suddenly, the empty place didn't seem as appealing as it had when he'd left the station. Besides, he should head to Lindsay's and tell Grandpa Joe this latest twist.

He ran for Lindsay's covered stoop. Her front door opened before he formed a fist to knock.

"You're soaked. Wait here." Lindsay must have seen his headlights through her window.

Yips greeted him next as Goliath scrambled forward, his paws clattering against the hardwood of the foyer as he ground to a halt. Mason hurried inside and shut the door behind him. The plump dog jumped on him, and Mason waggled his finger. "Down, Goliath."

The dog wagged his tail before giving in. Mason rewarded him with a "Good dog" and a scratch behind his ears. In no time, Lindsay returned with a fluffy blue towel and gray sweats, which looked familiar. "They're not Tim's." He must have been more transparent than he realized, judging from Lindsay's response. "They're yours from the time Chloe had her little accident. I kept them here in case of another emergency."

He chuckled and accepted the clothes. Goliath leaped up and sniffed. He must not have been impressed since he abruptly left.

Mason held up the sweats. "You forgot about these until just now, didn't you?"

She chuckled this time and tilted her head toward the guest bathroom. "Stop reading my mind and get dry, then join us in the playroom."

"Aye, aye, matey." He lifted two fingers to his forehead in a mock salute.

Lindsay rolled her eyes and walked away. The intriguing smile on her face caused him to sway slightly. This was Tim's widow, and he had no right to think of her in any other light.

In the guest bathroom, he splashed cold water on his cheeks before he swapped his set of sopping-wet navy sweats for the dry gray ones with the faintest trace of the lavender fabric softener Lindsay favored. He left the bathroom and found them all in the living room. With a few strokes, he rubbed his hair with the towel and watched the scene before him. Grandpa Joe was helping Chloe build a cabin with Lincoln Logs while Lindsay and Evan constructed something of their own. The serenity of the setting wasn't lost on Mason, and he credited Lindsay with the toasty atmosphere as opposed to the wet mess of the spring storm outside.

Even the soft instrumental music, something low and sweet with a Celtic flair, brought a sense of repose, something lacking this afternoon when he and Jordan came upon the scene at Timber River.

She'd even found an old blanket and pillow for Goliath, who was curled up on a makeshift dog bed. He didn't realize he needed this. Until now.

"What's that?" Mason asked and settled on the cream carpet. He pointed to the structure in front of Lindsay and Evan.

"It's a greenhouse."

"It's a dungeon."

Mother and son had answered at once, then both burst out laughing.

"I guess we didn't ask each other. It just happened," Lindsay explained.

Lightning flashed, spotted through the window, with thunder splitting the air a few seconds later. Her gray gaze met his, and something connected between them, an arc of electricity as potent as the storm. He shivered, too aware it had nothing to do with the weather and everything to do with this beautiful woman. She scrambled to her feet.

"How about some peppermint tea to ward off any lingering cold from the rain? Or I can put on a pot of decaf?"

She turned toward Grandpa Joe. "I bought more of that hazelnut creamer you liked the other night."

"Can we have hot chocolate?" Evan licked his lips.

Chloe separated herself from Grandpa Joe and motioned for Mason to pick her up. He did so, and she reached for his hair and giggled. "Mason's hair scwunchy."

"Crunchy hair? Not exactly the look I was going for, but it should be all the rage next season."

A loud clap of thunder rocked the house, and Chloe lowered her head to his shoulder and whimpered. Lindsay rushed over, but Mason comforted the little girl by rubbing her back. "It's just the air, honey, but it's more fun to imagine a story for it. Some say thunder is someone bowling a strike or maybe banging on a drum." Two rams butting heads with each other also came to mind. Sort of how he'd been feeling around Lindsay these days.

Chloe giggled, faced him and patted his cheeks. The lights in the house flickered, but the power didn't go out. The rain crashed with force against the windows, and again he met Lindsay's gaze. She checked her phone and then announced, "Severe thunderstorm warning and tornado watch. We're moving this party to the basement."

Grandpa Joe rose and clutched his back. "I think I'll stay up here and give the all-clear signal when it's safe."

A tornado siren pierced the air, and Goliath howled. Chloe tightened her grip on Mason, digging her little fingers into his back. He transferred her to Lindsay. "If you take Evan and Chloe, I'll be down in a minute with Goliath and Grandpa Joe."

Lindsay nodded and ushered her children to the basement. Mason went over to Grandpa Joe as the shrieking wind intensified. "Time to join them."

Grandpa Joe nodded. He tried to step forward and winced. "My back medicine's in my bedroom at your house. I can't make it downstairs like this. Take Goliath, and I'll wait out the storm here."

Mason reached for his grandfather's arm and finagled his way under him, so he supported most of his weight. "Goliath will follow you, and I'll get your medicine when it's safe. Come on."

With some effort, his grandfather made it down the stairs. As soon as they reached the finished basement, Lindsay helped with Grandpa Joe. Together they settled him on the sectional. Then she handed out candles and matches. "In case the power goes out."

Lindsay picked up the children's book she'd been reading, and huddled her kids around her. Even Goliath's and Grandpa Joe's ears perked up as her calm voice filled the air. Within minutes, rhythmic sounds of breathing and dog snuffles prevailed, and even Mason had a hard time keeping his eyes open.

What seemed like only minutes later, he opened his eyes. He shifted from his place on the floor and jerked awake, checking his cell's screen only to find it was already Thursday. His gaze went to Lindsay, her arms protecting Evan and Chloe cuddled against either side of her. He'd never seen her asleep before, with her honey-brown hair surrounding her like a soft cloud.

Lindsay was beautiful. The thought rocked him as her eyelids fluttered open. With a start, she blinked and looked around the room. He pointed toward the stairs, and she extracted herself, taking caution not to wake Evan or Chloe. His grandfather rested on the other side of the sectional. In spite of the circumstances, Mason wasn't in that big of a hurry to break this spell.

She rubbed her neck and joined him, her gray eyes still tinged with sleep. His gaze landed on Goliath, who peeked at them before returning to sleep at his grandfather's feet.

"How late is it?" Her whisper caressed his cheek, and he stepped backward. Anything to stop this type of reaction to Tim's widow. "Ten, eleven?"

He held up his phone. "More like five in the morning."

Her eyes widened, and she hurried up the staircase. He followed her. Wedding pictures hung on the closest wall. Was it just him, or was Tim frowning at Mason's reaction to his wife?

"Thanks for not waking the kids. I wanted to look at my messages," she said and extracted her phone from her pocket. When she scrolled, her eyebrows creased. "Aunt Hyacinth texted. Her house is fine, and she's meeting her business partner to check on Sweet Shelby's Tea Room."

Mason checked his messages, focusing on the ones from his coworkers detailing the tornado that had touched down outside city limits. His chief hadn't activated him to report for duty, so he texted him he was available if needed. A quick reply informed him everything was covered. He waited as three more dots appeared. He let out a breath as the reply indicated calls were limited to being about power outages and the like, without the need for extra paramedics at this time.

"I'm going home for Grandpa Joe's medicine."

"Oh, no! Your grandfather's back. I totally forgot. I'm so sorry. He needed that medicine."

Mason waved away her apology. "You did everything right. And your house has a basement, so I'm glad we were here. You kept him calm, and we all apparently liked the story you read to Evan and Chloe a little too much."

She chuckled, although her smile didn't reach her eyes. "Is that a polite way of saying I put everyone to sleep?"

"No. It's a polite way of thanking you for the kindness you provided my grandfather. And me."

Without hesitation, he leaned in and brushed her cheek

with a quick kiss. He quickly pulled back and left via the sliding glass door. Outside, darkness surrounded him, his lips still tingling from the contact with Lindsay's soft skin. The rain had stopped, and a mountain bluebird's predawn chirps cut through the silence. Her friendship meant everything to him. Why had he done something foolish, like kissing her cheek?

Mason retrieved Grandpa Joe's medication and brewed a cup of coffee in case he was called in. He poured his first cup and lingered, his normal confidence replaced by doubt. Should he bring up the kiss? Should he apologize?

Taking the last sip, he clutched the pill bottle and headed for Lindsay's, a sliver of orange and pink on the horizon heralding the beginning of the new day. The impact of last night's storm became evident in the light. He stopped and stared. Lindsay's vegetable garden, the one she tended so reverently, looked as though a giant had stomped on it, the row markers shredded like cheddar cheese. Nothing would be salvageable. All that work gone in an instant.

A brief rap on the sliding glass door and he let himself into her kitchen, wondering whether he should begin by telling her about her yard or face up to discussing the kiss.

He found her on her cell phone, her cup steaming on the counter with the tea bag hanging over the edge. As quiet as he could be, he checked on the occupants of the basement, still asleep. Upon his return to the kitchen, Lindsay was looking annoyed, her phone on the counter.

"What's wrong?"

"The tornado. It hit the botanical garden. My boss wants me to stay home until he evaluates the damage, even though there's no safety risk as far as anyone can tell. I hate it when others make decisions for me. I need to see it for myself." She glanced at the door to the basement.

"On top of that, their day care center sent out a text. They incurred some damage and are closed today."

Mason checked his phone, and his chief hadn't changed his mind. "I'll watch Evan and Chloe."

"I shouldn't be too long."

He grinned, knowing she'd lose track of time once she was there. "Take as long as you need. If I'm called in, Grandpa Joe is here." He held up his grandfather's medication. "This doesn't cause drowsiness, so he should be fine."

"Thanks." She grabbed her car keys and rushed for the front door.

He cleared his throat, and she glanced over her shoulder. "Is something wrong?"

"I love pink hippopotamus lounge pants, but you might want to change."

Her cheeks flamed and she rolled her eyes. "Where would I be without my best friend?" She grabbed her tea and hustled upstairs.

Where would he be without his best friend was the real question, and one he didn't want answered.

CHAPTER FOUR

THE DAMAGE WAS more extensive than Lindsay had feared. At Sycamore Station, she clenched her stomach, feeling as though she might be sick. Numbness overtook her, her bones weak at the sight of uprooted plants and broken stems. She reached down and rubbed a velvety cosmos petal between her fingers, frowning at the devastation of what was once beautiful and alive now reduced to debris and fleeting memories.

The canna flowers she planted a few days earlier were ruined, their remnants scattered and plastered in the thick, drowning mud. The circle for the memorial garden was destroyed. This was more than her workplace or a garden. It was her sanctuary. She loved these plants. Now she'd have to start all over.

She stood and faced Phillip. Protective goggles covered his eyes. "We have to postpone the opening." Lindsay didn't want to waste a moment driving her point home. "I can't guarantee we'll be ready in time."

Stone-faced, he examined the sycamore, some of its smaller branches lying on the ground, a gash evident just above her eye level. "The gardens are fortunate. With most of the damage relegated to this area and the Children's Play Zone, where Heather is going to oversee the cleanup—"

"Excuse me?" She couldn't believe her ears. "Those are my tasks. Overseeing the volunteer roster is also on my list of duties."

"And I oversee you. My wife is more than capable of simple limb removal and tidying up, so you can focus all your energy and attention on this area and on the damage to the visitor greenhouses on the western side." He moved the goggles to the top of his head and wiped off some sweat. "The tree will be fine. The gash isn't deep and the opening will continue as planned."

"The circle of flowers is destroyed, and I have to begin again." His stony face gave no sign her words were having an impact. "Can you at least postpone the opening date?"

"We're already going to lose visitors for the next two days while we make repairs, and we can't afford that at our busiest time of year. At least the space sycamore was spared from ruin. This is becoming an unnecessary discussion. We're wasting precious minutes. I expect a report with any revised budget estimates and so on by next Monday." He removed the goggles altogether, and his face suddenly softened. "My vacation in Wilmington already seems a distant memory. Heather and I do truly miss the place. Never mind, the fact is we need visitors back here ASAP. We're on the same side, Lindsay."

He strode away, and she surveyed the scene once more before starting out for the supply shed. The buzz of chainsaws whirring to life cut through the silence, so unlike the normal gleeful shouts from the Children's Play Zone. She paused with her hand on the latch of the fence. One of the oaks that provided shade for the giant playground had split in two before falling on the main wooden play structure, and she shivered. At least the tornado had swept through at night, rather than the busy daytime, with no injuries reported so far.

Her phone chimed the familiar ringtone of her mother, and she winced. She knew she'd forgotten someone.

She accepted the call but before she could say a word she heard her mother's voice.

"Why did I hear about a tornado from Hyacinth and not from you? Thank goodness my twin sister texted me and assured me she was safe, but what about you? Are you okay? What about Evan and Chloe? Should your father and I quit our trip and catch the next plane back to the States?" Her mother managed to convey all of that in one breath.

"Good morning, Mom. I'm fine and the kids are fine." Her mother Dahlia and her mother's twin sister, Hyacinth, were day and night. Hyacinth loved Hollydale while Dahlia roamed the globe with Lindsay's father, now retired from chiropractic medicine.

Dahlia and Jonah had sold their house prior to their around-the-world adventure, placing a deposit on a town-home in the new development near Sully Creek, which wouldn't be ready until late summer.

"There's no need to fly back from India. Everyone's fine, and I'd be lousy company seeing as I'll be putting in extra hours at the garden."

"Jonah, start packing the bags. Our grandchildren need us. Oh, Lindsay, those pictures you texted the other day are absolutely adorable."

Her parents' return was the last thing she thought she needed. Her mom had good intentions but in terms of practical help, it would be nonexistent. Same applied to her father.

"Is Dad there?" Lindsay waited until her mother passed her father the phone. "Please don't cut your visit short on my account."

"Oh? Wait a second. Your mother's tapping my arm—"

"Lindsay, are you spending every minute at work? That's not healthy, you know. When we arrive for the dedication, I'll teach you some new meditation techniques. It's the most divine experience." Lindsay listened as her mom went into detail.

Her mother finally stopped for breath, and Lindsay cut in. "Mom, I'm sorry, but Phillip moved the dedication up by two weeks. You'll miss the ceremony, but I'll be able to spend more time with you and Dad when you arrive."

"See, Jonah. I was right about that date. Your father double-checked the garden's website before he made our arrangements just now. It's settled then. We're coming home to Hollydale for the dedication. Hyacinth is having some work done to her bathroom in June so we're staying in your guest room."

Great. Now Lindsay had to air that room out and give it a thorough cleaning that would be good enough for her mother's inspection. In the meantime, Sycamore Station demanded her attention.

"Mom, I have work to do."

"Of course, darling. We'll talk more soon, and I can't wait to see your face when you and the children see your souvenirs. You're going to love them."

The goodbye stretched out for a while before Lindsay pressed the End Call button. She closed her eyes and counted. A tornado and her mother in one morning. She brushed her fingers where Mason's lips had skimmed her cheek. Tingles marked the exact spot, and she wasn't sure if that was a good thing or not, given as he'd hightailed it out of her house the second he'd realized what he'd done.

The first time a man kissed her since Tim had left on the morning of the helicopter accident. It was just a small peck on the cheek that hardly qualified as a real kiss, and yet Mason had run away faster than a rabbit being shooed from her vegetable garden. Hardly flattering, to say the least.

She pushed past the gate and reached the shed. What

would a real kiss from Mason feel like? Taste like? She shivered and hurried inside afraid she'd like the answer too much.

TWO SETS OF sparkling eyes gazed at Mason as though they expected him to sprout wings and fly around the room for their entertainment. After he'd fed Evan and Chloe steel-cut oatmeal with blueberries for breakfast while Grandpa Joe grumbled for doughnuts, they'd colored until his fingers cramped.

Then he'd fed the kids lunch and tucked them in for an hour of slumber along with his grandfather and Goliath. Nap time was now over, their supply of energy replenished, and they clamored for a new project.

The doorbell rang, and he sent silent thanks to whoever it was. He checked the peephole and spied Hyacinth waving and pointing to something that looked like a pie plate.

His mouth instantly watering, Mason opened the door, and Lindsay's aunt flowed inside, her sunflower scarf tied like a hairband around her curly gray locks. "Good afternoon, my sweethearts." She hugged Evan and Chloe, who crowded around her. "Who's ready for some pie?"

"Pie?" His grandfather echoed from the top of the stairs, and he and Goliath hurried down. "Hyacinth, you're a lifesaver. Mason insisted on an organic kale salad for lunch. A man needs sustenance."

What was wrong with kale? Mason was quite fond of it, and the crunch of the vegetable went well with the smoothness of his homemade pineapple vinaigrette. Evan and Chloe hadn't complained once.

Hyacinth patted his grandfather's cheek and then made her way to the kitchen. Like she was the Pied Piper, everyone, including Mason, followed close behind her.

"Aunt Hyacinth, what type did you make today?" Evan asked.

"Cherry crumble." She waggled her finger toward Mason, who came closer. "I know you like healthy food. This has oatmeal and the cherries are full of fiber."

"But how did you know we were here and not at my house?"

"Lindsay texted me that you and Joe are babysitting." Hyacinth opened cabinet doors, pulled out plates and started cutting the pie.

Mason hooked Chloe into her booster seat and handed her a small sliver of pie at the same time Hyacinth gave Evan his. "Thank you, Aunt Hyacinth." Evan bobbed his head before sitting next to his sister.

"Tank you," Chloe added.

"I've stopped by on my way from the tea room." Hyacinth clucked her tongue. "My business partner Belinda graciously consented to my leaving early so we can begin the gardening my niece won't mind us accomplishing on her behalf. Master gardeners like her are sometimes finicky, but we'll start by removing the debris."

"Since you're putting me to work, make mine a double slice." Grandpa Joe held out his plate like it was Oliver Twist's bowl.

Mason kept his growl to himself. Or at least he thought he had until his grandfather jerked his thumb toward the living room. Mason followed.

"What is your problem? And it had better be good since you're keeping me from pie," Grandpa Joe insisted.

"You hurt your back last night and could barely get down the stairs. Maybe you and Goliath," the dog jumped on Mason's leg when he uttered his name, "should stay inside so you don't get hurt."

"Nonsense. That nap and medicine worked wonders."

Grandpa Joe's mouth snapped shut, and he folded his arms. "I'm not twenty months old like Chloe. If I want to eat pie and garden, that's my choice."

He stomped into the kitchen, and Mason fought the urge to throw his arms up in the air. Hyacinth entered and placed a plate of pie and a fork into Mason's hand. "You look like you need this. I'll keep an eye on your grandfather while we're cleaning up Lindsay's yard. My husband, Craig, was quite obstinate that I not treat him like an invalid after his cancer diagnosis. It was hard to accept change, but we must. That was my gift to him and myself."

After pie and milk, they all headed outside, and Mason's gut wrenched at the devastation, more evident in the bright sunlight than at dawn. Chloe sucked her thumb, and Mason knelt in front of her. "Hey, sweetheart, what's wrong?"

Her big gray eyes, almost violet, filled with tears. "Mommy's gawden. Not pwetty like yesterday."

"Then we'll just have to make it pretty again, won't we?"

She nodded and removed her thumb. Gardening wasn't his preferred cup of coffee, but he'd do this for two of his favorite females and Evan.

Hyacinth assigned the tasks accordingly, and Mason helped Evan with the raking. A while later, they'd filled three garbage bags with yard scraps and stood back while Mason rested his chin on the tip of the rake handle. "Great job, E." He gave the boy a fist bump.

Hyacinth came toward them, holding a tall coppery stake sculpture thing that resembled a bare willow tree with multicolored bells hanging off each metal branch. "I'm so glad Lindsay stored this in her garage so her beautiful birthday gift didn't sustain any damage in last night's storm. This one has an especially significant meaning. You know Lindsay's maiden name is Bell, right?"

"Yes, ma'am." Mason kept from laughing, as he knew the whole story. Lindsay had stashed the metal structure away in her garage three months ago, not wanting to hurt her aunt's feelings by rejecting the gift.

"But Aunt Hyacinth—"

"Lindsay will be stunned when she sees it in the yard. Absolutely stunned," Mason interrupted Evan.

That was as close to the truth as he could manage.

Hyacinth beamed. "Evan, can you help Joe and your sister while Mason shows me where this goes?"

With no other choice, Mason set the rake against the house and picked up a trowel. He led Hyacinth to a spot in the front yard, shielded by some trees, and Hyacinth jabbed the wind chimes into the ground. "A bit of color makes the world that much brighter, don't you think?" Hyacinth pointed to the other helpers. "Spring air is glorious for people of all ages, and this type of activity will be perfect for your grandfather, don't you agree?"

Mason blinked, not sure which statement of Hyacinth's he was supposed to address. Instead, he nodded.

"You know, I really wanted to talk to you away from Joe and the wee precious ones."

He hadn't realized that, and he moved toward her. Since she was a good friend of his grandmother's, he had an idea about what was coming next. "Did Grandma Betty send you to check up on us?"

Did no one trust his judgment? For crying out loud, he was a paramedic. At work, people darn well better rely on him for split-second life-and-death decisions, and they did. Why didn't his friends and family do likewise?

Hyacinth reached out and patted his hand. "No, she didn't. Although now that you mention it, I sense tension in you. If you let it, gardening can be a most relaxing hobby, a chance for a person to get back to nature and allow life to spring up—"

"Lindsay's been telling me that for the past year."

Hyacinth removed her gloves and shifted them to her left hand. "And she's the real reason for this little chat. I'm concerned about my niece. You're her closest friend, so I'm assuming you have her best interests at heart. For the past few years, she's pruned herself by retreating into work and avoiding her friends until there's barely anyone left. She's surrounded herself with what's comfortable and familiar rather than allowing herself to blossom."

"Lindsay's a fighter, and she's doing her best to hold her family together." He dug his sneaker into the moist dirt and clenched the trowel, uncomfortable talking about his best friend behind her back. "I need to check on my grandfather. Leaving him alone with two small kids and a dog might aggravate his back."

Mason walked on.

"One more quick question if you don't mind." Hyacinth's pleading brought him to a halt, and he faced her. "Is Lindsay ready to date again?"

Shocked, Mason dropped the trowel.

He bent over and picked up the garden tool as Lindsay's truck pulled into her driveway. "You should ask her, but I'd wait until after dinner."

Lindsay slammed the driver's door, and Evan and Chloe ran toward her, enveloping her in a big hug.

"What's going on?" Her gaze landed on the bags of debris that Mason had dragged to the curb.

Hyacinth swept Lindsay into an embrace and then broke away. "You arrived home before we could finish our multitude of tasks. Why don't you go inside for a brief rest or shower? Maybe even enjoy a slice of oatmeal cherry crumble pie before helping us decide what you want to plant in your new vegetable garden."

Lindsay's face crumpled for a second before she blinked, her sad smile cutting Mason to the quick. "So everything's gone? The carrots? Snap beans?"

Hyacinth nodded. Mason longed to comfort Lindsay, but it was hard enough not to remember how soft her skin was when he kissed her cheek. A hug would do him in and would probably violate the friend code.

The bachelor track's the path for you, Mason. "Hyacinth mentioned it's not too late to plant zucchini. I have a recipe for zucchini muffins, and Evan and Chloe won't even guess that's the main ingredient," he said.

Lindsay's throat bobbed, and she exhaled a deep breath. "This is so kind. I can't change the weather, but I can change my clothes and help. I'll be back in a few."

Several ticks later, Mason excused himself and went inside. Lindsay was in the kitchen. Pie for dinner sounded good, so he snagged a piece. "Mind if I join you?"

She sent him a death glare. "Are you going to eat or talk to me?"

"If I stop eating, it'll only be to tell you crucial information that might save your life." He pretended to roll the ends of an invisible mustache.

"Save my life, huh?" She stabbed a small triangle of pie and brought it up to her mouth. "Sounds like I missed something diabolical."

"Worse than that. Your aunt wants to play matchmaker for you." He tasted the cherry pie and found this piece even more delicious than the first. It might be the pie, but more likely it was Lindsay's company. Even upset, something about her apple cheeks appealed to him and brought out another side to him. Why did Lindsay's presence suddenly impact him like this? He'd known her since Tim introduced her as his girlfriend and pulled Mason aside with the news she was *the* one, the woman who'd claimed his heart.

He'd lost one sister because of childhood leukemia and one best friend due to high winds taking down a helicopter flight rescue. Losing Lindsay, too, would be devastating. If he ruined this friendship because of his own selfishness? He had to back off and fast.

Lindsay finished sipping her milk. "Can you blame her? She and her group, I think they call themselves the Matchmaking Mimosas, took the credit for Jonathan and Brooke Maxwell's relationship. Here's another plum assignment right under their noses."

She popped another bite into her mouth as he pushed his plate away. Why did the thought of her moving on with anyone other than him irritate him as much as her moving on at all? Why did the first woman to intrigue him like this have to be the widow of the man he considered a brother?

He rose from his place at Lindsay's table and said, "After a day of gardening and kids, my motorcycle's calling me. It's been too long since I've tinkered with it."

Lindsay stood, her mouth agape. "Oh, no, don't tell me she tried to sign you up. I'll be absolutely mortified if she did."

She fell back into her chair, her cheeks flaming red. As much as he wanted to escape, he remained where he was. "She claims it's because she cares about the your future. Something about color and things blossoming."

Lindsay grimaced. "Caring is one thing. Making it impossible for me to meet you at the back fence later is another." She stabbed a piece of her pie. "You let her down easy, didn't you?"

"Hold on a second. What do you think your aunt said to me?"

"Why, she was trying to match us up, of course! After

Jonathan lost his Most Eligible Bachelor status, it was only time before they targeted you. Do you want me to tell her to leave your romantic future in your hands? Isn't that why you said my life depended on this conversation?"

He sat and brought his pie plate closer again. From her gray gaze, Lindsay believed he was the unlucky sucker, although settling down at all prickled his skin. Didn't it?

The fact Lindsay wasn't ready to date again should have cheered him up, yet her mortification at the thought of being set up with him was a distinct blow to his ego. This time he stabbed a piece of pie and brought it to his mouth, the oatmeal cherry cobbler now tasting like sandpaper.

The wobble in her smile let him know she expected an answer.

Mustering his strength, he produced a big belly laugh he didn't feel inside, and she joined in. "You know your aunt. She sees everything through rose-colored binoculars."

She reached across the table and covered the top of his hand with hers. That was the type of woman Lindsay was, warm and open, sweet and sharing. Until now, he didn't know he wanted something permanent, and someone like her. "Thanks for not bursting my aunt's bubble when she tried to set us up. Every once in a while, my ego needs a boost, especially after a bad day like today."

A sucker for punishment. That described him to a *T.* He cast aside his predicament by concentrating on her. "What happened?"

She finished off her pie, licking the fork clean, a blissful expression on her face. "My boss is overestimating my ability as a magician, and my parents are underestimating me. They're cutting their trip to India short just to fly in for the dedication." She winced. "When I put it like that, I must sound awful."

"So, the botanical garden was spared?"

"The tornado skirted the southern part, but the sycamore didn't sustain as much damage as Phillip and I originally thought. The tree will survive, but the rest of the memorial area needs a lot of work." She massaged the back of her neck. "And my boss is still committed to the new date."

"What new date?"

Her eyes widened, and a slow smile finally brought some color into her cheeks. "I haven't told you. This day might get better after all. The ceremony was moved up two weeks. Will you be able to attend now?"

He laid his fork next to his plate. "I won't be there."

"You claim he was like a brother to you, and yet you won't even come to the ceremony." Her nostrils flared, and those pretty pink lips formed a straight line before curling downward. "I don't get it."

Hyacinth burst into the kitchen and motioned to them. "Come outside. You have to see this."

Lindsay wasted no time in rushing outdoors, and Mason scrubbed his hand over his mouth, the tartness of the cherries now leaving a sour taste. Going to the ceremony would open memories better left closed, but staying away might cost him a relationship he couldn't bear to lose.

CHAPTER FIVE

"THAT'S NOT HOW you're supposed to plant seeds." Evan shook his head at Chloe. "Mommy showed us how to press one in the ground and cover it up, 'member?"

"Evan no fun." Chloe threw a few seeds down and then ran along the row, scattering more seeds as she went. Two unique personalities converging in one garden. Only time would tell which tactics yielded the most zucchini.

"You're such a baby," Evan scolded.

"Am not."

Evan popped his hands on his hips and glared at Chloe. Lindsay exhaled and took another deep breath before coming over.

To her chagrin, Mason followed. Never before had her judgment let her down to this extent. How could she be attached to someone who showed no loyalty to what she held dear? Once more, Mason had declared he had no intention of attending the dedication ceremony, and the other day he'd confided in her about Bree's condition but only when she was halfway in her house, rather than confiding in her outright. How could she still feel the undercurrent of attraction between Mason and herself? It didn't make sense.

Evan unfurled his dirt-crusted hand and showed Lindsay the remaining seeds. "Aunt Hyacinth let us plant the zucchini, but Chloe's doing it wrong."

Chloe's lower lip trembled before she burst into tears. "Am not."

Mason stepped forward and cleared his throat. "Evan, a gentleman should always be respectful of his sister."

Lindsay shook her head. "A gentleman should also honor commitments, don't you think, Mason?"

That familiar face, handsome even, was tinged with sadness. "My motorcycle's calling me. Evan, Chloe, see you later."

Goliath yipped and ran circles around Mason as her neighbor strode across their shared side yard. Joe whistled for the chiweenie, who circled one more time before heeding his owner's call. Joe reached into his pocket and threw a treat to the dog. Lindsay stared at the corner of the house where Mason had disappeared from view. The evening, full of promise and a shelter from the day's events, stretched out before her, longer now since their later fence chat was presumably canceled.

"Thank goodness that a lovely friend tended to the needs of my boxers, Artemis and Athena, after work, but I must get home." Her aunt looped her sunflower scarf around her neck and patted Lindsay's cheek. "My dear, don't let discouragement take root. Last night's storm wreaked havoc in your precious garden, but new plants will bloom and spread joy."

Her aunt left, and Lindsay walked over to Joe, who was clipping Goliath's leash onto his harness.

"I know Mason," Lindsay began. Or she thought she did. His walking away so easily left her doubtful of that. And if she was wrong about that facet, what else was she wrong about? "Once he starts on his motorcycle, it'll be hours before he emerges from the garage. Did you want to eat dinner with us?"

"At my age, I've learned never to pass up an offer like that from an attractive woman." He laughed. "Especially when you know your wife would approve."

Goliath yipped and jumped on her. Lindsay scratched behind his ear until he flopped on his back. She knelt beside him and gave him a good belly rub. "You're invited, too, Goliath. Joe told me what brand of dog food you eat, and I bought a bag."

Lindsay straightened and found Joe's gaze never wavered from where Evan and Chloe were finishing planting their zucchini seeds.

"Chloe looks so much like my Colette." Tears slipped down Joe's cheeks, and he batted them away with his free hand.

Was Joe having an episode? Who was Colette? He reached out and patted her arm. "I see your look of alarm. My memory's fine, m'dear. Surely you know about Coey. Mason always called her that since he couldn't pronounce Colette."

She shook her head, unsure of everything today. "Who's Colette?"

"My granddaughter and Mason's sister."

Concern overtook her once more at Joe's faulty memory, so she kept her voice as gentle as possible. "Oh, you mean Bree. I forgot to ask Mason if he heard from her during his shift."

Joe sagged against the side of Lindsay's house, and Goliath left her and licked Joe's pant leg before resting at his feet. "I thought you knew Peter and Tara had three children. Colette died of childhood leukemia when she was four. Bree was born two months later, too late to be tested as a bone-marrow donor."

"No, I didn't know that. Mason never talks about her." Lindsay's heart went out to Mason's parents. She'd seen Tim's parents during his funeral and would never forget the grief etched in their faces at losing their only child.

"Don't think he's forgotten about her, though. I'm sure he hasn't." Just then, Chloe ran over to him, and Joe smiled.

"All done," Chloe announced.

"That's a big girl." Joe bent down and tweaked her nose, raising his hand with his thumb tucked between his index and middle fingers. "Look at what I have. I have Chloe's nose."

Her daughter giggled, her curly honey-brown hair bobbing with her. "Want my nose back."

Joe pretended to paste her nose on his face. "But I need a new nose. That way I can smell when Goliath needs a bath." He sniffed his dog, who raised his head and lowered it again. "Ooh, boy. He's getting one tonight."

Laughter erupted, and Chloe fell on her bottom. Evan ran over. "What's so funny?"

"I have Chloe's nose," Joe announced, winking at Evan in an obvious ploy to try to get her son to go along with the joke.

"It looks great on you." Evan grinned until Chloe's lip trembled. He reached up and touched Joe's nose, then Chloe's. "It's back, Chloe. Don't cry."

Chloe sniffled and patted her nose. A huge smile broke over her face. "Yay!" Lindsay reached out to Chloe, who pulled away. "My nose, not yours."

Joe chuckled and gave her a salute. "Aye-aye, Cap'n Chloe."

Lindsay's head ached at everything that had transpired that day. She glanced at the house next door. She'd had such high hopes Mason would attend the rescheduled dedication. For the first time, though, she wondered why she'd set her mind on that. Was it for his grief process? Or was it for her wanting someone there she could lean on?

Would he be letting Tim down if he didn't attend? Or would he only be letting Lindsay down?

And did it matter as much now that she had more insight about why he might want to stay away?

MASON TIGHTENED THE leather washer and bolt for the motorcycle's gas tank. He twisted the wrench once more and made sure it was good and secure so the tank wouldn't scratch the paint, the washer acting as a needed buffer. Stepping back, he swiped his forehead with his arm and removed his noise-canceling headphones. Then he turned off the Do Not Disturb feature on his phone. No sooner did he do so than his phone rang with a call from Bree.

"I just wanted to say hi to my big brother before my surgery tomorrow." Her voice wobbled, and he understood.

"But I thought we agreed the next time you called me would be to say hi after the surgery." He tried projecting cool confidence while shoving the phone between his shoulder and head. Then he walked over to the supply shelf.

"I changed my mind. If something happens to me—"

He wouldn't let her go there. "Nothing bad is going to happen, only good. The doctors will remove the tumor, and then Tristan will send that group text to let us know you're okay."

An extended silence came over the line. "Tristan and I had a fight."

Seemed he wasn't the only Ruddick to get in an argument with someone today.

He switched the phone to his other ear. "Wouldn't Grandma Betty be better with this kind of thing? She's been married for over fifty years."

"I need to talk to someone who won't make everything glossy and rosy for me. Tris and Grandma Betty have been doing everything for me. It's worse with Mom emailing and asking if she should finish her thesis in the States. I've replied I want her to stay with Dad in Australia. His work at the rift there is important."

So she called her big brother. Did everyone regard him as honest and overly blunt? What if they were wrong? What if he was just a rebel with a chip on his shoulder? Some unidentified caller tried to interrupt, but Bree was more important. "You make me sound like the voice of gloom, but since I'm honest to a fault, you know any surgery has some inherent risks..."

"Thanks, brother dearest."

"But you're young and, until now, you've had no health issues. You've got the best shot there is to beat this. Don't worry, I'll call Mom and Dad and talk them into not asking for a leave of absence." He set the phone on Speaker, grabbed the bar end mirrors and set them on his workbench. "You know I'd be with you if you wanted me there. All you have to do is say the word. But I have confidence in the doctors and you."

"And you're still in Hollydale, where I want you to stay."

"Yep." Intense rapping at his side door jolted him. "Someone's here, Bree. I'm looking forward and you should, too. You'll come through the surgery just fine. I'm sure it'll be with flying colors. Love ya."

"Right back at you." Bree's voice sounded more hopeful and optimistic, perfect for tomorrow's surgery.

"Mason. I have dinner." Lindsay's voice, insistent and loud, reached him.

As if on cue, his stomach rumbled, and he opened the door. The brightness from the garage's interior was a contrast to the darkness outside. He rubbed his eyes and blinked. "What time is it?"

"Well past nine o'clock." Lindsay wove her way around the block with his motorcycle and set the aluminum-covered plate on his workbench. "After you rejected his phone call, he phoned me, worried about you."

He checked his phone. Good grief, that missed call was his grandfather. "I didn't realize it was him—I was talking to Bree. Thanks for the dinner. I'll let Grandpa Joe know I'm fine so he and Goliath can get some sleep on a real mattress. Good night."

Lindsay folded her arms and didn't move. "How's Bree?"

"Her surgery's tomorrow, and she's nervous." A bit of an understatement, and he didn't blame his sister one bit.

He opened the box with the bar end mirrors.

"Aren't you even curious about your dinner? For all you know that plate could contain a double bacon cheeseburger and French fries with a side helping of Carolina slaw." Lindsay moved, blocking his path to his tools.

"I trust you. You know what I like."

"But I didn't know you had another sister." The hurt and sadness reflected in her face cut him to the core.

"I don't talk about Colette."

"Why not?"

His jaw clenched, and he slid the first mirror out of the box. "She died a long time ago." He examined the mirror and muttered something under his breath.

"What's wrong?" She craned her neck.

"The mirror's cracked." He flipped it over for her to see. This setback would cost him a couple of weeks while he waited for the new part, and just when he was so close to finishing. He'd dreamt of feeling the breeze on his cheek as he sped along the curves of the mountain roads. "I'll have to order a replacement. It might take weeks before I can finish this now."

She picked up the plate of food, holding it out to him. "More time with your grandfather. Maybe that's not as bad as you think. Neither is eating your dinner hot off the grill."

He accepted the offering and peeled back the foil and found his favorite meal, grilled salmon and roasted vegetables.

"Unless you believe that superstitious nonsense about broken mirrors and seven years of bad luck."

"Come to think of it," he said. "Tim introduced me to you seven years ago."

"Ha-ha, hilarious." She rolled her eyes and a corner of her mouth lifted. "And we only met six years ago. You must have me confused with someone else."

Never. "Nope. Tim fell and fell hard." He grasped the fork and ate a bite of fish.

She leaned against the wall and watched him take another bite. "I think you underestimate yourself. You keep from falling so you don't get hurt."

His best friend was too perceptive at times. If he let himself, he could fall for someone like her, but never her.

He needed a distraction and time away from his house, from Evan and Chloe, from Lindsay. He chewed another bite and lost that battle, determined to win the war. "Tomorrow night at the fence?"

She met his gaze, and something crackled in the air. The hairs on his arm were sticking up. "How about earlier rather than later? I want to hear about how Bree's surgery went."

Of course she would. That was Lindsay. Even if she was upset at him, she still cared, and not just about him, but about every member of his family. "How's six work for you?"

"Great. Aunt Hyacinth is picking Evan and Chloe up from day care while I make dinner for the four of us. I'll have time to eat with them and find out about their day before our talk. Looking forward to hearing good news about Bree." She passed him, before turning back. "And more about Colette."

That was also Lindsay. Tenacious. She stuck to what she believed in. The broken bar mirror taunted him from its position on the workbench, and he threw it away.

CHAPTER SIX

LINDSAY KICKED OFF her left gardening clog into her walk-in closet while smiling at Chloe. Her daughter was chattering nonstop about riding in the caboose of the cardboard train at day care. Aunt Hyacinth rushed into the room, the scarf with colorful tulips, one of Lindsay's favorites, flowing behind her.

"There you are, my darling little buttercup." Aunt Hyacinth swooped Chloe into her arms.

"Are you sure you can stick around while I talk to Mason?"

"You only trust me to watch Chloe and Evan when they're asleep? I'll have you know Craig's nephews and nieces visited us often, and I seem to recall a certain little girl who loved playing pat-a-cake with her uncle Craig." Aunt Hyacinth's eyes glowed the way they always did when she spoke of her late husband.

Lindsay gave her arm an affectionate squeeze, and traded her other gardening clog for a pair of slip-on moccasins that would caress her feet. Her silver T-strap sandals with the two-inch heels winked at her next to her Wellingtons, and she caught a glimpse of her favorite green cocktail dress hiding in the far recesses behind her work blazers. What would Mason's reaction be if she showed up at the fence with a touch of glitz and glamour, a far cry from her ripped jeans and soft floral knit shirt?

Would he even notice? And why did she care? It wasn't

like she and Mason were destined to be anything other than best friends and next-door neighbors. Although lately she wondered...

Lindsay checked her watch. She pecked Aunt Hyacinth's wrinkled cheek, tapped Chloe's curly head and rushed out, only stopping at the sight of Evan and Goliath curled up together on the living room sectional while Joe rested at the other end with earbuds and a tablet, and one eye open and one eye closed. She hurried outside.

She wasn't too surprised Mason had beaten her to the fence, today's tie-dyed T-shirt a subdued mix of blues stretched out across his chest, drawing emphasis on how he kept himself in shape. From what she'd heard from his new partner's mother, a volunteer at the botanical garden, those hours at the gym had paid off last week in a rescue involving a group of teens who'd capsized while white water rafting. Mason hadn't mentioned it once to her.

For someone who drew the attention of many ladies, he never blew his own horn. His gaze was glued to his phone, and his fingers were flying fast and furious.

"Good news, I hope." She plopped into one of the Adirondack chairs and he settled into the other.

"Yes. Bree's husband, Tristan, is communicating via a group chat. Grandma Betty already called Grandpa Joe and told him everything went well."

"So, your grandmother will be coming home soon?" Although she was happy for Betty and Joe, she couldn't help but feel Mason and his grandfather needed more time together.

He shook his head and frowned. "They're going to do a scan next week to see if Bree needs any further treatment, and then Tristan has to leave again. Since my parents work in Australia, Grandma wants to stay put until Bree is in the clear."

Lindsay started to say something when the sound of car doors slamming from the direction of Mason's driveway caught her attention. "Are you expecting someone?" she asked.

"No." He looked as surprised as she did.

He headed for his front yard and peeked around the corner of his house. Then he rushed back. "You have to come with me."

She jumped up from the chair, which had been comfy after a day of constant motion. "What's going on?"

"Covered dishes. That only means one thing. Someone's trying to match me up with an unsuspecting female. You have to protect me." Desperation and humor clung to his voice, and he faced her. "Please."

"Since this is no doubt the work of my aunt Hyacinth, I guess it's my duty to help."

"Um, if I didn't make it crystal clear yesterday, your aunt wasn't trying to fix me up. She only has her eyes set on finding someone for you."

What? Lindsay hadn't seen that one coming, but before she could interrogate him further, he pulled her toward the house. "You better do the same for me someday, Mr. Ruddick," she muttered under her breath, but hoped was still loud enough for him to hear.

Mason released her, and her hand tingled where he'd touched her. Alarm skittered through her until a raindrop plopped on her nose. The electricity must be due to the weather, and not Mason. At least, she hoped it was due to the impending storm.

They approached the front stoop where two women were talking animatedly as if plotting their next move.

"Hello, ladies." Mason's voice flowed with the buttery smoothness of Carolina sourwood honey, Lindsay's favorite for her weekend tea.

The pair turned toward her and Mason. The shorter woman, Mitzi, the owner of the best beauty salon in town, held her hand to her chest, which contained one of the biggest hearts in Hollydale. Mitzi was one of her favorite people.

"Good thing Destinee is holding your grandpa's cheesy bacon chicken casserole instead of me—you scared the whatsit out of me, young man. Evening, Mason, Lindsay." Mitzi nodded at them, her gray bob accented with one bright purple streak, the same color as her bright tunic paired with black leggings.

"Evening, Ms. Mayfield—"

"It's Mrs. Thompson now." She beamed. "You know, every time I correct someone I think of how Owen practically glowed on the stairs of the gazebo on Valentine's Day. That might be, though, 'cause he was freezing. What was I thinking having an outdoor ceremony in the middle of a Great Smoky Mountain winter?" She chuckled and glowed herself before turning to the taller woman standing next to her. Destinee resembled a model with her hourglass figure and high cheekbones.

Lindsay's floral knit shirt and ripped jeans seemed almost shabby next to Destinee's sequined shirt and bright capris and stilettos.

Mason opened his door and unloaded the casserole dish from Destinee's hands. "Let me take that from you."

"Ooh, thank you, dumplin', and just so you know, I'm Destinee with two e's. That casserole was getting so heavy." The younger woman fluttered her eyelashes, thick with black mascara, and swept back her long, bouncy blond curls. "This is my momma's secret recipe, and it's so delish."

"Luanne is having her corns removed from her feet, so her niece Destinee, who's also a certified stylist, is filling in for her for the next couple of weeks before she heads back to Dillsboro." Mitzi entered Mason's house and looked around. "Where's Joe?"

"Grandpa's next door with Evan and Chloe." Mason smiled at Destinee, who flashed her shiny white pearls. "They're Lindsay's adorable kids."

"You love kids, too? I just knew from the way Mitzi talked about you we'd have so much in common. Dillsboro's just an hour away." Destinee leaned over and touched the ends of Lindsay's hair. "Oh, honey, before I leave town, you need to come into the salon. I'll get rid of those split ends in two seconds and shape your hair so it frames your face. You really ought to consider some gold highlights, too."

If Destinee kept talking, Mason might have to protect the blonde from Lindsay instead of Lindsay protecting him. Lindsay blinked back this unexpected twinge of jealousy and tried to ignore Destinee's flirting with Mason. Odd because the only time she ever felt riled up always involved Mason, and this had to stop. "Thanks for the suggestion. I'll keep it in mind."

Lindsay spied Mason fighting to keep from laughing. He wasn't hiding it that well. "Ladies, it was a pleasure." He placed the casserole on his counter and wound his arm around Lindsay's waist. "Lin and I have to get back to Grandpa Joe."

Lin? Before she could challenge him on the nickname, Mason ushered the two women out of the kitchen and his house. As soon as he closed the door, he pressed his back against it, relief written all over him.

"I thought they'd never leave." He returned and picked up the casserole. "This would be the worst thing for Grandpa Joe's angina."

Mason approached his trash can but Lindsay rushed

over. "You're right, but it would be an awful waste. My kids might like it, and we can guess the ingredients and report back to you. Sort of make it a game."

"Be my guest." He laid the dish back on the counter.

Lindsay eyed the casserole. "Then again if they love it, and I can't replicate it, I might have a revolt on my hands."

They both stared at the offering, and Mason snapped his fingers. "Wait a second." He whipped out his phone and sent someone a text. A ping made her that much more curious about the recipient. "My new partner, Jordan, is more than happy to have a homemade meal."

The first time Mason had talked to her about his job after Tim's death had sent a ripple of pain through her. Thankfully, that subsided after a few of their fence talks. "What happened to your last partner, Duncan?"

Mason opened his refrigerator, and pulled out a tray. "I made lemon garlic turkey meatballs earlier. Hungry?"

Another reminder she hadn't stopped to eat more than that protein bar with all the activity at the garden. "Yes, but what happened to Duncan?"

Mason preheated the oven and leaned against it. "He wanted a change. We keep in touch. He's now on his way to becoming a physician's assistant."

The doorbell rang, and he opened the door. On his front porch stood another of her aunt Hyacinth's closest friends, Tina Spindler, who held a large tote bag. By her side was Officer Jillian Edwards in her police uniform, carrying an aluminum baking pan, similar to the one Mitzi and Destinee had just dropped off.

Mason waved the pair inside. "Hey, Jillian, Mrs. Spindler. How are you both doing this fine evening? Let me get that bag for you."

Lindsay was beginning to see a theme in tonight's offerings, and it had nothing to do with food. Aunt Hyacinth and the Matchmaking Mimosas had struck again.

But if Lindsay knew one thing about Mason from the past couple of years, it was that he didn't have any trouble finding dates all by himself.

"Drew's mother lives in Florida, and she's a force to be reckoned with, so please call me Tina." She thrust the bag toward Mason, and he accepted it. "There's homemade chicken noodle soup and four other types of soup as well. I had today off, and your grandmother called. How's your sister?"

Mason gave them the good news about Bree while unloading the soups into his freezer. "And speaking of family, Grandpa Joe is next door. I'm sorry to take your food and run, but I need to check on him."

Lindsay held up her phone. "Aunt Hyacinth texted a minute ago. He's rocking Chloe, and my aunt is making a sun catcher with Evan. You stay with your company while I check on them."

Though she couldn't imagine Destinee and Mason together in any universe, Jillian and Mason had so much in common, considering they both worked as first responders. Her stomach tightened at the thought of him getting serious with someone.

Mason glared at her, but what was she supposed to do? Come to think of it, when he did become serious about someone, would she lose her best friend? It would take a strong woman to accept her and Mason's friendship. Then again, she knew Mason wouldn't settle for less.

Tina bumped Jillian's arm and tapped her watch. "We're not staying. I'm with Jillian's mother tonight while Jillian's on duty. Rhoda has early-onset dementia, you know."

Jillian's face turned grim, and Tina gave her a small hug. "I have appointments next week in Asheville to look at assisted living homes." Jillian passed her container to Mason as if it held a hot potato. "It's baked orzo with chicken. I remember Joe had a touch of angina last year, and it's heart healthy. Time for me to head to work."

Tina smiled and shook her head. "One evening you need to let me stay with your mom so you can go out and have *fun*."

Lindsay didn't miss how Tina's eyes widened at Jillian and she tilted her head ever so slightly in Mason's direction. However, Mason was harder to read.

Jillian shook her head ever so slightly, then whipped out her phone. "Well, Becks Porter has been after me to go to the Timber River Bar and Grill with her and her friends for a fun night with the girls. I've lost touch with quite a few people outside of work since my mom's diagnosis." Jillian glanced up from the screen and over at Lindsay. "Once we choose a night that works for everyone, I'll send you an invite."

"Thanks." Lindsay watched as Mason escorted Tina and Jillian out the door.

Mason huffed out a breath once they were gone. He turned off the oven and removed the hot meatballs, then placed them on a trivet on the counter. "What happened to your promise to save me from the matchmakers?"

"What happened to the guy who brought a different woman to each of mine and Tim's barbecues? He'd already have called Destinee."

This was a standoff, no two ways about it. Tension lit the air with his blue eyes flashing fire. He stepped toward her, and she hoped this time his lips would connect with hers rather than her cheek. Before either could end the standoff, the doorbell rang again. They both laughed. "You never told me you live at the Asheville Regional Airport with arrivals and departures every fifteen minutes," she said.

He peeked through the peephole before opening the door and waving in Fabiana Ramirez and her daughter Graciela. "Welcome."

The ladies entered, each carrying yet another aluminum pan. Fabiana's gaze went from side to side. "Ah, Lindsay. Thank you for the advice about the garden. My leaves are so much fuller and don't have little holes in them anymore."

"Any time. Glad those aphids got the message." They weren't the only ones, either. Lindsay stepped forward and relieved Fabiana of her offering, the fragrant smells of garlic and rice making her even hungrier. She stopped short of grabbing one of Mason's forks and tearing off the foil. "This smells delicious. What did you bring?"

"It's Graciela's favorite, arroz con pollo. So delicious and full of flavor." Fabiana smiled proudly. "Graciela made those brownies herself. She's a better cook than I am."

Fabiana stared straight at Mason while she spoke, and he reached over and accepted Graciela's offering. Three matchmakers, three different choices with distinct personalities. Lindsay didn't know whether to congratulate him or cringe. Aunt Hyacinth interfering in her dating life wasn't for her, and she was unsure whether Mason would appreciate the attention despite his initial reaction to his first guests.

Mason nodded at Graciela and graciously accepted the dish, placing it on the counter next to the others. "This smells wonderful."

"De nada." Graciela rummaged through her purse and pulled out a form. "I'm selling dog bandannas as a fundraiser for the animal shelter. I thought adopting a senior chiweenie was so sweet of your grandparents. Can I put you down for a blue one for Goliath, oh, and a plaid one, too?"

Mason got out his wallet while Lindsay held her hand over her mouth, hiding her laugh. "Um, how much?"

She named her price with a wide, encouraging smile. "It's for a great cause. The proceeds go straight to the shelter, purchasing needed supplies and food." She accepted the bill he held out to her and added it to the envelope. "The bandannas should arrive in a week. Goliath will be the best-dressed dog in the neighborhood."

Fabiana folded her arms and craned her neck. "Where's your grandfather? Betty will be upset if I don't send her a positive report. Anything to help one of my best friends, and she and Joe are just the sweetest couple."

Mason hesitated, his hand on the cabinet that held his plates. "Wait a second. You mean, you, Tina and Mitzi have all shown up tonight for my grandfather?"

She walked over to Mason and patted his cheek. "Apparently you aren't feeding Joe enough."

"So I gather. Soups, casseroles and now brownies. Just for Grandpa Joe." Amusement laced Mason's tone, so he wasn't envious or upset this attention wasn't for him.

"Of course. Who else?" Fabiana stood tall, her back straight, her dark eyes fierce.

Graciela met Lindsay's gaze and she grinned. "Oh, Mami. I'll explain it on the drive home." She tapped Mason's arm. "By the way, Jordan speaks highly of you. We baked the dessert together."

"I'll call Grandma Betty tomorrow and make sure she's well-informed about my grandfather's health." Mason opened his front door for the women and smiled. "And I'll make sure he doesn't go to bed hungry."

Graciela led Fabiana away, and Mason shooed Lindsay out the door, then followed her. "I'd like to escape before anyone else descends on my home. I'll put the food away later."

She held up a finger. "One second."

An advantage of being his best friend was her familiarity with his kitchen, having permission to raid it on his days off if she ran out of something. She piled some of Fabiana's arroz con pollo onto a plate and shoveled in a couple of bites before joining him outside.

She sat on Mason's front stoop. The delicious seasoning and blend of flavors helped her savor this moment even more. He stared at her. "Do you want to eat the rest of this at your house?"

"In a minute. I rarely get to enjoy a hot meal, and this is too good to miss without tasting every bite. Try some." She moved over when he settled next to her and she handed him her plate.

"No fork? Some best friend you are."

From the sound of his voice, his ego wasn't too bruised.

"Here, use mine. You won't be sorry." She fed him a couple of bites, and her cheeks warmed. "Oh, oops, sorry. Hard habit to break. Of course, you can feed yourself."

Their gazes connected, something different reflected in those depths, and she pulled the fork back. Nothing could change between them.

"I think we both know I'm an adult, Lindsay."

The seriousness in his voice floored her. Apart from his job, where he was professional and more than capable of performing his duty, Mason was often lighthearted and flippant. This new side of him? Caring for his grandfather, helping with her garden? Then again, he was still the same Mason underneath, escaping to his motorcycle the first chance he got.

A little breathless and a lot warmer, she jumped to her feet, taking care not to spill any of her dinner. "I've been away from Evan and Chloe too long."

They trekked the short distance to her house, and she

made sure she kept her hands on the plate. Before she entered, though, he tapped her shoulder. "Have a minute?"

"For you? Anytime." She smiled. "That's what friends do for each other."

His brow furrowed, and apprehension, something she didn't usually see in him, appeared on his face. "I hear Grandpa Joe at night sometimes. He's not sleeping well."

"You know how it is. New house. A different mattress. Unusual sounds. It's sweet that you're concerned. Betty will be back soon, and she sent her friends to help. That type of friendship goes far." She hadn't kept up most of her friendships during her grief. Mason was one of the few who held tight and wouldn't let go. The fact that her friends were drawing her back now brought forth another smile.

"I'm your best friend, right?" He flashed a full grin, and her stomach went to flutter mode. "You know you can count on me any time of the day or night."

"Like I'd need to call you at night." She scoffed, keeping her plate steady, and then softened her expression. "I do, however, reserve the right to call you any time of day once my parents arrive."

"Oh, that's right. I remember what that was like when your mom moved in for a month when Chloe was born. Geesh. Still that bad, huh?"

"Worse. You know, I'm an only child and she's always hovered. Sometimes she takes over and does everything herself."

He nodded. "It happens. Are you done with your fork yet?"

"You can get your own from my kitchen." She moved her fork so he couldn't reach it.

"I wouldn't dream of taking something that someone else claimed first. Although it's a good thing Jordan claimed that casserole. I'll take it to him on our next shift."

The reminder of his profession with its inherent danger was helpful as they entered her house, and she guarded her food from Goliath, who jumped up, his little sniffer quite active. She'd do well to guard more than her plate.

What if she acted on her feelings for Mason and lost him the way that she'd lost Tim? In their type of job, especially, there were no guarantees.

CHAPTER SEVEN

SOMETHING SCRATCHED AT Mason's bedroom door. He turned over, pounded the pillow and then placed it over his head. The scratching became more insistent, and Mason bolted upright in bed, the pillow slipping to the carpet. Goliath's persistence must mean he needed a visit to the great outdoors, or...

Grandpa Joe!

Mason rushed down the hall with the chiweenie yapping and nipping at his heels. He threw open the door to Grandpa Joe's room. *Empty.* For the first time, the robust aroma of coffee reached his nose, and he hurried to the kitchen. In front of the refrigerator, his back to Mason, stood Grandpa Joe. He turned and shook his head. "Where do you keep the real bacon?"

Goliath sniffed at his leash, his signal for his morning walk. Mason waited for some acknowledgment from his grandfather of his dog's need for his morning ritual. Instead, the scowl grew deeper.

"Good morning to you, too, Grandpa Joe. Your dog wants to go outside, and egg whites are healthier for you. They're quite delicious when you get used to them." Mason would never be known for his tact, unlike Lindsay, who'd find out what was wrong with a sweet smile and a snack. In his experience, there wasn't time to beat around the bush.

Grandpa went over and poured himself a cup of coffee and returned to the fridge. "You're out of cream. A man needs sustenance to take his dog on a long morning walk."

"Good thing I bought extra turkey bacon for breakfast then."

Goliath yipped and headed toward the back door. Mason opened it and let the dog have free reign outside in his fenced yard. His walk would have to wait until later.

Maybe food cooked for him would perk up his grandfather. "How would you like your eggs this morning? Over easy? Boiled? Scrambled?"

"In Tennessee with my Betty. Not that I don't like spending time with you."

The problem crystallized, and Mason understood his grandfather's mood better. There was something sweet about how his grandparents' love endured this long. "I miss her, too, Grandpa."

Mason bustled about the kitchen, pausing to let the chiweenie back inside. "How about an egg-white omelet with onions and peppers?"

"How about adding cheese and ham to that? A man needs some protein." The grumbling reassured Mason that all wasn't lost yet.

He cracked eggs, separating the yolks and then whisking the whites. "The egg whites are a significant source of protein, but you convinced me."

His grandfather's eyes lit up, and he licked his lips. "Make mine so the cheese oozes out."

Mason opened the refrigerator and plopped a container of Greek yogurt in front of his grandfather. "Here. This has more protein than cheese, and it's much better for you."

Grandpa Joe shoved it away. "I'm not that hungry, anyway."

Undeterred, Mason cooked two omelets, delivering one to his grandfather. "What time do you need to be at the community center?"

"Brooke gave me the day off since I'm scheduled for

all day Saturday." He cut into the omelet and dropped a piece to the floor. Goliath snatched up the morsel. "Good thing, too. It'd be hard to pass the reception desk and not see my beautiful bride's face."

Mason borrowed a cue from his next-door neighbor and counted to ten. "Grandma's not dead, either. She'll be back soon."

"True, but I don't have anything to do today. Chloe and Evan are in day care."

Part two of the equation was now solved. Lonely and bored. He had to get his grandfather out of the house.

Mason took his first sip and spit out the coffee with a muttered curse. "What did coffee ever do to you?"

Grandpa Joe sipped his and shrugged. "Tastes good to me."

The way his grandfather had brewed it, this would strip the paint off his chopper. Come to think of it, Georgie Harrison, the restoration mechanic at Max and Georgie's Auto Repair, had notified him his new bar end mirrors had arrived, and she had personally inspected them to ensure they were not broken this time. A trek downtown was what this paramedic ordered. "How about we walk Goliath together this morning?"

"Come to think of it, he loves walking along Main Street and sniffing all the good food."

His plan backfired, and Mason sighed. "The Night Owl Bakery makes those raspberry Danish you love, right?"

"Only on Thursdays." His grandfather perked up. "Wait, that's today."

"Then we'd better hurry before Paige sells out."

At Sycamore Station, Lindsay extracted a soil sample from under the famous tree and then glanced around. Satisfaction at her slow but steady progress flittered through her. She'd spent most of the previous week cleaning up the damage from the tornado. The greenhouses had occupied most of her time, but they were back up to speed. Now with the tilling and fertilizing of the soil complete, she'd spent the morning with volunteers planting the new cannas and cosmos flowers donated by Jasper and Jules's Garden Center.

Her revised plan ensured something would bloom year-round with the winter irises and early daffodils, the ones that pushed up in January, providing a splash of color when most of the other exterior flowers and plants were dormant.

Lindsay returned to her rolling cart and examined her itinerary. She headed to the larger of the two greenhouses and entered the employee area. Suzie, the assistant greenhouse horticulturist recently back from maternity leave, glanced up from the Venus flytrap.

"Those new screens you suggested are such an innovative improvement. That zipper is so much easier to use than those old clips. Our electric consumption is down, too. We should see some real savings soon." Suzie removed her gloves and sipped from her water bottle. "And thanks for switching weeks with me on the snack schedule. You saved my morning. Elijah finally slept through the night, and I forgot to set the alarm. I wouldn't have had time to stop and pick up anything for tonight's staff meeting."

Snacks? Meeting? Lindsay kept her smile constant, not letting on that she'd forgotten about the switch. "I'm glad the screens are a success. They'll make my case for the new moisture-control monitors that much easier tonight." She glanced at her watch. "Time for my lunch break."

She left her cart behind and hightailed it to her truck. In no time, she parked near the gazebo downtown, a short distance away from the Night Owl Bakery. The gazebo, made with timber harvested for Hollydale City Hall, captivated attention for miles around.

Under normal circumstances, she'd linger and admire the tulips near the gazebo, but she didn't have any time to spare. A selection of petit fours, cookies, mini eclairs and tarts from the bakery ought to suffice for tonight's staff meeting. Mason would cringe at the treats with nary a vegetable platter in sight. The one time she brought fresh celery, broccoli and cherry tomatoes with a tasty homemade vinaigrette, Phillip glared at her throughout the meeting.

She walked toward the Night Owl Bakery and rubbed her eyes. Sitting at one of the café tables was Mason. He held on to Goliath's retractable leash. The small dog yipped and ran straight for her, jumping on Lindsay's legs.

"Let me guess. Grandpa Joe?" Lindsay ordered Goliath to get down and rewarded him by petting behind his ears.

"I thought this might cheer him up. He's missing Grandma Betty."

"And you're bribing him with sugar?" She cocked her head to one side and frowned. "That doesn't sound like the Mason Ruddick I know."

"A guy has to have some surprises up his sleeve." Mason grinned and reeled Goliath back his way. "Speaking of surprises, shouldn't you be at work?"

"I forgot I'm the designated snack provider for today's staff meeting." Her gaze widened, and she bit her lip. "Hold on a second. I need to call Aunt Hyacinth to find out if she can pick up Evan and Chloe from day care since I have to stay late for the meeting." She slipped her phone from her pocket.

Mason's fingers made contact with her hand holding the phone and she stopped, noticing the shock from his touch. He gave no sign of a similar reaction, a relief, she thought. Instead, Mason pointed toward the window where she saw

Joe taking a bite of a Danish. "Let me bribe Grandpa Joe with Chloe and Evan," Mason said.

"Excuse me?"

Goliath yipped at her high-pitched squeak.

"I'm on their approved checkout list, right?" He waited until she nodded. "We'll pick up the kids. Grandpa Joe loves spending time with them. It'll do him some good."

"I can't keep taking advantage of you."

"Nonsense. And besides, before you know it, Grandma Betty will return, and I'll get back to the single life. For now, though, he needs something, something I can't give him."

"Like Danish and other baked goods?" She couldn't resist teasing him a little, considering her heart was wrapping itself around how much Mason already anticipated a return to his old lifestyle.

Goliath flopped down and Mason rubbed his belly. "I'll feed them dinner."

"When you phrase it that way, how can I resist?" Lindsay chuckled and glanced at her watch. "Between the tornado cleanup and the class I'm giving at Jasper and Jules's Garden Center for Earth Day, I'm swamped."

"You're the lifesaver. Literally. This might save Grandpa Joe." He smiled and Goliath leaped into his lap, and Lindsay's heart melted at the sweet sight.

Lindsay hurried into the bakery and grinned at Joe, who held up his Danish, the impishness in his eyes a match for his grandson's. "You wouldn't believe how good these are. There are only a couple left. Make sure you buy one for Evan and for Chloe and one for yourself."

She laughed and nodded. "They're one of my favorites, too."

He smacked his lips and left the bakery. Lindsay went up to the counter and explained her dilemma to the owner,

Paige, who assured her she had a selection of goodies the botanical garden folks would enjoy.

Lindsay ordered five cupcakes for dessert as a thank-you to Joe and Mason. While she waited for Paige to box the treats, she glanced out the window at Goliath, jumping on Grandpa Joe, who accepted the leash from Mason. In such a short time, Mason had made strides with his grand-father to the point where he was going out of his way to find what the older man needed. If Mason was becoming more perceptive at reading emotions, she'd need to keep her growing feelings for him close to her vest. Mason made it clear that everything would return to the status quo when Grandma Betty was back, his path on the bachelor track the one for him.

She didn't need another hint he had no intention of set-tling down.

CHAPTER EIGHT

MASON SNIFFED HIS WRIST and frowned before transferring the salmon from the prep board to the grill. That new cologne Grandpa Joe had insisted he try on at the Smoky Mountain Emporium this afternoon was really pungent. It even overpowered the seasoned fish. Shuddering, he closed the lid and went inside, only to find Lindsay crossing into the kitchen and peeking into her oven.

"Do you like what you see?" He snapped the tongs for extra effect.

Lindsay clapped her chest with one of her hands. "You scared me."

He gestured to his apron and flip-flops. "I'm scary? I like to think I'm quite lovable. A real sweetheart, if I do say so myself."

She rolled her eyes and pointed to the oven. "You know I was talking about you sneaking up on me."

"I could say the same. I thought you'd arrive home much later."

"Short staff meeting."

He laughed. "I didn't think there was such a thing."

"Me either, but after a long day, I'm not complaining. Besides, I never criticize anyone who's cooking my dinner. What's in there?"

"Oven-baked jasmine rice. Since Grandpa Joe had a Danish today, I thought it might be a way to slip some cauliflower and zucchini past him." He spotted the famous pink box from the Night Owl Bakery on the counter. "And what's in there?"

She blushed a becoming shade of pink. "Red velvet cupcakes."

"Did I hear red velvet cupcakes?" Grandpa Joe and three other smiling faces popped into the kitchen.

Evan and Chloe licked their lips while Goliath wagged his tail. The timer pinged, and Mason used an oven mitt on the rice. His grandfather stared at the casserole dish as if it had two heads. "What's *that*?"

Mason recited the list of ingredients. Chloe folded her arms and plopped on the floor. "Unh-uh."

Lindsay reached for her. Chloe scrambled into her arms but wouldn't meet her gaze. "You know Mommy's rule. Try at least five bites or no cupcake."

Chloe held up three fingers. "Four bites?"

Evan came over and raised her pinky finger. "That's four."

"He's right." Lindsay moved Chloe's thumb. "But I said five and I mean five."

"Except for anyone who gets the senior discount at the Holly Days Diner, right?" Grandpa Joe grimaced and kept a wary eye on the rice dish.

"Those special people don't have to eat five bites." Mason nodded and clapped the tongs for effect once more as his grandfather broke into a grin. "They have to eat ten bites."

Lindsay's laughter followed him outside while he removed the salmon from the grill. Throughout dinner, Goliath went from person to person, looking for morsels of fish. Evan snuck him several pieces, and Goliath parked himself next to the four-year-old.

After dinner, Lindsay shooed everyone into the backyard. "Mason cooked, so I'll clean up."

Evan faced Mason. "Mom signed me up for T-ball. Can you teach me to catch?"

Guilt flittered through Mason. Tim should be the person Evan was asking for that honor. Still, it would be his privilege to fulfill Evan's request. He moved toward the boy, when his grandfather picked up one of the gloves on the patio.

Grandpa Joe touched Evan's shoulder. "I used to be pretty good with a baseball and glove. I taught my son Peter a trick or two, enough so he was the star shortstop on his high school team."

Mason stepped back and let Grandpa Joe take the lead.

Evan and Grandpa Joe made their way to a grassy area with Goliath on their heels. Mason stayed with Lindsay. "I'd be more than happy to help since you worked all day."

"I'll be fine." Lindsay pushed him and Chloe outside.

With some reluctance at leaving Lindsay's side, Mason escorted Chloe to the patio and settled next to her. Grandpa Joe was less than a yard from the young boy and tossed him the ball, obviously building his confidence with some easy catches. Then he lengthened the distance between them and tossed one with a little more force. It flew past Evan, who backtracked and fell. Goliath trotted over and began licking the boy's face.

Evan took his time getting up, and Mason left Chloe's side.

"Evan?" Mason didn't like how disoriented the boy's brown eyes looked.

Evan blinked, his pale face matching the blond hue of his hair. "Sorry, Grandpa Joe. I should have caught that one." His giggle didn't have its usual pep. "Goliath, I can't taste that good."

Grandpa Joe whistled, but the dog stayed at Evan's side. "Goliath." His grandfather neared, the annoyance of his tone matching his expression until he took a long glance at the little boy. He neared Chloe. "Come on, little girl. Let's go inside."

"Cupcake?" Chloe licked her lips and patted her stomach.

"We'll see. Mason needs a moment with Evan." Grandpa Joe's clear concern proved Mason wasn't imagining something was wrong. "I'll tell Lindsay."

Was the boy having an allergic reaction to something? Or was this an asthma attack? "No need. I'm taking him inside."

Mason swooped him into his arms over Evan's protests with Goliath hovering around the bottoms of Mason's jeans.

"I'm not little like Chloe. I can walk."

"Hey, you're practice for me. I have to stay in shape. Next month, I have to show my boss I can lift a hundred pounds and drag fifty. Your mom wouldn't be happy, though, if I dragged you inside." He pretended Evan was a barbell for a brief second. "So, you're the one doing the favor for me."

A slight giggle turned into a noise that sounded like Evan was whistling. Lindsay met them at the sliding glass door, and Goliath squeezed through before Lindsay slid it closed. "Joe said something was wrong. What's happening?"

Mason mouthed the words "asthma attack" and Lindsay grabbed her purse and extricated one of Evan's inhalers. Mason deposited Evan on the living room sectional. The whistling was now replaced with a harsher, wheezing tone. Goliath jumped up and stayed near Evan's side.

Lindsay handed Evan's inhaler and spacer to Mason. "I'm getting my phone and calling his pulmonologist."

She left while Evan curled up on his side, away from

Goliath, his eyes closed. Mason's paramedic training took over. He tapped the boy's shoulder, and his eyelids fluttered open again.

"I know it seems natural to want to take a nap, but when you're having an asthma attack, it's best if you sit upright. Can you do that for me?" Mason said in a firm but gentle voice. He tamped down his nerves. This wasn't just another case; he loved Evan very much.

Goliath thumped his tail against the cushions.

"I don't like asthma. Chloe can have it for me."

Mason chuckled and shook his head. "It doesn't work like that. We get what we're dealt with." Ironic, since he'd been thinking along those same lines not even an hour ago.

He checked Evan's pulse, which was about eighty. As long as it kept under ninety, medical attention at home would be sufficient. Evan's fingertips turned blue, and that sent off alarm bells. Mason uncapped the inhaler and gave it three firm shakes. He reassured Evan and then covered his face with the mask connected to the suction part of the spacer. Activating the measured-dose inhaler, Mason instructed Evan how to breathe and had him hold his breath while Mason counted backward from five. Lindsay appeared next to Mason on three, nibbling her thumbnail, while her gaze didn't leave Evan.

Evan repeated the deep breath as Mason relayed soothing instructions, waiting for the medicine to take full effect. After a few minutes, Mason removed the mask and spacer away from Evan's mouth. "How are you doing?"

"A red velvet cupcake would get the yucky taste away."

"Humor and a complete sentence. I think you might get that cupcake soon." Mason glanced at Lindsay, who sat next to Evan, her arm tightening around his shoulders.

"I just called your pulmonologist. She knows Mason and says he's a good judge of whether we need to take you to the ER." She met Mason's gaze, worry clouding her gray orbs. "Do I need to arrange for a babysitter for Chloe?"

"Grandpa Joe would gladly volunteer, except Evan doesn't need to go. I'll monitor him for the next hour and continue taking his pulse, but as of now, the rescue inhaler seems to be doing its job."

Goliath swiped Lindsay's fingers with his tongue, and Lindsay pulled back. Her face turned almost as ashen as Evan's, and she glared at the dog. "Certain triggers exacerbate asthma, don't they?"

Mason moved his fingers to Evan's neck and calculated his pulse again while Goliath nudged closer to the boy as if he could sense Lindsay's disapproval. "Yes, but Evan has been around Goliath for a couple of weeks now. Surely Goliath isn't the trigger. He'd have had a reaction before now."

Almost on cue, Evan's breath sounded as though he were blowing through a whistle. Lindsay stood and glanced around the room. She walked over to Goliath's leash and called for the dog. Grandpa Joe appeared at the doorway, a cupcake with half the wrapper removed near his mouth. "What's wrong? I thought Evan was okay."

Mason approached Lindsay and kept his voice low enough so only she could hear. "I'm concerned, too, but the medication is working. Evan's recovering. And he's learning to manage his asthma well."

"Goliath could be the cause. I don't think he needs to be around Evan."

But everywhere his grandfather went, Goliath wasn't far behind. "Can we talk about this later? Grandpa Joe'll be flustered to think any of this was on account of his dog. Please don't embarrass him like this. He loves these kids as though they were his own. It's the only thing that's kept his spirits up since Grandma Betty went to Tennessee."

She glanced at Evan, whose breath was coming in more natural spurts, the whistling diminishing with each second, and then faced Mason. "As soon as the dog moved away, my son started breathing normally. I think that's obvious proof, don't you?"

Mason found it hard to dispute her logic, but Evan and Goliath had been best buddies for the past few weeks.

"I'm old, but I can hear perfectly fine." Grandpa Joe's voice sounded from behind, and they turned to find him there, crumbs and icing around his lips. His back hunched, he clipped Goliath's green leash to his collar. "I'd never do anything to hurt these two little ones. I'm sorry, Lindsay. I'll keep Goliath away from the kiddos. Come on, Goliath."

With that his grandfather moved toward the door, and the evening came to a halt. While Lindsay hadn't directly called out Grandpa Joe, her rejection of Goliath seemed too quick, a gut reaction rather than a measured examination of the facts.

This was why it was better not to get too attached. Good things always seemed to come to an abrupt end.

"Evan should be good, but if his pulse rises above ninety, call his doctor. If it goes about a hundred and ten and stays there for over five minutes, text me and we'll take him to the ER immediately."

"Mason."

He shook his head. "Later. I have to check on Grandpa Joe. He's my responsibility."

Mason couldn't look at Lindsay as he followed his grandfather and left for home.

CHAPTER NINE

LINDSAY STUCK A BOOKMARK in the gardening journal and turned out her lamp, before burrowing under the thick duvet cover. After all, what else was she supposed to do about Joe and Goliath? If the dog triggered Evan's asthma, Goliath would have to stay away. She hadn't meant for Mason and Joe to take the rejection personally.

She turned over and exhaled. When had every conversation with Mason evolved into an argument? At the botanical garden, she had the reputation of staying calm in any crisis. She could coax plants, which others were ready to gut for dormancy, back to life.

Yet lately, the air around her and Mason buzzed with the expectancy of something different on the horizon, some change too ominous to ignore. The awful part was she liked that too much. She squeezed her eyes shut even tighter, determined to rid herself of any feelings crossing over the friendship line.

A squeak in the floorboards of the ceiling snapped her eyes wide open. Then something scurried above her, and she flicked on the lamp once more.

Light flooded her bedroom, bathing the soft blue walls in a peaceful glow. Everything was tranquil and orderly, the way she liked it, from the picture of her wedding day on her bureau to her trundle seat at her bay window. With nothing out of place, she assured herself she was hearing things. Her hand reached for the lamp, but more overhead noises alerted her to the fact that something was invading her attic. Her heartbeat accelerated, and she spied her phone on its charger by her bed.

Mason had invited her to call day or night, but that was before he trailed his grandfather out the door. Besides, it might just be something small frolicking in the attic. Lindsay was a competent woman, and she'd check the attic tomorrow. Then she'd call the appropriate company to remove whatever was up there.

She pounded her pillow and went to turn out the light. Ignoring the unwanted sounds would be for the best tonight.

Except tossing and turning didn't help any. Whatever was scurrying around up there had invited friends and it now sounded like they were having a party. She flopped onto her other side and the duvet slipped off the bed. Out of reach of the cover, she huffed and got out of her warm sheets, only to find the temperature in her bedroom had plummeted.

Glaring at the ceiling, she didn't have a choice between taking action or snuggling deep under the covers. Whatever animal sought refuge in her attic might have damaged something. If she investigated now, she could determine whether it was loose insulation or some sort of stray animal. Then she'd be back in her nice, warm bed in mere minutes.

With a sigh, she swung her feet onto the carpet, the plush fiber cushioning her toes. A chill nipped the air, and she shivered. She grabbed the flashlight Tim had insisted on keeping in the top drawer of their dresser in case of emergencies and tiptoed into the hallway, taking care not to wake up Evan, who was her light sleeper. It would take a bullhorn to wake up Chloe. At least the attic door was on the opposite side of her house from their bedrooms.

A check of the thermostat, four degrees cooler than her preferred preset temperature, elicited a groan. Was the furnace broken or was some animal nibbling on the wires?

She pulled down the squeaky attic door and the stairs descended into the hallway. A quick glance confirmed neither of her children was out of bed. She fought the flutters in her stomach. Flashlight in hand, she entered the unfinished attic, the beams and insulation daunting. She quelled her fears and found the problem, her laugh of relief tamping down those pesky nerves. Somehow, the flap of the furnace filter had opened and was banging against the metal, leaving the air filter exposed. She exhaled at the simple solution. Balancing on the wooden beams, she crossed over and closed the flap. The furnace clicked on, and she all but cheered. To think she'd almost called Mason over something like this.

Halfway back to the stairs, something long and furry with a big bushy tail caught her eye and scampered across her feet. She screamed and dropped the flashlight, the clatter on the wood echoing in the night. Stumbling, she pitched forward and reached for something, anything, to regain her balance. Instead, she lost her footing, falling into scratchy pink insulation. The floor below her gave way. Her bare feet broke through the wood while bits of dust and plaster went up her nose. Falling, she cried out and her heartbeat accelerated. Until she realized she was wedged in a hole. Trapped, her chest was above the hole, and her legs dangled below. She was stuck and couldn't pull herself up. She tried not to panic. The flashlight was close enough where a beam slipped through the crack and illuminated the guest room below. Now was time to panic.

"Mommy?" Evan's voice came from the direction of the stairs and he coughed.

"Stay down there." She didn't want to think about what

the dust and insulation would do to his asthma. "Do you remember how to use Mommy's phone?"

"Yes." He coughed again, and she hoped this wasn't the beginning of another asthma attack.

"Call Mason and then release the bar from the sliding glass door so he can come inside." Gripping the beam with all her might, she tried not to think about falling to the floor. "And hurry."

IF IT WEREN'T for the panic in Evan's voice over the phone, Mason would have thought he was dreaming. He hurried next door, where Evan grabbed his arm and dragged him upstairs.

"Mommy's legs are in the ceiling."

He'd heard of minor reactions to the measured dose of asthma medication, but this type of vivid dream was one for the books. Once he reassured Evan everything was fine, he'd wake up Lindsay and warn her she might want to keep better tabs on her phone in the middle of the night.

Mason stopped short outside Lindsay's guest room. A most attractive pair of legs were dangling from the ceiling. His chest heaved at the sight until he realized the rest of her must be holding on in the attic. This nightmare wasn't a dream. "Hold on, Lin."

He found the stairs leading to the attic and rushed up them, then pulled her to safety. She clutched him close, her chest puffing in and out, a classic sign of hyperventilation. He grabbed the flashlight and then helped Lindsay down to where Evan waited at the bottom of the steps.

"Mommy!" He clutched her leg before she was even off the staircase.

She sent him a shaky smile. "Thank you, Evan, for being such a great helper."

Her voice was also shaky, and she leaned against Mason. "Thank you for coming over."

"Any time."

She brushed his cheek with her lips, the kiss imprinting itself into his stubble. She stumbled, falling back. Her shiver alarmed him, and even the dim light didn't hide her ashen face.

"I could have fallen straight through to the floor."

He pulled her close, and she leaned into him. He kept still, giving her as much comfort and time as she needed. He longed to kiss her, to reassure her everything was all right, but he'd settle for being here for her. Anything else would cross the line.

Eventually, he let go of her. "What happened?" he asked.

"A squirrel, I think."

Why hadn't she called him earlier? He'd save that question. "Let's get you warmed with a cup of tea and then I'll stay here in case Evan or Chloe need me while you take a shower."

He started for her staircase, and she rested her hand on his arm. "I have to see the damage to the guest room first. My parents are planning to stay there."

For the dedication. She didn't have to say the words. They hung in the air like the faint dust coating the carpet. Even this attraction wouldn't change his mind about attending.

"Hello, is everyone okay? I heard Mason hurrying out of the house and came to check up on everyone," Grandpa Joe called out and then appeared at the foot of the stairs. "Chloe? Evan?"

"Chloe would sleep through the zombie apocalypse, and Evan's fine." Lindsay's voice still sounded shaky, a sign she might be going into shock.

Mason escorted her to the kitchen and settled her at

her table. Then he started the stove top for some peppermint tea while she told Grandpa Joe what happened. By the time he found the tea bags, Evan's head rested on the table, his even breathing reassuring after last night's episode and the dust particles that could have brought about another asthma attack.

Lindsay's teeth chattered, and he knelt by her and gazed into her eyes, searching for dilated pupils, or even ones that weren't equal in size. "Do you have a headache?"

"No, and I didn't hit my head so I don't have a concussion."

He realized his grandfather was nowhere to be found. "I'll track down Grandpa Joe and ask him to watch the kids while I take you to the ER for observation."

"There's no need for that, and I'm not scaring Evan again. What I have is little bits of insulation pricking my arm, and I'm cold because a squirrel or mouse was in my attic and was messing with my furnace causing it to turn off."

"You should have called."

The teakettle whistled, and Evan stirred before falling back asleep. Mason started for the stove, but Lindsay passed him and prepared her cup of tea by herself.

"Things ended badly between us tonight," Lindsay said, pouring steaming water into her mug.

"We're both looking out for people we love."

"Yes, but well, I have to stay strong for me. I don't like other people handling everything for me. Take my mother, for instance. First, she wanted me to move in with dad and her. Then she wanted me to stay in bed and let her wait on me hand and foot."

"Which she did for a while."

Lindsay dunked the tea bag until water sloshed out the sides of her cup. "And now my boss believes his wife can handle the volunteer roster, which is on my list of duties, and effectively do my job. I'm not some fragile flower like the ones blooming at the garden."

Her eyes blazed and he nodded his head. "I never said you were fragile."

"Good news!" Grandpa Joe entered the kitchen.

"I thought you'd gone home." Mason glanced at the sliding glass door, then at his grandfather.

"While you've been checking out Lindsay, I've been checking out her guest room and the furnace. It's working again."

Mason's chest tightened. If his grandfather figured out Mason's feelings for Lindsay were growing stronger, he'd have to do better at hiding them closer to his heart.

Lindsay groaned and closed her eyes. "Give it to me straight. How much damage did I do to the ceiling?"

"You'll need some special drywall, wooden cleats, mesh tape, and compound. That won't set you back too much. Thank goodness you don't have popcorn ceilings. Then I'd have to turn you down."

"I'm not following."

"I'm going to fix your ceiling." He grinned and tilted his head toward Mason. "With his help, of course."

Her eyes widened. Then she pulled Mason into the living room. "I thought your grandmother wanted you to monitor him because of his angina. Won't working on my ceiling be the worst possible thing for that? Should I let him do this?"

"He's been in construction and the like all his life. He's great at repairing things. I'll tell him if he feels any dizziness, fatigue or nausea he should stop immediately." Although he and Lindsay were now in need of repair, too. He just wanted their easy friendship back. He was beginning to think it was too late for that. "This project is exactly what he needs. And he's offering himself. He wants Evan and Chloe around."

She looked unconvinced until she peeked into the kitchen. Her face softened, and he kept himself from staring at her pink lips. "He's looking at Evan as though he misses him already. I know you think I overreacted, but I'm not convinced that I did. Goliath must have been the cause. For some reason, though, this past month you've been getting under my skin worse than this insulation." She cringed and ran her fingers through her hair, disheveled and cute with a chunk of the fiberglass insulation sticking out.

"Let me." He reached over, brushed it away and tried not to notice how soft her hair was, even with bits of plaster and dust turning it from honey brown to white.

He folded his arms over his chest and added distance between him and Lindsay, whose compassion was becoming a distraction that had nothing to do with the late hour. She tried rubbing some of the pink fiberglass fragments off her skin.

"You and Joe will keep an eye on things, or in this case, the ceiling, while I take a shower?"

He nodded, and she gave him a grateful smile. "Looks like the Ruddick men are riding to my rescue tonight."

"You didn't need rescuing, just a helpful hand." He grinned, happy to get this conversation back on safe ground. "Apply some antibiotic ointment liberally to those scratches. An infection is the last thing you need."

"A literal hole in my ceiling is the last thing I need, one I hope will be fixed before my parents arrive. Joe will ask for more help if he needs anything, right?"

"Yes, ma'am." He tapped his wrist, the one that remained bare unless he was on his shift. "Um, I have to report in the early morning hours."

"Then I'll hurry. Be back in two shakes."

Mason waited in the kitchen, watching Grandpa Joe, who watched Evan lovingly. Lindsay was true to her word, returning in no time with a smile.

"All fresh again." She hugged Grandpa Joe, and a light whiff of lavender caught Mason's senses. "Thank you for the offer. I know you'll do an outstanding job with the ceiling. Just make sure you let us know if you need anything, and I'm sorry about Goliath."

With that, she nudged Evan, who trudged upstairs. Next, Lindsay waved and closed the sliding glass door behind him and Grandpa Joe.

Mason flicked on his phone light, illuminating the path between his and Lindsay's houses.

Grandpa Joe chuckled. "Wait until I tell Betty about this. Just when I thought nothing interesting would happen."

A longing swept over Mason. His grandparents shared a special bond which distance nor anyone else could ever break. What would it be like to open himself up to a powerful love like that for his very own? Did he even dare try?

CHAPTER TEN

WAS IT JUST Lindsay's imagination or was the cart Joe pushed through the aisles of Farr's Hardware getting more weighed down by the second? Drywall, wooden two-by-fours and fiberglass tape already rested there. Who knew so much was involved in fixing a gaping hole in her ceiling? Chloe tugged at Lindsay's capris, and she picked up her daughter.

"When's ice cweam?" Chloe stuffed her fingers in her mouth, and Lindsay removed them.

"Soon." Lindsay was also anticipating the trip to Miss Louise's Ice Cream Parlor. "Joe's finding stuff to fix the guest room for Mimi and Pop-Pop's visit."

Lindsay's mother didn't like the usual grandparent names and chose something she believed had more flair.

"I love Grandpa Joe." Chloe reached for the older man, his delight as plain as the wire glasses resting on his nose.

He accepted her, and she nestled her head on his shoulder. "And Grandpa Joe loves you."

Mason moved toward the rolling cart with Evan on his heels, taking care around the other Saturday shoppers. With hero worship in his eyes, Evan asked questions about every power tool in sight. To Mason's credit, he was taking it all in stride.

Lindsay kept her gaze on Mason, seeing what a lot of women in Hollydale saw in him, and more. That grin of his was charm personified, and he made you feel like you were the only person in a crowd of thousands. Yet he rarely showed people that other side of him, the one that craved solitude with his motorcycle, valued honesty and being forthright, the side with a strong core of steel.

Who was the real Mason? The charmer? The rebel? The paramedic next door? As far as she could tell, those were all facets of his personality. To her dismay, she found herself thinking about him more than she should.

"Is this the right one, Grandpa Joe?" Evan turned his attention to the containers of joint compound and pointed to a white tub with thick green letters.

Mason's grandfather shook his head. "I like the one with the red writing better. It's more expensive, but it lasts longer. Can't go wrong with quality. I knew the minute I met Mason's grandmother, she was the one for me. Her spunk and spirit are quality stuff. Same as your mom." He smiled at Evan, who was struggling with the heavy tub, and handed Chloe back to Lindsay.

Then he grabbed one side of the handle and indicated Evan to get the other. "Next time I'm sure you'll be old enough to load it on your own." He helped Evan swing the tub into the cart and then gave him a fist bump. "Good job."

Little beads of sweat popped onto Evan's forehead. The smile faded from Lindsay's face as Evan's breathing became staggered, more of a whistle sound than his normal quiet intake of air. Joe must have noticed, and his face became ashen. "I didn't think about animal dander."

Neither did she. If Evan had this severe reaction when he hadn't even been around the dog, how could she allow Joe over at all?

Joe backed up and jostled a pyramid of paint cans. Mason reached over and lifted two fingers to Evan's neck. No sooner had he done so and Evan started coughing and raised his fingers to his neck, obviously struggling for breath. Mason glanced at Lindsay and shook his head. "I came here to meet you straight from the station after I finished my two-day shift."

"Hold that thought while I get his inhaler."

Lindsay's fingers rattled against her purse, and she grasped Evan's canister. If she banished Joe from her house, Mason might take that as a personal affront. That would be two more gaping holes to the ones already marring her life. She shook the canister, and placed the mask over Evan's mouth and squeezed, counting aloud.

"Lindsay, I wasn't even near Goliath."

"Don't make me say it out loud." Her voice sounded ragged and she focused on Evan, refusing to look at Mason's face lest she lose her nerve. "Please."

"How can this be a reaction to animal dander? I haven't been around an animal for forty-eight hours."

Chloe took that opportunity to run off. "Chloe!" Lindsay glanced at Evan, needing to be with him.

"I've got her." Mason sprinted down the aisle and grabbed Chloe. He carried her back like a sack of potatoes.

Chloe wrinkled her nose and wriggled as if trying to escape from his grasp. "Smelly. Ick."

"Gee, thanks. You know how to bruise a guy's ego, don't you?" Mason sniffed his wrists and held out his palms to the toddler. "So, you don't like the new aftershave and cologne Grandpa Joe bought me last week?"

"What?" Lindsay almost dropped the canister of asthma medication before gathering her composure. She gave a reassuring nod to Evan and counted backward calmly once more, giving the medicine a minute to take effect. Then to Mason she said, "What new aftershave?"

"The day we went out for Danish, and oh…" Mason whooped and swung Chloe around in his arms, receiving a glare from a nearby customer. "Chloe, sweetheart, you get extra sprinkles on your ice cream!"

Grandpa Joe straightened, that pyramid of paint unsteady for a brief second. "It's not Goliath, then?"

"Highly improbable if you ask me." Mason laughed and then grimaced when he caught sight of Evan. "Sorry, not trying to be insensitive to your asthma attack, Ev, but this is awesome news. It's this new brand of aftershave, not Goliath at all."

The plastic mask didn't hide the smile lighting up Evan's face. For the first time in a long time, in Farr's Hardware of all unlikely places, those gaping holes didn't feel so deep.

CHAPTER ELEVEN

LINDSAY WINCED AT the hole in the ceiling. It hadn't seemed quite so big when she missed the rafter and slipped through, but in full daylight, with Joe and Mason next to her, it was enormous. If she had actually fallen through the ceiling onto the floor, she could have sprained her ankle or even broken her leg.

Or worse.

She brushed her cheeks with the back of her hand. At least she hadn't heard any scurrying noises at night. After the trip to the hardware store, they'd celebrated at Miss Louise's Ice Cream Parlor and Joe decided on an impromptu weeklong trip to Nashville before he started the repair project. In her spare time, she'd cleared away the debris and vacuumed the cream-colored carpet. Between her work schedule and Mason's extra shifts, every minute had rushed by, but now it was time to deal with the aftermath.

She lowered the goggles over her forehead until they rested comfortably on her nose. Mason and Joe moved the bed against the wall and placed a blue plastic tarp over the furniture. Prepping the room and configuring the workspace would be the first step toward patching the hole. Gloves in hand, she glanced at the ceiling once more. It all caught up with her, and she shuddered. Her breathing became shallow, and her heartbeat accelerated.

Mason came over and reached for her shoulders. "Excuse us for a minute, Grandpa Joe. We'll be right back."

Mason escorted her downstairs and out to the backyard. The vivid pinks of the azaleas seemed to drive home the life around her after the flat dullness of the dust and tiny particles coating the guest room.

"You won't go there." Mason sat in one of the Adirondack chairs, and she sagged into the other.

"The only place I was going to was back to my guest room to start getting everything under control."

"I meant back into the grief."

How did he read her mind like that?

"I'll be all right. It just caught me for a second." She breathed in and rose. "Each spring I have to prune the crepe myrtles in the front yard and then they bloom again. I have to do the same in a way." She took a step forward. "Evan and Chloe ought to be waking up from their naps. I need to make them a snack. There'll be enough for you and Grandpa Joe, too."

"That reminds me. Last night I found Grandpa Joe's snack stash. He needs to eat healthier foods again. I've got something that'll be perfect for everyone."

Lindsay gnawed her lip while he disappeared via the fence. Somehow, she had to put some distance between them. One first responder had already been taken from her; she didn't want to fall for another, who'd made his position as a confirmed bachelor all too clear, anyway.

She went inside. Evan was in the living room, already awake from his nap, playing with the plastic birds. She went and checked on Chloe, who held out her arms for her mother's embrace. Lindsay obliged and cuddled her daughter.

"Sugar and spice and everything nice." She carried Chloe into the hallway. At the open doorway of the guest room, she moved Chloe's arm up and down in greeting.

"Look who just woke up, Grandpa Joe. How about some fresh air and a snack, and then we'll start again?"

"You won't have to repeat that offer twice." Grandpa Joe came over and tweaked Chloe's cheek, a spring in his step.

They headed downstairs, where she repeated her offer to Evan, who put the plastic birds into the container and followed them out to the patio. Mason wasn't back yet, and Joe, as the last one through, closed the sliding glass door behind him. Chloe toddled over to him. "Pick Chloe up?"

Joe reached for her hand and sat in the other Adirondack chair, bouncing her on his knee. "How's this instead?"

A giggle served as her daughter's affirmative answer. Evan picked up a plastic bottle of bubbles and started blowing them around the yard.

A clatter at the fence brought her to her feet. The gate swung open, and Mason had something tucked under his chin and both hands occupied with platters of food. Before she could reach him, Goliath darted through Mason's legs and headed right for Evan, who dropped the bubbles. He fell backward in the grass, laughing as the dog licked his face. Her heart thudded as she ran over, joined by Joe, with Chloe a distant third.

"Evan, are you okay?" she asked.

Joe called Goliath, who moved away with some reluctance before he sniffed the air and followed Mason to the patio table. Lindsay looked to Evan, but he ignored her and scrambled to his feet. "Hey, boy. I'm glad you're back. I missed you when you were in Nashville."

Pulled in two directions, Lindsay didn't know what to do. Part of her wanted to trust it was the aftershave while the rest of her didn't want Evan to suffer through another attack. Evan ran to the table and scrunched his nose.

"What's this?"

"Hummus and pita bread." Mason dipped a triangle of

pita into the creamy golden mixture and ate it. "Delicious. Homemade, too."

Goliath tried jumping on the table, but Mason had placed the food out of the dog's reach. Lindsay went over and put her hands on her son's shoulders. "How are you feeling?"

"Sorry about spilling all the bubbles."

Bubbles. Though Lindsay could have used his peak air meter, this might be a better way for unofficially measuring his reaction to Goliath. "Why don't you try a bite of what Mason brought us while I run to the garage?"

In no time, she returned with two bottles of bubbles, one for Chloe and one for Evan. "Hey, mom. Hummus isn't half bad," Evan said, waving a pita.

Mason chuckled and passed a plate to his grandfather. The man's blue eyes sparkled when he winked at his grandfather. The breeze ruffled Mason's thick auburn hair, and Lindsay's insides melted. "Want to try?" he asked Grandpa Joe.

That charisma of Mason's was a little too potent. When she became involved with another man, it would be someone unlike Mason. Someone who didn't push her or tempt her with that dimple in his left cheek.

"Maybe later." Joe kept his eyes on the kids while Lindsay opened the caps on the bottles.

Soon Evan and Chloe ran around the backyard, blowing bubbles with Goliath, yipping on their heels and trying to pop them with his snout. So far, it would seem as though Goliath wasn't the culprit of any asthma attack. Seeing her children happy with the chiweenie, she didn't mind, although she did feel foolish about how she'd jumped to conclusions.

She sidled next to Joe. "Mason would love it if you tried some of his hummus." She dipped a piece of pita into the creamy concoction and handed it to him. "And I'd love it if you'd accept my apology."

"Nothing to apologize for, m'dear." He accepted it with a grimace. "You know I think the world of Evan and Chloe."

"Can I ask a personal question?" Lindsay ate a delicious bite while Mason chased the two kids, tickling Chloe before releasing her and going after Evan.

"As long as you don't mind a personal answer." He chuckled and came close to eating the pita before lowering it to the plate again.

"Why are you here rather than staying in Nashville? I know you miss Betty."

"I came back to keep an eye on things while Betty helps Bree. Our home is in Hollydale and I check on our house on my way home from work."

Lindsay reached for a napkin and brushed off the hummus on her lip. "You and Betty have lots of friends. Someone would do that. There must be more to it than that."

His gaze went to Mason and the children running around the yard, having fun on this bright spring day, Goliath's yips in chorus with the chirps of the cardinals and the giggles of her kids. "Ah, but I also have my regular cardiologist check ins, and besides, jobs at my age aren't easy to come by, and the new director's done a bang-up job. I don't want to desert my post."

"Or your grandson?" Lindsay's gaze went to Mason pretending to fall on the grass while Evan and Chloe piled on him.

"Betty and I worry about him, all our grandkids, really. Right now, Bree and Mason need us, and it's nice to be needed. Bree knows it and is thankful for it. Mason, though?"

"Stubborn like his grandparents, huh?"

Joe laughed. "Only his grandfather. Betty's patient

yet feisty. She keeps me on the up and up more than anyone knows."

He jutted his chin at the cheerful group and chewed the pita and hummus. "Same recipe as Betty's."

"What a coincidence."

"Not really. Mason gave Betty the recipe." He winked at Lindsay and turned back to the antics. "And let's just say I exaggerate a bit. Betty knows I sneak out for ice cream, but it's an excuse so I get to spend more time with Mason. He doesn't push me away when I bring over the sherbet."

Joe chuckled and Lindsay did the same as he left her side and joined the others.

MASON REMOVED THE bar end mirrors from their box. Georgie and Max's auto shop always ordered the best products. Pure steel was pricier than some of the alternatives, but it was worth it. With everything he'd need at his fingertips, he moved the plug away from the left handlebar and used a smaller expansion sleeve for a tight fit. Losing a mirror during a lane change would be disastrous. He tightened the nut with his wrench and stepped away from the bike.

His phone rang, and he laughed as his grandmother, who as always went through her elaborate ritual of identifying herself. "Bree is doing so much better. Her eyes almost show that Bree spirit again. You and I both know that type of spunk goes a long way in the fight."

If anyone had spirit, it was Bree.

"Glad to hear it." He had regretted not going with Grandpa Joe to Nashville, but duty had called and his sister insisted he should stay in Hollydale.

"Speaking of spunk, how's Joe?"

"Ornery as ever. He's lonely without you." Although this afternoon with Lindsay and the kids had done them all a world of good. So much that Grandpa had even eaten the creamy vegetable risotto for dinner without a complaint. Afterward, Grandpa had headed out to walk Goliath while Mason tackled this next step on his bike.

"While he was here, he didn't make much sense, talking about holes and cologne and pretty ladies hugging him in the middle of the night."

Mason explained everything and reassured her once again that he was keeping an eye on his grandfather. When he hung up and started to pick up his wrench, once again, that feeling that someone cared that much clutched him tight, and he left the right bar end mirror where it was. He needed to get away from this garage, away from the gardener next-door.

After crossing the walkway to his house, Mason grabbed his wallet and jacket. He searched for his grandfather so he wouldn't wait up for him. He checked the hook where Grandpa Joe kept Goliath's leash. *Still empty.* That must have been one long walk.

Or they went over to Lindsay's. He hurried outside and there in his spot on her patio, resting in Mason's favorite Adirondack chair was his grandfather, bouncing Chloe on his knee and laughing while Goliath and Evan played Frisbee.

Orange and pink hues dotted the horizon, and dusk was beginning to claim the day. Lindsay caught sight of Mason and waved him over.

"Evan hasn't had an attack all evening, and Goliath's been here the whole time. Isn't that the best news?"

The happiness on her face caught him off guard. He wished he hadn't become so close to her. It seemed wrong to think that, but he had to listen to his head from now on and not his heart. How else would he keep himself or her from getting hurt? He couldn't stay, not tonight. "It is. Since things are under control, I'm heading over to the Timber River Bar and Grill."

He started to stride away, glad he had his keys in his pocket. Then he felt Lindsay's hand on his arm. He wanted to acknowledge the touch, but he refused to let himself.

"Mason, what's going on? Did you get some bad news about Bree?"

"No, but I feel like the walls are closing in." The huskiness in his voice came off harsh, yet it took all his resolve to not join in the cozy evening.

"Sure, but you seemed happy earlier playing with Evan and Chloe—now you're acting…" She pursed her lips and her gray eyes darkened to the color of a turbulent sky. "Just so you know, sometimes you get me all mixed-up. You're shaking us off like I shake dirt off my gloves." She stepped back.

If she thought she was mixed-up, it was nothing like the confusing mess of emotions swirling around him. He wanted nothing more than to have what his grandparents laid claim to for the past fifty-six years. And yet?

He couldn't claim anything with Tim's widow. No matter how attractive she was, inside and out. No matter how his heart raced when that scent of lavender came his way, acting on the attraction? That would belittle Tim's memory.

He resisted the urge to kiss her, though it was the very thing he longed to do. "Maybe the best way I can honor Tim is to leave and get that drink."

"Huh?" Confusion lurked in her eyes, and she folded her arms over her chest. "If that's not the oddest excuse I've ever heard, I'll eat those morning glories."

As much as he'd like to take her in his arms and throw away all the excuses in the world, he couldn't. "Lindsay, trust me on this one, okay?"

"What do I tell your grandfather, the kids?"

"The truth. Sometimes people need space."

"There's something else going on, something under the surface." The glow of dusk surrounded them, highlighting the golden streaks in her short honey hair and the glint in her gaze. "Something neither of us wants to admit."

She was right. They were both flirting with danger, something below the surface that could undermine their friendship and threaten to rip apart everything he held dear.

If he stayed another minute, he'd kiss her. Then there'd be no more laughter while they built trellises together, no more sunsets with his beer bottle clinking her flute of Riesling, no more evenings by the fence. The air crackled around him, and she licked her lips almost as though she wanted him to kiss her, but she herself said she could never fall for another first responder.

He wouldn't want them in a position where she had to go against her own words. He nodded and pointed toward Grandpa Joe. "Tell him not to wait up for me, okay?"

"I've seen you run before, but I didn't think you would run from something that should be out in the open." Her expression accused him of the very reason he needed to escape.

Those gray eyes would be the undoing of him if he let them.

"Friends should give each other space. We're friends, right?"

What if she said no, that they were more than that? He held his breath. What if they were on the verge of something special?

"Since you've made it clear you don't want to be here, go." She glanced down and scuffed the grassy dirt with her sneaker. "And you're right. There's nothing going on here."

With that, he turned on his heel and left.

CHAPTER TWELVE

FLIPPING ON THE portable fan, Mason turned and assessed Lindsay's guest bedroom. He hadn't liked how he'd left things with her a week ago. Since then, he'd filled in for a sick colleague for five days. Then on his two days off, Lindsay stayed at the garden later than usual. Grandpa Joe mentioned how hard she was working on the display, only taking time to eat and tuck in her children. It was hard to get back in someone's good graces if they weren't around.

From the looks of things, she and Grandpa Joe had made little progress since Mason had made for the bar and grill.

Was he doing this for her, or was he trying to win back their friendship by facing this gaping hole?

No, he wasn't here to regain her favor. He was here because he'd made important realizations that night, nursing his lone beer alone for hours. First, he and Lin made a great team. As friends. If one of them had to get things back on the right footing, he'd volunteer and somehow stop looking at her kissable lips.

So for now, he'd tackle the ceiling. He'd used his spare key to enter Lindsay's house. He'd fix this and save his grandfather from extra exertion and prevent Lindsay from receiving a litany of questions from her mother about her middle-of-the-night slip.

With his keyhole saw in hand, Mason climbed the ladder, which was positioned over a drop cloth so there wouldn't be more damage to the carpet. Taking care there were no wires in sight, he cut an eighteen-inch square in her ceiling. Then he pushed away the excess insulation. He descended and collected the wooden two-by-fours he'd insert into the attic opening.

Then he heard footsteps.

"What are you doing here?" Grandpa Joe asked from the open doorway, his white coveralls a clue he'd come for the same purpose.

"Fixing the ceiling."

Grandpa Joe harrumphed and checked the consistency of the joint compound Mason had mixed. "A little watery, but it'll thicken before you apply it."

Mason climbed the ladder and positioned the wooden strips where he wanted them. "I've got it covered, Grandpa. You can take Goliath for a walk or maybe have a nap. Can you hand me that drill and a couple of those coarse dry-wall screws?"

"I don't need a nap." Grandpa Joe harrumphed and passed the screws to him. "Why do young whippersnap-pers always think old people need naps? Why do you think you need to do everything for me?"

Mason whirred the drill and screwed the strips into place. Satisfied, he descended and found his grandfather waiting for an answer. "This whippersnapper would never underestimate you—it was only a thought. And as for the ceiling, I had some free time. End of story."

"End of story, you mean end of discussion? Not quite." Grandpa Joe took the drill and picked up the premeasured drywall square. He climbed the ladder and scowled at the open space. "I thought Peter and I taught you better than this. Never cut corners. Anything worth pursuing is worth a little effort. Where are the arrows?"

Mason went and located a pencil and made the appro-priate marks on the ceiling and the square. Then he removed the two screws from his pocket and drilled one in, followed by the other.

His grandfather checked his work.

"All I meant is you could go and have some fun, Grandpa. No use in the both of us hanging out in here."

"This isn't drudgery for me."

Come to think of it, it wasn't for Mason, either. It had been a long time since they'd worked together, like when Mason was young and Grandpa Joe taught him how to construct a treasure box for his mother's birthday present. "Sounds like you're telling the wrong person to go home." Grandpa glared and flipped the fan to the next-highest speed, the wind rippling the curtains.

Once again, his grandfather wasn't listening to him. He loved Grandpa Joe and only wanted the best for him. Instead, his grandfather was like a force of nature Mason couldn't come to grips with. What would Grandma Betty say when she returned if Grandpa Joe wasn't the same as how she'd left him? "Aren't you supposed to be at the community center?"

Grandpa Joe examined the different size putty knives. "Brooke didn't schedule me for this afternoon. I've been doing overtime on the weekends, same as you. Keeps my mind off Betty and Bree, but I'm here now spending time with my grandson."

Since he crossed into adulthood, Mason had thought he no longer needed these bonding moments with his grandad. Maybe he did after all.

"Any word on when Grandma Betty is coming home?"

"Not soon enough, but Bree's progressing nicely. Love is what matters. But enough about me. Why are you avoiding Lindsay?"

"I'm going to put the tape around the perimeter, okay with you?" Without waiting for acknowledgment, Mason climbed the ladder. "And I'm not avoiding Lindsay. My extra shifts aren't about me. My new partner, Jordan, is getting his feet wet. He's the one filling in while Gina and Darius are out. I'm just monitoring him."

Mason ripped off a chunk of the tape with too much force, and the roll landed on the drop cloth. His grandfather tossed the roll up, and he caught it. "Thanks."

"And I suppose you skulking away to the Timber River Bar and Grill last week had everything to do with Jordan and nothing to do with Lindsay?"

Mason taped the other three sides of the perimeter and smoothed them flat against the ceiling. He had to come down off the ladder sometime. "Okay, that did have everything to do with me and Lindsay."

"Glad you can admit that. It might be time you make some other admissions to yourself, too."

"Admissions are only worthwhile if you intend to act on them." Which he wouldn't.

"You should act on your feelings before someone else does, but you need to realize that for yourself."

Grandpa Joe slathered joint compound onto a three-inch putty knife and climbed the ladder, muttering something under his breath as he went.

Mason stirred the remaining joint compound, making it an even consistency. Grandpa Joe had been right about it being too watery before. "Are we tag teaming this job then?"

"Guess so. That ought to give me enough beauty time to prepare for my date."

Mason's jaw dropped, and his hand slid, causing the joint compound to spill onto the carpet, rather than the drop cloth. He tried to scoop the sticky substance back into the container, fuming that his grandfather had the nerve to stand there, smiling.

"I heard you wrong. Did you say *date*?"

"Yep." His grandfather came down the ladder. "Your grandmother even knows about the date and is quite supportive."

Mason had missed something, or he'd wake up any minute now. He pinched himself and cried, "Ouch."

"Don't look so appalled. The date's with Chloe, and we're planting a flower tonight at Jasper and Jules's Garden Center for Earth Day. Lindsay's teaching the workshop." He guffawed and stirred the compound. "Like I'd mess up a good thing. Your grandma's the best."

Grandpa Joe laid the putty knife on the makeshift table.

"Grandpa." Mason wanted to prepare him for what would happen when his grandmother returned. "Shouldn't you pull back from Chloe and the Hudsons before you get too involved? Once everything's back to normal, you'll be spending your time with Grandma Betty. Chloe might get attached, and then when you don't come around as much anymore, she'll be devastated."

"Who says I plan on abandoning them when Betty comes home? They'll gain a grandma instead of losing a grandpa." He rearranged the tools on the table. "You can never have too much family. Lindsay, Evan, and Chloe are part of ours now. The demonstration at the garden center starts at six thirty if you want to see Lindsay in action."

Grandpa left, and it was Mason's turn to mutter something under his breath. His grandfather made him wonder who was taking care of whom here. Mason might be the person Grandma Betty enlisted to watch over Grandpa Joe, but it sure seemed as though he was taking care of Mason instead. Still teaching him a thing or two. Maybe it was time to listen and learn.

JASPER AND JULES'S GARDEN CENTER might be one of Lindsay's favorite places. Their selection of native plants of

Western North Carolina, along with Jules's eye for container design, brought fans from as far away as Raleigh and Charlotte. With Joe's kind offer to take Evan and Chloe home after Lindsay's presentation for children and their guardians about how to grow flowers from seeds, she now had ten minutes for window shopping before ending her day.

Customers milled about the shop, chatting and choosing various plants and equipment to purchase. Lindsay eyed the long lines waiting to cash out with carts filled with trees, annuals and every garden implement available. She approached the fairy garden display and considered whether Chloe might be old enough for it yet.

"Lindsay, I thought you'd gone."

She turned and there was Jules, patting down a strand of her pixie-cut white hair. An inch shorter than Lindsay's average frame, Jules was a dynamo of energy.

Jules reached into her apron pocket and pulled out an envelope. "Here's the small token of appreciation we gave our workshop leaders. I wish it could be more."

Lindsay pushed Jules's hand back. "Can you donate that to the botanical garden instead?"

"It's a gift card, or else I would. Why don't you use it to buy the materials for a fairy garden for Evan and Chloe? Kids love them. We do a thriving birthday-party business on the weekends where each child leaves with an aquarium that has all the trimmings and a mini display." Jules picked one up for Lindsay's examination. "For those with younger siblings, we include a mesh lid that's childproof."

"I'll bring Evan and Chloe back after the dedication ceremony. They enjoyed tonight's class and especially planting the marigold seeds in the little clay pot they painted first." Almost as much as Joe had, from the look on his face.

His smile had widened when he told her Betty had

called with good news right as he'd pulled into the last available parking spot at the garden center. She was finally coming home this weekend.

A timer pinged, and Jules smiled. "Time to award a door prize." She thrust the envelope at Lindsay. "Better yet, use this for a gift for yourself. Considering how many extra people you squeezed in for the workshop, I'll make a special starter fairy garden that's childproof and pretty for your kids. It'll be in my office the next time you drop by."

Before Lindsay could dissuade her or return the fee, Jules disappeared in the crowd. Lindsay marveled over the different fairy gardens in the different aquariums, each unique, each beautiful.

"Which is your favorite?"

Lindsay glanced over and there was Mason. That urge to brush the thick auburn lock of hair from his eyes, just to touch him, swelled in her, and she steadied her impulse. She should be mad at him about how they parted a week ago, but she had to be honest with herself. He called her bluff and, in doing so, it cooled anything going on between them. She should feel relief, but instead she struggled with everything he forced her to feel once more.

"You know this is Jasper and Jules's Garden Center and not the local auto parts store, right?"

"Grandpa Joe said you had a presentation tonight. Is it over?" Mason picked up one of the aquariums. "What does a mermaid have to do with gardening?"

"Yes, it's over, and that's a terrarium fairy garden. Later this fall, the Children's Play Zone at the botanical garden is going to have a display with gnome houses and more. It's a great way for parents to introduce their children to gardening and talk about the natural world around them." She stood on her tiptoes and tried not to inhale his fresh scent of soap and sandalwood and spring that was as aromatic as a bunch of roses. "The typical fairy garden also recycles materials available on hand. It's particularly appropriate since today is Earth Day."

"Is that why it's so crowded and why someone gave me a blue ticket when I entered?" Mason replaced the aquarium on the shelf and pulled out the ticket.

"Good evening to our customers who stayed with us until the end since you must be present to win our grand prize." Jules's voice came over the loudspeaker. "The winning number is two-four-six-eight." Jules chuckled. "Who do we appreciate? Mother Nature. Don't forget to plant a tree, go green and recycle. Make every day Earth Day."

Mason pocketed his ticket without looking at it, and Lindsay scowled. "Aren't you going to see if you won?"

"No. I'm sure someone else did."

"I haven't heard any shouts of glee. Give me your ticket." He rolled his eyes but handed it over anyway. There they were, the four correct numbers. She grabbed his arm and shrieked. "You won! Come on—Jules has been bragging about that basket every hour. I want to see what's in it."

Without thinking, she launched herself into his arms for a hug. The full contact with his hard chest sent alarms ringing through her. Not because there was anything wrong with the hug, though, but because everything was right. She jerked away and glanced at her clogs, too conscious of him and the undercurrent still between them.

"Will they give it to someone else if I don't claim it?" His expression gave no sign the embrace counted as anything but a congratulatory hug. Instead, he bent over and examined the closest display, which happened to be a coordinated group of houseplants. "I need a plant in my house. Something to welcome me home after Grandma Betty collects Grandpa Joe. Is this one easy to maintain?"

"It's a philodendron. It's great for removing toxins from

the air, but it's toxic to pets." Vetoing his selection, she went over and picked up a calathea instead. "This will be perfect in your living room. It likes a bit of shade and you only have to water it every week or two in the spring and summer. It's perfect for a bachelor. Now let's claim your prize."

"I'm not a gardener, Lin. Let someone who loves gardening win the basket." He examined the calathea from every angle and returned it to its spot.

"It's a basket, Mason, not a lifetime commitment."

He scoffed and tapped the terra cotta pot. "Trust me. I know the difference, and yet it seems all this is better suited to someone who has their yard mapped out."

"This isn't about the basket, is it? Are you saying people shouldn't branch out and try new things? And bachelor or not, we can still socialize." Her nostrils flared, and she reached for the calathea. "I'm buying this for you as a present."

"What I'm saying is you need someone like you." Mason glared at the calathea. "And I don't need a gift."

"Everyone loves gifts. It's like breathing. Besides, it'll add some color to your life. Your living room is monotone brown. A little green will go with the scheme just fine." She started walking to the end of the checkout line before changing direction for Jasper and Jules's office.

He followed her, and said, "I don't love gifts. It means you're obligated to someone."

She halted, and a cart skimmed her leg. "Don't stop in the middle of the aisle when it's close to closing time," muttered the woman who bumped into Lindsay and who now rushed toward the checkout.

Mason stared at the cutest display of gardening boots in a variety of prints from chickens to flowers to bumblebees. Next to it were a variety of wooden racks for boot storage. Lindsay stood in front of him, moving the calathea leaves aside so she could see his face better. "Gifts aren't obligations."

"Everything's an obligation."

"Family's not."

They glared at each other, and she kept hold of the ticket next to the terra-cotta pot containing the calathea.

"If I claim the basket, can everything return to the way it was?" he asked.

"If you claim the basket, will you let me buy this for you?" she asked.

The intercom crackled. "We are closing in fifteen minutes. Please take your purchases to the nearest register and thank you for shopping at Jasper and Jules's Garden Center. We open tomorrow at ten."

Lindsay blinked first. "This calathea needs a home. Chloe will name it for you, but she's twenty months old so you'll probably be stuck with a plant named Greenie."

"I'll accept it if we start talking at the fence again."

"Isn't that one of those obligations you just claimed to hate?" The electricity between them zinged, and she stared at his body language, the vibes coming off him spellbinding and strange. Well, not really, but she hadn't seen him like this around her, only around women he brought to social occasions or the like. Women he was interested in romantically.

"Our talks aren't obligations, Lin. They're fun. Both of us went into them needing a little levity and a shoulder to lean on during a tough time. I knew that's all they were, same as both of us know you'll end up with an extra houseplant if you buy this for me."

Did he think she only talked to him as an escape?

The fence talks were more than a way to end her day. He'd become her best friend. They'd shared everything over those countless hours. She'd assumed those times meant as much to him as to her, but had she been wrong? She'd best retreat before he bruised her heart.

Though it might be too late.

Still, she couldn't believe the meaningfulness of those talks was one-sided.

"It's a risk I'm willing to take."

"You always make it tough to say no to you." He reached for the plant and grinned. "Don't say I didn't warn you, though, when this ends up in your kitchen."

And, just like that, he'd given himself an out when he thought he needed it. That was Mason in a nutshell. She wouldn't give up. Not yet.

"But you'll claim the basket?"

"Will it make you happy?"

You'd make me happy. She discarded the thought. Being happy by herself and for herself was an adjustment, and the last time she loved someone, the fall had come without warning, breathless and hard, leaving her broken.

"Surprises make me happy." She hedged, wanting to be careful and cautious. No use getting burned by someone who had no intention of forming a commitment to a plant, let alone a person.

"Okay. We'll claim that basket before they put the merchandise back on the shelf."

On the shelf. Had she been on the shelf for the past few years? Or had she been going through the motions, playing at living so she could stay where it was safe, a place where she couldn't get hurt?

Jules was using the intercom to announce the store was now closed when they found her. Mason presented the ticket to Jules, and Lindsay peeked at the overloaded basket, and it was even better than she'd expected. Inside, there was a window box that held glistening metal tools and sharp shears. A green-and-gold reusable tumbler sat on a cozy green-and-gold blanket; a watering can, packets of seeds and an envelope nestled out of reach under the protective plastic wrap fixed with a bright green bow.

"What's in the envelope?" Lindsay asked.

"A one-hundred-dollar gift certificate with an added consultation for his yard with a design and maintenance plan." Jules accepted the ticket from Mason with a smile. "Glad one of Hollydale's first responders won the basket."

"Thanks. Is the yard consultation transferable? I'd like to give that to my grandparents."

Jules nodded. "Joe and Betty? For them, sure."

Mason pointed to the calathea. "And I'd like to buy that now if it's still possible."

"Actually, it's a gift from me." Lindsay reached into her purse and pulled out the envelope with the gift card Jules gave her earlier in the evening. "You sure have been handing these out tonight."

Jules reached over, clipping the tag off the houseplant. "People come in and spend three times as much when they bring a gift certificate. Besides, your presentation brought in customers, most of whom purchased something afterward, and we only awarded one grand prize. The rest of the door prizes were small, like a free flower, and only given on the hour."

Mason tried to hand the basket to Lindsay. "Grandpa Joe told me what time I was supposed to be here for the workshop. Since I missed it, please have this."

She nudged it over to him and picked up the calathea plant instead. "No, you won that fair and square. I'll help you spend the gift card, but it's time to bring some color into your yard, and I'm just the person who can do it."

CHAPTER THIRTEEN

MASON OPENED HIS back door and carried the bag of groceries into the kitchen. Something was wrong, but what? He had the answer almost as soon as he asked the question. There'd been no greeting. Not one hello, nor a dog racing up to him.

What was going on? Where was Grandpa Joe? Where was Goliath?

He lowered the groceries onto the counter and called out their names.

Checking the hook where his grandfather kept Goliath's leash and spying it empty and that Joe's jacket was gone told Mason what was up. Until now he hadn't realized how he'd grown accustomed to having the two of them greet him when he came home from shifts or errands. How had he never noticed the silence before?

Probably because Lindsay and the kids lived next door.

He'd placed the last container of yogurt in the refrigerator when the creaking of the front door signaled someone's return. The chiweenie flew to his side, greeting him with jumps and swipes of his tongue on Mason's jeans. His grandfather wasn't far behind, his grin stretching from ear-to-ear.

"Excellent timing. I just finished putting away the groceries. Is that why you're smiling?" Mason teased and bent down and gave Goliath some attention. Grandpa Joe peeked in the freezer.

"Any chance you bought butter pecan? And I'm not smiling because I got out of helping you. I talked to my beautiful bride during our walk." His grandfather's eyes glistened with love. For a moment, Mason was a little jealous.

"I didn't buy any ice cream, but how's Grandma Betty?" Mason straightened and folded the reusable bags. "And Bree?"

"Tristan's going to California for a business trip." Grandpa Joe's smile faded. "Betty's not coming home for another two weeks."

The normally jovial tone Mason loved hearing was missing, and he felt a need to cheer his grandfather up. "Why don't you visit her again and stay until you both come home? Surely they can do without you at the center for a couple of weeks."

"Trying to get rid of me that easily?" His grandfather nudged Mason's ribs.

Far from it. "I want what's best for you, Grandpa."

Was that a tear in his grandfather's eye? It must be the light.

"Ah, that makes this old heart proud to be your grandfather."

Mason gulped and shrugged. "I can keep a watch on your house if that's the problem."

Grandpa Joe shook his head. "Goliath has a vet checkup this week, and I have a couple of doctor appointments myself." He unclipped Goliath's leash. "And then there's my job. It's something I love doing."

Where did Mason see himself at his grandfather's age? A fair question, and one he'd never asked himself. Did he really want to be alone or on his own that far in the future?

Last week at the garden center, Lindsay had hugged him, her softness and excitement melding into him. Every spark of him had come alive for those brief seconds while they connected. After, she'd skirted away from him, giving him enough space to come to his senses.

"There are other jobs." Mason poked at the tile floor with his sneaker. "Why Hollydale? Why not move somewhere else you might like and enjoy?"

Although the question was finally out in the open, Mason was almost afraid of the answer.

"For one thing, you're here. So are our friends, many of whom are my family. They need me too." His grandfather arched an eyebrow and shook his head. "I'm seventy-five, Mason. I want to be useful to the town I love. Hollydale is special, it's my home."

His grandfather never ceased to amaze Mason.

"All right, Grandpa. Good to know. I suppose it's time for me to make dinner."

"It's too nice of a night to sit at home on a recliner eating a boring old supper."

They looked at each other and burst out laughing. "Is that a hint that you don't want me to make my legendary barbecue tofu bowl?" Mason exclaimed.

"*Legendary* is a word I wouldn't place in the same sentence as anything you made."

Mason flipped his grandfather's phone over and noted the time. Almost seven on this Saturday night. "I hear Mark at the Timber River Bar and Grill introduced a new veggie burger that's as good as beef ones."

"How about you try that while I order the real thing?" His grandfather perked up, so did Goliath. "Sorry, boy. You'll have to stay here and guard the house."

More laughter bubbled on Mason's lips. Goliath would merely lead a burglar to the refrigerator and wait for a snack. "It's a date then?"

Grandpa Joe nodded. "My calendar hasn't been this full in years."

A date with his grandfather on a Saturday night. Bachelor-track Mason would have once scoffed at the idea, but so what? This was what he and Grandpa Joe needed.

MASON MOVED THE pager around in his hands. A half-hour wait for a table in Hollydale?

"Do you feel like waiting that long?"

"If it's this or tofu, we'll stay here," his grandfather grumbled.

"There are nights I don't have time to eat on my shift, so a half-hour wait is nothing."

"Do you know that's the most you've ever said to me about your job?" Grandpa Joe leaned against the brick exterior of the bar, the late sunset and this sudden spring warm spell allowing them to wait outside rather than in the crowded interior.

"That can't be right. Surely I've mentioned details to you and Grandma Betty over Sunday dinner."

Grandpa Joe arched those bushy eyebrows of his and shrugged. "Name the last time you've eaten with us on a Sunday."

Mason searched his mind and couldn't remember when until he stumbled onto a memory. "I brought Lindsay and Evan and Chloe with me between Thanksgiving and Christmas."

"More like she brought you." Grandpa Joe chortled as he zipped up his jacket. "Not to mention that was months ago."

What was this? Attack Mason Week? First Lindsay accused him of not being grateful for gifts and gave him a hard time about their friendship, and his lawn, and now his grandfather was arguing with him after that heart-to-heart talk back at the house. Was Goliath the key to his getting along with Grandpa Joe? He couldn't take a dog everywhere, could he?

His grandfather shivered, and Mason fingered the buzzer once more. "Do you want to go somewhere else? Or should I check to see if they can seat us at the bar?"

"I'm not Evan or Chloe. I closed my jacket because I was cold, and I'm already warmer. I can wait like everyone else."

The tension between them lingered, and Mason relented. "Grandma Betty would never speak to me again if anything happened to you."

"And what about you?" His grandfather folded his arms across his chest. "How would you feel if something happened to me? Would you volunteer to work so everyone else could mourn my loss instead of you?"

That punch out of nowhere hurt more than the time a confused, angry patient clocked Mason's jaw. The buzzer lit up and vibrated before he could respond. Not that he knew how.

They remained silent as his grandfather opened the door for him. Still stunned, Mason handed the glowing buzzer to the hostess, unable to hide his trembling fingers. Grandpa Joe laid his hand on the back of Mason's hand. "I'm sorry. What I said was cruel and over the line."

Mason didn't know which was worse, the fact his grandfather's statement was blunt, or that it rang true. "Sometimes the harsh truth is a good wake-up call."

"Nothing excuses unacceptable behavior. Not age, not hunger, nothing." His grandfather followed the hostess, who seated them at a table next to a group of four women who were sharing a basket of wings.

"Joe!" His grandfather's boss, Brooke, jumped up with a smile. "It's wonderful to see you. When did you get here?"

His grandfather rose and stepped closer to the others. "A while ago. We waited outside." Grandpa Joe's cheeks reddened as the other three ladies joined Brooke in bragging over him.

"How's Betty?" More questions about their family followed.

At his earliest opportunity, Mason grabbed a menu and inspected the offerings. He peeked around the menu and spied his grandfather smiling and joking thanks to the attention from Betty's friends and the community center's director.

His grandfather had hit too close to home with his question. Tomorrow night at the fence he'd have to talk to Lindsay, make her see why he didn't want to attend the plaque ceremony. If he could convince her, maybe they could talk to Grandpa Joe together. His decision had nothing to do with mourning or grief, and everything with how he wanted to remember Tim. She'd understand. Deep down, he believed that, as much as he believed Grandma Betty would be home again when the timing was right.

Mason decided what he'd have to eat just as his grandfather, his ruddy cheeks glowing, finally pulled up his chair. Their server tapped Grandpa Joe's shoulder. "Where have you and your pretty bride been hiding lately?"

Despite the size of the noisy crowd, she listened while Grandpa Joe recited his story. Then she wrote their orders on her pad and scooted to another table. Brooke came over, leaned in and hooked her arm through Grandpa Joe's. "Mason, would you mind if we borrowed your grandfather for a minute? We'll return him—we promise."

"Be my guest." Mason rose and pointed to the other room. "If I'm not back when my order arrives, throw me a line and come get me. I'm going to see if anyone's up for a game of pool."

LINDSAY TESTED A dart in the back room of the Timber River Bar and Grill. Behind her, someone broke a rack of balls, and laughter ensued from the crowd surrounding the pool tables. She'd always preferred darts anyway, especially since her uncle Craig had taught her how to cast them. Even though she hadn't played for years, throwing something with a sharp point suited her mood.

An order for Asheville's Botanical Garden arrived at their facility today, only compounding a lousy week that had started with discovering that a contractor installed a subsurface drainpipe near the Children's Play Zone, rather than the Azalea Pathway. After a week of backbreaking work, she'd jumped at her aunt's offer to babysit Evan and Chloe so she could come here with Jillian and her friends for a fun night.

Except Jillian had deserted the table when the owner of the local outfitter appeared at the bar and Lindsay took that opportunity to escape to the back room with the pool tables and dartboard.

"Need a teacher?" Mason's voice sounded from behind her, and she faced him.

The low lights of the room glinted off his auburn hair, her gaze lingering on the black T-shirt, different from the tie-dyes he usually favored. It made him look even more attractive. She retrieved the bar's dart case from a shelf and handed it to him. "A bit presumptuous, don't you think?"

"That you want to learn to play darts? Why else would you be in here? Unless you're escaping people." Mason strolled toward the table and opened the case. "Hmm. Good quality."

He removed three darts from the case and then explained the rules and the scoring. After the rough week she'd endured, teaching him a lesson about presumptions was going to be fun.

Mason stood behind her, close enough for his breath to graze her cheek. The spicy scent of his cologne made her senses go haywire. Missing his friendship at the fence was only part of it. She'd missed his deep laugh and his ready wit. She'd missed him period.

He guided her shoulders and lifted her arm. "Balance your weight forward and keep a good grip on the dart, but make sure it's not too tight."

She nodded as he closed his hand over hers, the dart between her fingers, ready to throw. A sudden noise from behind caused the dart to go off course and into the wall, missing the dartboard completely. He shook his head and stepped back. "Then again, this might not be a good idea."

Already she missed the close contact. It was the best thing about her week so far, apart from the brief snippets of time she'd spent with Evan and Chloe at bedtime. "What? Are you worried word might get out that you're not an excellent teacher?" She leveled a challenge, knowing he wouldn't back down from that.

He laughed, and the server approached with a tray of beer mugs with frothy tops and several bottles. She delivered a bottle to Mason, and Lindsay ordered the same. There was something about the back room of a bar with a pool table and a dartboard that cried out for a beer rather than her usual Riesling.

An older man came up to them, his scowl visible in the dim light. "You two playing a game or what?"

Lindsay held her hand out to Mason to shake it. "Come on. I promise no one will get hurt in the course of our friendly game, and it might do us both good."

Mason nodded. "Sorry, mister. One game, but it shouldn't take long."

Lindsay smiled wryly and nodded in return. The man

grumbled into his beer and signed his name on the waiting list. "I'll be back in twenty."

The server brought Lindsay her beer, and she sipped it for courage. There was something distinctive and nutty about the taste that she rather liked. She could get used to the flavor.

"How about we just play a simple version called three-oh-one where we start with that many points and work down? To start, you have to shoot a double bull's-eye, that's one in the exact middle, and then the points are deducted from there." He proceeded with his first throw. "We each get three practice throws. Watch to see how it's done."

The first dart landed under the twenty in the double-score section, the second in the single bull's-eye zone and the last was a perfect bull's-eye. He might give her a run for her money. "That's some serious casting. Have you had the same type of week I've had?"

"Just a terrible night." He approached the board and yanked out his three darts, not blinking at her slip of the tongue that gave away she knew something about darts. "It seems you're not the only one who's taken note of my intention to skip the dedication ceremony," he said.

She wasn't surprised he hadn't changed his mind. "Who said something upsetting to you?" She stepped to the line and purposely threw them in the single-score range of the one, two and three. "That's good, right? I hit the board."

"Not quite, unless you're playing a game called Around the Clock, where you start with one and end up at twenty. Grab your darts." He sipped his beer and motioned to the board. "My grandfather thinks I should go to the ceremony and spoke his mind about it."

"How about you tell me the real reason behind your decision not to be there?" She went to the board and gripped the darts. "And not some convenient excuse. I want the truth this time."

"The person who did better in the practice round usually gets to go first. Does that work for you?"

She nodded. She only had one intention: closing out the game on her first turn. Once Uncle Craig had joined Aunt Hyacinth and their guests, Lindsay would spend hours practicing her throwing technique, enjoying the time away from her overprotective mother.

"As long as you come clean." She sipped her beer and settled on the stool next to the table.

He sat next to her and took a long moment to finish off his beer. "Grandpa Joe might have to drive me home." He set the bottle on the table and looked at her. "I don't want to remember Tim as a name on a stone or on a nice plaque. He was more than that, you obviously know that. Seeing him in that sense when he should be here with you and Evan and Chloe…"

The raw voice matched his bare honesty, revealing the real reason he didn't want to be at the botanical garden.

"It's about how he lived his last moments, Mason. Doing his duty. This isn't reducing him to a line on a plaque—it's a way for his memory to live on," Lindsay tried to explain.

"You believe in this. Your voice, your stance. And that's a good thing. But for me, this is different and personal." He glanced at her, and something like regret flickered in his blue eyes.

He stood and they resumed their game. He hit a bull's-eye. Twenty points. But her confidence in the dart lessons her uncle taught her remained, although at this rate she worried she wouldn't get a chance to prove herself.

On his next throw, he hit another dead center. Here he was, running the board before she even had a turn.

"I understand your point, but I don't understand—why don't you tell Joe that? The same way you just told me."

"I could use the moral support when I do." He threw another dart and reduced his points by eighteen.

Maybe a distraction would help. "How about this? We'll make our game a little more interesting. If you win, I'll talk to your grandfather for you."

"Great. Seeing as I'm ahead and having seen how you throw, that's a done deal," he said in a teasing tone.

"What if I win? What do I get?" She kept her tone light enough for him to believe there was no chance of that happening. Sure, she was playing him a bit, but she wondered what he thought would match an honest heart-to-heart with Joe.

He eyed her and then removed the three darts from the board. He returned and shrugged, that gleam a little too sparkly for her taste. "You've worked eight days in a row, haven't you?" She nodded. "If you win, you do something that doesn't involve gardening. Try something new."

She sipped her beer, considering his offer. "I won't have time for that for about seventeen more years."

He squinted at the dartboard and then at her. "I remember those barbecues where we had so much fun and there was music and games and… What happened to that woman?" He turned bright red. "Not that I saw you as you then."

"You saw me as Tim's wife then."

He relaxed his shoulders. "Exactly."

But did he see her in a different light now, the way she noticed everything about him? She couldn't pinpoint what quality she first saw in him, but his unexpected layers drew her in and fascinated her. The same man could gently explain something to Chloe one minute and then his blue eyes could turn navy when his gaze made contact with Lindsay's the next.

She sipped her beer, growing more and more accustomed to the full richness of the taste. "I understand."

"Do you?"

They were dancing around something they'd started by the fence a year ago. This attraction went deep down to her bones.

"I understand more than you know."

"Well, you should have more fun in your life. You need people."

"And you don't?" she asked.

"Trust me—I'm learning to navigate the boundaries with my grandfather every day."

To Mason's credit, he'd been working on his relationship with Joe, something neither of them realized needed the same fine care as an orchid. A beautiful flower, but one notoriously difficult to grow, requiring a delicate balance of sunlight, temperature and water.

"What are we waiting for, then? We have a bet, and that guy will be back soon."

Mason cast another dart and reduced his score by ten just as the pool players burst into loud cheers. In the process of throwing the next dart, he missed.

"Oh, that's a hard break."

He removed his darts and settled on the stool. "Then again, I can't get too comfortable. I'll put you out of your misery soon enough," he said.

Except this wasn't misery.

She set down her beer and grinned at him. "Hold that thought." Extra pressure rarely bothered her. She hefted one of the darts and then rolled it in her fingers to gauge the weight of it and how that would affect her throw. She stepped to the line and let the first bull's-eye land in the middle of the board. She flashed him a smile. "Wow, you're a brilliant teacher."

She concentrated on her next aim and went on a run before throwing her last dart, another bull's-eye to end the game. She wiped her hands and pulled the three darts out of the board.

His mouth gaped, and his eyes narrowed. "You've played before."

"You assumed I hadn't. Never presume." She placed the darts in the case. "Sometimes you can tell someone you're capable, but sometimes you have to batten down the hatches and just deliver."

"Message received." His lips twitched before let loose with a laugh. "And I thought I knew everything about you."

"I hope there's still a lot to learn." He nodded and smiled at her. "What are you going to try that doesn't involve gardening?" When she put his darts away too, he asked, "Are you secretly a pool shark or do you want to come back next week for a game?"

The grumpy man returned and arched a brow.

"That's our cue to leave." She started to walk away. "Besides, I have to get back to my group of friends I deserted. See you tomorrow night at the fence." She waved and returned to the booth in the back corner with Becks Porter and the others.

Becks smiled and introduced Lindsay to Penelope and Kris, who looked familiar.

"I was wondering if you'd walked home," Becks said. "I ordered several appetizers, and they should be here any minute. I was just telling Penelope and Kris about my recent investment, a couple of abandoned buildings by Sully Creek. I'm starting a soccer complex, which should keep me busy for a while. Penelope's reviewing the contracts for me. She's my lawyer." Becks placed her glass on a coaster and scooted over on the bench, making more room for Lindsay. "Jillian's still at the bar, but, in the meantime, the rest of us single ladies have to stick together."

After a hard divorce, Becks had moved back to Hollydale. The food arrived, and the evening passed with jokes, stories and laughter. Sitting back after a last bite of bread pudding, Lindsay spotted Mason helping his grandfather with his jacket.

She noticed Kris watching him as well, and then Kris faced Lindsay, her brown eyes highlighting her flawless skin. "I know I should know you, but I just moved back to Hollydale. Have I seen you around the elementary school? Perhaps one of your children is in my class." Kris reached for a peanut and popped it in her mouth.

"Evan's four and Chloe's not even two yet. Somewhere else maybe?"

"Most likely I've seen you at The Busy Bean. My mom owns the coffeehouse. Wait a minute! You live next door to Mason, don't you? That's where I know you from." She snapped her fingers. "Mason and I went to one of your barbecues ages ago."

"Oh, that's right. I'm sorry I didn't recognize you. It's been a while." Lindsay felt bad she hadn't figured out the connection quicker.

Kris gestured in Mason's direction and then broke into a chuckle. "We dated a couple of times, but that ship sailed away ages ago. He let me down gently, and then I met my daughter Gigi's father. In the end, it all worked out. I was never sure Mason was the serious type about relationships, anyway."

Lindsay had seen how Mason treated his romantic relationships, making it clear all along he wasn't that interested in something permanent, but this confirmed it. Who was the real Mason Ruddick? The grandson who fretted over his grandfather and took Joe's criticism to heart? The paramedic who reassured Evan after his asthma attack? The genuine guy who held her close after she almost fell through the ceiling, so close she could feel his rapid heartbeat?

There were obviously more layers to him than the one he cultivated as the fun, footloose, single guy about town.

She could fall for the man if given half the chance, but then what? He'd simply tell her the same thing about not wanting to settle down once he was ready to move on. And she'd risk their friendship in the bargain.

No, she had to keep her feelings to herself, not only for herself, but for her children, who'd be devastated without Mason in their lives.

And wouldn't she feel the same?

CHAPTER FOURTEEN

SPRING WAS IN full force, beautiful one day with a hopeful promise of summer, the next overcast and cold. The cooler temperature was more than enough indication Mother Nature had some surprises in store before the gardenias bloomed in June. At Sycamore Station, Lindsay shivered and rose from the flower bed. She brushed the soil off her gloves and glanced around. The memorial circle was now 60 percent complete, a mere two weeks until the ceremony.

"You're the person I've been searching for." Her boss's authoritative voice boomed and she joined him at the base of the sycamore tree.

"The fungicide worked well." Lindsay examined the tree for any further signs of deterioration but found none. "By now, we'd have known if the gash caused more damage, so I think the tree's in the clear."

"Good, good, but that's not why I'm here," Phillip said.

If this was about her reminding Heather she was planting the hostas too close together, Lindsay might take the rest of the day off. As it was, this was now the tenth day in a row she'd worked.

"Excuse me, but we'd like to take a selfie with the sycamore." Two visitors, one with a selfie stick, were polite in their request, and Phillip ushered Lindsay over to her rolling cart.

"I've been talking to Heather." Phillip picked up a spray bottle and examined the nozzle.

"I spent hours that day replanting hostas—"

"No, no, I'm speaking personally, not professionally." Phillip flashed a smile before examining the cannas in the circle. "What are your plans here?"

She looked to the lamb's ears for the border to go along with the creeping phlox.

"I'm planting these, deadheading those flowers and then checking on the greenhouse filtration system."

The two visitors left the area just as new people arrived.

"Well, I'm checking in with employees. Nice to see attendance is good today. That lovely sycamore's one of our biggest attractions, isn't it," Phillip said, as if Lindsay didn't already know this. She could almost see the dollar signs in his eyes.

"We should have closed it off until the grand opening." She placed the water bottle he'd taken back in the cart. "Can this discussion wait?"

"Let me rephrase my earlier question. What are your long-term plans?"

"Continuing on like always." She loved her job, so much so that she and Tim had argued days before the accident about her continuing to work after Chloe was born. Lindsay sipped from her water bottle and considered why Phillip would ask something like that. One possibility hit her like falling timber. If attendance figures continued to free-fall, Phillip could be looking to downsize the staff. "Is there something wrong with my performance? My evaluation's not for another three months."

"You're right, it's not, but didn't you mention something about Tim's parents driving here from Wilmington for the dedication?"

Phillip came all the way from the main administrative offices to the southernmost tip of the gardens to ask about Tom and Donna?

"I did, and they are." She liked her home and being near Aunt Hyacinth in Hollydale, and the kids loved the mountains and their friends. That precluded any possibility of a move. "What do my in-laws have to do with my schedule or job performance?"

"Didn't you see that email I sent you from the director of one of the largest botanical gardens in the state? He and I happened to meet during my recent vacation to Wilmington and hit it off, having adult children and being the alumni of the same college. He called me this morning to let me know he's retiring."

"Good for him. If he's looking for a mountain cabin, Robin at Cobb Realty is amazing. Comes highly recommended."

"You haven't responded yet about whether you'd be interested in the Wilmington posting, the one with the larger salary and better benefits. Closer to Tim's family, too."

"I'm sorry, Phillip. I still don't think I'm on the same page. I didn't think I needed to answer that email since I wasn't planning on applying." She rubbed her eyes and reached for her pruning shears. "If that's all, I have lots of things to do before the greenhouse filtration system."

"But you'll look at the email and give the job some consideration?"

"Only if you do the same." That slight exasperation in her voice was unlike her, but she couldn't help it. "Now that you also have a tie to the area, Phillip, and your youngest started college, a new challenge might be right up your alley."

"Heather wouldn't hear of it, but it would be a raise and advancement for you, something you're not likely to find here."

"Oh, ok-ay. Thanks for telling me." Satisfied he'd leave her in peace, she set about her duties and he hurried away.

MASON ATTACHED A manual block sander to a pole in Lindsay's guest room. Then he climbed the ladder. Grandpa Joe walked in, whistling a Beatles tune.

"Good afternoon. Lovely day, isn't it?" His grandfather came over and inspected the joint compound, which Mason had already prepared for the next step. "Perfect, absolutely perfect. I just got off the phone with Bree."

Mason laid the pole across the top rung of the ladder and rushed down. "Did she get her scan results?" *Please let her be in the clear.* Otherwise, the doctors would have to order chemotherapy or radiation or both. He whipped out his phone. He checked his texts. "Hmm, no update."

"There aren't any yet. It was a simple grandfather, granddaughter chat, that's all."

It must be the day for that type of talk as he'd spoken to Grandma Betty earlier, reassuring her he was looking after Grandpa Joe. They'd laughed over his grandfather's first taste of turkey bacon, which he'd proclaimed pretty good.

"Okay, then." Mason climbed the ladder once more, not wanting the joint compound to set. Sanding the ceiling first would allow for a more even coat of mud.

"Are we still on the second coat?" Grandpa Joe asked.

"Yep." He'd half expected his grandfather to have done this step by now. "You won't be able to tell anything ever happened by the time Lindsay's parents arrive for the dedication."

No sooner had he said the words than he wanted to take them back. He'd opened a hornet's nest. If only he'd won that bet with Lindsay, she'd be beside him for moral support or even be the one doing the talking. Although the way she'd surprised him and thrown a darn good dart curled his lips into a smile. Just when he thought he'd known everything about her, she kept him on his toes. Made his toes curl, too.

His smile faded. Losing that dart game was probably for the best. Lindsay shouldn't be the one dealing with his grandfather. He needed to speak up.

"Most people wouldn't know anything about their neighbor's parents." Grandpa Joe glanced around the room. "You and Lindsay are close, aren't you?"

"We've been friends for a long time, but our patio and fence conversations didn't take off until a year ago. Now she's my best friend."

He'd arrived home one night and found Lindsay in her backyard, staring at the stars; at first, he'd thought something had to be wrong, but there wasn't. Apart from a woman trying to come to terms with what life had dealt her. And not just for her own sake, but for the sake of Evan and Chloe, too. She waited until he finally came over and spoke to her, then she opened up about her day. Pretty soon the floodgates gaped, and he found her the easiest person to talk to. When she glanced at her watch, they laughed at how three hours flew by so fast.

Ever since, he'd discovered an appreciation for how she held everything together. And how her beauty radiated from within.

Grandpa Joe stirred the compound and whistled more of the song, moving his hips in time to the rhythm. "There's not a doubt in my mind that you never noticed her as a woman while Tim was alive, but now you have. What's next?"

Nothing. It was obvious she was still in love with Tim. She was so committed about the dedication.

"We go on with our lives." Mason finished sanding the ceiling and descended the ladder. "As friends and nothing more."

"You won't get anywhere with that type of attitude. Sometimes you have to go for it. Did you two have a fight when you played darts? I noticed you were a trifle cross when you came back. I, on the other hand, had a fantastic time that evening." He started whistling an old Stones classic, moving his shoulders in time. "Don't wait up too late for me tonight. I've got a miniature golf game with friends, and then tomorrow it's Karaoke Night at the Timber River Bar and Grill. I'm thinking about 'Born to Be Wild.'"

Taken aback by his grandfather's sudden full social calendar, Mason located the three-inch putty knife on the makeshift worktable and added enough mud for the application of the second coat. He climbed the ladder once more, wondering if his next call should be to his grandmother. "Isn't it time to act your age?"

With broad strokes, Mason covered the lines of the fiberglass tape with the joint compound, taking care to trace the rectangular perimeter. He came down and swapped out the smaller putty knife for the larger version, scooping up enough mud for the interior of the rectangle where Lindsay had fallen through. Like a yo-yo, he stepped up to the plate once more.

"You left a glob at the corner. Smooth it out." Mason glanced at his grandfather, who stopped whistling and folded his arms. "I'd say you were the one acting younger than Chloe with this attitude."

And now back down again. There wasn't anything else Mason could do for the ceiling until this coat dried, then he'd apply the third one before sanding everything and painting it smooth.

He faced Grandpa Joe. Maybe he should just be honest with the man.

"I leveled with Lindsay about the real reason I don't want to attend, and she seemed to accept it. I don't want to feel as though I'm reducing Tim to fine print on a plaque.

The ceremony is for those who want one. I can understand that." Mason rubbed at his jaw.

"I see where you're coming from. Don't think I agree with you. Showing respect to Tim should be embraced no matter what the circumstances." His grandfather leaned in and patted his shoulder. "But you're my grandson and I want to make sure you're feeling alive and living life to the fullest."

Mason blinked. Of course, he was living life to the fullest. "That's what I do. Live for the moment."

"Without anyone at your side."

Life was easier that way. "Makes it a lot less complicated to hit the open road whenever I want."

His grandfather looked at him hard. "That works up to a point. I love you, Mason, but is it that you're afraid you might end up on that plaque? And if so, you're wondering who'd make sure they spelled your name right? Who'd keep your memory alive?"

Had that been the problem all this time? It could easily have been Mason on that helicopter. Was it guilt for Tim dying? Or was it guilt about being the one who lived? Was that the reason he didn't want to go to the ceremony?

Mason placed the lid on the compound. "You and Grandma would keep my memory alive. Mom and Dad. Bree." He'd also like to think Lindsay would remember him.

But that would be selfish of him to expect her to mourn him.

"What about Jordan?" Grandpa had been listening.

Mason gathered the putty spreaders so he could wash them. "I see what you're doing."

"What I'm doing is living." Grandpa lowered his hands and performed a smooth putting motion. "Eighteen holes of fun surrounded by a group of kind people. Can't beat that at my age."

Grandpa Joe crossed the threshold, and Mason called out. "Grandpa Joe!" His grandpa turned to him. "Can you understand why I don't want to go?"

"Oh, I understand perfectly, but remembering someone by honoring their service shouldn't be an issue." He returned, reached up and patted Mason's cheek. "It's all in how you see things. For instance, there was once a gaping hole in that ceiling. Now it's being repaired. It doesn't mean it wasn't there. It means hard work and effort fixed it up, and that took time and sacrifice, but it was worth it. Think about it, Mason."

His grandfather left, whistling once more. If Mason went to the dedication, he'd be seeing how much Lindsay still loved Tim. He clenched his fists, unwilling to hold on to hope he had something to do with the spark of life reignited these days in Lindsay's eyes.

But if he didn't attend? He'd risk losing the respect of some people he cared about most in his life.

LINDSAY CARRIED THE tray of homemade guacamole and chips, her thank-you to Mason for the work on her ceiling earlier today, to the small table between the Adirondack chairs. Then she rearranged her glass of wine and Mason's beer before she sat and looked to the west.

The silhouette of the Great Smoky Mountains provided the perfect backdrop for the full moon, rising high. In the distance, a barn owl screeched, starting its nightly hunt. She settled back and let her neck muscles relax against the headrest. Comfortable, she closed her eyes for a minute, only to open them when a chill descended on her.

A quick peek at her watch bolted her out of her chair. She'd fallen asleep for an hour. She checked the chair next to her. No Mason. Then she checked the guacamole. No indentations there. He'd never arrived.

Hustling inside, she reached for her coat, needing warmth as the nights were colder in the mountains than other parts of the Tar Heel State. She also grabbed the nursery monitor she kept for such occasions.

She knew where Mason was.

She knocked on his garage door. Sure enough, he opened it, a narrow gap that wasn't an invitation to enter. "Lindsay."

"I know my name. Funny how you forgot about tonight."

He ran his hand through his rumpled hair. "Who says I forgot? I finished my bike."

His shiny motorcycle took center stage in the middle of the garage. She squealed and elbowed past him. "It's beautiful!" She glanced at him, his excitement radiating from him. "Can I say that?"

He covered the rearview mirrors with his hands. "He's sensitive. Handsome at the very least." He winked, and she grinned.

"And thanks for your work on my ceiling, Mason. It looks great." Only ten days until her parents arrived. A series of yips caught her attention, and she glanced around. "Is that Goliath? Where's Joe?"

Mason looked surprised now. "I lost track of time, and Goliath needs to go outside. Grandpa Joe is fine, but he's sort of embraced the bachelor life."

"Goliath can run around my backyard while you explain what you mean by your grandfather acting like a bachelor when he's devoted to your grandma Betty. This might take a while, and I need to be closer to my house." She raised the nursery monitor.

Within minutes, they settled on her patio, and the active dog begged for a tortilla chip. She couldn't resist the little fellow.

"Now he'll keep wanting more." Mason scooped some guac in a chip and downed it. "I didn't eat dinner. Thanks."

She rolled her eyes and went inside, checking on her kids before grabbing a plate of leftovers for Mason and returning. Mason picked up the chicken quesadilla and bit off a good chunk.

"What's this about Joe?" she asked.

He polished off the first quesadilla and washed it down with a sip of beer. The second and third disappeared in a flash. Goliath ran over to her feet once more. She slipped him another chip.

"When you and I were playing darts, he accepted an entire month's worth of engagements." Mason reached for the last quesadilla and chomped on it.

"Isn't that what you wanted?" She loaded a tortilla chip with guac and ate it before tossing another to Goliath.

"Maybe at first, but things change."

She reached for another chip, and her fingers brushed his, that electric spark almost making her jump. Her gaze met his, and that intensity jarred her. Yanking her hand back, she blinked when Goliath jumped onto her lap and licked the salt off her face.

"Calm down, Goliath." The dog settled, his eyes heavy. "Good dog," Mason said.

She petted Joe's dog until gentle snuffles of sleep overtook the little chiweenie.

"So, you don't want your grandfather having fun while your grandmother's out of town? And, in case you forgot, we have a date with Joe tomorrow at Jasper and Jules's Garden Center to spend your gift card." She kept her voice as soft as possible; Goliath's snuffles were quite adorable.

"When you put the question like that, I sound rather

controlling if I stand in his way." He laughed and ate another chip, the intensity of a minute ago gone, replaced by that laid-back goofy grin she loved so much.

"There are words to describe you, but *controlling* is not one of them."

He met her gaze once more. "And how would you describe me if someone asked?"

Caught off guard, she wanted to make an excuse and retreat to the house, but the weight of the dog prevented that. The Mason of a month ago wouldn't have asked that, assured in himself and his reputation. Now it was almost as if he was allowing her in, valuing her opinion of him.

"I guess it would depend on who asked and why. Take the other night. Destinee would have loved it if I'd pulled her aside and told her something personal that would get you to notice her."

A wry smirk crossed his face, and he scooped more guac and ate another chip. "And what would you have told her?"

"For me to have said that, it assumes you've noticed me."

His soft gaze confirmed what they both knew and couldn't avoid anymore. He'd noticed her, not as Tim's widow but as Lindsay. Her heart skipped a beat. Mason stood, his hands reaching for her, then pulling her up, much to Goliath's dismay. The dog snorted and curled up on the deck. Mason cupped her face, his hands warm.

"I think we both know I have."

"Hello?" Joe's voice called out from Mason's yard. "Goliath? Mason?"

Goliath's ears perked up, and he yipped a welcome to his owner. The chiweenie zipped through the open gate.

"Goliath!" Joe's voice sounded panicked. "Come back here!"

Mason hurried after the dog. "Goliath!"

Lindsay grabbed the bowl of chips, hoping food might aid in bringing back the dog. A noise from inside the house stopped her, and she opened the sliding glass door. Evan was standing on the step stool, reaching for a cup. "I was thirsty and heard Grandpa Joe. Is Goliath okay?"

Her phone pinged a text with one word appearing on her screen. Safe.

She nodded and poured Evan some water. "Mason let me know he's okay."

If only she could say the same for her heart.

CHAPTER FIFTEEN

MASON DROPPED THE tailgate of Lindsay's truck. "Was all of this necessary?"

She gave one emphatic nod and started removing his myriad purchases. "Your lawn has been in serious need of TLC for years. I've been itching to help you plant perennials and hostas and more, but you weren't ready until now."

Until his grandfather had moved in with him, that is, and began sharing his wisdom daily, he'd never considered himself ready for everything life offered most people. Maybe it wouldn't be selfish forming attachments even with the risks associated with Mason's particular career.

"I think we bought out the store this morning. Do they have new stock to replace all the plants and flowers we purchased?"

"Jasper and Jules have been at this a long time. They're experienced at inventory." Lindsay handed Evan a small bag of soil, so he'd feel useful, but nothing too heavy, while giving Chloe a box of sidewalk chalk. "Jules was right when she said the gift cards pay for themselves. I'm just glad everything checked out with the sycamore, and I was able to join you at the nursery earlier than planned."

His phone rang, and he looked at the screen. "Can you carry on without me for a few minutes?"

After she nodded, he connected with Bree. "Hi, sis. What news?"

"I must have the wrong number. You have the same

voice as my brother, but you're what I would call chipper." She laughed, perhaps the first genuine laugh since her diagnosis.

"And you're sounding more like the—" he caught himself before he said the word *old* "—like Bree. So how was your scan?"

"I'm on the mend. No chemo, no radiation. My margins are clear."

He closed his eyes, gratitude washing over him, and he fell into one of Lindsay's Adirondack chairs. "That's amazing, Bree. I'm so happy for you and Tristan. And Grandpa Joe too."

"About that."

Hesitancy was back in her voice, and he was glad he was sitting down. "Why do I have a feeling Grandma Betty hasn't booked her return flight yet?"

"Because she hasn't. I have more news. You remember Tristan went on a month-long work trip." Excitement now dominated her tone, and he let out the deep breath he'd been holding. "He received a promotion."

"And, let me guess, more hours, so more responsibility, and more time Grandma Betty will be spending with you?" Would he have to be the person who'd convey this message to Grandpa Joe?

"You're only mostly right. The reason I need Grandma Betty is we're moving to Atlanta! We'll be closer, and after we're settled in our new house, we're driving her back and Tristan and I will visit with you and Grandpa."

"What about your treatment in Nashville? Your doctors?"

"They have those in Atlanta, too." That teasing note he hadn't heard in a long while also reassured him. "By then, I'll even be finished with the scarf I'm knitting you."

"Scarf?"

"It started as socks and it still might end up as a blanket. I'm not sure yet. Grandma keeps clucking at me, and she says I'm already a pro at dropping stitches." Voices sounded in the background. "Gotta go. Realtor's here. Give Grandpa Joe a great big hug for me. Love ya."

"Right back at you." Mason stared at the silent phone. He rubbed his temple before standing and placing it in his pocket.

He found Grandpa Joe helping Hyacinth unload the last supplies from the back of the truck. The two of them appeared deep in conversation, so Mason glanced at the sky, the dome a perfect blue with nary a cloud in sight. Once everyone scattered for lunch, he thought, he'd head out for the first time on his motorcycle and figure out how to break the news of yet another delay in Grandma Betty's homecoming to Grandpa Joe. Albeit a temporary one. For now, he wanted nothing spoiling this moment.

Goliath barked and ran over, nipping Mason's heels. Mason moved toward Lindsay, but first paused and watched her nimble fingers. She knelt by the row of bushes at the side of his house, her face shielded with a light blue wide-brimmed hat.

He approached, and she glanced up. "Was that work or family?"

He wasn't sure there was a difference. As far as he was concerned, his fellow paramedics and first responders in Hollydale were like family to him.

"That was Bree." He knelt beside her.

She placed the trowel on the dirt and focused on him. "How's she doing? Any updates?"

Lindsay leaned in toward him as though her whole day pivoted around his answer. This wasn't simply casual interest. She cared about Bree and Grandpa Joe and Grandma Betty as if they were members of her family.

While Lindsay's lopsided smile and soft curves accounted for the physical pull, he found himself in a deep hole of attraction for this intelligent and intriguing woman.

"There's a fresh problem on the horizon."

"Did something else show up on her latest medical test?" Lindsay reached out and touched his arm, her instant support another quality he found endearing.

"Her prognosis is good." He glanced toward Grandpa Joe, his face animated as he described last night's golf outing to Chloe, his voice exaggerated for extra effect. "However, there's news on the Grandma Betty front, and it isn't great."

"Make yourself useful and dig with me as you fill me in. This is your yard we're making beautiful."

They worked in sync and talked about Tristan and Bree's latest update. He couldn't help but peek at Grandpa Joe, Goliath at his feet, playing with Chloe. "We're growing closer, but I'm concerned about him moving back home before Grandma Betty's return."

"Aw, that's sweet. So, it's his possible reaction to yet another delay and not the move that's worrying you."

"It's both, and hey, I'm not the worrying type." Mason reached for the next plat of impatiens and lifted one from its nesting place. He then planted it, smoothing the mound in the same manner as Lindsay had.

"You're so cute sometimes."

"Only sometimes?" He grinned.

"You're insufferable all the time, and cute most of the time." She grinned back, her sly smile wide enough for conveying she was in on the joke.

"The lady thinks I'm cute." He collapsed backward in the grass, and Goliath ran over and licked Mason's face.

Lindsay laughed and reached for his hand to pull him upright. "And insufferable."

"Well, you're cute all the time." He tapped her nose affectionately, the shock sparking through his body, too aware of her as more than just his neighbor.

It took a herculean effort not to kiss her right in front of everyone. More and more, every time he did anything with her, he was finding it harder and harder not to kiss her.

Her eyes widened, and she rose as if the change in their relationship was now irrevocable.

Goliath yipped once and then returned to Grandpa Joe's side. "Abandoned by a dog."

"You'll live." Lindsay gathered the gardening implements and stepped back. "That looks a sight better, doesn't it?"

Even though he knew she meant their handiwork, he only had eyes for the woman standing beside him, her honey-brown hair glinting in the spring sun, her wide cheeks blooming pink. "Yes."

She faced him and tapped his arm with her gloves. "We need a cold drink. Follow me."

She went over to the small refrigerator in his garage and handed him a bottle of water. "Now that we've stopped for a break, you can fill me in on the rest of that phone call. For someone whose sister is moving closer to him, you don't seem that excited."

"She'll have a different set of doctors, and her support system in Atlanta won't be the same. I just want her to stay confident. She's gotten such good care in Nashville."

She sipped from her reusable water bottle. "So, you think a support system in place outweighs job advancement? Is one more important than the other?"

"I didn't say that. Bree's situation is unusual." He uncapped the bottle. "For the most part, though, I believe if there's something you want, go for it."

Why couldn't he go for it with Lindsay?

Tim, Colette, my job. All of that held him back. If he gave all of himself, he wouldn't be able to run anymore.

But the spark between them soared again, warming him from head to toe. For a second, he considered pouring the bottle of cold water over his head. Then a calmness came. Taking a chance on her would be worth everything. "Lindsay—"

"Have you ever been to Wilmington?"

"Of course. It's a great surfing town. Love the A-frame barrels there."

She paused and took another drink. "Tim's parents live there, you know."

"No, I didn't." Or at least he didn't remember that. "But Bree is moving to Atlanta, not Wilmington."

"Their botanical garden is searching for a new director. I don't think Bree would be qualified for that."

No, but Lindsay would. Suddenly he felt as though that cold water had drenched him. "You're definitely qualified, probably overqualified."

She sighed and focused on her aunt Hyacinth who peeked at them for a second, but she backed away. "As far as support systems go, mine is here, but Phillip thinks I should apply for the job and go for it, as you said."

"Is the job right for you?" His heart thudded while awaiting a response. Hiring Lindsay would be the best thing any organization could do for itself. Dazed, he bumped into a row of waiting planters.

"The pay's great as are the benefits, including an extra week of vacation, plus Tim's parents would become more active in the kids' lives."

What about us? He kept from shouting out.

If Lindsay moved from Hollydale, another person he cared about would be gone, and it wouldn't be just Lindsay who'd leave, it'd be Evan and Chloe, too.

Yet he couldn't ask her to stay. Not for him.

"Sounds like you have a lot to think about. I'd best get back to work. It's my yard, and I can't slack off." He hurried off and ran into the exact person he was looking for, his grandfather.

Grandpa Joe backed up. "Haven't seen anyone in that much of a rush since your grandmother moved to save those chocolate chip cookies that almost burned."

"Speaking of Grandma Betty…"

Grandpa Joe held up his hand. "I already know. Bree and Tristan are getting a fresh start. A new house, a new lease on life. Can't beat that for my granddaughter. My bride will be back soon enough."

Mason opened his mouth to reply, but no words tumbled out. He should have known Grandma Betty would tell Grandpa Joe. Of all the different reactions, this wasn't one he'd expected.

Same as he hadn't anticipated Lindsay going anywhere. And what did he expect?

For Lindsay to meet him by the fence every night for the rest of her life?

For them to grow old together, her single and alone in her house and him in his?

Nothing stayed the same forever, not even the best things life had to offer.

He scrubbed his chin and stared at his grandfather. "How can you stay so calm? Don't you sort of feel like she's pushing you away by staying there so long?"

"My Betty's as true as the day is long." He patted Mason on the back. "There's so much in this world that changes, but Betty's my constant, no matter where we are."

Goliath ran toward Joe, and his grandfather bent and picked up the small dog. The children and Hyacinth also found their way over.

"My dear, your cheeks are too pink." She waggled her finger at Lindsay. "Gardening should be a delight, a feast for the eyes and a balm for common ailments such as heightened blood pressure. You need an evening free of concerns, no matter how delightful," she glanced toward Evan and Chloe, "those concerns are."

Lindsay eyed him, and Mason shrugged. "I've been saying that for weeks."

Hyacinth let out a little cheer and clapped. "That's the perfect solution for this quandary. Our Lindsay needs time to herself." She adjusted her flowing floral-print scarf. "Sweet Shelby's is having a special pie tasting test this afternoon until early evening. Only a few friends and repeat customers who'll give feedback on what new savory items and desserts will work with our existing menu. Joe and the children can be my guests. That's one advantage of being the owner, or at least, the co-owner."

Lindsay frowned and picked up Chloe. "Thanks for offering, Aunt Hyacinth, but you've done so much for us today."

"Nonsense." Hyacinth bored her gaze into Mason and arched her eyebrow. He received her message loud and clear, without her even speaking a word. He gave a subtle nod of alliance. "I have to leave early to help with the preparations," she continued. "But I insist on having them along. Spoiling them over one dinner by their aunt won't hurt them. And no one can resist my pie, so that's settled. Joe, would you like to tag along tonight with the kiddos? What about you, Mason? Are you coming to Sweet Shelby's later?"

"Pie? Sign me up." Grandpa Joe rubbed his belly and turned toward Lindsay. "I can drive them in my car if you're okay with that."

"Yes. That is unless Mason's going."

Everyone waited for his answer.

"Uh, no. I'm working tomorrow so it'll be an early night for me." With his grandfather occupied, there was no better time to get a first ride on his motorcycle.

"I must go. I'll see the three of you tonight." Hyacinth tweaked Chloe's nose and Evan's before leaving.

Joe reached for Chloe and motioned for Evan. "How about lunch now so we'll be hungry tonight?"

In two seconds, everyone except for him and Lindsay filed out of the garage. Even Goliath opted for the backyard.

Lindsay frowned. "Do you feel like we've been set up?"

"Not at all. Your aunt was clear—this evening's about you, and it'll give you time to reflect on what you want." He stepped back, almost tripping over a rake. "I mean as far as the move."

From there, he left without another word. Tonight would give her time to think about what was best for her life, especially that job in Wilmington. He couldn't stand in her way. He cared too much, and if leaving Hollydale would be the best thing for her, he'd have to say goodbye.

The thought made his stomach hurt. If this was what caring for someone did to a person, made you feel empty and twisted, maybe he was better off alone.

LINDSAY HAD A quick shower and put on fresh clothes, but then wasn't sure what she should do next. The house was almost too eerie since she wasn't used to the silence.

Why hadn't Aunt Hyacinth asked her to come with them? She loved pie almost as much as she loved the thought of a night to herself.

Everyone else, though, had other plans. Becks and Penelope were reviewing paperwork, and Kris was heading to Asheville to see the latest animated movie with her mother and daughter. She went over to Mason's garage and banged on his door, releasing her frustration on the innocent wood. Mason opened the door enough for her to see the helmet in his hand. "Don't worry. I'm being as quiet as a mouse so you can enjoy your night off," Mason said.

"Hello, Lindsay. How are you after a morning of work and an afternoon of making my yard look the best it's ever been, Lindsay? You could start with some pleasantries, you know?" She elbowed her way into the garage.

Mason's motorcycle took front and center with his tools hanging in place on particleboards and surfaces clear of parts. If it weren't for the faint whiff of oil and paint, she wouldn't even guess he'd built it here from the ground up. She walked over, a quiver of apprehension running through her. She'd never ridden a motorcycle before.

"Thanks for the hard work. It's a changed yard. It's terrific." He clicked on a button and the main garage door opened.

She noticed the motorcycle's silver metallic paint. "Silver. Interesting choice. Why not something else?"

"It stands out without standing out. It's also a suitable alternative to other colors that show off the dirt and grime more quickly." He tucked the helmet under his arm. "I'll see you later?"

"Nope. You lost a bet, and I'm collecting on it." She enjoyed asserting herself. It felt good.

"Okay." His voice was wary, almost as if he was backing away from her.

Good thing she was persistent. A gardener had to be patient, and something told her the fruit of her patience this time would be worth waiting for. "Stop assuming you know everything about sweet ol' Lindsay. I'm full of surprises."

"I don't like surprises, remember?" He rested his helmet on the worktable and placed his elbow on it. "What do you need? I only have a little light left, and I want to get rolling."

"Perfect." She pointed to his helmet. "You got an extra one of those?"

"Why?"

"Because I'm going with you." She went over and straddled the bike before she lost her nerve. "This holds two people, doesn't it?"

"I've only driven around the block once. This is the genuine test." He arched an eyebrow and shook his head. "I can't take you. What if we get stranded on the road or something goes wrong?"

"You put it together, right? With the intention of it working?" She waited for his nod. "That settles that. One helmet, please."

He went over to the cabinet and pulled out a spare. "This is the smallest one I own."

"Good to know I don't have a big head."

He stared at her for a long moment. "If you're really going, you need to change first. Pants and a jacket along with gloves, okay? Boots if you have them."

"You won't leave without me?"

"A bet's a bet."

"And you'll throw in dinner? I'm in the mood for fried chicken." She grinned.

"Sounds good."

"Bet aside, would you have taken me, anyway? If I had asked nicely." She smiled and patted the seat, the rich leather hiding a layer of thick foam.

"I don't know, to be honest." He laid both helmets on the workbench. "I'm used to traveling solo."

He'd driven that point home ever since she'd met him. "Then it's a good thing I accepted that bet, isn't it?" She hurried off before he could change his mind.

Or before she could change hers.

CHAPTER SIXTEEN

MASON SWERVED INTO the gravel parking lot for the hiking trail that led toward Pine Falls. This was a new sensation, having someone's arms around him with the spring breeze rustling his jacket, the miles disappearing under his feet. Not just anyone's arms, either. Lindsay's.

He cut the engine and removed his helmet, taking a deep breath of the clear mountain air. The Great Smoky Mountains were in their full, breathtaking beauty this time of year. Many tourists came to Hollydale in the fall for the foliage when the leaves went out in a blaze of glory. They didn't know what they were missing in spring—his favorite season. There was something about the hint of cherry blossoms in the air, the wildflowers springing up alongside the river and the trickle of that river giving rise to a full crescendo.

Holding his hand out, he assisted her as she dismounted, her trembling fingers not lost on him. Catching a ride on a motorcycle wasn't for everyone. Lindsay struggled with the chin clasp, and he unhooked the strap for her. She removed the helmet. Her pale face sent alarm bells ringing.

"Lindsay." Her name was but a breath as a crash of feelings flooded through him. "Lin?"

"Where do I put this?" She held up the helmet and he took it from her. She started removing the knapsack from her back.

Mason opened the pannier and swapped the take-out

containers from the Holly Days Diner with the helmets. For a few seconds, he let his disappointment wash over him. What had he expected? For her to be as entranced about motorcycles as he found himself about gardening.

He loaded the knapsack with their reusable water bottles and the containers.

"Ready?" He pushed off, but she stopped him at the base of the trail.

"What's with being gruff? It was your idea to stop for the food and to come to the trail."

"You're right. I'm sorry, I just have a lot on my mind." He didn't want to bring up her and the kids leaving town, not when she was standing there looking so open and hopeful.

She nodded and tugged on his sleeve. "Then let me carry something. C'mon. Don't be stubborn. I let you pay for my dinner, the least I can do is carry it. Smelling my fried chicken will make me walk that much faster, although I'm not sure I'd be in such a hurry for your vegetable plate."

Reluctantly, he extracted the water bottles from the knapsack and handed them to her.

"Not fried chicken, but it'll do." She smiled.

This late in the day, other hikers weren't starting out, but they passed a good number of people returning to the lot. Too many for any conversation and the rocky path also demanded most of their attention. When he thought about it, he didn't mind the silence. Not with the possibility of her moving to Wilmington still unsettled.

The river rushed alongside them. With each step, the muted sound of the falls became more pronounced, as did the incline. She stuck with him, matching him step for step, stride for stride.

They came upon a rock outcropping with water dripping over the lichen surface, an overhang tall enough to shelter hikers. She pulled him under the rocks and inhaled. He did the same, the dampness and the earthy scent filling his lungs.

"Thank you, Mason."

"For what?"

"I would have missed out on this moment if you hadn't suggested the hike. I'm so busy making the gardens beautiful for others and our yards a sanctuary for ourselves that sometimes I forget the simple majesty of the world around me. Timber River, the red maples, the flowering dogwoods. Nature for the sake of nature. You're right. I needed the reminder."

The crest of the mountains surrounding them stood out on the trail. Sharing this with someone was different, he reflected, than usually hiking on his own. No matter how many women he'd dated, he hadn't opened up to any of them about his grandparents' and parents' long marriages or losing his sister and best friend.

Had he used those losses as excuses, ways to keep on a path familiar and level rather than hiking a treacherous trail with a trusted someone by his side?

"There's a flat rock near the falls where we can sit and eat," Mason said.

They made it the rest of the way, with Pine Falls cascading sixty feet into a pool of water. Some hikers milled about while others watched in wonder. Lindsay moved the water bottles under her arm and, with her free hand, squeezed his. "This is perfect. Aren't you glad I won the bet?"

"You're quite the con artist."

Her cheeks pinkened, and they settled at the last unoccupied spot on the rock. He unstrapped the knapsack and lowered himself to the gray slate.

"I love everything about tonight. Thanks for my first motorcycle ride."

Mason stopped unzipping the main compartment. "I thought you were scared. Your hands trembled and your face was flushed."

She put his water bottle in front of him. "Maybe my trembling hands had nothing to do with the ride itself."

"Then why were you shaking?" Her chin snapped up, and she leveled her gaze at him.

He leaned back and almost fell off the rock. Opting to keep this light, he said, "My driving's not that bad." He gave a weak smile and brought forth the food, fried chicken for Lindsay, grilled vegetables and rice pilaf for himself. Even now, she shivered when she accepted the disposable container. "Are you cold?" he asked.

"Not cold, just wondering why you're shutting me out."

Her lips pulled into a straight line as she opened the container. She bit into a drumstick and chewed while he struggled with his emotions. He dared to look at her. He shouldn't be noticing the best qualities of something that would be gone too soon. The thought of her moving away crushed his heart and kept him on his side of the rock. He had to hold back.

"I'm just trying to enjoy the scenery, like you said." His smooth voice didn't match his shaky interior.

"Just so you know, that won't work." She breathed out and closed her container. "Maybe I enjoyed that ride with my arms around you too much. Maybe the reason I was trembling was *you*. I might regret this, but I haven't thought of anything else on the trail."

She leaned into him, her fingers gripping the sides of his jacket, pulling him close. Their gazes met, and she licked her lips. The roar of the falls had nothing on the roar of his heart. "Well, I am hard to resist."

"I'll never be able to keep your ego in check now." She grinned before he curled his arm around her.

With a slight nod, she closed the gap, and her sweet lips brushed his. Her fingers threading through his thick hair.

The kiss was pure Lindsay: truthful, blossoming, giving. The kiss deepened, and he smelled lavender and poppies and everything beautiful. Some barrier inside him broke open, like floodgates letting in water to a thirsty town.

Just as with the unending waterfall, he wanted to keep kissing her, to keep this feeling of one constant thing in his life going. This kiss was what he wanted, something he would cherish, a reminder that at the end of a bad day where everything went wrong, there was someone open and joyful, and waiting for him.

So he in turn could be that someone for her. For Lindsay.

Chuckling, Lindsay broke away. "Dinner and scenery and lack of interruptions. I can see why this must be a popular dating spot for you." Her face drained of color, and she shrugged. "Not that this is a date. It's..." She glanced at him as though he'd have the right answer.

"A bet, won fair and square." He waited for her nod and then he opened his food container. He devoured the rice pilaf, and also kept an eye on her. "You're wrong, though. You're the first person who's walked this trail with me."

Her face went from ashen to rosy in less than ten seconds. He liked her different expressions, whether here, by the fence or downtown. He especially loved the shades of pink on her cheeks, at times revealing her innermost self.

"I'm one of a kind. Thanks." She tossed her hair back and offered a grin.

He speared a bite of grilled zucchini. "Have you been out on a date since Tim?"

Why every topic during their nightly conversations had come up except this one, he couldn't say. Maybe, on some level, he hadn't wanted to know.

"A couple. They ended before they began."

His phone echoed somewhere in the deep recesses of his backpack, and he broke away. "Sorry, but I have to check in case it's a work emergency." He looked at the screen. "It's my brother-in-law. I should take this."

Before he could say more than hello, he was hearing the news. "Bree wasn't feeling well this afternoon after she talked to you. It happened suddenly. She's having tests done." Worry consumed Tristan's voice. "Your grandmother and I are in the emergency room."

"I can be there in a few hours. I just have to throw some things together and find someone to cover my shift."

"Hold on." Muted voices came over the line, and Mason strained to make out any of the words.

Mason stared at the waterfall, the constancy of the flowing water no longer a romantic refuge. Lindsay's hand covered his; he thought he should pull it back, but didn't.

"That was Bree's doctor. She has an infection, but they're confident they caught it in time. She'll be on an antibiotic drip and if all goes as expected, she'll be discharged in the morning." Relief came through the line. "Your grandmother wants to talk to you."

"Stay with Joe." His grandmother sounded older than her usual self, but steady. "We'll keep Bree safe, and then we'll plan a long weekend for you and Joe to come get me at the end of the month." Grandma Betty was quite emphatic, too much so for his taste.

"Grandma, I can be there…"

"Mason, trust Tristan and me. I'll be back in Hollydale soon enough, where I won't get to see my granddaughter as often as I'd like. With you there, I know my Joe has someone looking after him." He must get his stubborn streak from his grandmother rather than his grandfather.

"Wait a minute. Lindsay's right here. I'll ask her if she'll watch Goliath. Then I can bring Grandpa with me."

"If you're with Lindsay, let me talk to her."

He handed over the phone to her. Lindsay pressed the phone to her ear. "Hello, Mrs. Ruddick… Oh yes, Betty."

He caught Lindsay's eye and they smiled at each other.

He tried following her conversation with his grandmother, but gave up and ate his dinner, not tasting anything. He stared out at Pine Falls.

Lindsay tapped his arm with the phone. "She said it's your call, but she'd feel better if you stay here. Bree's doctor doesn't think she's in any real danger."

"Grandpa Joe needs Grandma Betty. I'll take him with me."

"She also said to tell you she wants to finish your knitted blanket with Bree, and they'll give it to you at the end of the month together."

"Did the two of you plan everything out?"

"You probably also missed me promising her that I'd make Joe my world-famous meatballs tomorrow night." She smiled and shrugged. "But only if you think you should stay. Betty's concerned, but not controlling. There's a difference."

Mason glanced at his disposable container, which was empty, and then hers, which was still half full. "Are you going to finish that?"

She chuckled and clasped hers to her chest. "Next time order your own fried chicken."

Next time? Could there be a next time? He'd love to kiss her again, sure, but what if things changed between them? What if she and the kids moved to Wilmington? As much as he'd like to take a chance that he could find the type of rare love his parents and grandparents had, this wasn't the right time to try. He might have to leave for Bree's side at a minute's notice, and Lindsay might be permanently leaving.

Three days on the job would give him some perspective. He'd never been so thankful for a long shift in his life.

IN THE SMALLER of the two greenhouses on the western side of the botanical garden, Lindsay checked the labels on the plants she finished transplanting and jotted some notes. A new employee called in sick today, and so Lindsay had done double duty, arriving at six this morning. Waving goodbye to one of her assistants, she stretched and yawned. How could thirteen hours have passed so quickly? A long shift but a fruitful one as she caught a mistake in the soil levels for the rare North Carolina plant exhibit scheduled to open next week. The extra alkaline wouldn't have helped the *Cardamine* flowering plant and monitoring the sulfur addition was a must so the roots wouldn't scorch.

With the sulfur added, she started her rounds and found one of the timer's screens blank. After she changed the batteries, she texted Aunt Hyacinth and let her know she was running late. She rubbed her eyes, then headed along the employee's path to the main building. To her surprise, Phillip flagged her down. "Something's come up and I'll be out of the office for the next two days."

Her jaw dropped. The dedication was a little over a week away, and she'd been doing twelve-hour days and several weekend mornings, giving her all.

Phillip opened the door for her. "It's not what you think."

"I was just thinking I've been working a lot of hours, and I'd have loved a break." Frustration at everything boiled over. "My kids are only little once, and I've put in overtime on this project, the rare plant exhibit and my other duties."

"And Heather will also be away, but she's arranged for extra help for you." Phillip kept talking and walking until they arrived at her office. "There will be a group of high school students, coming to assist you for the community service hours."

Lindsay groaned and retrieved her purse from the bottom drawer of her desk. Then she exchanged her green blazer for her coat. "The last time that happened I had to explain the difference between the blade and the handle of a trowel to more than a few of the kids."

Phillip shook his head, propping her door open. "She personally talked to the agricultural teacher. All these kids are looking for careers in the field and have experience with landscaping."

That sounded more promising, but she wouldn't hold her breath. "The supplier said the substitute plants I ordered should arrive by ten tomorrow morning, so the help would be appreciated."

He went over to her desk and examined her pink stapler with her name written in Sharpie on the top and also on a label affixed to the bottom. "Did you give any more consideration to that position in Wilmington?"

"Yes, I've given it more consideration, and no, I'm not applying. I have no desire to become the director of any botanical garden. I'm all about the plants and flowers. I'm glad you're the one in charge of the budgets and keeping the donors happy."

That stapler became that much more interesting to him, as he never raised his gaze. "You wouldn't even be interested in applying for my position then if it became open?"

"Nope." Funny, she expected a boulder on her shoulder, but relief was a small price to pay for speaking her mind to her boss.

"Good to know." He placed the stapler back on her desk. "See you in two days."

"Why are you taking time off so close to the ceremony?"

Phillip zipped up his jacket. "Heather and I have done nothing but talk about Wilmington since we left, so I've applied for the position. My interview's tomorrow."

"Good." *Oops.* That came out a little too fast. "What I mean is…"

"No need to explain. Heather's picking me up here and we're driving tonight."

It'd been a full day, and Phillip was interviewing for another job. Thank goodness tonight was Mason's first night off in three days. She missed their fence discussions and needed one.

A yearning to see him swept over her. She sank into her office chair. This wasn't just a need to talk life over with a friend and a cup of coffee at The Busy Bean. This was about something else. Something more. In the past few months, a casual chat had developed into an intense connection. That kiss proved the attraction wasn't one-sided or a mere crush, and it wasn't a friendly peck on the cheek, either.

When they'd first started these backyard chats, she'd gone along with them because Mason was so safe and so off-limits. What better person to chat with than a perpetual bachelor who liked his freedom? What better person than her husband's best friend who'd keep her at arm's length?

When did something easy and comforting become something that skirted the edge of disaster?

That kiss, tender yet mind-boggling, dynamic and breathtaking, left her reeling and wanting more. She hadn't ever meant to be anyone but a friend to Mason, especially with Tim being their common link. Yet here she was, thinking about him—his character as loyal as the perennials that grew every year, his personality as colorful as the flowers she loved to surround herself with.

And yet there was no one worse for her than Mason. He lived for the moment, whether it was an unplanned trip to surf, or hike, or even his job, dedicating himself to that brief window of time when he had to stabilize a patient and rush them to the hospital. She tended to her garden and her children, where patience and a steady hand guided the day. For the first time in years, she was reconnecting and expanding her circle of friends.

So his kiss caused her heart to crash in her chest, the same way the waterfall collided with the rocks.

She craved solidity and constancy, two attributes that would never describe the man who didn't wear a watch unless he was on duty.

She found her keys and exited the garden, stopping for a minute to chat with the night security guard before driving home.

The drive didn't take long and Chloe greeted her at the door, where Lindsay swept her into her arms, nuzzling noses with her daughter. Chloe giggled.

Aunt Hyacinth came into the living room, removing her apron, the one with the sunflowers. "Dinner's in the oven. A lovely chicken pot pie with my signature flaky crust. Do let me know whether the dish is as delicious as it is fragrant. Belinda and I wish to accommodate our customers who would like to partake of something heartier, and you're my taste testers."

A loud crash came from upstairs, followed by a wail. Lindsay quickly lowered Chloe to the carpet and ran toward the sound.

Lindsay rushed into the guest room at the same time Mason descended from the ladder, paintbrush in hand. She flicked off the speaker, playing rock and roll. Evan was sitting on the floor, his lower lip jutting out. He burst into tears.

"Evan, are you okay? When did you come in here?" Mason shucked his protective goggles and kneeled beside Evan, laying his hand on her son's shoulder.

Evan cried louder and pointed to an overturned can, where paint was pooling on the beige carpet. Mason set the paint can upright. Evan wailed, and she tried to console him.

"What happened, Ev?"

He sniffed and scrunched his eyes shut. "I only wanted to help Mason. But I tripped and the can fell over and—" Then crying began afresh.

She hugged Ev and sighed, seeing the huge glob of white paint on the beige carpet. Her parents were set to arrive in three days. Moving the bed might cover the spot.

Mason disappeared, and she let go of Evan. "You knew Mason was in here painting the ceiling. Sometimes adults need helpers, and sometimes they don't."

Mason returned with dish soap, a black garbage bag and two rolls of paper towels. Chloe toddled in behind him, and he handed Evan the soap. "No use crying over spilled paint. We need to clean this up while it's still wet. Chloe, you can mix the bubbles with your mommy, and Evan, you can scrub with me."

Chloe giggled but took her job of using a paint stirrer to mix the water and dish soap to heart. After another fast hug, the four of them set to working and within minutes, the carpet looked better, although Lindsay would still have to rearrange the furniture so her mother wouldn't notice.

"Sorry." Mason pulled the plastic drawstring of the

trash bag closed. "I thought I had closed the door. I didn't hear him enter."

"I'm sorry, Mommy." Evan sniffled once more, and she kept still for a second, monitoring his breathing and reaction to the paint fumes.

Nothing. At least that was one relief. "Accidents happen." Something beeping sounded in the distance, and Lindsay tapped her forehead. "That must be the pot pie. If Joe's not doing anything, you can call him and see if he and Goliath want to join us for dinner."

The rest of the evening progressed smoothly. After helping with the kitchen cleanup, Mason threw the dish towel over his shoulder. "I'll put everything away in the guest room before I take Grandpa Joe home."

She glanced at Joe, reading a book to Evan and Chloe. "I'll come with you and check on the stain."

They went upstairs, and Mason's phone rang. "Is it Bree?" Lindsay held her breath until he shook his head.

"It's work."

He stayed in the hallway, and she examined the spot and the furniture arrangement. There should be enough room to move the bed, but until everything was put away, she'd have to leave it as is. Mason joined her, but his face reflected something was bothering him.

"What's wrong?"

He grimaced. "Tomorrow's crew is out sick. Jordan and I are covering their shift."

"Be careful. Even if you're okay with the extra shifts, watch over him and keep your guard up." She examined his eyes, weary enough after a recent three-day stint.

Without warning, Goliath rushed into the room, barking playfully. He zigzagged in the open space and headed toward the table with the paint supplies. Mason scooped him up before the dog caused another accident. "Nope, not today, Goliath." He stopped at the entryway and glanced over his shoulder. His gaze fell on her and she wondered what he was thinking now.

Maybe she hadn't been the only one dwelling on that kiss and hoping there'd be another. It had been one thing, though, to realize he was wrong for her but to have kissed and just walked away from it was another. Should she bring it up? Why hadn't he? Did that mean he wanted to forget all about it? The accident with the paint might not have been the only one to have happened recently.

Rather than aiming for the dartboard and seeing whether another kiss would score a bull's-eye, he'd swooped out, conceding before anything began.

He was right. Their kiss was an accident, one that could cause irreparable damage to their friendship were it to happen again.

She'd gotten the hint. If only her heart had gotten the hint before the kiss, though.

CHAPTER SEVENTEEN

LINDSAY OPENED THE refrigerator and peeked into the container with the chicken pot pie. There was just enough for three servings. She placed the leftovers on a cookie sheet and opened the preheated oven. *Thank you, Aunt Hyacinth.* After her exhausting day, heating dinner and getting Evan and Chloe ready for bed were on top on her short list of evening activities. Since Mason was working and Joe was elsewhere, she'd paint the guest-room ceiling by herself after Evan and Chloe were asleep. She plugged in her coffeepot, eager for one last caffeine surge even this early in the evening.

Her doorbell rang, and she glanced at her watch. She wasn't expecting company. The doorbell rang again, and she clicked on the coffeepot before checking on Evan and Chloe, watching their favorite animated cartoon in the living room, and then she peered through the peephole.

No, it couldn't be. Not this early. The muscles in her shoulders tightened. Her parents had arrived one week ahead of schedule.

"Lindsay, darling!" Her mother rapped at the door. "Are you there? I see your truck in the driveway. It's your mother."

"Mimi! Pop-Pop!" Evan and Chloe scrambled off the floor and ran toward Lindsay.

After a deep breath, Lindsay opened the door, her

mother on the stoop, her father at the trunk of their rental car, unloading the luggage.

Her mother never changed. White bangs protruded from her silk scarf with a jungle pattern of leopards and elephants hiding her cap of short hair. Dahlia was one of a kind, and she sailed inside, her black stilettos sinking into Lindsay's carpet. "Evan and Chloe! Look at you two angels. Are you eating enough? When was the last time you went outside? Your cheeks seem pale." She bent and patted Evan's cheek, then Chloe's, before blowing air kisses on either side of Lindsay's cheeks. "Lindsay, dearest. You have dark circles under your eyes. Don't you fret about anything. Mother is here, and I'll do everything I can to make sure you get plenty of rest."

Her father, the same as ever with his lanky frame, rolled two suitcases along her walkway with two smaller ones stationed next to the car. Barefoot, Lindsay rushed out and helped him. "Let me get those for you."

"Nonsense. This way I'm balanced." He laughed as though he'd told the funniest joke. Up close, there were a few more crinkle lines around his gray eyes. "I know where your guest room is. I won't be but a minute until I can join you all."

She gasped and bit her lip. The guest room still had paint cans and drop cloths everywhere. "Put the luggage in my room, Dad."

She'd finish the ceiling tonight and then once it dried and everything was back where it belonged, she'd put her parents there and then sleep in her bed again. For now, the living room sectional would suffice for her bed for a couple of nights.

Her mother faced her. "Your room? Is there something wrong with the guest room?"

"Mommy almost fell through the ceiling in the middle

of the night and Mason helped get her out and there was a big hole until Mason and Grandpa Joe fixed it and then I spilled paint, but Mason wasn't mad at me." Evan blurted all of that out before Lindsay could stop him.

"A man? And the middle of the night?"

Right. Her mother would zero in on that. "It wasn't a big deal. You remember Mason Ruddick, don't you? He was Tim's paramedic partner. He moved in next door, and now he's my best friend." Even though her feelings now had changed.

"Hmm." Her mother's expression didn't change.

Dahlia started for the stairs, and Lindsay smelled the fragrant aroma of tonight's dinner. "You're early. I wasn't expecting you. I don't think there'll be enough chicken pot pie for five." She glanced at Chloe. "I might have something in the freezer for Evan and Chloe."

Her mother stopped halfway up the staircase. "Don't be silly, darling. Of course, your father and I don't expect you to cook for us."

"So, you ate on the way here?" Lindsay stepped toward the kitchen, not wanting a burnt crust.

"At six in the evening? Hardly." She waved her hand dismissively. "That's far too early for dinner. No, I'll freshen up and then your father and I will take you and the children out for our repast. Dominic's is one of my favorites even after traveling almost everywhere."

"Dominic's is rather elegant, and I thought they recommended reservations. Mario's Pizza is more Evan and Chloe's speed."

"Then again, your father and I probably have too much detritus from the plane trip for such a fine establishment as Dominic's." A grudging acceptance, but Lindsay would take it. "Before we leave for the next leg of our trip, I insist on taking you and Mason there for dinner. It'll give your father a chance to get better acquainted with him. It won't be that long before our townhome is finished, and we'll be returning to Hollydale for good."

Her mother started walking again.

"Mason and I aren't a couple." And another stop. This time her mother turned and smiled.

"Thank goodness your father and I arrived when we did. You need someone to pamper you. Since Dominic's is off-limits tonight, let's settle for the Holly Days Diner. I've already booked us appointments at the new spa the day after tomorrow. You know, at that wellness center, started by Patsy Appleby's daughter. We're having the works. A facial, mani/pedis, everything."

Lindsay counted to ten while her mother went up the staircase. "I can't go. I have to work."

"They won't miss you if you show up relaxed and beautiful, especially with that ceremony in only a week. Think of all the cameras and news agencies. You need to look your best."

Lindsay rolled her eyes and clutched the newel post. "The gardens will look their best, and that's what people are coming to see."

"We'll discuss this at dinner."

Something smelled like it was burning, and Lindsay rushed into the kitchen. After reaching for an oven mitt, she pulled the pot pie out of the stove and clanged the baking dish on the stovetop. A burnt mess stared back at her, and she no longer had an excuse to reject her mother's invitation. From here, she could see her patio and the fence, and more than ever, she needed the support of her best friend.

Although a kiss would be even better.

MASON PULLED INTO his driveway, and Jordan parked next to his SUV. Mason clicked the key fob, and his garage door opened, revealing the beauty that was his new motorcycle. In the glow of the setting sun, the silver metal gleamed. He waved at his new partner, who followed him to the bike.

"I haven't driven it over a long distance, but it accelerates well, and the brakes work on a pin drop. Following the proper maintenance and regular precheck procedures, this one ought to last forever." A twinge of something that almost felt like betrayal ran through Mason while he stared at the bike.

"Hey, Mason, are you finally home?" Lindsay's voice called out from the yard.

"We're in here," he called back.

Lindsay stopped in front of his garage. Her gaze went from Mason to Jordan. "Oh, hi, I'm Lindsay Hudson."

She extended her hand to Jordan, who shook it and nodded his head. "Jordan Bonetti."

"Oh, you're Mason's new partner. Nice to meet you. I'm glad to see you're taking an interest in Mason's motorcycle. Being friends away from work builds a better team."

Jordan eyed the bike. "The framework is sweet. Can I examine the exhaust first?"

"Go ahead."

Jordan lay on his back and scooted toward the bike. "The exhaust is solidly built. I'm impressed. How much are you asking for it?"

"What?" The word burst out of Lindsay, and she grabbed Mason's arm. "Mason, can I see you over here for a minute?"

Mason followed Lindsay out to the driveway while trying hard to ignore how much he liked being in her presence. On this spring day, everything in the neighborhood was in full bloom. The pink tulip trees were her favorite, but then again, everything in a garden was Lindsay's favorite. Everything about Lindsay screamed out for love and he didn't think he'd ever be ready. She needed someone predictable, not someone who wanted last-minute motorcycle rides into the sunset,

"Oh, first, my parents arrived yesterday. They're watching a movie with Evan and Chloe tonight. I've already seen it so I'm meeting Becks and Jillian at the bar and grill, but never mind about that. He's under the impression you want to sell your motorcycle."

"That's because I asked him if he wanted to buy it."

"What? You've been working on it for years. You can't just sell it like that." Lindsay snapped her fingers.

Mason folded his arms over his chest. "Why not?"

"You poured hours into that bike. For the past year, you've talked about nothing else but the trips you're going to take on it, driving to the beach, to the mountains," Lindsay sputtered and imitated him, folding her arms across her chest. "You love this bike."

"I love the challenge of this bike. Welding parts, painting it, seeing it come together, but now that it's done, I'm off to the next adventure. Something new, something different."

She winced. "That's it? You're willing to just walk away from something that's so meaningful to you?"

The disappointment welling in her eyes was almost too painful for him to watch.

"Something new will strike my fancy and that'll be that."

She'd done more than strike his fancy. He could see himself with her every day, waking up next to her, loving her, yet he wasn't convinced he was what was best for her. Someone else would give her everything she deserved.

Seeing how hurt she was, however, almost stopped him in his tracks. More than anything, he longed to sweep her into his arms and tell her they should face the future together, but he couldn't.

"I see." Comprehension lurked in that beautiful face, which almost penetrated the armor he'd built around himself, but didn't. "You can sell the motorcycle, but you should know that you can't sell what it represented. You still have to face whatever led you to spend all that time ripping it apart and putting it back better than ever."

She turned on her heel and rushed away. A hand brushed his shoulder. Mason faced Jordan, who let out an enormous yawn. "I'll think about the bike, but I'm too tired to test drive it tonight. Four days in a row? That's some heavy workload."

Jordan kept talking, but his words were lost on Mason.

Lindsay'd pierced his armor.

LINDSAY SWIRLED HER straw around her glass of Cheerwine cola and stared at the bubbles rising to the top. She'd left Mason's driveway only a few hours before. Was he waiting at the fence for their nightly talk while Goliath strutted around the yard? Or was he picking out his next motorcycle to build? A newer, flashier model…

"Earth to Lindsay." Her friend's voice cut through the noise of the crowd at the Timber River Bar and Grill.

Lindsay faked a smile at Becks and Jillian, who sat on either side of her. "Sorry I'm not better company tonight, Becks."

Becks shrugged. "Nope, don't apologize. That's why we're here. To support each other." She picked out a fried pickle from the appetizer plate. "Secretly I'm enjoying a night away from Nat's baby shower preparations."

Jillian nodded and selected a fried mozzarella stick, dunking it in the marinara sauce. She faced Becks. "What's this I hear about your former fiancé moving back to Hollydale?"

"Huh? Carlos has come home? Last I heard, he's fighting forest fires out of state." Lindsay noticed how Becks' pink cheeks had turned as red as her pixie cut. Becks reached for another fried pickle. "Not that I was keeping track of him or anything. See, Lindsay? Everyone needs to share and listening is what friends are for."

Friends. For too long, she'd put aside her friendships thinking that she could manage her grief alone, but that wasn't the case. She needed them as much as they needed her. She wished she could say the same about her next-door neighbor.

"Thanks." This time her smile was genuine.

"So, why aren't you better company?" Becks grinned. She was tenacious to the core.

For the first time tonight, Lindsay was hungry, and she reached for a chicken wing. "My parents arrived early for the dedication. Mom is still upset with me about turning down her offer for a spa day with her. She'd scheduled it for tomorrow. However, I did say I could arrange a night out with the girls if they were willing to babysit. They said yes, which was sweet, so she and Dad are watching a movie with Evan and Chloe."

"Isn't that a good thing that they're here?" Jillian dabbed her napkin at the corners of her mouth. "Oh, maybe it's Evan? Does his asthma give you cause for concern?"

Lindsay brushed some of the ranch dressing onto the chicken. "My dad knows what to do in case Evan has an asthma attack."

"Please keep the rest of this fried food away from me." Becks pushed at the appetizer tray. "Wouldn't your next-door neighbor pitch in during an emergency? Do your parents have Mason's contact information?"

Lindsay bit into her chicken wing with a little too much

force and the ranch dressing splattered everywhere. She swallowed and then wiped away the sauce. "Mason is…"

She couldn't finish the sentence.

Becks sipped her drink, her gaze not leaving Lindsay. "Mason is what?" She placed her elbows on the table and leaned forward. "We won't tell anyone."

"He's loyal and infuriating. He's charming and obstinate." She placed the rest of the wing on the small plate. "He's selling his motorcycle when he's worked so hard on it, and he's not coming to the ceremony."

"And you're upset about all of this, why?" Becks asked.

"Same reason I'm upset he hasn't kissed me again." The words had slipped out faster than she could stop them.

Becks glanced at Jillian, who placed her hand over her mouth to hide a laugh before looking at Lindsay. "We kind of suspected you guys were close. Did you tell him that? About the kissing?"

Lindsay picked up her appetizer again. "No."

"You should." Becks passed a napkin to Lindsay and squeezed her hand. "I'm no Mason Ruddick, but if you need a friend at the ceremony, count me in. I'm sure my mom will watch Pippa."

Jillian checked her phone for the time and then gave her regrets as she was scheduled to work. But that she'd come out at all and joined them touched Lindsay.

Her friends had rallied around her tonight. Becks was also texting Kris and Penelope about their attendance at the dedication. Becks held up her thumb, her indication more people would be backing Lindsay's efforts at the botanical garden.

With the support of her friends, she'd somehow make it through the next few weeks and she'd be there for her friends, too.

She wasn't alone, and that felt good. She reached for another wing in celebration.

CHAPTER EIGHTEEN

LINDSAY TURNED ONTO Holly Cove Lane and soon was parked in her driveway. Dread knotted her stomach at what her parents might have done on this, the fifth day of their visit. Yesterday, Saturday, she'd arrived home to find her living room rearranged and a new, larger television hanging over her fireplace mantle. Her mother mistook her stunned silence for joy. But this wasn't like the bell wind chime Lindsay didn't care for but had kept in her front yard ever since Aunt Hyacinth had staked it there. The television was a massive and expensive purchase made without consulting her, a complete disregard for the sanctity of her home.

Somehow, she'd have to screw up the courage and tell her mother thank you, but no thank you. She never had a problem telling Mason what she thought, so why was she hesitant to tell her mother the truth?

Mason.

Then again, she wasn't being honest with herself. She hadn't told him about how her romantic feelings for him were strengthening. Losing that friendship connection would be devastating, and yet? This strain was equally draining. She couldn't decide what was better, though, the thought of never having their fence talks again or the thought of never kissing him again.

She sighed and took the keys out of the truck's ignition. *The kisses. Definitely the kisses.* Time to find out if her mother made any changes or purchases today. Maybe she'd been so occupied taking care of Evan and Chloe, she hadn't had the chance to even rearrange a coaster.

With that hopeful thought in mind, she bounded into her home and stopped at the suitcases lined up in the foyer. Her breath stuck in her lungs. She hadn't expected them to leave Hollydale so soon. No, that wasn't right. Maybe the owner of the bed-and-breakfast had a cancellation and called her parents about the early vacancy.

No one greeting her, not even Evan or Chloe, brought a frown. "Mom? Dad?"

Her mother emerged from the kitchen, a disposable cup from The Busy Bean in hand. "Your father is playing in the basement with Evan and Chloe." She set the cup on the closest end table and grasped Lindsay's hands. "I have the most wonderful news, darling."

Lindsay braced herself. "Are you leaving before the dedication?"

"No, dearest. I talked to Lucie Appleby. Oh, what does she call herself these days?"

"Lucie Spindler."

"That's right." Her mother squeezed her hands and smiled. "Well as you know, I was at her fabulous retreat at the edge of town, and her salon isn't half bad. It's a shame you weren't able to make our appointment on Friday. When I was there, we spoke about the cabin her husband lived in while they were dating and now it's available for rental."

"So, you and Dad will stay there for the next week?" Lindsay glanced at the number of suitcases in the foyer. Somehow the luggage seemed to multiply in the short time her parents had stayed here.

"With you and Evan and Chloe." She clapped her hands, a look of delight gracing her expression. "Even though it's the weekend, I've arranged for a construction company to come and take care of the ceiling in the guest room starting tomorrow. They'll also rip out all the carpet and put in hardwood floors, which are ever so much better for someone with asthma. Carpets can trap allergens, you know. Your father is very sensitive to that sort of thing, and he had to use his rescue inhaler this morning."

Lindsay broke free of her mother's grasp. "Why didn't you tell me about Dad's asthma attack before I left?"

"You had already gone to the botanical garden. You seem to be there all hours, by the way." Her mother tapped her own cheek. "I'll call and talk to Lucie about a facial that will do wonders for the bags under your eyes."

"Thank you, but no thank you." She was now grateful Evan and Chloe weren't here. They didn't need to see this confrontation.

"I'll pay for it, of course." Dahlia tightened the animal-print silk scarf around her shoulders. "If you're concerned about money, which must be an issue for you as you didn't hire someone to fix the ceiling, don't be. Your father and I are only too happy to help our only child. And, of course, while we're here, we need to go to Asheville to buy some quality clothes for Evan and Chloe."

"Mother, please stop." Lindsay waved her hands in surrender. She glanced at the suitcases, three of which looked familiar, since she saw them in her closet every day. "Wait. Did you pack for me?"

"Of course, darling. You were working, and the construction crew will be here bright and early tomorrow morning. You need your beauty sleep and those hammers?" She visibly shivered.

"You had no right to go through my things and pack for me. Mason and Joe helped me with the guest room out of the kindness of their hearts. It was the neighborly thing to do." There was that word, *neighborly*, when her feelings for Mason were beginning to be anything but neighborly. "Thank you for offering to have the repairs done, but I'll get to them when I can afford them. I can also afford to make sure *my* children have clothes."

Dahlia huffed and raised one curved eyebrow. "I was in labor for forty-eight hours with you. I think that entitles me to show a little concern."

"A little concern, yes. Doing everything for me, no."

"Well, I don't have to stay where I'm not wanted." Dahlia made her way to the door that led to the basement.

"Mom, that's not true. I want you and Dad here but as guests."

Her mother swung the door wide open. "Jonah, it's time to go to that delightful guest cabin." The patter of footsteps up the stairs preceded laughter and excited shouts. "Sorry, darlings, only Mimi and Pop-Pop are going. You two are staying here."

Evan and Chloe reached her. "But Mommy, Mimi said it's going to be a party and we get to stay up late." Evan gazed at her with those enormous eyes.

"And I get a new teddy." Chloe also looked at Lindsay as if four against one would work.

"You have a perfectly good teddy bear, and I'll be dropping you off at day care in the morning so it's bedtime as usual tonight." Groans met her words, but Lindsay remained firm.

Her father reached the top of the stairs. "What's this I hear? Your mother has a perfectly reasonable plan."

"That she didn't run by me first." Lindsay folded her arms across her chest. "But she had no problem informing my children without asking me if I approved."

"Because I knew you'd be unappreciative and wouldn't think about our comfort, including your own." Dahlia raised her chin. "Fifty hours in labor and for what?"

By tomorrow, the number would probably reach sixty. "I appreciate what you're trying to do, but I have to raise Evan and Chloe my way, and that means being strong enough to stand up for myself. I hope you both understand that. And you're both more than welcome to stay here."

"We'll be staying at Lucie's. I made reservations at Dominic's for tomorrow night in a private room to accommodate Evan and Chloe if that's not too presumptuous on my part." Her mother's icy tone didn't slip by unnoticed, but at least she was still talking to Lindsay. "Since we'll be returning to India as soon as the ceremony is over."

Jonah frowned at Lindsay. "I understand, honey, but you could have agreed to this."

Yes, she could have, but not at the expense of her self-respect. "We'll be there tomorrow night."

Her parents spoke little as they departed, and soon Lindsay was left with two crestfallen children. "But Mimi said she wanted to look out for you." Evan bit his lip, and Lindsay's heart went out to her son and how considerate he could be.

"You know how the tulips are blooming now?" She waited until each child nodded. "They require a lot of work and attention from the moment the bulbs are planted until they grow, and it's like that with parents and their children. Parents help little ones until they can be themselves and blossom."

Their faces were still scrunched up. They might be too young to understand what transpired, but not too young to help her outside. After they changed into older clothes, she hustled them into the sunshine flooding the yard with springtime warmth.

Ever since Lindsay could remember, she'd sought refuge from her overprotective mother at her aunt and uncle's house, the wind chimes and bright colors a place of nurturing and happiness. There'd be darts with Uncle Craig while her Aunt Hyacinth would show her how to care for plants and flowers. Then they'd share a meal and laugh over one of Aunt Hyacinth's pies before her mother would arrive to take her home.

The truth was she'd always felt a connection with Aunt Hyacinth.

The splash of color Lindsay had added to Mason's yard boosted the basic design. Not that it mattered to him that much since Mason only rented the house, not wanting to settle down and own a property.

He'd made it all too clear he didn't want to settle down at all, selling the bike he'd invested so much in for such a long time.

If she didn't know better, she'd think he was pushing her away on purpose. Same as any prospect of a future relationship with him. Even their yards didn't mesh together, their approaches to life too different, too substantial. And yet, there was something about Mason that made her yearn for a second glance. Maybe their friendship was the base layer and romance could be the topper, which would lead to something real and lasting, not a simple flash in the pan.

Lindsay looked at his house with longing, but the scene with her mother held her back. She put herself out there once today, and that led to a disaster with her kids' disappointment still lingering in the air.

No, it was better to hold back.

GRANDPA JOE GLANCED out the window, and Goliath jumped on his lap, trying to peek out, too. Mason cleared away the rest of the lunch plates, aware his grandfather had picked up on the tension between him and Lindsay. He and Grandpa should get away from the house and do something together for the rest of the afternoon.

"Grandpa, how about a visit to the Night Owl Bakery?" That had distracted him once before. "Or we could see if the fish are biting at Sully Creek?"

His grandfather turned away from the window. "Lindsay, Evan and Chloe are outside. I think Goliath and I will see if they need any help." He snapped on Goliath's leash. "Are you coming?"

"In a minute. Let me finish cleaning up first."

Nothing had gone right with Lindsay since his grandfather came to visit. Not that he could blame Grandpa Joe for his mistakes. Here his best friend was a vibrant, caring woman, who raved about and loved the thirty-one different types of peonies and could also cast a mean dart. He kept her at arm's length, and he wouldn't blame her if she finally listened to him and stayed away.

She and Tim had truly loved each other. He couldn't be a replacement for his best friend. He kicked himself for that very idea. But had he actually been depriving himself of happiness out of some sort of guilt? And what about Lindsay's happiness? He looped the dish towel over the oven handle. If he truly cared for her, he couldn't get in her way.

Distance between them didn't seem the answer, though, so he started for the back door. Mason's phone pinged, and he checked the screen. A reply from Jordan. Mason scanned the text. Jordan understood why Mason had changed his mind about selling the bike. His throat clenched at how close he'd been to giving up his motorcycle. Not having it around would only represent something else he'd missed out on.

With that settled, he joined his grandfather and Goliath in Lindsay's garden. There she was, showing Chloe and Evan how to harvest zucchini.

"You've been patient for forty-five days, and now it's time to reap the rewards," she told the kids.

Was a relationship like that? Could her patience with him lead to new adventures and something beautiful down the line?

"That's a good way to think about life in general, kiddos," Grandpa Joe's voice broke through Mason's reverie, and Lindsay looked their way.

She sent them a smile. "How's Bree doing?" Lindsay plucked another zucchini from the ground.

"She's much better, left the hospital last week, and she's now packing boxes with Betty," Grandpa Joe replied.

Lindsay rose and patted Grandpa Joe's arm. "You and Betty are my role models. I'm glad you're so supportive of each other."

"She's the best." Grandpa glanced at Mason, then at Lindsay again. Why was Mason reminded of the Cheshire cat?

Chloe tugged at Grandpa Joe's sleeve. "Chloe wants a hug."

He complied with her wishes. "Evan and Chloe, I'm at your service. It's time to collect zucchini."

The children led him to the first row, and Mason cleared his throat. "Lindsay, do you have a minute?"

Lindsay lingered but looked his way. "Is there something you wanted to say to me?"

So much, too much. "I'm not selling the motorcycle."

"That's good. You'd have regretted it before the ink was dry on the title transfer. If you'll excuse me, I have vegetables to harvest."

She moved away, and it occurred to him that he really didn't like the space growing between them. "Want to meet at the fence later?"

"I don't think so." Lindsay stooped to examine some flowers. "I've had one of those weeks. My mother is being domineering, I'm under pressure from my boss regarding the Wilmington position and I feel like I've lost my best friend."

Mason glanced at her driveway, but he didn't see another car. "Where are your parents? I don't see their rental."

She scuffed the ground with her gardening boot and then covered the mark. "They told me in no uncertain words how ungrateful I am about not allowing them to hire renovators and not giving them permission to fix me."

"You're not broken."

"Try telling them that." Her smile was forced, a far cry from the usual happy feature he craved seeing.

"I will. Anytime," he told her and meant it.

Her muscles loosened, and the smile became more genuine, more an extension of her true self. "Thanks, but I'm the one who needs to do that. Not you. Seems we both need to learn to talk to our relatives."

"Mom! Come look at my zucchini. I grew it all by myself." Evan held up his green gourd.

Lindsay hurried over, and Mason followed. Chloe's face was the miniature version of Lindsay's as she concentrated on pulling hers off the vine. She plucked off a huge zucchini and fell on her bottom for her efforts. Mason rushed over and knelt beside her. "Are you okay?"

"Mine's bigger than Evan's." She laughed until her giggles became hiccups.

Evan scowled and jutted out his bottom lip. "Mine's gonna taste better."

Lindsay stood between them and placed both zucchinis in a basket. "Gardening's not a competition at this house. You both did a magnificent job."

They seemed to accept that, and she helped them harvest the rest. She'd taken what could have escalated into a fight and made each child feel special.

It wasn't long before the kids grew tired, and Lindsay

asked Grandpa Joe to take them inside. Mason could have kissed her for that alone, as his grandfather was also looking wilted, although he'd have been the last to admit it.

Lindsay kept harvesting the zucchini, and Mason worked beside her. She glanced his way. "I thought you disliked gardening."

"I seem to like it if there's a certain someone around." She had no reply so he knew cute, charming lines weren't what she wanted to hear. She wanted more from him, and he liked how she wouldn't settle for anything less than his entire self. "Okay, here's the truth. Without you, I might not be outside gardening. I'd be on that motorcycle heading to who knows where. That doesn't mean, though, this is something I don't enjoy. It's not the first thing on my list, but it's now on my list."

"Because of me?" She sounded a little flattered and a lot skeptical.

"Partly." He cut the last of the zucchini and tossed it in the basket. "There's a peace that goes along with doing this, the same type I find with the wind all around me and the road flying under my feet. I wouldn't have found that without you."

He scrambled from his position and offered her his hands. She accepted his offer, and he helped her stand.

"So, what you're saying is gardening could become something you look forward to, something like a hobby?"

Her light tone expressed much more. He swept that errant strand of hair behind her ear. "You, Lindsay, could never be a hobby. You're the real deal. Twenty-four seven and worth every second."

She raised her chin, her lips full of sweet promise. Without another word, he leaned down and kissed her. More than coming home, the kiss held the promise of light and hope, and everything he never dared to dream could come his way.

Her lavender scent entranced him, and he deepened the kiss, the taste and feel of her as heady as the first ride on a motorcycle after a long winter. He wound his hands through her honey hair. He couldn't get enough of her, and he wasn't sure he ever would.

Lindsay broke away and, out of the corner of his eye, he swore he glimpsed Grandpa Joe peeking out from the window, smiling before he replaced the curtain.

"Are you sure, Mason?" She sounded torn. "Many people love the idea of gardening when they're at a nursery and everything is alive and vibrant around them, but then they bristle at the work and dedication that goes into cultivating something sustaining and real."

The subtext wasn't lost on him, and he used his willpower to stop from kissing her again. That wouldn't solve the issues between them, although the appeal of her soft lips pulled him toward her once more. With Lindsay, though, it wasn't just mere attraction. He wanted to be around her and share the simple pleasures of life with her; it was a new feeling that he'd never experienced. "I won't deny that gardening is appealing."

Would this last? The plants and flowers Lindsay loved so much provided a glimmer of beauty for a short time, and then poof, they went out in a blaze of glory. He saw that same question in her expressive eyes.

"There's more to gardening, you know, than meets the eye." She led him to the basket of vegetables. "You'd think these zucchini would be uniform, since they came from the same batch of seeds and were planted in that patch of soil receiving equal sunlight and water."

"So?"

She smiled and held up two of the zucchini. "This one,

though, was in Chloe's patch." She raised the larger one. "Where she randomly scattered fertilizer. She's more spontaneous while Evan is more methodical, but both vegetables will end up tasting delicious in your zucchini muffins."

"I can handle methodical. You follow a set of instructions for a motorcycle, and you get a finished product that purrs along the highway."

"And, in your line of work, you know the procedures that are best for each patient." She tapped her hand against the zucchini and threw it back in the basket. "You're calm in crisis situations, but you're a rebel at heart. There can be rebels in gardening. Chloe's zucchini's proof of that. It's not staid or boring."

This part of Lindsay fascinated him, the side of her that was calm and knowledgeable on the outside but could still be open to new experiences, like her first motorcycle ride. Somehow, she turned his idea of relationships upside down. "You make gardening sound like a team effort."

"You say that like it's an awful thing. Teamwork's not a terrible concept. There are advantages of leaning on someone."

She walked away, leaving him behind. She was right, but the prospect of leaning on someone and then having them disappear from his life wrenched his heart in two. Even now, there was a chance she'd be moving to Wilmington. It was hard to want to join a team when the star player's transfer was imminent. For Mason, it was time to step back and let her bloom.

CHAPTER NINETEEN

WITH ONLY FOUR days to go until the dedication of the memorial plaque, Lindsay wasn't sure she had enough time on this Tuesday evening at Sweet Shelby's Tea Room for Natalie Murphy's baby shower, but here she was nursing a cup of raspberry herbal while her parents spoiled Evan and Chloe, promising to get them to day care tomorrow morning.

Aunt Hyacinth and her frenemy-co-owner, Belinda Chastain, had transformed the elegant private room into a celebration of fun for the impending arrival of Miss Murphy, Natalie and Aidan's second child after they'd adopted his nephew Danny, who seemed quite happy to be gaining a sister. Pink-and-silver balloons formed an arch at the doorway, and more balloons surrounded the table with a pink tablecloth and a three-tiered strawberry cake.

All around her, thirty-five women, give or take a few, wearing pink string necklaces with safety pins on them, milled about in groups talking to each other, laughing and exchanging the pins if anyone was caught saying *baby*. Lindsay fingered her necklace and wondered whether anyone would miss her if she ducked out and finished planting the impatiens at the botanical garden.

"Whatever you're thinking, the answer is always yes." Becks, the co-host of the shower, was at her side. Although they were identical, Becks's cropped red hair always made it easy to tell them apart, along with their different fashion styles. Natalie preferring sundresses while Becks always sported shorts or jeans. "Except if you're thinking of leaving early, then the answer is no."

Becks's dry sense of humor was one reason they'd been friends in high school, although they'd lost touch when Becks moved across the country. Now their friendship was going full steam again, but one thing bothered her. "Tell me again why we didn't stay in touch." Lindsay raised her voice so Becks could hear her over the din.

"That's on me. Sometimes when you lose yourself in a person and it doesn't end well, it takes a while to find yourself again." Becks sipped her cup of tea. "I don't think I ever extended my condolences about Tim. Sorry I didn't make it home for his funeral or reach out after he died."

"This isn't exactly the type of conversation I expected to have at a baby shower."

"I get your pin. You said the b-word."

Lindsay unhooked her safety pin and handed it over to Becks, whose necklace sported a fair amount of silver.

"Natalie's a much better partygoer than me. I'm too competitive." Becks shrugged as another woman approached.

"You two look like you're not discussing the forty-nine different ways to change a diaper. Count me in." Georgie, the other cohost, tapped her foot. "I knew we should have held this at the gazebo. Only the best events take place there."

She grinned, and Lindsay remembered the day Tim escorted her to Georgie and Mike's wedding at the gazebo in the heart of downtown Hollydale. It was the last formal event they attended together.

This is a celebration of new life. Not that she'd ever forget Tim and the life they'd shared, but she had to keep living.

"Except for the ones at the botanical garden. I've heard those are pretty decent." Lindsay raised her teacup and smiled.

"My stepdaughter Rachel is enamored of the wishing fountain there. Mike and I didn't know she wished for a new member of the family, and that same night Natalie announced she was pregnant. We haven't taken her back to the garden since." Georgie laughed and then turned to Lindsay. "Isn't the dedication coming soon?"

"This Saturday." Lindsay nodded and tried to deflect the attention away from herself. "By the way, when is Natalie due?"

"In two weeks." Becks clutched her lower back and squirmed. "I shouldn't have run those extra three miles this morning. I've had a backache all day."

"Before I return to my hostess duties, the same as someone else should be doing," Georgie cleared her throat and glared at Becks, "what's your guess about time, date of birth and weight of the baby, Lindsay?"

"I'll take your pins, thank you very much." Becks pounced with glee and added Georgie's four to her growing collection. "This is fun."

Lindsay glanced at Natalie, who was speaking to her son, Danny, and her mother, Diane. If she didn't know better, she'd guess Natalie was due much sooner from the way she was carrying the baby quite low. "Um, tomorrow, and six pounds even?"

"I hope not, but you're not the first person at the party to guess she won't go another two weeks before the baby comes." Georgie waved goodbye and returned to the crowd, giving a five-minute warning for the pin game.

"That long until cake?" Danny's question brought a round of laughter, and Becks clutched her back again.

Lindsay moved toward her. "Are you okay? Did you

put up the decorations for Aunt Hyacinth? Maybe you wrenched your lower back muscles."

"I'm fine, but I haven't felt like this since Pippa was born." Becks mentioned her daughter and then waved away Lindsay's concern. "Listen, we have to plan on those Girls' Nights Out becoming a regular event. The first couple were such stress relievers for me. Jillian's under all sorts of pressure with her mother, and Penelope's trying to make more friends in Hollydale."

Lindsay saw straight through her transparent friend. "I'm guessing you won't take no for an answer, huh?"

"Darn right. I'm persistent. It's one of my best traits." Becks laughed. "Time to hostess. The things I do for my twin sister." She strode away, waving enthusiastically at a couple of late arrivals.

Aunt Hyacinth floated by with a tray of mini tartlets. "Would you like one, my darling niece? I especially recommend the strawberry rhubarb." She selected one and placed it on Lindsay's plate and then added a couple more. "I'm sweetening you up on purpose. Could you be a dear and help with the cleanup?"

Since her parents had Evan and Chloe tonight, she was able to say yes. She'd help here, check on that one problem with the thermostat in the smaller greenhouse and get an extra early start tomorrow. "Sure thing."

"Lovely, my dear. Isn't this so beautiful? A celebration of future life coming into the world. My one regret is Craig and I weren't blessed with children, but I'm so fortunate to have you and Evan and Chloe."

Aunt Hyacinth sailed away, offering her selection of desserts to the next taker. Regrets and life? Would she regret not telling Mason of her growing feelings for him? She filed that away for later reflection and joined Kris as Becks announced the next party game.

Mason bounded up the front steps of Sweet Shelby's Tea Room. He'd promised Hyacinth he'd break down the tables after Natalie's baby shower in exchange for leftover pie for the paramedics' staff kitchen. Not a bad deal if he did say so himself.

The main area of the tearoom was empty, reflective that serving hours were over. He peeked into the gift shop, and there was no one there either.

"Hello," he called out, but only silence answered.

He then grabbed his phone from his back pocket, confirming this was the time Hyacinth had asked him to be here. It was, so he repeated his greeting.

Lindsay, a sight for sore eyes in a beautiful floral dress that brushed her knees, came around the corner from the kitchen. "I thought I heard you." She wiped her hands on a towel. "Everyone's busy at the moment and Aunt Hyacinth had to run home to let out her dogs, but she'll be back in a little while."

Their gazes met, and they burst out laughing. "Hmm. Likely story, huh? What excuse did she use to get you here? Gosh, gee, where I happen to be…"

He slipped his phone back into his pocket and flexed his muscles. "Hey, I'll do anything for pie."

Lindsay arched her eyebrow. "Ever get the feeling you're being set up with your next-door neighbor?"

He stepped closer and gave her a warm smile. "Don't you think we're past that stage?"

"Hello?" Natalie came from the kitchen, making a beeline for Mason. "You're a paramedic, right?"

Uneasiness skittered down his spine. Those words rarely led to anything good. "Yes," he drawled and took in Natalie's appearance. "Are you in labor?"

"No, I'm… Oh my, this baby packs a punch. Ow!" Natalie cried out and reached for a chair.

Mason tossed his keys to Lindsay. "My SUV is parked in the back lot. There's a medical bag in the trunk with supplies. How fast can you get it?"

"In a minute. Two if you want me to call 9-1-1."

"Take two then." Mason laid his hand over Natalie's before reaching to her neck and taking her pulse rate.

"Take three minutes and call my husband too." Natalie breathed in and out. "E-e-e, o-o-o." And she kept repeating the mantra, along with panting breaths.

"I don't have Aidan's number." Lindsay reached the door. "I'll call him on your cell when I get back."

Mason searched for the best place for Natalie to lie down. "Natalie, the truth is the baby might be here before we can get to the hospital."

She practiced her deep breathing techniques and began to move. "The private dining room." Her knuckles turned white. "I don't want my baby being born in a gift shop no matter how pretty it is."

She wailed again and dug her fingernails into his shoulder. If the contractions were coming this close together, his instincts were telling him the baby would be delivered here. He helped her to the room decorated with pink-and-silver balloons.

Lindsay rushed in with his bag, and she brought Natalie's twin sister with her. "Well, this explains the backache I've had all day." Becks knelt beside Natalie and held her hand. "Did you have sympathetic labor pains when Pippa was born?"

"Hello?" A male voice called out from the other room. "Natalie? Becks? Anyone here?"

Becks rose. "I'll explain to Aidan what's going on while you find out if my niece is going to be born in a tea room or the hospital."

Natalie cried out again. "Hurry!" Her teeth ground together. "Something's happening."

Mason turned to Lindsay. "Do you know where your aunt keeps the clean linens?" She nodded. "Bring whatever you can and a pot of hot water."

He focused on the mom-to-be and slipped on a pair of gloves he took from his bag. "Your water broke during the shower, didn't it?"

She nodded and gulped. "I've heard first babies take forever."

"This one is in a hurry to meet you." *Forget the ambulance.* He'd likely be delivering this baby. A man with short black hair wearing jeans and a blue Oxford shirt with the sleeves rolled up rushed into the room, and Mason recognized Natalie's husband. He ran over and clutched Natalie's hand.

"The baby's not due for another two weeks. I don't understand." Aidan glanced at Mason, his eyes full of concern. "Is Natalie okay? I can't lose her or the baby."

Natalie cleared her throat. "I'm right here, Aidan, and I'm fine, just rather busy." She stopped and let out another cry. "The baby, though, didn't get the memo about the due date."

"But we have a birth plan all written out to a *T* mapped everything to the smallest detail, and it's at home." His deep voice sounded more fraught with every word. "Your suitcase…phone list…the baby's going-home outfit!"

"Aidan, listen to me." Natalie performed more breathing exercises and pulled him close to her face. "I know you love your plans, but babies sort of throw plans out the window and sometimes they decide when they want to be born."

Lindsay returned with table linens and hot water. Mason took a hard look at everyone. "Well, this baby is saying she wants to be born in the next minute. You two are the father and sister, right?" He waited for affirmation. "You're supporting the mom-to-be." Then he faced Lindsay. "And you're helping me deliver the baby."

Lindsay met his gaze, released a deep breath and nodded. "It's good that we're on the same team then. Natalie, you're doing great."

Mason met Natalie's gaze. "You are doing great. The baby's about to crown."

In less time than it took for his motorcycle to accelerate, the baby made her entrance into the world. "Congratulations, Mom, Dad. You have a beautiful daughter."

Although the new father seemed shell-shocked, he kissed his wife and whooped as if he'd scored the winning touchdown. Gina and Darius, two of Mason's fellow paramedics, arrived. He updated them and then stood back for them to do their jobs.

They loaded Natalie onto the stretcher and swaddled her daughter, who gave a lusty wail, breaking the tension. Gina and Darius were about to roll mom and daughter away when Natalie held up her hand. "Wait." They halted the stretcher; Aidan hovered next to her. "Mason and Lindsay, thank you. I'd like to introduce you to Shelby Diane, named for Aidan's late sister, who was my best friend, and for my mother, who is still very much alive. You two are Shelby Diane's godparents whether or not you want to be." They all chuckled.

Aidan murmured his thanks as well, and he and Becks accompanied Natalie out of the tea room. Lindsay collapsed into a chair and Mason settled beside her, not taking his eyes off the beautiful brunette. She was everything he needed and wanted.

"We're a good team, you and I." He might have just

stated the obvious, but today proved what she'd already told him.

Before Lindsay could respond, Hyacinth sprinted into the private room. "There's an ambulance in front of the tea room, and I couldn't get in here any sooner. Is someone hurt?"

Her eyes clouded over with concern, but Mason reassured her. "Natalie and Aidan's daughter decided to come a little on the early side. She and mom are fine. They're on their way to the hospital."

Hyacinth clapped and wiped a tear from the corner of her eye. "How beautiful. What a momentous event for their little family." She glanced around the reception area. "You two have had a full and special day that you'll remember forever. Why don't you go celebrate? I'll clean up and then drop the pies for the first responders at the fire station on my way home."

She ushered the two of them out of the restaurant before either could protest.

"You don't have to walk me to my truck. The lot was full, so I parked on Timber Road a couple of blocks away." Those were the first words she'd uttered to him since Shelby made her grand entrance.

"I want to walk with you." Not just tonight, either. There was something about Lindsay that he'd never expected to find, least of all next door. Her soothing spirit restored his battered soul, which he hadn't even realized had been so wounded from Colette's and Tim's deaths.

He reached for her hand, and she allowed him to take it. The bright red buds of the maples would soon give rise to green leaves, and the air was fragrant with lush blooms. A crowd of teenagers entered Miss Louise's Ice Cream Parlor while a family packed up a picnic basket from the spot on the grassy knoll in front of the gazebo.

He and Lindsay reached her truck and stood on the sidewalk. He didn't want to break the spell yet, but even after magical moments, life continued. Speaking of which, her usual shadows were nowhere in sight. "Where are Evan and Chloe?"

"They're with my parents at the cabin they rented until Saturday." She looked at him with expectation. "Are you coming to the dedication?"

There it was. The wedge keeping them apart. He loosened his grip and leaned against the bumper. "I don't think so. It doesn't bring Tim back."

She reached into her purse and pulled out her keys. "I never said it would."

This might always stand between them. "Lindsay."

She held a finger to his lips. "Before you say anything else, I have to check on the smaller greenhouse. Why don't you come with me and I'll give you a peek at the site? A preview might help you change your mind."

Mason wasn't too sure of that. However, he didn't want this evening to end on a sour note. "How about dinner first?"

Lindsay patted her stomach. "I ate too much at the shower, and I'm pretty proud I kept it down while delivering a baby."

"You're my first choice for a delivery partner any day of the week." His skin grew flushed. "I'm going home to shower and change, then I'll grab a quick bite and meet you at the botanical garden. Say an hour from now?"

"Sounds good. See you then, godfather."

CHAPTER TWENTY

MASON DROVE INTO the garden's parking lot. Lindsay's truck was nowhere in sight. His cell phone confirmed he was ten minutes late. He leaned back and wondered where Lindsay was. Then again, it wasn't every day someone delivered a baby. He was impressed at how she'd kept her cool and coped throughout, not to mention locating those supplies so quickly. No doubt that adrenaline had finally caught up with her, and she needed a minute.

Now he and Lindsay had yet another special moment in their lives that no one could ever take from them. Life with Lin next door was turning out to be one adventure after another. Could he hold back from kissing her and return everything to the way it was a few months ago? What if she moved? Did he even want to imagine life without her in Hollydale?

He reached for one piece of the spicy tuna roll he'd grabbed at the new Asian fusion café after he'd showered and changed. The stop had taken longer than expected, as the gossip chain had already spread the word about Shelby Diane Murphy's sudden arrival into the world. Everyone wanted the scoop, and he stopped counting the number of times he retold the story.

The first two pieces of sushi disappeared in no time, and he dipped the third into the wasabi sauce. Then he scanned the lot once more. Cars and trucks had left, but none had parked the lot. Where was Lindsay? It couldn't be traffic, not in Hollydale.

After he finished the last bite, worry began to skitter through him, and he wasn't the anxious type. Lindsay loved this place. With that greenhouse issue to deal with, she'd be here unless some other emergency arose. He was gripping his phone when her truck barreled into the lot and stopped next to his SUV.

From his spot, he saw her sitting behind the wheel, staring off into space, her lips mouthing numbers slowly one by one. Concerned, he exited his SUV and rapped on her window. "Lindsay?"

She blinked and hopped out of the truck, her normal smile nowhere to be found.

"Did something happen to Evan or Chloe?"

"They're fine." Her voice sounded faraway, and she clicked her key fob. "Nothing will happen to them on my mom's watch."

He trailed after her as they went past security, and even though he had a good six inches on her, he struggled to keep up with her pace. His side started cramping. He must have eaten too fast. "I need to sit down for a minute."

She glanced over her shoulder. "We're almost to the wishing fountain. We can sit there."

Even with dusk surrounding them, the rose garden shimmered with the velvet petals awash in vibrant color, the aromatic sweet perfume surrounding him like a cloak. At the center of the square loomed a sculpted fountain with water spouting out of a mermaid in a soft whisper. No wonder Lindsay spoke of this facility with such pride. There was genuine artistry in the floral arrangements and the stonework.

He followed her to the edge of the water and sat close to her. "Want to talk about what's bothering you?"

"Why would you think that?"

Everything about her screamed just that. Her shoulders were stiffer than his starched uniform pants. "We just delivered a baby together not even a couple of hours ago. That can be an incredible high, or it can be scary. I have to admit working in tandem with you was the highlight of my year." He paused. He had to say something even though she added distance between them by swinging her legs, bent at the knees, onto the ledge and encircling her arms around them. "And the way we kiss each other. As hard as I've been fighting this, that's special. Extraordinary, really."

She frowned. Whatever happened in the past hour or so was a genuine worry. He and Lindsay hadn't even started, and they might already be over. He'd never felt this type of agony about a relationship before.

"I've never seen you in action. I mean, on the job, responding to a call. Although you were there to help Evan that time. And now today." She stared at the water in the fountain. He shimmied out of his jacket and held it out to her, but she shook her head. "I'm not cold. I'm sad. I don't believe I could take it if something happened to another person I loved in the line of duty."

Her words knocked him back. She'd been thinking about this, about them, and she might already have shut him out.

The full implication of her words hit him like a breaking wave. Did she love him? Her face showed no emotion, so he couldn't tell if it was just a thought or what she really felt.

"You know I'm a paramedic. I love what I do."

"Especially since each call brings something new, something that could be dangerous and risky."

"There's risk in everything, Lindsay. Even caring holds an element of risk." A risk he was finally willing to accept.

"Do the rewards make it worth the pain?" She still wouldn't look at him.

Were there rewards once someone was gone forever? Colette, Tim, both taken way too young. "I don't know, but risk shouldn't hold you back from anything."

She laughed, a wry sound that twisted his gut even more. "You hold back on the front end while I hold out after my heart's already involved."

Her hand flew over her mouth as if she'd realized what she'd said. He scooted right up to where she was sitting. "Hmm, your heart's involved? I take that type of ailment seriously. I have a reputation as a charmer, you know."

"Oh, I can't ruin your image." Her smile shared that she accepted all of him. She had an inner sense of when to go along with him and when to challenge him.

Although the pull to kiss her was strong, chemistry wouldn't solve their problems. Grandma Betty and Grandpa Joe had the type of love that worked through life together, even when they were in different states. A bond like that could make the tough patches easier, but without him and Lindsay ever being on the same page, how could they connect at that level and make it through the good and the bad?

"Maybe we should talk about why you were late tonight?"

"This makes a change. Mason Ruddick wanting to talk and not run to his garage and work on his motorcycle." Their gazes met, and everything stilled.

The sunset soaked their surroundings in a pink glow, and the woman beside him radiated beauty more substantial and deeper than any of the showy roses. It might sound corny that her calmness rounded out the side of him that loved speed and excitement, but that was the unvarnished truth.

She was more than the woman next door, more than his best friend. Somewhere along the way, in the past year, he'd fallen in love with her, and that scared him as much as his profession scared her.

He wasn't sure if this fear helped or hurt the situation. "Lindsay—"

"Do you know Tim wanted me to give this up?"

"What?" This was an integral part of her, and he laughed at the very idea. "Tim would never ask you to do that."

"Yes, he did." Her seriousness reflected in the twilight brought an end to his mirth. "The day before his last shift he asked me to stop working after Chloe was born. He wanted me to stay at home with her and Evan until they were both in school. I didn't even have to think about my answer. I told him no. I love my job—I love this."

A tear slid down her cheek, and she brushed it away with the back of her hand before he could do it for her.

"He never told me." Even if he had, Mason hadn't known Lindsay well at that time. He'd seen her at the barbecues and chatted on a casual level, but that was about it.

"And I haven't told anyone until now. Part of me always wondered if he volunteered for a longer shift because of our fight." Her voice was rough as if she'd struggled with this for two long years.

"That could have been part of it, but honestly, Lin, he also knew I was looking forward to my date that night." Deep down, Mason had struggled with whether he should have been on that helicopter rather than Tim. He'd had that in the back of his mind when he rented the house next to Lindsay's so he could watch over her, only to learn she could more than take care of herself.

Lindsay sighed, the whisper melting into the mountain

breeze. "We both know Tim." He noticed her use of the present tense, but it wasn't in a bad way or in denial. "He wouldn't have volunteered if he didn't want to be there."

They both suffered with guilt over the past, and for what? It wouldn't change things, any more than a plaque would, and it might hold them back from the future.

"You've been keeping these feelings inside you all this time? You never mentioned any of it before." And Lindsay had always been more open than him.

"I couldn't tell his parents we fought, and who was I going to confide in?"

"Me." He'd thought their friendship had been cemented over those fence-side chats they'd had so often. "You're my best friend."

"And I don't want to lose my best friend. We need to go back to the way it was for us before Pine Falls."

Decision time. He looked hard at the poised woman on the ledge, and he knew his answer. "We don't have to lose each other. We might end up gaining so much more."

She stilled, and the soft sound of the fountain carried the night. "The thought of losing you was why I was late tonight. I don't know if I'm scared of losing my best friend or losing something more. You yourself have thought something might happen to you. That's why you made Chloe and Evan your beneficiaries."

The raw emotion in her face made him want to sweep her into his arms until she was happy once more. Yet the memory of Tim hovered between them.

But if they didn't address Tim, could he ever move forward with Lindsay?

"That was just me being practical. I'm not planning on going anywhere, but I can't promise that won't ever happen. Same as you. Same as anyone." He placed his hand under her chin and tapped it with two fingers. "I can't be someone else, other than who I am. And I'll never be Tim."

Her gray eyes narrowed. She seemed to see through him like no one else ever had or ever wanted to. "I've seen you, the real you. The serious side of you around Evan and Natalie and Bree, but you like being laid back like no one else either."

"I like to leave the world behind."

"It's not a light switch, you know. You care all the time. More than you let on."

Until now, he'd let the blithe side of him make the world think he was only that. That was one reason he felt so much for Lindsay. He didn't have to pretend or put on a façade when he was with her. She knew the real him and still wanted to stick around.

"It's the same with you but in a different way. You love working here, you're tough and determined, but you love gardening at home just as much and there you're open and almost carefree."

"So much seems uncertain right now. I don't even know what's going to happen here in the long run. Take that Wilmington position, for instance."

The one she'd talked about. They'd be lucky to have her, but where would this leave them? Mason rose, antsy and ready to release some of this nervous energy. Changing topics came to mind. "I bet Wilmington has nothing on this botanical garden. I should have visited here properly long ago. What's your favorite spot?"

"Choosing one would be hard. I can't. I love this spot, though. There's something wistful about the fountain. It merges the natural with the whimsical." A lot like Lindsay herself. When she allowed it, her peaceful side merged with her playful self, surprising and complex.

He reached into his pocket and pulled out two coins, then handed her one. "Make a wish."

"What?" She laughed and shrugged. "The wishes don't come true. We use the money for our outreach program."

"What?" He placed his hands over his heart and pretended to faint. "Wishes don't come true?" He waggled his finger at her. "Don't tell Evan or Chloe, and definitely don't tell Grandpa Joe and Goliath."

"Very well." She snatched one of the coins from him, closed her eyes and threw it into the fountain. Then she opened them again. "There."

"What did you wish for?"

She laughed. "You know I can't say, or it won't come true. That's part of Wish Making 101."

He tossed in his quarter and pulled her close. "There's a way to disprove that. I wished I kissed you."

"That's not technically true if I kiss you first."

She leaned in and kissed him, his breath stolen from the sudden move. He wound his arm around her waist, pulling her toward him. Since she instigated the kiss, he wasn't sure whether that technically meant his wish hadn't come true. He was too happy to care. If she moved to Wilmington, whether he'd follow her there remained to be seen.

Until then, he kissed her back and believed this might be the best fifty cents he'd ever spent. A taste of paradise right here in Hollydale.

LINDSAY RUSHED BACK to the fountain, hoping Mason would still be there. After their incredible kiss, she'd received an urgent text from the night horticulturist in the biggest greenhouse regarding that broken thermostat. With the problem finally solved, she rounded the corner, half expecting Mason would be gone.

Her breath caught as she drank in the sight of his strong

features in the dusky gloaming. Those broad shoulders, the bright indigo of his tie-dyed shirt, and that ginger hair were familiar but new, leaving her breathless. Though she'd never expected her heart to open to someone else, let alone the paramedic next-door, Mason was hardly typical. A rebel, a charmer, a family guy at heart, all rolled into one.

A great kisser, too. Her toes still tingled from their latest kiss. As she'd swapped out the broken thermostat, she considered whether there'd be more kisses tonight. The notion her relationship with him might end up like his previous ones with women had also weighed on her. But she already felt this was different. From what she could tell, this relationship was unchartered territory for both of them.

If she only had herself to consider, she wouldn't care, but she was Evan and Chloe's mom, too. As much as Mason made her tremble in the best way, she needed to know he cared, some indication he'd fight for her with that Mason intensity.

She neared the wishing fountain enough to see his jaw clench, and he moved his cell to his other ear.

His knuckles were white around the edges of the phone, and she hurried over before placing her hand on his shoulder. A speck of dirt marred the fabric of his T-shirt. She brushed it off and he ended his call.

Underneath his stubble, his tanned skin had become pale. "What's wrong?"

"That was Bree."

She held his hand, ready for whatever news he shared.

"She, Tristan and Grandma Betty went to Atlanta to close on a house and for her first visit to a new primary care provider. Her bloodwork revealed Bree has anemia from her treatments and probably from the bout with that infection."

That muscle tic in his jaw was back, and she leaned into him, hoping that would relax him and comfort him. "What's anemia, and can they treat it?"

"It's an iron deficiency, making her feel tired and list-less. She outlined what the doctor advised her, basically plenty of rest and a new diet, rich in leafy greens, beans and certain types of meat. If her red blood cell count gets any lower, they'll admit her and give her a blood transfusion."

She heard a *but* in there. "What else are you holding back?"

"I'm packing tonight and leaving as soon as I can find someone to cover my shift. I'm driving to Atlanta and doing what I should have done weeks ago. Making sure my sister is taken care of." His blue gaze stared straight ahead.

If he was in Atlanta, he wouldn't be here for the dedication. "I know this is a lot to ask, especially since your sister is fighting cancer, but can you postpone going until after the ceremony? We're talking hours, not days or weeks. You can leave for Atlanta straight from here." Her heart thudded against her chest. She'd put everything into this project.

Tim had wanted her to quit work, and here Mason didn't want to celebrate her work with her.

Then again, was she in the wrong? His sister was undergoing treatment for cancer. Although the initial results were promising, Bree had faced an uphill battle with setbacks ever since.

He shook his head. "I've waited too long as it is, and Grandpa Joe needs Grandma Betty back."

"I'm just asking you for a couple of hours." She blinked and wanted to say more, but her throat choked up, her words inconsequential. Had something wonderful slipped through her fingers? "You'll be rested for the drive if you take off later in the day." Driving right after a two-day shift would be brutal if he couldn't find another paramedic to cover for him.

"Bree needs me."

"You didn't fail Colette and Tim, you know."

He froze. She remained in place, too, letting her words sink in, offering absolution he might have needed to hear for some time now. His throat bobbed, but he kept silent.

"I know Bree and your grandmother need you." She wanted to reach out and assure him, whether with words or a gentle touch, but she also had to stay strong for herself. "I'm only asking for a short delay. This memorial is many things to me—I'd like you to support my work."

All of this was too overwhelming. Her secure little bubble was gone. For a while now, Mason made the world around her bloom again. More than that. She'd seen him look out for his grandfather ever since Joe arrived, and many others too. These past few weeks, she'd seen through the cute charm and uncovered the substantial man underneath. One who loved his family, lived his life with candor and grace. She and Mason shouldn't have meshed, but she'd fallen head over heels in love with him.

"She sounds fragile."

Lindsay hesitated. "She must be if she asked you to drop everything and come to Atlanta to be with her."

Silence greeted her, and she inhaled the sweet scent of the roses all around her, too aware of how often those thorns had pricked her. "She doesn't know you're coming." Lindsay clenched her fists by her sides. "Does she?"

"I do things on the spur of the moment. You know that. I go surfing at a minute's notice and don't bother with a watch when off duty."

"You've repeated your mantra to yourself so often you believe it." She stepped toward him. "Deep down you distance yourself as soon as you think anyone is getting too close. You hide behind your reputation and run from your problems when it's convenient."

She borrowed a page from his playbook and ran.

CHAPTER TWENTY-ONE

SEEKING THE COMFORT of her living room, Lindsay rubbed her forehead and considered what her grandparents must have gone through raising Dahlia and Hyacinth.

"Hyacinth, you must listen to me. Lindsay is my daughter, and these are my grandchildren." Her mother threw her animal-print scarf over her right shoulder. "If I want to employ a housekeeping service to allow Lindsay to enjoy extra time with them, what business is it of anyone's except mine? It will make her life so much easier."

"While the beneficence of doing what you can to make someone's life easier is a sweet notion, dear sister, Lindsay's a grown woman and can make her own decisions." Her aunt threw her sunflower scarf over her left shoulder and winked at Lindsay. "You've raised a beautiful daughter, Dahlia, who intertwines kindness with intelligence. Did you ask her if she wanted you to pay for a housekeeper or did you forge ahead and hire the service?"

This little tête-à-tête had gone on long enough. If Lindsay could hold her own against Phillip, she could stare down her mother and her aunt, the two most formidable women in her life. She was made of sturdy stuff.

"Thank you both for your insights." Lindsay stepped into the middle of the fray. "Mom, my mind says thank you for the offer of a cleaning service, but I must decline. I don't want a housekeeper." The minute those words were out, she winced. She must be clueless to turn down that kind of offer. *The principle, Lindsay, it's the principle.* With that reminder, she stiffened her shoulders. "Aunt Hyacinth, that bell chime, um, thingamabob in my garden is beautiful, but it's not my taste and I'd love to donate it to the botanical garden. I know the perfect spot for it."

Her aunt's face wilted for a second before her usual radiance came through. "I was wondering when your inner courage would allow you the generosity of telling me the truth. And the joy of spreading the wind chime's beautiful colors to a multitude of visitors is a gift in and of itself."

Lindsay interrupted before Aunt Hyacinth could really get going. "I love both of you, but it's been a long day and I'm going to tuck in Evan and Chloe. I've been awake since four. The memorial is in less than two days. I hope you both can still make it."

She ushered them to the door and threw it open, only to find Joe, his face ashen, phone in his hand. The poor man looked like he was close to collapse. Something must have happened to Bree or Betty.

"Joe?" She glanced around for Goliath, but the chiweenie wasn't anywhere in sight. "Is it Betty?"

He shook his head, and his eyes looked vacant and shocked. He opened his mouth, but no words came out.

Aunt Hyacinth and Dahlia hooked their elbows around Joe's and pulled him inside to the sectional, where he slumped down into the cushions.

"Is it Bree?" Lindsay sat next to him, but he didn't meet her gaze.

If something had happened to Bree before Mason traveled to Georgia, he'd be devastated, and they'd never be able to get past her asking him to delay his trip. Lindsay reached for Joe's hand, only to find an ice-cold block. She rubbed his hand, trying to bring back some warmth and blood flow.

Joe blinked, then focused on them. "It's not Bree. There was an accident at work. Mason's at Dalesford General." He clutched her hand, and she squeezed back. They'd support each other. "He's unconscious."

A sense of dread overtook her. She'd never even told Mason she loved him. Lindsay's emotions spiraled, her world fading around her at the thought of anything awful happening to Mason.

Aunt Hyacinth came over to her. "There's always hope, sweetheart. I've often found that searching for that hope and acting on it precipitates a better outcome."

Her mother knelt in front of her until Lindsay had to meet her gaze. "Although my twin sister put a flowery spin on it, as with everything, she's right. There's no use sitting around here if Mason needs you. Hyacinth knows Evan and Chloe better, so she'll stay and I'll drive you and Joe to the hospital."

Should Lindsay go to the hospital? Or would she be an unwelcome reminder? When they'd last talked about this exact possibility happening, she ran away. The truth sank into her bones. Loving Mason was worth the risk. Any risk.

He was worth so much more.

The next minutes passed in a blur. Before she knew it, her mother had taken charge, and, for once, Lindsay was thankful. She stared out the rental car's backseat window while her mother drove her and Joe to Dalesford General.

Once there, Dr. Wang delivered an update about Mason's condition, serious with the next four hours being the most crucial for his head injury.

"Can I see him?" Joe asked. It was as if he was aging before Lindsay's very eyes.

"We're running tests. After that." The doctor gave a tense smile and nodded before leaving them.

The shock finally was wearing off. Lindsay asked, "Does Betty know?"

Joe replied, "I called her, but Bree has a doctor's appointment tomorrow morning and they may do more tests, so she can't drive. Tristan's on a flight home from his latest business trip."

"Then I'm going to get Betty." Lindsay jumped up and clutched her purse. "Mom, will you and Dad watch Evan and Chloe while I drive to Atlanta tonight? I'll be back before sunrise."

"No, I can't let you drive alone at night." Her mother stood as well.

"Mom, I'm capable of…"

"I'm going with you. I'll be the passenger and sleep on the way. Then after we pick up Betty, I'll drive back. You can talk to her or sleep then." Her mother came up to her and slipped an arm around Lindsay's shoulder. "It's me or your father, but he'll take an hour to get ready."

Lindsay was grateful. "What are we waiting for? We'll call Bree and Betty on the way."

MASON BLINKED AND realized he was in bed with strange noises happening all around him. Why was he at home? He should be at work. His head grew fuzzy. Hold it. There was a patient waiting inside the ambulance. He just had to close the rig's doors, but then the pain came. He licked his lips and tried to sit up. Instead, he found himself connected to wires. The quiet beeps of the monitors registered, and he jolted awake.

By his bed, Grandpa Joe slept in an uncomfortable-looking chair, and a nurse, whom Mason vaguely recognized, entered the dim cubicle and rolled a cart toward him. "Well, hello, sunshine. Glad to see you're awake so I can take your vitals."

"What happened?" Mason tried to sit up once more, and the nurse gave him a stern look. He worked through the pain in his head until he remembered her name. "You're Sunny, and you call everyone Sunshine."

"That's good." She pressed a digital thermometer to his forehead. "Do you remember your name and why you were brought in today?"

"Mason Ruddick." He reeled off his date of birth and other relevant statistics before the pain blocked out everything else. The dark wall frustrated him. "I don't know why I'm here."

She clicked her tongue and checked the monitor behind him. "Your temp's normal, and your vitals are good. You have a concussion, so take your time. Don't force it. According to Jordan, you hit your head hard on the patient's lawn ornament after a freak accident involving a Great Dane, a skateboard and a gnome. You've rambled a few times, always something about Lindsay, but you're finally coherent and awake. That's a positive sign. Dr. Wang will check on you soon, but the scans were normal. No swelling or bleeding. If you don't fall asleep again, you'll be transferred to a room for overnight observation and hopefully discharged in the morning."

His grandfather stirred. "Mason."

"Grandpa Joe, how long have you been here?"

His hands went to his chest. "Thank goodness you're awake."

"What time is it?"

"A little past nine at night. I've only been here for about an hour." He pointed to the digital clock above the door. "The sheriff came by the house around eight. He'd heard I was staying with you."

"I want to leave, Grandpa, now. I'll be all right. Can you tell them?"

Grandpa Joe cleared his throat and laid his hand gently on Mason's arm. "Listen to the nurse, okay? You need to take it easy and follow orders rather than pushing your limits."

Mason leaned back against the pillow. "Please tell me you didn't call Grandma Betty or Bree or Lindsay." The image of his neighbor's beautiful face swam before him. In fact, there were three of her. He moaned. This was exactly what Lindsay feared. This accident ended any hope of them ever getting together. "They don't need to be worrying about me."

Sunny popped back into the cubicle. "Dr. Wang said to let you know he's running a little late, but I filled him in on your condition. He'll come by probably in a couple of hours. If you fall asleep again, I'll wake you up per standard concussion protocol. We'll transfer you to a room once Dr. Wang signs off on that."

Mason breathed in and out and tried to focus.

"Jordan and your boss checked in on you, but they were called away. Your boss is covering your shift." Grandpa Joe kept talking about the accident, but Mason turned away, too afraid to ask about a certain woman with honey-brown hair. "And Lindsay's concerned about you."

"Can we talk later?"

What would he even say to Lindsay? He yawned and the next thing he knew, someone pushed on his arm, and he blinked away. Sunny was taking his temperature. "Dr. Wang had a priority case come in, but you're next on his list." The nurse smiled and checked the thermometer and then recorded his vitals. "How you feeling, Sunshine? Everything hurt yet?"

Muscles he didn't know he had screamed their reply, but Mason wanted his home, to see Lindsay's house, to see his motorcycle before going inside and sleeping away this monster of a headache.

His grandfather squeezed Mason's hand, the coldness seeping into Mason's skin. "I'll be fine, but I'm worried about my grandfather." He tried to smile, that charming one that usually convinced a patient that everything would be fine if they did as Mason asked, but it only intensified the pain. He gave up and spoke from his heart. "Is there an extra blanket, preferably one from those warming racks that you could spare for him?"

Sunny glanced at Grandpa Joe and waggled her finger at him. "Mr. Ruddick, I've asked you a couple of times if you needed anything. You should speak up. I'll be right back." She winked at Mason. "I'll pluck one from the middle, that way it'll be nice and warm."

"Thanks." Mason laid back and admitted the doctor wouldn't discharge him tonight. Not by a long shot. He closed his eyes, washing away the disappointment.

"Mason?" The worry in Grandpa Joe's voice made him open his eyes. His grandfather had aged a couple of years since Mason left him in the kitchen drinking his cup of coffee with Goliath begging for a morsel of turkey bacon.

"How's Goliath? If he's home all alone, why don't you go let him outside and get some sleep? I'll call you in the morning before they release me."

Speaking of calls, where were his phone and his watch and his multi-tool? He glanced around before his head started to ache again, telling him to stop moving. His grandfather pointed underneath his chair. "I was wondering when you'd ask about your belongings. They gave me your personal possessions in a plastic bag. It's all here and inventoried." He gave a small laugh. "It's not often a grandfather has his grandson's credit card."

Sunny ducked in with a blanket and hurried out again. It must be a busy night in the ER.

Mason fingered the edge of the white sheet covering him and found he was still in his paramedic uniform. If he stayed the night, he'd probably be presented with a lovely hospital gown to change into. "Could you bring me some regular clothes in the morning? And if you see Lindsay, tell her…"

After she'd ended their conversation and left the garden, he meandered along the path. Lindsay had created an unforgettable repose where visitors could get lost in a world of beauty. Peace and calmness. She'd brought those back into his hectic lifestyle.

Knowing Lindsay the way he did now, he'd never ask her to give up such a crucial part of herself.

Still, he thought, the best way to show he supported her career was not to stand in her way. If she was meant to spread her wings and provide her talents to the Wilmington garden, he had to let her go.

Everything once again looped back to the problem they confronted last night. She wasn't his to begin with. This injury only confirmed what she feared.

"Tell Lindsay what?" Grandpa Joe prodded. "Mason, don't shut me out. It felt like I lost you tonight, and we've shared too much these past few months for us to stop communicating now."

Mason took a deep breath. Hadn't he learned anything? Facing his fears about his family, those he'd lost and those he'd lose if he didn't show them his authentic self, that was what Lindsay gave him the courage to do. "Okay, Grandpa, then I need to start off with something important. I haven't forgotten Colette."

Grandpa Joe's brow furrowed. "I never thought you had. Even though we don't talk about someone every minute of the day, it doesn't mean they're gone from our hearts. Different people have different ways of mourning, and you were such a good brother to her. Same as you are with your sister, Bree."

Mason shook his head and winced at the pain shooting through his temple. He stayed still until it was manageable. "A good brother would have been in Nashville every chance he got." And he hadn't helped in Atlanta, either.

"Bree knows you love her. She knows we both love her. Why else would Betty and I have stayed away from each other for so long? There's the house, the town and I need my job at the center and your life is here. In fact, there's a certain next-door neighbor who's part of that life, you know? What are you going to do about it?"

What could he do? Last night Lindsay accused him of distancing himself from her, and then this incident drove home the fact he wasn't immune to workplace injuries.

"Nothing."

"What? Haven't you learned anything from your grandmother and me? I love Betty, and I've treasured every minute we've had together." The blanket fell off Grandpa Joe's lap as he scooted forward. "You have a wonderful, vibrant woman next door who's in love with you."

"No." The word ricocheted around the room like a boomerang as one glance at his heart rate monitor confirmed it had skyrocketed.

Sunny rushed in with a look of alarm. Mason took a few deep breaths and his levels returned to normal. "What's going on? I thought I heard someone shout *no*," she asked.

Grandpa Joe gave a weak laugh. "My grandson is rather obstinate sometimes. He gets that from my side of the family, I'm afraid."

"If this happens again, I'll have to ask you to go." Sunny

narrowed her eyes at his grandfather and then left, muttering under her breath.

"Are you saying Lindsay doesn't love you? I have eyes, perfect vision. She does. Or you don't love Lindsay, which I know you do." Grandpa Joe picked up right where he left off, and Mason gave serious consideration to buzzing for Sunny.

However, having the nurse do Mason's dirty work didn't sit right. "Lindsay told me last night I don't face up to my problems. I run."

"Smart *and* beautiful." Grandpa Joe leaned in, his face lighter since Mason had regained his bearings. "Why don't you snap Lindsay up before some other lucky fellow does?"

"Because Lindsay *is* my problem."

"Oh." A woman's voice from the doorway caught his attention. Not just any woman's. Lindsay's. "I'm your problem?"

"Joseph Ruddick. Here I've come all the way from Georgia in what's practically the middle of the night, and you're lying there talking about another woman!" Grandma Betty appeared from behind Lindsay, a gleam in her bright eyes. "Is that any way to greet your wife?"

Moving faster than Mason had seen him in years, Grandpa Joe rushed to take his wife in his arms. "Elizabeth Ruddick, if you don't know by now you're the love of my life, I won't ever be able to convince you of that. I'm never letting you go."

This moment. This was what Mason had dreamed of having while being too skittish to commit. Even with announcements over the intercom and the thrumming noises of the ER, his grandparents only had eyes for each other. Fifty-six years hadn't dimmed their love. Some might think his grandfather didn't care as much as he did since Grandma Betty had stayed away for so long, but it was just the opposite, it was that he loved her this strongly and deeply that they could do that.

After a few minutes, his grandparents pulled out of their embrace.

"Mason, how are you?" his grandmother asked, coming to his side to squeeze his hand.

"I'll be okay, Grandma. You're a sight for sore eyes, though."

His grandmother nodded. "Lindsay and I have been really getting to know each other. Oh, I should let you have a few minutes with the woman who was nice enough to drive me here from Atlanta. Thank you, Lindsay, I'll never forget such kindness. We'll be back to check on you, Mason." She nudged Grandpa Joe's ribs and they quietly slipped out the door.

Mason drank in the sight of Lindsay. With every depth of his being, he loved her, but he wanted so much for her and he still wasn't sure that included him. He wished that it did.

He'd believed he had learned how to hide his feelings and thoughts rather well over the years. Being a paramedic, he'd adapted a mask for any given situation.

Lindsay settled into the chair. "I talked to Bree while your grandmother packed. Your sister sends her love. Tristan, too. He arrived just as Betty and I were leaving."

Bree. The accident couldn't have come at a worse time. "How is she?"

"She's okay. She said to tell you to call her when you feel up to it."

"I will."

A long silence followed. He was torn between wanting to wrap his arms around Lindsay and knowing that wouldn't be best for her. For her future.

Lindsay winced and then stood, the harsh screech of the

chair leg against the linoleum ramped up the pain in his head. "This isn't exactly the kind of welcome I expected. Although, to be honest, it occurred to me on the drive back to Hollydale that I've never told you how I feel about you."

He had to let Lindsay go so she could soar wherever she chose to land. Wilmington, Hollydale…

"Let me speak first. We had a fun couple of months, Lin." He kept from cringing at his words. Anything to allow her to thrive. Ending it first was the right thing to do before he could hurt Evan or Chloe or Lindsay. "After I'm out of the hospital, it's on to new adventures. You know me, I never dip my foot into the same water for too long."

Lindsay pointed at the IV line. "Is that fear going straight into your veins? Because I don't believe the man I've gotten to know over the past year is the one talking right now."

Mason kept his gaze on the clock over the door. "Maybe this accident has reminded me of the real me."

"Since you can't go anywhere, I'll take this opportunity to tell you what your accident taught me. For one thing, I discovered I can be in the car with my mother for five hours straight if it's important." He gripped the thin mattress so he wouldn't look at her and see the fire he knew would be lighting up her eyes. "And love is important, Mason. It's worth fighting for."

"Love?" *Keep your eyes on that clock, Mason. Do not look at Lindsay.* He was doing this for her and Evan and Chloe. "Who said anything about love? We're friends who kissed a few times. I'm your rebound. Thanks, and you're welcome." *Forty-eight, forty-nine, fifty.* How many seconds would he have to lie to get her to buy into this phoniness act?

"That's a low blow."

"Well, life is too short to tie yourself to one person."

She sat down again. "Life is too short to throw away the best thing that will ever happen to you because you're scared."

He laughed. "I ride a motorcycle, shoot darts in bars and rush into situations I know nothing about so people have a chance to live. That doesn't sound like someone who fears life."

"You're not scared of life. You're scared of me and you're unwilling to fight for a love that's powerful, that you don't understand, something that might make you happy."

You didn't hear that. He'd crack in a second, and she had so much ahead of her if she played it safe once more. A job she was proud of, two kids who loved her, friends, more family, a town that thought highly of her. All of that couldn't include him. "You misjudged me. I'm not the man you thought I was."

She stood and crossed to exit the cubicle. "You're right. You're not. The Mason I fell in love with showed me how to live again and get out from under the rock where I was hiding. He showed me predictability is no way to move forward." She met his gaze, tears clouding her gray eyes. "Instead, it's a dash of unpredictability here, lots of laughter there and a firm foundation with hot kisses thrown in for good measure."

His muscles tensed as she walked away. He waited for the relief to wash over him, some sort of signal he'd done the right thing by letting her go. Nothing like that came. It was the opposite. He was pretty sure he'd just made his biggest mistake yet. Yesterday she'd accused him of purposely putting distance between them, and today she'd told him he was afraid to live. Everything he'd hit home to her about as they sat and watched the sunset together so many times. During the course of the past few months, she'd won his heart, which would twist every time she closed that sliding glass door behind her, and he'd head to an empty house without acknowledging his true feelings for her.

He might be a rebel, but for too long he pushed everyone away. He'd been his own worst enemy when his greatest adventure had been next-door all the while.

He heard his grandparents' voices in the hallway and screwed his eyes shut, hoping they'd get the hint and leave.

"Come on, kiddo, that's the worst acting I've ever seen, and your father, Peter, is terrible at it." Mason opened his eyes and found Grandma Betty hovering over him. "That's better. We've spoken to your parents. Tara said she and Peter will text us their flight arrival time once they arrange their work schedules, and Bree and Tristan are coming for the dedication this weekend. Tristan went to school with Tim, you know."

"But her appointment and tests. She can't come." He sat upright. "Her treatment, the long car ride."

"Bree's a fighter, and her own person." Grandma Betty puffed out her chest. "Like her grandmother."

Mason knew it was true, but still, it didn't seem right. His head pounded. He craved rest and let them know.

They were quick to leave, and then he was alone. *Alone.*

But that was how he wanted it, wasn't it?

CHAPTER TWENTY-TWO

LINDSAY ATTACKED THE potting soil with a spade, today's early staff meeting still on her mind. It was their last chance to get together as a group before tomorrow's ceremony. Meanwhile, Phillip's last day would be a week from next Friday. Until a new director was hired, everyone would take on extra responsibilities, but thankfully none of hers revolved around administration or fund-raising.

A couple of her coworker friends had approached her afterward about whether she'd be applying for the director's position, but interviewing for her boss's job wasn't on her radar. She loved what she did best: growing plants and trees and getting her hands dirty. That phone call with the plaque company two months ago proved how much she didn't want to be the new Phillip. Schmoozing and worrying about revenues and receipts weren't her calling.

Although, that day resonated since it was the beginning of how her friendship with Mason had bloomed gloriously before wilting away to nothingness.

No, not nothingness. Never that. Thanks to Evan and Chloe and her friends and family, her life was full and rich. She stuck the spade into the dirt with a vengeance. How one man could not see the nose on his face and realize he was running away from love was beyond her...

"Good morning, darling daughter. So, this is your workplace, is it?" Dahlia whipped off her designer sunglasses and peered at Lindsay, who was elbow-deep in soil.

Unsure of the reason for her mother's sudden appearance, Lindsay decided she'd take a wait and see approach.

The mother who'd accompanied her on the Atlanta drive was someone she could see having lunch with and talking to regularly. Somehow, her mom had been more relaxed and less overbearing than the woman in front of her with her manicured nails and stylish dress, a contrast to Lindsay's dirty khakis and blunt, short nails. "Yes, and I love it."

Dahlia swung a basket covered with a red plaid napkin onto the worktable, a warm aromatic smell of cinnamon, nutmeg and sugary goodness overcoming the mint and other herbs in the greenhouse. "According to Betty, who dropped them off at the cabin this morning, these are zucchini muffins with cranberries." Lindsay peeked and found six plump muffins. "And I didn't come here to start a fight."

Lindsay removed her gloves and plucked one of the muffins out of its nest before removing the paper wrapper. "Why did you come here?" She sank her teeth into the crumbly delight.

"To see something you love. You're obviously passionate about this place." Dahlia slipped off her animal-print scarf, her short silver hair perfect without one strand out of place.

"Yes, I am."

"I helped your father out with the billing and the like, but I was never enthralled the way you and Hyacinth are about your vocations." She ran her hand over the untidy worktable, her hazel eyes, so like Aunt Hyacinth's in shape and color, but shrewd and cool unlike her aunt's amiable warmth.

"Is that why you travel?" Her mom's admission conveyed so much to Lindsay, even more, as it also was her mother's way of offering an olive branch, one she'd accept.

"Perhaps."

Lindsay prodded her. "And?"

"Why did I hear from Betty instead of you that you and Mason are finished?"

The sweet, dense muffin lost all flavor, and she swallowed a bite that might as well have been the paper wrapping. Lindsay rested the other half of the muffin away from the others. "What can I say? I thought we were planting a redwood, and Mason didn't feel the same way."

Suddenly, Lindsay choked up, and her mother opened her arms. She flew into them, her mother's strong citrusy perfume suiting her and soothing Lindsay. She let the tears fall and then stemmed the tide. Stepping back, she gasped at the wet stain on her mother's caramel-colored silk shirt. "Sorry about that. I'll pay for the dry-cleaning bill."

"I'm not sorry, and you'll do no such thing." Her mother lifted her chin. "After the ceremony, would you and the children like to accompany your father and me on a small vacation?" She held up her hand. "It's a gift—I know you can pay for your own trips. This'll be a getaway from the memories swirling around you. What do you say?"

Lindsay sniffled. "I say you really mean for me to get away from my next-door neighbor for a while, don't you?"

"That and I want to send your father to talk to him. Other similar retributive thoughts have also entered my brain."

Her mother's raised eyebrow left Lindsay in no doubt that Mason wouldn't get off lightly. She almost felt sorry for Mason. "You missed your calling. You should have written crime thrillers."

"There's still time for anything, darling."

Anything except a relationship with the man who'd

lifted her off the ground and moved her to new heights. One for whom adventure lurked around every corner. "That's a nice thought, but it's not always true. Once a storm is over and a flower's stem is broken, it's gone forever."

"Except sometimes that flower can brighten a room, or the rosebush can be saved." Her mother examined her bright red manicure as if her life depended on it, and it hit Lindsay.

Her mother was fighting for her.

"Dahlias are perennials." Lindsay searched for some way to bridge what she knew about the flower with what she knew about her mother.

"They're also vivid and hardy. You know where you stand with dahlias." Her mother met her gaze and nodded, then reached for the end of her scarf.

With the dedication tomorrow, Lindsay didn't have any time to spare from her duties, so she picked up the spade, reluctant as she was to stop this conversation with her mother. "Will you please quit hovering and let me do my own thing?"

"Of course. I'm glad, though. You wouldn't have confided in me like this before, if your dad and I hadn't made this trip home for the ceremony." Her mother tied the scarf around her neck and reached for the basket.

"I've learned about me over the past few years." Lindsay started transferring the plants into larger pots, adding a scoop of wood ash to neutralize the soil. "My friends have waited in the wings, and now when I need help, I ask for it."

Her mom smiled. "I'd say you have an excellent support system in Hollydale."

She'd need that support even more, given her heartache over Mason, the last man she'd ever expected to fall in love with.

Lindsay kept her focus on the plants and gripped the handle of the trowel tighter. "Are you and Dad still coming back when your townhome is finished?"

"Your father wants to come home sooner. He mentioned something about a group of his friends who fish at Sully Creek most mornings. Fishing, of all things, makes your father happy."

"Would cutting your trip short make you happy?"

"I hadn't realized how much Evan has grown since we've been gone, and Chloe didn't recognize me." Her mother's voice was low and less stern.

"What makes you happy?" Lindsay stilled her fingers, still halfway in the pot, and looked at Dahlia.

"Well, travel often satiates my curiosity." Her mother's gaze grew distant, as if she was remembering a certain trip or locale, before the keen perceptiveness returned. "However, I think we will be staying closer to Hollydale after this. Connecting with my family is a new challenge, and I never back out of one, especially when someone hurts my little girl."

Lindsay swiped at her eyes with her arm and occupied herself once more. This time she placed the dug up plants on the cart. "I've known Mason for a long time." She gave her mom a rueful smile. "You always think you'll be the one who's different from all the others before you, but sometimes you're not."

Her mother smiled back. "Oh, darling, I'd endure this for you if I could."

"I know." And for the first time, Lindsay believed that. "But you have to let me make my mistakes and recover from them. Just be there with some jelly beans when you've come home for good, okay?"

"I'll make sure there are extra cherry ones, just for you."

Her mother knew her favorite flavor of jelly bean? Dahlia left, and Lindsay stood there, her mouth agape.

ON THIS BRIGHT SATURDAY, Mason reveled in the feel of the sunshine soaking the back of his neck and his face. Finally appreciating the outdoors, he hadn't done anything like this since his accident, which he still didn't remember well.

Given the doctor had told him to lay off his motorcycle until he visited his general practitioner—that wouldn't be for another two weeks—Mason had found other things to do, so he wouldn't be cooped up inside. He had to; until his doctor cleared him to work again he had to find ways to stay busy.

The jays and crows in the backyard were creating quite a ruckus, he noticed, and yet the noise he really missed came from Evan, Chloe and Goliath.

As much as he'd once tried to have his grandfather live next door, he missed Grandpa Joe and Goliath deeply ever since they'd returned home with Grandma Betty. But not as much as he missed Lindsay. He craved another chance to feel her silky hair, to taste her sweet lips and to talk. Thanks to his stubbornness, that would never happen.

He pulled out another weed and added it to the stack he'd accumulated. To his surprise, the exercise was quite calming, almost fun, really. He'd have committed to this a long time ago had he realized how therapeutic it could be.

His grandparents' small SUV pulled into the driveway, and he rose. Grandma Betty soon made a beeline toward him, her dark sweater matched with plaid pants for today's ceremony. He'd made his excuses last night when he'd said good-night to his parents and Bree and Tristan.

"So, you meant it then." She popped her hands on her hips and glared at him.

He brushed the dirt off his gloves. "Good morning, Grandma. Guess this means no hug?"

That glare became more blinding than the afternoon sun. He knew avoiding the botanical garden today might mean no hugs for a long time. He was hoping his grandmother wouldn't be that cruel.

"Have you not come to your senses about Lindsay yet?" She stared at the pile of stems and discards he'd set aside. "Wild mint is not a weed. Didn't you smell it when you plucked it?"

"Concussion, remember? My sense of smell is haywire." Mason tapped his head. "And I didn't ask you to get involved in my love life."

Grandma Betty stooped and picked up one of the stems. "Do you know all the uses of wild mint?"

"No, but I take it you're going to tell me." The sun hid behind a cloud, a shadow falling over his grandmother's face.

"Well, you should listen to your grandparents. We know you better than you know yourself sometimes." She came over and waved the stem at him. "Wild mint can be used to keep away animals you don't want in your garden. It's also an herb for tea or a salad, and it's quite beautiful in full bloom."

He didn't miss the parallels to Lindsay. She'd kept away the grief and the loneliness, their kisses were full of flavor and she was always beautiful, whether she was halfway through a ceiling or standing next to a waterfall. And he'd run away faster than a motorcycle accelerating on a stretch of deserted highway.

The way he figured it, it mattered less whether his and Lindsay's time together lasted for months or years... While he'd prefer blowing out fifty-six candles on a sheet cake celebrating their anniversary, same as his grandparents, it

was the intensity of the love that counted. His next-door neighbor certainly captivated him, made his stomach do wild cartwheels and stopped him in his tracks.

And he'd blown it.

All he could think about was distancing himself so neither of them would get hurt, and the look on her face told him he'd succeeded in doing just that. He'd hurt her by pushing her away.

"I'm afraid, Grandma." He leaned against his house for support. "Here I am, a paramedic who goes anywhere they tell me to try to save a person, but I couldn't save myself from hurting Lindsay. I love her."

"Love makes everything sweeter. We're all afraid sometimes." She stepped over his new hostas and joined him by the house. "Joe says you're old enough to know your own darned mind and to trust you. But I told him last night at bedtime you'll never take that first step toward Lindsay without our help." She checked her watch. "I have somewhere you need to be."

He shook his head. "I can't go." He scuffed the dirt with his boot. "It should have been me. It could be me in the future."

"But it wasn't. You can't change that, just like we can't change what happened to Colette. Here's the thing, Mason." She laid her hand on his arm and squeezed until he met her gaze. "Your sisters are strong and have made tough choices. Colette may have succumbed to cancer, but she gave her all while she was here. Same as Bree is fighting now, and the rest of the time, she's embracing everything she can."

"It's too late for me and Lindsay."

"Is it?" She whispered into his ear, "I know why you pushed Lindsay away, but you're wrong. Distance in miles can make a heart grow fonder, but distancing yourself?"

She turned and started to walk away.

Mason held out his hands. "You're leaving me like that without answering your own question? It's like you stopped in the middle of the sentence that tells me how to win at life, love and everything."

Grandma Betty stopped, but only smiled a *Mona Lisa* grin before climbing into the car. What secret was she holding back about love? He wanted to know.

He stared long and hard at Lindsay's house and thought about everything it represented. His neighbor had become his best friend while he rambled on about his cases. She'd never said a disparaging word when he left her for a late-night date or another session with his half-finished motorcycle. While he couldn't pinpoint a particular minute, everything had changed between them. One day her hair went from plain ordinary brown to smooth honey strands and her eyes were no longer simply gray but the color of a rippling river before a storm.

And seeing her stuck in the ceiling? That was definitely the moment he knew there was no going back.

Shaken, he entered his house and closed the door quickly, not wanting Goliath to get out. Except the senior chiweenie didn't live here any longer.

He chided himself again. In the past few months, Lindsay and Evan and Chloe had become his home, his heart. Lindsay was so kind, so smart to give him space when he needed it and to tell him off when he needed that too. And just be there for him the rest of the time.

Lindsay was everything he didn't know he needed. Until now. And he'd responded by shutting her out. Now it was too late to sit outside with her and a bottle of beer and a glass of Riesling and set things to right.

Or was it too late? Was there still hope they could be together, whether here or anywhere else? He chuckled at how well Grandma Betty did know him. If she'd told him the answer outright, he would have scoffed and done the exact opposite.

He always thought he needed what Grandma Betty and Grandpa Joe had. He was wrong. What he needed was his best friend to become his partner, his love, his life. Lindsay was not only his best friend, but so much more. A future without her would be boring and empty.

He ran up the stairs, hoping he still had enough time to let her know he'd come to his senses.

CHAPTER TWENTY-THREE

TWO YEARS AGO, she'd said goodbye to Tim, not knowing it would be for the last time. She'd been inwardly fuming because he wanted her to put a pause on her career. Two days ago, she'd said goodbye to Mason. However, she'd known it at the time and had been outwardly fuming because he wanted to distance himself rather than take a chance on love.

So here she was, at a ceremony she'd been anticipating for months, wanting to be anywhere else than wedged between her aunt Hyacinth and her friend Becks. Most of all, what she wanted, despite Mason's stubbornness, was a future with him. She wanted him to wake up to the hard truth that sometimes people didn't come home. That didn't mean love ended; it just meant the people left behind had to find a way to go on.

That was what this memorial rock signified to her. A way of showing Evan and Chloe that Tim's sacrifice hadn't been forgotten and that they would go on.

For this new relationship to end like it did? Her heart broke yet again. She questioned giving Mason space for him to explore the idea of the two of them, when that space had provided distance for him to run away rather than embrace the risk of loving someone.

Their time wasn't a waste, though, and she wouldn't trade it for anything. He'd awakened in her the need to become part of Hollydale again. Reconnecting with friends and finding a new relationship with her mother might not have happened without him and their nightly talks, when she'd laughed at his anecdotes and stories, and embraced the colorful world around her.

During that time, Mason had transitioned from her charming playboy neighbor to her loyal, brave friend who'd taken up a spot close to her heart. Someone whose spirit for adventure and the open road unlocked something profound in her, something she'd never connected with. That time at the waterfall sparked a special moment and she'd always remember it.

When they delivered Natalie's baby together, her feelings for Mason only deepened. That slow burn grew. Mason caring for those in need showed her a side of him he didn't brag about or show off for attention. That was another layer to him, one he hid behind a smile and that ginger charm.

Making house calls in the middle of the night wasn't a bad way to capture her heart, either. Those kisses curled her toes.

The mayor handed her a pair of scissors and she stopped dwelling on what might have been. With Phillip leaving for Wilmington and a new director on the horizon, announced today, one with innovative ideas about attracting visitors and community programs, the botanical garden's future look stronger than ever.

Lindsay smiled at the crowd as the relatives of other fallen first responders took their places next to her. On cue, she cut the ribbon and then she walked to the front row of the reserved seats, searching the crowd for the person she knew wouldn't be there. Her gaze met Betty's. Mason's grandmother sent her a regretful smile, one that told the complete story. Mason wouldn't come for Tim, for Betty or for Lindsay.

With a sigh, she settled into the folding chair and checked on Evan and Chloe. This was one of the few times when both sets of grandparents were in their midst. Lindsay faced the front again, knowing her kids were well cared for and loved.

The commemoration continued with words from Mayor Wes, his somber stories washing over her. Polite applause brought her back, and she began clapping after taking another quick glance around. This time she made eye contact with Penelope and Kris, both of whom waved and smiled in support. Still no Mason, and so she faced the truth.

Mason really wasn't coming. There'd be no more patio talks, no more motorcycle rides, no more waterfall kisses. Mason didn't want her in his life, and she'd have to accept his decision, no matter how much her heart ached.

Phillip placed his program on his folding chair and approached the dais. "Thank you for being here today. This memorial rock is a loving tribute and the culmination of hard work, and a team that came together for a worthy cause. I'm sad to announce this team will no longer—"

"Don't go!" a voice called out from the back of the crowd. Mason's voice. It rose over Phillip's speech, over Sully Creek, over the pounding of her heart.

She looked and there was Mason, running down the aisle, his formal dark suit, pressed shirt and tie standing out in the mostly casual attire of the attendees. He rushed up to the podium, leaving a stunned Phillip with no choice but to yield the microphone to Mason.

Mason's gaze searched the crowd and landed on her, and his entire face lit up. Then his eyes widened as he caught sight of Tim's parents. He gulped and loosened his tie. "This might not be the best setting to tell someone you love her, but I couldn't risk waiting another moment. Please understand. Today, this ceremony, that plaque are all fine testaments to the first responders who died as they performed their duties. Just as their sacrifices aren't forgotten, neither should it be forgotten that they were people, people like you and me, with dreams and hopes, and most importantly love.

"My friend, Tim Hudson, whose name is inscribed on that rock understood risk. And he understood love. I'd trade anything, including my life, for him to be here, giving this speech, instead of me." Mason stopped and gulped for air, emotion twisting his face. A tear fell and she could see him exhale a deep breath. "I hope Tim's children will always know his love for them was endless. And they do have their mother, Lindsay. A beautiful, kind, compassionate person who deserves to be loved and cherished. Until this year, I never had the chance to know her, but now, I'm up here to thank her, in front of our family and our friends, for being the radiant woman that she is and to ask her not to move to Wilmington." He took another deep breath and exhaled. "Lindsay, if do you accept that job, look for a house with a vacancy next door because I'm moving there, too, supporting you every step of the way."

Lindsay glanced around, half expecting people to be angry or upset at the interruption. Instead, all eyes were on her, many faces with tears falling, others grinning from ear to ear. From the seat next to hers, Lindsay felt Aunt Hyacinth nudge her. "You better go put that man out of his misery and tell him the truth."

She turned to Becks, who nodded her agreement. "That's the type of speech that makes you believe in love again."

Lindsay hurried to the dais. She ignored the emotion caught in her throat, no ready smile coming to her rescue. She wasn't sure whether she should address the crowd or Mason, but decided she'd better take care of the guests first.

Lindsay stepped up to the microphone. "Thank you, Mason, for coming and…for what you said. Mason's also a first responder. And yes, every one of the inscribed names represents someone who lived and breathed, laughed and cried, and was someone we loved and cherished. It takes courage and guts to remind us of that." She turned to Mason, who nodded as the crowd applauded heartily.

Phillip came forward again and she left the dais, tugging Mason along with her. She noted the curious eyes of the onlookers and didn't stop moving until they reached the privacy of the fountain. Then she remembered she was angry at him. "Why did…"

He'd taken out a handful of coins and now dumped them into the fountain. "I need all the help I can get."

A flash of gold on his wrist caught her attention. "What's that?"

He laughed and pushed up his sleeve. "My watch?"

She unclasped it from his wrist, stopping short of throwing it in the fountain too. She handed the watch back to him. "Why did you come after all?"

There was a time to give him space and a time to confront what they both needed. Now the latter approach prevailed. Any chance they had at a lasting relationship demanded nothing less.

"For the right reasons and the wrong ones." He glanced to where sounds from the ceremony could still be heard. "I'm here because my next-door neighbor is the best horticulturist in the world."

"Am I only your neighbor?"

The tension between them zoomed to a fever pitch, the look in his eyes gave her his answer.

With her breath coming fast, he caressed her cheek and kissed her. The whisper of the fountain couldn't match the beating of her heart as the kiss filled her with hope.

She broke away and licked her lips, the taste of him still there. "Do you go around kissing all of your neighbors like that?"

"Only the attractive ones who get stuck in their ceilings." The corners of his mouth rose and then assumed a serious, straight line. "I won't run away again, except to follow you."

"I'm not moving. Phillip and Heather are the ones moving to Wilmington."

"What?" He sat on the edge of the fountain and placed his hands over his face. "Come to think of it, I guess that explains why there are no moving boxes or anything like that at your house. I just ruined a ceremony and for nothing."

"Maybe, maybe not." She sat next to him. "You spoke from your heart about love and sacrifice. I think it was much better than a predictable, prepared speech."

"Can you spare a little change and some more love for your next-door neighbor?"

She shook her head. "No."

His face fell, and he closed his eyes for a long while. Pain marked their depths when he opened them. "I see."

"No, you don't. I meant, no, not like this." She tugged off his suit jacket. "This isn't the Mason I know and love."

He grinned and widened the gap between the first two buttons of his dress shirt to reveal a tie-dyed t-shirt underneath. "He's still here." His expression grew serious again. "I love you, Lindsay, and the thought of losing you forever was more than I could bear."

"Does this mean another trip to Pine Falls?"

"First, I should probably tell you why I ran all those times." His somber expression remained. "I was scared of losing someone again."

"I was scared of finding someone again."

Mason looked at her then and his expression was so genuine, so heartfelt that she knew she'd never forget it. He quickly kissed her, until footsteps sounded behind them. With great reluctance, Lindsay broke away.

There stood Mason's grandparents, giving each other a fist bump. Then Joe brought Betty into his arms, and they stole away.

"Grandma and Grandpa will never let us live this down, you know." Mason laughed. "Part of the reason I didn't want to commit to anyone was thinking I'd have to live up to what they have. Fifty-six years is a long time, and yet with you, it would seem like fifty-six seconds."

"Is that a promise?"

"You better believe it."

Never had the roses in this garden come so alive with their fragrant spring blooms. Such splendor, she thought, and she was grateful. A life with Mason would be unpredictable and spontaneous, and that was the sweetest perfume of all.

EPILOGUE

MASON PUSHED THE last suitcase into the SUV. "I think we're finally ready." Lindsay nodded and turned to Grandma Betty and Grandpa Joe. Goliath was off in the distance, cuddled next to the kids' new puppy, Coco. Evan and Chloe were playing nearby.

Lindsay said, "Now, if Evan has an asthma attack…"

"His nebulizer is right here, and his emergency inhaler is always with the adult in charge. Your written instructions are quite complete." Grandma Betty winked and pointed at Mason. "I raised his father, so I'll keep these two alive for a few days."

Mason smiled and said to Lindsay, "We need to leave before your new boss forgets something else and you can't get away for a couple more hours."

The good news was her boss was a genius at drawing visitors to the garden, with the bad news being that he'd realized how otherwise invaluable Lindsay was. The two of them had come to an understanding after Jules had offered Lindsay a job, with Lindsay seriously considering taking her talent elsewhere. Now her boss only got in touch during regular business hours, not any time it suited him.

"Wait a minute. I almost forgot something." Lindsay ran inside the house and emerged with a big, decorated box. "Your wedding present."

"You didn't have to get me anything," Mason said. Just having her beside him when they woke up in the morning was enough, her honey-brown hair splayed across the pillow.

She held the box away. "Does that mean you don't want it? I know it won't compare with Bree's news she's cancer-free and in remission…"

"Thanks for that visit with them, and only a week before our wedding." He unloaded the box from her hands and ripped off the paper much to the obvious dismay of his new wife.

Lindsay had taken the time to collect each ribbon and cut off a bit of wrapping from every gift for their album.

He broke into a wide grin once he had the box open. "His and hers motorcycle helmets?"

"Even better." She waited for him to take one from the box and then clapped. "A tie-dyed helmet for you, and a white helmet with a rose on the side for me."

Grandpa Joe pointed to the bike. "What are you two waiting for? It's time to ride off into the sunset."

Mason went over to Lindsay, sealing his thanks with a kiss. She beamed and slipped her arms around his waist.

"So, now the fun begins?" she asked.

"I thought it had already started." He leaned in. "I reserved a patio room for our honeymoon, overlooking the beach, and a bottle of your favorite Riesling."

"And next month it'll be a family vacation in Georgia, with a weekend stop at Bree and Tristan's home. We've found the best of both worlds."

To think the adventure of a lifetime had been waiting for him next door. With their family looking on, Mason followed Lindsay onto the bike, knowing they'd have to head to Pine Falls.

The future was in front of them and a gift neither of them would ever take for granted.

* * * * *

WESTERN

Rugged men looking for love...

Available Next Month

Finding Fortune's Secret Allison Leigh
Healing The Rancher Melinda Curtis

The Little Matchmaker Catherine Mann
The Cowboy SEAL's Challenge Julianna Morris

The Triplets' Secret Wish Cathy Gillen Thacker
A Starlight Summer Michelle Major

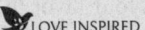
LOVE INSPIRED

The Rancher's Family Legacy Myra Johnson
The Texan's Truth Jolene Navarro

Larger Print